FROST LIGHT

Frost Light

DANIELLE BULLEN

Danielle Bullen

Gloir dó Dhia
For all that is written, said and thought.

Gloir do Dhia.

Cover art: Annie Parsons
https://annieparsonsart.com

Editor: Hannah Rebecca Wilson
https://www.tangledlight.com

First Printing, 2022

To Mr A.
Thank you for the 'kick'. It was needed.

To Phoebe.
For whom this book was completed.
Thank you for telling me this story was worth reading
when I wasn't sure it was worth writing.

For Lydia.
My favorite sunshine girl.

Glossary

Frostland Words

Pakem: father, or dad.

Mamé: mother, or mom.

Civ: lady or woman.

Kif: Girl, woman. Usually a form of affection or tenderness.

Nie: definite no. Hard no.

Va: yes, or more casual, yeah.

Grandmere: grandmother

Amani: pet name for grandmother.

Amrif non: A flakey pastry traditionally made in honor of winter.

Cava: Sir, a word of deference or respect, generally given to strangers.

Cregf: Chief or lord.

Calli: A sheep like creature, usually about the size of a hair sheep, with thick, water proof wool that will fetch a high market price if cared for correctly. They smell, however, so the wool has to be given the correct treatment. Calli themselves have large, sharp teeth, that serve them well on the islands they are from, with the thick, harsh heather grass and weeds.

Eider tree: a short, thorned shrubbery, that only produces a few flowers and thereby, a few seeds every year. Pale pink blooms and not much to look at.

Cavene: A race from the Frostlands, generally tall and known for their harsh temperaments, excellent senses of smell and taste and for being mercenaries in foreign countries.

Landlot: word for people, in general, of any race. This word is commonly used anywhere that speaks a common tongue in place of people to refer to the general population.

Lot: Slang for landlot.

Region and country names

Frostlands: A major country that is largely inhabited by some of the harsher races directly above the Drylands.

Wan Core: A wind current that comes off the ocean and warms the lower and middle part of the Frostlands and Drylands, cutting specifically through the mountains and giving the land several more months of warmer weather.

Drylands: The country directly below the Frostlands, separated by the mountain range of Kriviar.

Settling Lands: A small portion of land in the upper part of the Frostlands that has recently been discovered as being worth inhabiting, making it a prize for any cregf brave enough to send people up to claim it. Up to this point, most settling attempts have been largely unsuccessful, as there has been an influx in settlers leaving for the Fresh Isle, and the land has proved harsh.

Fresh Isle: A country to the Southeast, over the ocean. It is about a 3 month journey by sea and has seen a massive upsurge in immigrants after a period of particularly hard political turmoil ended about a year back.

People and place names, reference.

Oanéka: (OHN-i-kah)
Alvea (Ahl-ve-uh)
Marin: (Mh-AR-in)
Gyaith: (Guy-ith)
Crith: (Kri-th)
Goran: (Gohr-on)
Pevi Likloré-Morfonnen: (Peh-VE) (L-IK-lohr-mor-fun-nen)
Orien: (o-RI-ahn)
Yorevali: (Y-or-VA-lee)
Mavikah: (MAH-vi-KUH)
Paun: (Pah-N)

Chapter I

Yore should never have said yes. This is madness, coming here.

Children should not be accountable for the debts of the father, not even once they are grown. I shake my head, my hands clenched on my arms. *Everything is brown and barren here, except the evergreens that go on and on, stretching up the tiny mountain until the air is gone. Even the rocks are brown. Evergreens and stones. That's all that is here. No one should be trying to settle this place. There isn't anything here, nothing worth settling.*

I turn away from the window where the shutters are not done up, and there is a shuffle from the back, from above—an uneven step and then a drag. *Alvea's limp.*

The door opens, across the room at the front, and there is the smell of wood on the wind. Yore is moving quickly, stooping low to make it through the tiny doorway that leads inside. My brother's brow is furrowed, his golden hair cropped too short for winter and curling on the breeze. His broad shoulders shift, and he drops the load of wood in the bin beside the kitchen stove that splits the room. His gaze flickers round. He brushes the dust from his shirt to the floor. "Where's your sister?" His jaw shifts into place, eyes settling on the stove.

I flick my eyes away, back toward the dishes that are dry now, that should be put away. "*Our* sister is in the loft." I lift a plate. "She hasn't come down yet."

He straightens, and his brow furrows deeper, that strained look and he turns back toward the door. "Make sure she eats when she does." The door thuds shut behind him.

I purse my lips. *Am I to keep track of her? She is a woman, and she can manage herself, as she's always done in his absence.* I lift the dishes from the cloth and set them in their places. *Dishes away, from last night, and then? There is not enough to do without my garden to tend, no one to talk to. The air is foolishly cold for the ninth month, up here, high in the Frost Lands. There is little left of life out in the forests already. Back home... Home I could have started Autumn crops now, and they would have time to grow. But it is already as cold as the eleventh turning here, above the Wan Core where living things do not grow. In this cottage, waiting silently for someone to come. Who lived here before us, so close to the stream? Why did they leave? Were they paying a debt too, like us? Did they finish out their time? Was the debt theirs?* I purse my lips.

There is the tap and brush, tap and brush of uneven steps on the ladder: Alvea's. She steps onto the floor beside the ladder, her head held high, and her dark hair pulled carefully back. *Her hair is always careful, dark and tended. Yore's is light, like gold, and ruthlessly short. And mine, mine is wild and colored, like sunsets and amber and blood.*

She steps in front of the counter space where the bread pans sit and lifts the bread slice from the counter. "Good-dawn." Her voice is low.

I nod and lift another dish, setting it where it goes. The wood is smooth under my fingers. "Gooddawn, Alvea. Are you weaving today?" I glance at her over my shoulder.

She looks at me sharply, her dark eyes scolding, hard. *Foolish question. But what else is there to say, to ask?* Her lips tighten. "Va. Of course." *Of course, because we have already scrubbed the house, scrubbed the floors. Of course, because we have already mended the cloth and the wood. Of course, because there is nothing more to do, but cook and haul in water, only a few times a day. There is no one here, to converse with, but each other. No one to bother with gossip and town, because there is no town, not for fifty, or a hundred miles.*

I look away. *She took the bread. So, I don't have to worry about her, like Yore said.* I turn, setting a dish in its place; the last one and it's done. They are all up. *I should have moved slower. What day is it? I cannot be losing count already. We have not been here more than a fortnight. Fourteen days. It will be the middle of the month, surely. So bread. Bread day will be tomorrow.*

And what today? I'll clean the floors again. Scrub the upstairs. Make soup, that takes long. Slice the tubers as thin as I can and the carrots long. I brush a strand of hair out of my face and smooth my skirts down. *That's enough. I can make it take long enough, stretch out. I will stretch it out to fill the space and time of today. No wandering. We should have brought the ingredients, rather than making soap before we came.*

* * * * * * * * *

My knees ache, and the hem of my dress is soaked with the water from the floor. *It's clean though. Again.* I swallow, swirling the spoon in the soup. The tubers are cooked, broth-soaked in. *It's ready. And dusk hasn't even fallen yet. Yore won't be in for another hour at least.* My teeth are clamped, my muscles aching at the back of my head. *Needlework then. I'll set to my needlework early.* The soft noise of threads through the loom scrapes the air, and the tap of a foot. Alvea's hands are moving the waft through the warp threads on the loom. *She hasn't taken a break all day.* There is no color in the cloth that she is weaving. It's bleak and gray, calli wool, all undyed and bland, like a sheep's. *So like sheep and not.*

I grab my needlework from the mantel where it's sat, useless, and my fingers lift the needle, purple thread hanging from the side of it. A flower. *Like the dahlias and bachelor buttons that will be blooming back home, the last of the season, but for a few weeks. I planted so many this year, to outshine the herbalist's garden for color, to add something to get people talking, make them think. There must have been a bushel of bulbs, every color I could get ahold of. And I'll never see them bloomed, never see the bursts of petals. No color. No life.* My throat is thick. *There wasn't much point in it anyway. It would not have made them like us any more. They had already decided against us, from the minute pakem left.* I drop into the chair, turning my head toward my sister. She's behind the small floor loom, hands still weaving, like yesterday and the day before and the day before. *Say something to her, say anything. No more of this silence.* I open my lips. "The evergreens are nice."

Her eyebrow twitches, just slightly irritated. "Va. If you care for needles and sap and green."

I shake my head. "There is not only the green." I slip the needle through, faster now and it brushes the side of my thumb, scraping against the skin. "There is also—." *Brown. There is also brown.*

She looks up, and her eyes say everything that her mouth doesn't say. *Like she knows what I never finished, what I never spoke. Foolish.* I stick the needle in, faster now, the purple thread is eaten away a little more by the white of the tiny cloth. *At least we do not have snow yet. Only miles and miles of evergreens, broken only by death, water and the tops of the mountain.*

A mewling call cuts out, sudden and sharp. My head whips toward the window. *The calli. One of them must have gotten out.*

I stand, moving across the room toward the only unshuttered window, and press my face against the glass. The shed is barely visible through the panes, our almost-barn. Yore is beside it, his great, sturdy figure bolting back and forth, hat nearly off his head, coat flapping. There is something in front of him, bolting back and forth, the same movement that he is making, its gray and fluffy, a little higher than his knee. Yore bolts, and he is on it, pinning it down and it's struggling and kicking its hooved feet and fighting. He stands, his face slightly red, the thing in his arm. The long, stringy tail of it dangles over his arm, the only thing from a distance to say that this creature is a calli and not a sheep. It lifts its head, mewls, that high, scratchy call, its pointy teeth visible for a moment and Yore is turning back toward the barn-shed, his shoulders easy under the weight of the animal though its legs are down past his knees.

A sheen is spreading over the window, my breath against the glass and Yore and the calli are vanishing behind the fog of it. I pinch my lips and turn toward the door. *I don't want to go out. It's too cold.* My hand is above the knob. I glance toward the window and pull my hand away. *He doesn't need my help. He's got it.* I turn back toward the chair.

Alvea's hands are still spinning over her work, perfect finger motions sending the threads deftly to their places. *It's always perfect. She does not make mistakes on the loom.* "Are the calli not lose?" She doesn't look up at me.

I pick up my work, shake my head. "One was. But he has it caught already." She rolls her eyes, and her hands have not paused, still weaving the strands together. Her foot is to the side, that awkward bend to it beneath her skirts, in her thigh from the break that never healed well. Her other is squarely in front of her, perfectly placed. *Controlled.* I roll my eyes and drop the needlework on the mantel. *It's pointless to try. I can't focus. I can't focus on that. It isn't supposed to be too cold for gardening yet. There is still supposed to be time for dirt and hands and green. It's not the time for winter and all things brown and dead. This is wrong.* I turn away.

"I thought you were doing cross stitch." Alvea's voice is curt behind me, the brush of the threads on the loom continuing.

I shake my head, and move toward the kitchen, shove the sleeves on my dress up. "It's too early for that." *And there is no point in doing it, with no one to sell it to out here. It can't help pay for anything that was bought before we came here. We can't buy anything else until we can go home. I can't focus.*

My fingers land on the wooden bowl, and I slip them across the edge. It's smooth, clean. Govi's work is always smooth, always so beautiful. *But this bowl was a scrap.* So he said, the woodcarver with kind eyes and hands so large they could wrap around logs. *"Take it, Oanéka. I have too many and this one is flawed. Too flawed for me."* The surface is beautiful and clear, only the tiniest of nicks in the top part, a flaw in the wood, not the work, and it is barely visible, the tiniest mark above the intricately carved centaur and snowflakes. *Govi. How can we repay your kindness if we are stuck out here?* Will his aged bones hold up until we return? Or will we find him gone, whenever we go back? He was the only one who would stop to ask about my garden.

Surely they won't make us stay the whole time. They'll call us back eventually and all will be well. Maybe in the spring. Spring. *That would be lovely, to come back to the village, back home in time for the flowers to be planted, and seeds sown? It would be perfect.* My lips are tight. *Would they want us to come home?* I shake my head and clear my throat. "Is tomorrow bread day?"

Alvea shakes her head. "Nie. Two days."

My heart sinks, eyes widening. "Two days?" My voice is too high.

She looks at me, gaze sharp. "If you had learned any other skills when they were offered to you, you wouldn't be so edgy." I purse my lips. *It is too late for that now. It cannot be changed, not anymore. They said there is not another person here.*

I turn away, back toward the kitchen, and press my hands sharply against my skirts. "I'm not fidgety. I just need something to tend." *I can't cope with this, with all these miles and only Yore and Alvea to talk to.*

"Stop pining, Oanéka." My eyes snap back toward Alvea. She is watching me, her eyes wide and dark, like grand-mere's were, back in the village. *They are filled with that emotion again that I can't read.* "It will get you nowhere." She says, hands moving, always moving. "This is what we have. Leave your garden and the plants be."

I snort, shake my head. "I'm not pining. And I wasn't thinking of my garden." My fingers lift the bowl from the counter and set it on the shelf beside the stove. I turn, stirring the soup over the fire. "I told you. I want something to do. And I'll find something." *I always have.*

She shifts, and her hands are busy with the loom again, eyes on me. "You had better." She glances at me. "Why don't you go see if you can find someone else out here, if you are going to be like this?"

My eyes snap to hers. "There aren't any other people out here. Yore said everyone down there said this place was empty."

She lifts her hands, shifting her fingers on the thread. "Well if you are going to fidget, it would at least give you something to do, to try and find someone."

I shake my head, stir the soup a little faster. My chest heats. *She doesn't need to waste my time. It doesn't affect her. She can just sit there and weave and weave for hours, and she has no reason to meddle in what I am doing. She never did before, so why now? She will just be there, weaving and weaving, things that are no longer useful to anyone. What will we do with all that she will make through the winter months? What will we do with anything we make, that could be beautiful, and would once have fetched a price? We are missing the season of selling, the season when people want to buy what she has to sell.* My eyes flick to her loom.

She doesn't look at me, her fingers set perfectly around the wool threads, calli wool, thick, water repelling and cleaned perfectly by someone's hands back home. *That would have fetched a high price, if we'd had time to finish and sell the piece before we came.* I shake my head. *There is no need for money now, no need to scrape. We are here.*

There is a mewl again, the sound of calli, this time muffled by something out toward the shed. The soft threading of Alvea's loom mixes with the crackling of the fire, low, quiet. *Curse it. There isn't enough to do. It's too quiet, and there isn't enough out here.* I fold my arms. *She didn't need to bring up others. There are no others out here. That was the warning we were given, after Yore had already said yes, and sent us all to this place.*

Chapter II

My hands lift the bowls, and they knock together, sounds rough and hard and loom stops. "What are you doing?" Alvea's voice is strained, the loom stilled.

I set the bowls together on the workspace, turning for the flour bag. "Making bread."

The loom is still not moving. "And what do you plan on doing tomorrow when the bread was to be made? Sit idly? Do nothing?" Her voice is low.

I grit my teeth. "I'll worry about that then."

Her lips twitch, that movement of condemnation on me, and mine tighten. *She doesn't get to scold me. She has done this before, moved the days around. I can do what I want today and figure out tomorrow, tomorrow.* I set the flour sack down, dust off my hands. Across the room, there is a scraping sound, the door opening, and there are footsteps—Yore's, heavy, long. They pause, beside the fire bin and he is setting wood down. He stands, and a frown crowds his features. "I didn't think it was bread day yet." He dusts his hands off, watching me.

My lips tighten, and I wipe my hands pointlessly on the apron over my skirts. "It not. It's tomorrow."

His frown deepens, feet shifting. "Then what are you doing with that?"

I lift my head and grab a scooping bowl from its place on the shelf. "Making bread." I turn. "I'm not waiting until tomorrow." I set the bowl on the counter.

His eyes dart to me, and there is that shoulder tensing, and he turns, snatching the door handle. The door is open and shut again that burst of cool air swirling into the room. *Why would that be a bother to him?* I frown, grip my apron. Alvea's mouth tightens, and the loom is moving quickly now, thudding and thudding against the shafts. *I shouldn't have said anything.* My lips shake. *I might have just said it was time. It doesn't seem to matter what day we make it out here, what day we do anything. There is no structure. No one to bother with.* Alvea's leg is awkwardly to the side, her posture sharper than before, and her lips impossibly tensed, a white line on her face and her eyes are focused on her hands, as if she needed to watch to make the lines perfect.

My lips are tight, pinched.

Water mixes with flour, and it looks like mud within the bowl, pasty, grimy. Brown and dull like everything else out here. *And it's all well and good.*

* * * * * * * * * * *

My steps are heavy on the floor, stockings slapping the wood. *There is nothing to do. Nothing. There should be something. There is always something.* My eyes flicker. Food is over the fireplace, and the floors are clean. *Again.* The bread is made, yesterday. I pause, and turn, walking back toward the window. *The floor is still too clean to wash again. There has to be something. I should have learned another skill, beyond housekeeping and gardens. They seemed like enough back home. They were always enough before, things to do each day. Before we came to this frozen wasteland. But here there is nothing. I can't do this. There is nothing to do, and nothing of beauty to look at beyond the empty trees.*

My hands tighten on my arms and there is the brush and brush again of Alvea's loom. I move over to the pot above the fire, grab the spoon handle jutting from the soup pot. The steam is thick, and it clings, clammy against my skin and sleeves, sticking them to each other. I stare at the ground, stirring, my arm twisting over the pot over and over. *How much will my flowers have grown since we left? Will anyone have tended them? Any of the people who claimed they would care for them, see them through the season after I had done all the work for them, for months and months?* Pain sizzles across my hand. I hiss, and jerk my arm back, the spoon slick in my fingers. *Only a steam burn.* My hand is red, slick with the dampness of the steam.

Foolish. I'm losing my mind.

I miss my gardens.

* * * * * * * *

Yore is still in his chair, his head bent a little forward, hands busy with the rope in them, weaving it, weaving, the knots he never stops weaving. His hand slips, and he stifles a curse. *Why didn't he just blurt it out? He used to curse aloud, the words he learned in the docks and taverns, spreading their filth to the corners of our home. Why would he not now? When he came back from working on the docks, on the evenings when he showed back up, it always came out easily enough then. Always came out.*

I purse my lips and look down. I shift my hands beneath the fabric, press the needle through again, the thread catching and pulling through. *Needlework.* My fingers tighten. *There is no point in it, not now. We are here, during the best months to sell it, before winter sets in, when everyone is in their homes, hosting and sharing during the long months. No one wants to buy needlework in the spring, no matter how carefully or beautifully done. They will be going to the fields, not to the house.* My eyes flicker to Alvea, and my heart sinks. *What if she doesn't want to return when the time comes? It would be a long journey, for only a few days there, with the few people who will still want to see us. If they even remember us.* I swallow and push up from my chair. My throat is tight. "I'm turning in."

Yore looks up, his golden eyes swirled dark with fire, those eyes that match mine, look for look. *Despair.* I force a smile, force it and it chokes my throat. "Rest well, Yore. Rest well, Alvea." She looks up, and her eyes hold nothing of Yore's, of mine. *Dark. Ready. Determined. She is the weak one and in twenty-one days, we have failed, and she has not. Does she already know that she won't go home in the Spring? Has she already decided? I'll be stuck here with her, Yore will go alone, and we'll have to stay, because none of us should stay alone in this empty place.* I turn, and clamber up the ladder, hands dragging me up, and there is emptiness, emptiness everywhere and I don't know if they responded to me, if they said anything to me. *We are lost. Five years. Are five years not worth it to save a life?*

Not all men die in the war.

I shake my head, jerk the ties of my dress loose under my arm. *And not all women keep faith while they are gone.* Foolish, foolish. *I can't think like that.* I can't. *It's worth it, for Yore. It's worth it for him.* I pull the laces free. *But what has he ever done for us? He wasn't ever there, when we needed him. He didn't stick around. He was always gone, always somewhere else.*

My lips are trembling, and I shake my head, drop against the thickness of the cot. Something clatters below—Alvea's loom. *I wouldn't trade my brother's life for comfort. I wouldn't trade it. I wouldn't trade him.*

But not all men die in the war. Maybe it wouldn't have been a trade

Chapter III

My steps are heavy on the floor, window to the back. Back to the window. *I don't know what to do. I could stitch together cross stitches to make a blanket. Or I could cross stitch a blanket. Or learn a larger method of needlework. Make a whole blanket of something. But that would be dull work, tedious. I don't have the mind for that, and we do not have the thread.* This is foolishness. Utterly foolish. *I cannot help Yore and Alvea if I am losing my mind in here. I can be of little use if I can find nothing to do.* I turn by the window, start back. *I could take up wood carving?*

Alvea's head lifts. "Oanéka." Her voice is sharp.

I spin, my eyes meeting hers. "What?"

She drops her hands from the loom. "You need to find *something* to do other than pacing."

My hands clench, arms cross. "I wasn't pacing."

Her eyes narrow. "Va. You were. And you need to go find something else to do."

I shake my head, turn half away. "I am trying to find something to do. That's why I was pacing."

Her eyes twitch on the edge of my vision. "You have to go outside. Do something. Take a walk. You can't do this today. Get out. Go outside. Don't come back until later." Her voice lowers. "Much, much later."

My hands tighten on my arms. *Walk?* I swallow. Alvea's face is tense, her eyes wide, pleading and threatening at the same time. I look away. *There isn't anything to be done outside.* I glance back toward her, and her eyes are still set, on me. *I can go. For her, I can go outside for today. And then what tomorrow? I will figure out tomorrow, tomorrow.*

I slip my feet into my boots, jerking the laces shut. They are stiff, awkward, the last purchase of the spring before the snows ended. I pluck my shawl from the rack, and my fingers grip the door, pull it open. There is cool air against my face, brushing across my skin.

The sky is gray out here, clouds high in the sky, like a sheet over the heavens. I jerk the door shut, and the boards of the porch squeak under my feet. My fingers wrap the shawl around my shoulders and clamp my hands over it. *Now what? Where is there to go?* The forest edge stretches out, just beyond the trickling stream, bare trees and limbs like barren arms. To the left, the stream travels down the nearly even ground, until it curves out of sight where the tiny field ends in trees. To the right, there is the shed, the fence, with calli inside. And there are more trees behind it. *Then I am bound for trees, wherever I go. I'm not following the stream. And I'm not getting close to the calli.*

I swallow, and my boots tap the porch, stepping off it. My feet skid on the creek bed, the dirt loose beneath my feet. I grit my teeth and step down onto the surface of a rock. The moss doesn't move, like it would back home. It sits still, dry and clinging to the rock beneath as though it will never leave. I step again, and the next rock is the same, covered with moss that does not slither. The bank is beneath my feet, with the flat bed of the creek where the water doesn't reach. The tree branches are above my head, their twigs scraping the top of my hair.

I step, leaves crunching beneath my boots and the air is crisp on my skin, cool. *The woods. I've not been in them since we came, by the wagon that left again.* They have no flare, no color. *No beauty.* Only the curling reaches of trees, tree after tree after tree. *There has to be something worth seeing. Maybe beyond these trees there is something different. There has to be something. Or else, why would anyone want to settle here? Why would anyone choose this place to claim for their people? There was always something to see at home, so that you did not notice the lack of things to do. There was always something happening.*

I step forward—a stick snaps beneath my boot. *There has to be something worth seeing out here. There must be something.* My hands grip my skirts, and I bolt through the trees, my legs pounding beneath me. The air bites at my cheeks, pulls at my hair, and branches are high and low, brush along the trunks of the trees. brown. Brown. Brown. Evergreen and brown and the evergreen again, blurring together into a whirl of nothing. Boulders and trees and boulders again, on and on in the never-ending reaches of trees. *There has to be something else here.* My lungs ache, I push, moving around the trees. My lungs burn, gasping, feet slow. There is a down tree across my path, branches jutting empty toward the gray coated sky. I press a hand against my side, stare at tree, suck in a breath and another and another. *More green and brown. There has to be something else. This land surely can't be all just this. Back home, there was something worth seeing in the winter too, wasn't there? Isn't there anything out there, to watch when the months get long?*

My breaths cut my throat, air cold in it, sharp, and the wind bites at my skin. It stings, the same way winter feels back home, but it's too early. *There will be too many months of winter here, with it beginning now. We are too far north. Back home, we had five months of it each year, except for the hard ones, and then we were done. But here, it's only the ninth turning, and the leaves are spread all over the earth, everything dull and lifeless. Seven months of winter, is that too large a guess? Seven months of cold, lifeless barrenness? What if there is nothing beautiful in this oncoming death of winter. Seven months of it. Barren. Empty. Lifeless. There is no one around to lighten it, no village to celebrate with, no family to cheer. Just us, three of us alone in the vastness of the empty forest, and we know each other too well to cheer. There is only emptiness, and footsteps in the leaves. There isn't any more family to cheer at home anyway, now. We are all that's left there.*

Something flickers, color swaying in the still breeze. My head whips around. A burst of the palest pink deep in the branches of an eider tree, short and wild. *A dried eider flower.* My lips twitch, pulling upward, and my feet drag me forward. *Color. Eider flowers. They grow here too, flowers drying on the short, tiny trees. Color. Something still brushed with beauty out here. But its dead, only a dried bloom, clinging to the last bits of the branches.*

But it surely will make Alvea smile. They could somehow make the cottage a little brighter, if there are more of them. Even dried flowers can do that. "I can collect them." My voice is loud in the empty forest, and the stillness is broken, though my words were only a breath. I step forward, and pluck the flower from its branch, thorns long and gnarled beside it, stick clinging to my skin, tough and grainy. There is another, on the other side of the brush, and out in the woods, there is another tree, tiny, with flowers upon its empty branches, and another beyond that, color in a lifeless forest, blooms with no life left. *But at least they are there, proof that somethings do grow in the summer months here, even if the winters are long.*

I look down at the flower, pressed against my stomach. The petals are thin, more delicate than the thinnest paper that Yore has brought home, the palest of pinks in the gray light of the midday sun. Thin and pale, like everything in winter, though snowfall has not even come yet. *How do these still cling to their branches, when the warmth of summer has gone, and the leaves have all fallen? How have the petals lasted this long in this world?*

My fingers twirl the flower, and the petals brush against the fabric of my dress, each one catching for barely a moment and they go on. *It is beautiful, in its own way. They are not what I hoped for, but maybe in searching for them I'll find something else. They are enough, for now.*

I look down, and there is a fern, small and close to the earth beside a tree. *A fern. Still alive this late in the season.* There is another one, beside a root, further away, and another. *Frost must not have hit them yet. They are still beautiful, still alive, each leaf curling with twenty tiny versions of itself beneath the winter sky. There is still green in this world, even up here. There is still life.*

* * * * * * *

The trail cuts off through the tree, some small little path in the woods. The sky is clear blue and beautiful overhead, and my boots are lighter on my feet. I tug at my shawl, lifting my head, and there is a song in my throat. It vibrates, and I smile, humming and stepping, adjusting the few eider flowers cradled in the crook of my arm, pale pink against the gray of my shawl.

Three days of hunting flowers. None of them still alive, but they would not be, after these months anyway. The air is drier here than at home. But there are plenty of smaller plants still alive, trees hung with the last leaves of autumn. I lift my eyes, and there is another dusting of pink, another spot, faint and pale off in the brush. *Another hour of searching paid off.*

I hum, step forward, pluck the flower from the plant, cracking the stem. Below, the ground dips down a little, boulders cluttering the earth as though they all chose to gather there, down where the earth comes together. *I wonder how Elnial chooses where He lays the boulders and stones.* I step forward, around the boulders, up the other side of the open space, and under the trees again. There are a few more small plants tucked under a tree. My eyes flicker down to the three flowers clutched in my hand. Their colors are all nearly the same, though they came from three different bushes, a crushed one next to the first.

There is a scuffling, leaves rustling, and something is moving. My eyes snap up. I freeze.

A stag, behind a tree, not more than the length of six sheep from me. His head is lowered, hooves shifting the leaves, kicking them, moving them beneath his nose, and the rack upon his head speaks of nearly as many summers as I can boast, fifteen at least. His hide is dark, deeper brown than the trees around, and he is not watching, not listening for me. A stag. He steps forward, walking, moving, nose still to the ground rustling the leaves. His shadow passes between the trunks, great height under the low branches, hide shimmering in the sunlight. I shiver. A stag. There is a howl, high in the forest, off somewhere. I grip my skirts, pulling them around me.

The stag's head barely lifts, his ears tipping that way, and he is stepping forward, a careful pace between the trees. I move forward, after him, through the branches of the trees. He's walking toward a group of large evergreens, through the lowest branches that nearly hide him but for the white of his beautiful tail shining in the sunlight. I step under, ducking, and the branches tug at the strands of my hair, pulling the curls free. He's gaining, getting further away. I step forward faster, and there is a small clearing, more trees, evergreens mixed with brown trunks. He is moving around a large boulder, the pale green moss nearly the same color as his coat with the traces of winter. He's beautiful. His pace is slow and easy, searching the earth, coat glimmering in the sunlight, antlers reaching for the sky. I smile.

Something rings through the forest, metal, familiar. I freeze.

The stag's head snaps up, and he leaps over the boulder, a snort as he is gone through the evergreens, beyond sight. My heart drops into my stomach. He's gone. My lips purse. *But how could he leap that rock, standing still?* There was no momentum. A single jump, and he was gone. My heart sinks. He was beautiful, so beautiful out here beneath the trees. Our paths will not likely cross again.

There is the ringing sound again, echoing through the trees and bouncing back, and another, another strike, like an axe hitting wood. Exactly like an axe striking wood. I swallow, turning away from the boulder. Did Yore venture out into the forest? Would he cut wood so far from home? I step slowly, leaves barely rustling beneath my feet, toes pressing against the end of my shoes. If he is, then he will be seeking silence. I grip my skirts, the flowers still clutched in my hands, feet quiet on the earth. There are trees ahead, some small trunks, and thick, great evergreens like the ones I pressed through. I step around them, move carefully beneath the branches. The trunks are getting larger, big, old tree branches not brushing my head anymore as I duck, but still not near the height of the forests back home. I press my hand against the trunk, move carefully. The ringing sounds again, and again, twice close together. I purse my lips and lift my eyes, stepping around a tree.

There is a man, standing beside a cottage, not the length of two sheep from me, an axe in his hand cleaving a log in two, face gleaming with sweat, and he is big, at least as big as Yore, shoulders broader than his, hair dark as the shadows I just walked from, bound at the back of his neck. He is dressed in rugged clothes, like ours, and he cannot be much older than Yore or Alvea, the big man with a beard as dark as the shadows of the trees. His eyes flicker up, to me, and he pauses, axe cleaved into the log. His hands flex on the handle, ripples coursing up his exposed forearms. My heart shrivels. I step backward.

His eyes narrow, brows low. He moves forward, just barely. I scramble back, and my foot thuds against something, hand fumbling with the thing behind me. A tree trunk. I swallow hard, press my back against it. There aren't supposed to be other people here. They said there was no one else settling in this land. That was why the cregf needed us to go.

"What are you doing here?" The man's voice—it's sharp and deep, and his eyes are forbidding, like I've trespassed on him. There is someone else in the forest. Someone else here. My heart half lifts, thudding still. His eyes are on my face. Calculating like Yore when he would get into brawls back home, at the docks and taverns. They are deep in his face. The hand on the axe shifts, moving up the handle—I shift with it, sideways, away. What happens if he wields that?

He moves forward, pulling the axe free from the log. I scramble away, moving to the side of the tree behind me. "What—" his voice is harder now, low, "—are you doing out here?"

I press my hand against the tree, purse my lips. I could run. Could I outrun him? He is tall. My eyes flicker to the logs around him, many of them, split on the ground. He's big. Strong. Maybe I could outrun him. Maybe his height or size would slow him down enough?

He shifts, just slightly and his hand is a little looser on the axe, eyes soften a little. "You shouldn't be here. You should get back to your family before night falls." He turns, dragging the sleeve of his thick tunic across his face, swiping away a stream of sweat. How can he be sweating out here? I pull my sleeves down over my chilled fingertips.

"It's not far." The words are out of my mouth and his eyes snap back to me, hand tightening on the axe again, whole body tensing with it, like a hound watching its prey.

Something crosses his face, and I can't read it, can't tell what it means. His eyes narrow, on me. "Dark is coming on, fast." He lifts the axe, gripping it with his other hand. "You should get moving, and get back to your family, if you have one. It would be wise not to wander about the forest next time. There are things that could catch you out here, this late in the day." My eyes flicker upward, keeping him at the edge of my vision, and there are clouds, gray clouds, here and there in the sky that is paling with the last evening light, no longer the pure blue from before. It's late. Too late. I should be home already.

There is a bark, loud and crackling through the forest.

My head whips back, a scream ripping from my throat. I slam my back against the great tree, and there is a hound in front of me, or a wolf, bounding my way. Fast, too fast. I lift my arms above my face and shrink. The man's voice snaps something, harsh.

The wolf stops, snarls, baring its huge teeth at me, only feet away. I could try to run. It would stay. I might could get away if I move now.

"Don't move." The man's voice again, and my eyes are stayed on the wolf. It is huge, fur pale red, thick and wild, a shaggy mane. Its eyes are narrowed, teeth bared, thick and white. "If you run, she will chase you." The man says. My eyes flicker to him, and back to the wolf again. Is that a threat? The wolf steps forward, one slow step, close to the ground. The man shifts, lowering the axe. "Gyaith, come." The wolf's head lifts. She is still growling, eyes on me. She steps sideways, toward the man, head lowering, teeth bared at me, growling. She stops beside him, and his hand drops upon its head. It's his hound. His dog. Not a wolf. And it's a girl? I swallow, pull my arm away from the tree, step backward.

He shifts his hand on the hound's head. It's nearly at his waist, her eyes still on me. How big would she be, if she was standing over me now? "Who are you?" My eyes snap to his, and they are watching me, hound under one hand, axe hanging from the other.

"A landlot." I blurt, and he stares at me, like he doesn't know what to do. Because I just called myself the most obvious thing in the world, and exactly what he knows I am. Curse it. I lick my lips and shake my head. "I mean. I... I am... I..." I grip my skirts in my hand, lift my head. "My name is Oanéka. I didn't mean to startle you. I'm sorry. I didn't know anyone was here. I didn't think there was anyone here." My heart is cold, shriveled.

The hound growls, and the man's hand shifts on the axe handle. His eyes look confused, a brow lifting a little. "Oanéka. You would be better off not stalking people in the forest from the quiet of the trees. Lots who live this far north don't normally take kindly to that sort of thing." My face warms. I look down, press my hands against the tree behind my back. He lifts a brow, eyes slanting toward the hound.

I shake my head. "I was not trying to sneak up on you. I didn't know you were there until you knew I was there. I thought you might have been my brother. We were told there was not anyone else out here. I'm sorry."

His eyes flicker up from the hound for just a second, and he shifts, his gaze flickering to the sky. He half nods, eyes moving back to me, calculating like the hunters at the bars. "Come here." My head snaps up. What?! His eyes flicker to the hound, and back to me. They narrow, just barely, his hand shifting on the hound. "If you don't, she'll believe you are a threat. She needs to smell your hands before you can go. Come here. I don't want her tracking you down tonight."

I clamp my hands over my arms, and my teeth are too tight, jaw clenched. I can't do this. What if she bites? What if Yore finds out? He would be furious. I found a big man in the woods with a mammoth hound and walked up to him.

But I have no choice, and the threat of a hound dog.

My legs inch forward, heavy under my skirts, and the hound growls again, lowers her head. I swallow, and the man nods toward me, his brow half lifting. I inch forward again, and I am beside him, the hound beneath his hand, head so high it is above his belt and higher than my elbows. It's huge. Oh, lands it's huge. It lowers its head, and growls, baring its teeth, eyes on me. The man snaps out a word, fast and sharp and the hound straightens, mouth shut, eyes still watching beneath his hand. I can't tell what he said.

He is watching the hound, eyes even and steady in the lines of his face. "Put out your hand." My hand shoots out, and the dog snaps, snarling, the man's hand clamping down on her muzzle. I jerk back, my heart is thundering in my chest. Oh lands. I'm going to lose my fingers. I'm going to lose my hand. Oh lands.

"Slowly, put out your hand." The man's voice is low, harsh, his eyes half hidden beneath his brows. I swallow, and my heart is in my throat. *I'm going to die from a wolf. There won't be anything for Yore and Alvea to find, if they even could.* I lick my lips, inch my hand forward, and the hound is growling again, its body still as a carving, eyes watching like it is going to rip me to pieces at any moment. My hand inches forward further—the man says something, a low word to the dog. She isn't moving, a growl still rolling from deep within her chest. My fingers brush the top of her head.

The growling stops. My heart goes with it.

My hand is on her head. Now what do I do? My heart pounds in my throat.

The man shifts, stroking the hound's neck and the creature relaxes a little, eyes still on me, too close to mine. Her nose could touch mine if she just moved a little up. The hand is still stroking her head. "Her name is Gyaith. You might speak to her. Before you move."

My fingers are still on the edge of her head, half blocking one eye as she moves. Speak. What to say? "Gooddawn, Gyaith." Dawn? It's not dawn, it's evening, growing dark. Curse it. My face warms. I purse my lips. "Or even. Goodeven. Your coat is..." Lovely? "Beautiful." She shifts her head, a half-growl rumbling through her head, through my hand, and my feet barely stay in place. I should not have said that. Foolish thing to tell a hound. She doesn't care if her coat is beautiful.

The man shifts. "You should go back." He is watching me, eyes scanning my face, still narrowed. I swallow, my fingertips brushing the hound's head, and his is on her neck, almost a grip. The hound is still. His eyes flicker to mine.

I look down, my eyes meeting the hound's. I shiver. "I know. Will she let me?"

"Va. Step carefully." His hand is still on her neck. I step backward, slowly, and the hound doesn't move, still and staring beneath his hand. He is a big man, beside a big hound. I step back again, and my heart is still in my throat, pounding, pounding. She didn't attack. He looks up, eyes still lost in a shadow so that I cannot read them. "Are you traveling through?"

I shake my head. "Nie. We..." Should I tell him? It is too late now. "We are here, for now."

His lip twitches, like Alvea's does when she is disgusted or disturbed and tries to hide it, and his hand shifts on the hound. "How far?"

I shake my head. "Not far."

His eyes flinch and he shifts sideways, just barely. "Can you make it back?"

My head is nodding. "Va. It's just this..." I turn, and the trees all look the same. Evergreens after evergreens around his hut, all huge like the ones I came through. My stomach sinks, heavy and it hurts. I don't know where I came from, which trees they were, which way to go. I should have been paying more attention. What happens if I can't make it back? Can Yore find me?

He grunts, moving away from the hound. "Describe the hut. I am assuming you didn't build it with all the empty ones around here?"

I turn, and he is watching me, eyes high above and unreadable still. "Nie. It's by a stream. Are there other empty ones around here? My brother said ours is about a forest's pace from the mountain. The cabin has two floors, a shed, and there are carvings in the front posts."

His brow twitches, just barely, and if I was any further away, I would not have seen it. "The Moni hut." Moni? A dwarf name? "Follow the path there—" he gestures off, toward the front of the hut and the empty spot in the trees, "until you reach a patch with no evergreen. Cut across it east, away from the setting sun, until you reach the stream and follow it down. You'll meet the cabin." He knows the place?

I swallow. What if he is wrong? How could he know every cabin in the area? There must be others he doesn't know, and what if he is wrong, what if I get lost out here, alone? There is no time for him to be wrong. My path is too long, if I can even find it. It is his way, or darkness will be here long before I find my path. But what if he is wrong? Is he trustworthy? My eyes flicker to his, but he isn't looking at me, but at the sky.

I nod, and half turn. Should I turn my back on the hound? I grip my skirts. "Thank you. Goodeven to you." My eyes flicker to the hound beside him. She is still watching me, her eyes closer to the ground than before, head a little below his hand.

"Goodeven." Dismissal. He has turned away, moving around the hut, the hound following him.

I turn, stepping around the logs on the ground, and force my back to straighten, my head to lift. His cabin is like ours, but there is only one floor, and the wood is rougher, no carvings in the logs that hold up the roof of the porch. I forgot to ask him why he is here, what he is doing out here. Should we know? The door is higher, taller, and it is all alight with the last of the setting sun, shadows deep and dark. My heart sinks. It's late. Later than I thought. Dark clouds are rolling in, pushing back the beauty of the sunset color. It's too late. I break into a run, and my hair clings to my face, in my mouth; I brush it back, turn up the path. The evergreens end, leaving only the dead brown of barren trees. East. Away from the colors of the setting sun. A stick crackles behind, somewhere off in the trees. Maybe there is a deer, or the hound is following me. I turn—there is nothing, only the end of the evergreens and empty trees.

The dead trees roll down ahead, off around boulders and dead brush, until the evergreens begin again. East. Just east. My steps are heavy and light, legs ache. The light is fading too quickly. I stumble around a boulder and slow. The trees are closer together, crowding in and it's dark between them. Branches brush my hair, catching it and pulling it free from the binding.

What can I do if I don't make it back before dark? If the moon isn't out? I move around a tree, and down tiny slopes, and leaves cascade, slipping over my boots and rustling to a stop. My legs are tired. I step again, around a tree, and another, and there is another boulder in the way. My skirts swish, brush against my legs and the air is colder, a brush of it against my face. Trees, trees, never-ending trees stretching on, across the forest floor. *What if I don't find the creek bed?*

There is the sound of water. The stream. I stumble, and a rock clatters against another, down into the darkness. My legs weave around a tree, and another, and there is the water, small and dark, trickling around rocks through the creek bed. *Find the stream, and then... Up? Down? Which way was it? If I am wrong, I can follow it back, can't I? Up or down?* My eyes flicker toward the sky. He must have said down. The clouds roll overhead moving toward the mountain and the last of the setting sun.

Down then. I turn, and the creek is flowing along beside me, cutting through the night.

The stream turns, through a thicket, and there is a boulder, huge and bare in the last light. Stones clatter under my feet, and are gone beneath the dark of the water, without even a splash, the water so close. It's nearly dark, and there is a pale stream of light, cold and glittering off the stream below. The moon. I look up, and the light is gone, rolling behind a cloud, leaving darkness behind.

"Oanéka!" Yore's voice, a call through the trees ahead. My heart lifts. I chose correctly. It was the right way. I'm not lost.

I swallow hard, lift my skirts. "Here!" My voice carries, high and piercing and something flutters out of a branch beside me—a bird. I flinch. Something is moving between the trees and the creek, in and out of shadows, huge and looming in the last of dusk. Yore lifts his head, his eyes bright, face a tight line in the shadows and light.

"Oanéka." He moves forward, and stops, feet from me. "Where were you? What were you thinking?" His voice is sharp, irritated, and it's better that I can't see his face very well in the falling dark.

I wrap my hands into my skirts, clench them. "I went too far on a walk. I'm sorry. I meant to be back sooner than I was." Wind cuts through the trees, chilled and sharp, and he shifts, sideways, his face out of the wind and out of the light. I shiver.

His head is shaking. "Alvea has food over the fire. Let's go." He turns and waits for me to go ahead. Like a lost sheep. I grit my teeth. Did he even wonder if I was alright? I step, and a stick snaps too loudly beneath my feet. But I didn't get lost. I made it back.

That means that the man with the axe did know which cabin it was. Moni, a dwarf name. That would explain the etching in the wood posts, the doorway that is short, that Yore has to stoop through. It must have been built by dwarvish settlers. Have there been dwarvish settlers? They said something about that once. But I cannot recall what was said, who said it, back in the village. There were not any dwarves in the village.

Yore is silent behind me, his steps loud and crackling on the leaves, over the rocks that splash now, with the lip that must be over the creek. "Where had you gone?" He says. His voice is low, irritated still.

"I was looking for eider flowers." Curses. My hands are empty, wrapped into the folds of my skirts. I must have dropped them when the hound startled me, back at the axe-man's hut.

"Does that mean that you have to come back after dark?"

My eyes snap up. "Nie. What does it matter to you? I made it back. I'm here." My voice is a little too high.

He snorts. "You were lost." He moves around something, stepping off the path beside the creek.

My foot slips, skidding—rocks splash in the water below, clattering against each other, and are gone. Lost? I grit my teeth, jerk my foot back up. "I wasn't lost. I knew exactly where I was going." I pull my skirts, and the wind brushes cold, throwing hair across my face.

Light glitters on the stream, steady and small, warm and orange. I lift my eyes. The one unshuttered window of the cottage. Something in the darkness ahead, a space in the trees with the darkened sky, the moon rolling behind the clouds and rimming them with silver. I swallow, and squint, staring at the stream. The light of the moon is faint on the water, and it's hard to tell rock from stream. Yore brushes past me, his shoulder barely touching mine, and he steps across the stream, two quick steps that I can't follow. My jaw tightens. There is a dark shape in the water below. It must be a rock. I step forward, and my foot meets with something solid. I step forward again, another one, and again, and the last one is a little further away, too far for my legs to easily reach. I grit my teeth, and jump, and there is a hand, gripping my arm, pulling me up the bank.

Yore's voice is low, barely brushing my ears, an irritated mutter. "Should have built a bridge." He steps up the slope, steps too long. I jerk my arm away. Yore has stopped moving, solid and dark beside me. Is he waiting for me to go first, again? I'm not one of his lost, foolish calli.

I grit my teeth, and stomp up the steps to the door, and yank it open. Warm air pours out, hitting my face, and there is Alvea, standing up sharply. Her face flinches, just barely, and her hand presses against her leg betraying the pain there, hidden in her face. "Oanéka. Where were you?" Her voice is sharp, harsh, like Yore's. "We were worried."

I step to the side and toss my shawl over the hook on the wall. "I went walking."

Her brows draw low, and her eyes flash over me, scanning my hands. "Where? What were you doing?" Her eyes meet mine again.

I stoop, and grip my bootlaces, tugging them, and tugging again. They are chilled, cold, half frozen. It's getting too cold out there. "I was looking for some eider flowers, but I dropped them when I was startled by a man and his hound."

Alvea's face pales sheet-white, her eyes widen, hope glinting across them. "There are lots here?" Her voice is low, barely a breath.

A step creaks on the floor behind me. "What man?" Yore's voice is sharp, hard.

My fingers fumble with the laces of my boots, red hair dropping over my eyes in a mass. I shove it back, grip thc laces again. "He was by a cabin. I came upon him, and he sent me home, told me how to get back after calling his hound off." My fingers pause. I never asked him his name. "I don't know who he was. But his hound was massive." I have no idea what his name was, the man with the axe in the wood. I didn't think to ask about it.

"So, you didn't find your way back on your own." Yore. My head shoots up. His voice is curt, amused.

I grit my teeth, jerk my boot off. "Nie. He told me the way. He knew our cabin, said it was called the Moni cabin. That's a dwarvish name, isn't it?" My eyes lift to Yore.

His arms are crossed, large over his chest, a smile at the corners of his mouth, almost smug. "It is, va. Many of the settlers who tried to live here were dwarvish. There was a colony of them that left the house of Stevnar to go north and claim their own territory a year or so back."

I straighten, press my hands against my knee. "How do you know that? Isn't Stevnar one of the lower clans, down south?"

Yore's mouth twitches, barely down, the smile still there, less smug now, almost normal. "Stevnar is a cregf, not a clan. And Storna is a middle clan, not so far from ours. There were often travelers from there at the lake docks." My head snaps up. Yore never speaks of the docks. His face darkens, he looks away, jerking his hat back onto his head. "I'm going to do the calli." He grips the door, and jerks it open, gone into the night. He still won't speak of them. And he didn't take a lantern. I purse my lips, fingers slipping on the laces of my boot, and my hair is in my face again, blocking my vision. When did it fall out of my braid?

Alvea shifts, moving her hands against her skirts. She hasn't moved from her place, her posture stiff and elegant, but it's too sharp now. Her eyes are wide, earnest, sharp, hopeful. They shift to me. "You met a man? There are really people out here? What was he like?"

She sounds relieved. I turn, brush my hair back from my face, the red curls tangling in my fingers. I shake my head. "It was just one man... he didn't mention any others. But he is here. He isn't very friendly though. I would not go back there." Her face falls a little, and she straightens, masking it behind those eyes again, the eyes that are grandmere's and not.

"Well," she steps forward, even, "one man is hopeful. We are not alone, and that... that is hopeful. It is hopeful. Maybe it won't be so barren out here, after all this." Won't be as barren as we thought it would be, when Yore came home from a summon to the cregf, the only time we'd ever been summoned, only to give us the word that we were leaving, that we were going nowhere, to save him from going somewhere, after he'd been gone for months. Alvea nods her head, her chin still high. "It is hopeful."

I swallow and turn away. Hopeful? One man? Is one man alone, with a hound as tall as my chest hopeful? One man with an axe that didn't care for me being there? Is it better than being alone, knowing there is a man who does not want us to be here, didn't want me anywhere near his hut? I straighten, drop my boots by the door. It gives Alvea hope. Her eyes are alight, spark still barely there, her hands lifting bowls, setting them on the counter.

I look down. I dropped the eider flowers. Those will be wasted on the ground beside his hut, ground into the earth or left there to rot, or be blown away by the winter winds that will be here too soon.

Chapter IV

I lift a dish, humming a little at the back of my throat. The waft stops, and Alvea's hands are suddenly still on the weaving.

I turn, setting the dish on the shelf, and flick my eyes half to her. "Alvea?"

She is sitting by her loom, hands gripping the top of it, eyes set. She turns, toward me, face still. "You should go get Yore. It's time to eat." Her voice is tight and sharp, irritated.

I frown, dropping my hands. "Why are you upset?"

She folds hers perfectly in her lap and doesn't rise. "I'm not. It's time to eat. Go get Yore from the shed. Now. It does not do to wait on things that will be better at present." She brushes off her skirts, hands sliding perfectly over the dark fabric over her skin.

I scowl. "If you aren't irritated then why are you talking like that?"

She smiles, perfectly, and stands, her limp hidden beneath her skirts and that posture, like it is when she is annoyed or frustrated at me. "I'm not irritated. I am quite happy." She smiles, but it clings to her lips, not reaching her eyes. "Will you please go get Yore?" I frown and brush a curl out of my face. Fine. I turn and slip my feet into the walking shoes by the door. My socks are nearly too thick for them, a gift, a hand-me-down from the woman down the road the day before we left. They were made for her, fitted to her feet and not mine. She had a new pair.

My fingers grip the doorknob, pull it open and there is air, brisk and cool on my skin. My steps sound hollow on the porch, sharp over the sound of the running stream. There is a strange mewling call, one of the calli. I will never get used to their cry. I hop to the ground and turn. The shed is small, a contrast sharp against the nothingness of beyond. There is a calli in the little yard, its shaggy wool short, head lazy, straw jutting out of its mouth from where the sharp teeth must be. Nasty, stinky things. Its tail flickers, long, with that strange tuft of hair on the end, slapping its thick coat.

I press the door open, and the dirt floor thuds beneath the clogs on my feet. "Yore?" Something calls beside me, sharp and high. I jump, heart thundering in my chest, eyes darting to the floor. A calli stares back at me, vacant sheep eyes, long off-white snout and straw aimlessly chewed in its mouth. Just a calli. I suck in a breath and turn away. There is nothing in here, but shadows, calli and a pile of straw strone across the floor. I lick my lips. "Yore?"

"I'm outside." The voice is muffled, somewhere out behind the walls.

My breath heaves, and I turn, tightening my arms over my chest. It's cold out here. The door taps shut, handle clicking into place behind me, and I step around the fence, turning. Yore is standing where the fence ends, his arm is above his head, height stretched to its full extent, his hand gripping a branch, tugging on it. I frown. "Yore?"

He fumbles with the branch, jerks. There is a snap, cracking, and the branch is in his hand, colliding with the ground by his feet. He turns and tosses the evergreen branch in with the calli.

I frown. "Can they eat that?"

He turns, his expression dry. "They eat dried heather. They can eat anything. What do you want?" His arms fold over his chest, eyes emotionless.

I nod, back toward the hut. "Alvea says it is time to eat. Why did you break that branch?"

His brow lifts, and he nods, slowly, toward the shed. "It was going to hit the roof in the winter. I don't want the damage." He shifts his jaw. My mouth twitches upward, and he scowls. "What?"

I shake my head, brush a strand of hair out of my face. "Just thinking of all the girls who are in love with your jawline back home. They used to say it was cut from the softest stone, didn't they?"

His face flushes, barely visible in his bronzed skin, but there, and he turns his eyes away. "They used to say a lot of things."

I laugh, and it echoes in the trees. His eyes crinkle in the corners. That's good to see. "They did. They said we were crazy for coming out here."

His smile vanishes, and his eyes flash, those honey-colored eyes that are the same as mine, the same as our pakem, who failed. "Because I'm ruining your chances of living, right? Taking you to an empty wasteland, ruining your lives?" His voice is sharp, eyes burning into mine.

I shake my head, grip my skirts. "Nie, Yore, they were being foolish. You weren't being crazy. You weren't ruining chances, neither of ours. Alvea had nothing waiting for her there." Ruined our chances? This isn't all his fault.

His eyes narrow. "I wasn't?" He shakes his head, jaw tightening, shoulders clenched, and he is turning away from me. "Tell Alvea I'm not hungry. I have something to tend in the forest."

My lips snap together. "Yore." He doesn't stop. I did this, again. I caused a rift again. "Yore, you should come in. Alvea is in a sour mood. It will make her happier to see you. Please. Please don't go out there."

His breath snorts, a scoff, feet still carrying him away. "It won't. Go in, Oanéka, or you'll catch your death out here dressed like that." My arms tighten. Dressed like what? I shake my head, and turn back, toward the house. Alvea is going to be irritated. She always is, when Yore doesn't come in. He didn't need to react that strongly. It was barely a slip up.

I step onto the porch, and drag the door open, air cold where my hands were on my arms. Alvea is in the kitchen, her hands moving, gathering the dishes, setting the table. She turns, a brow raising at me. "Is Yore behind you?"

I swallow, fold my arms. "He said to tell you that he's not hungry and had something to tend in the forest."

Her mouth tightens, a thin line and her eyes sharpen, darker. "He what? He can't have anything to tend that is more important than eating. That's foolishness." She steps forward, toward the door, and her movements are uneven, one step, one hobble, hands clenched.

"Alvea." I reach out, too far away to reach her. "Please don't. He'll be furious."

Her eyes narrow, and she leans toward me. "He'll be furious?! We don't spend all morning making food for him not to eat it. The least he could do is just come in!" She spins back toward the kitchen, and her steps are sharper, one step, one hobble. She grabs a bowl and shoves it back onto the shelf. "Just because Pakem is gone doesn't mean he can do whatever he wants. I thought he'd changed. I thought he was going to do better." Her words are sharp, sharper than her eyes were, and they are bitter.

I thought we'd all changed. I have, I'm aimless and empty, but Alvea is sharp and curt again, her back straighter than her leg can hold, and Yore is gone, off to skies know where. But we came here to share this with him, didn't we? This was all for him. Alvea is right. We shouldn't have to suffer anymore just because he is angry at the world and won't acknowledge where we are now. This isn't right. This isn't fair, to be here.

* * * * * * * * * *

Alvea's hands are working quickly with the threads beneath her fingers, her head bent low over them. I purse my lips. She's been quiet all day, still quiet today. I swallow and move toward the door. I can at least go get a breath. "I'm going for a walk."

Her head tilts up. "Don't get lost this time." She turns her eyes back down. My lips tighten. 'Don't get lost this time?' *I wasn't going to get lost. I didn't plan to lose my way last time.* I grip my shawl, jerk it over my arms, and pull the door open before me.

The porch is hollow beneath my steps, and the air is chill through my shawl, and maybe it's colder today. *Foolish. This is all foolishness. She could have been nicer about that. I'm not trying to cause problems for her, or to bother her in there.*

She never bothered me about what I did back home. 'Don't worry about it, Oanéka. I've got it. I'll tend that.' I shake my head. *I don't understand why it bothers her so much now, what I do in there, or out here. She could be more kind about it. I would pace back home, wouldn't I?* My heart freezes. *No. But mamé did, before she left. She used to every day.*

I step on a rock, and the creek rushes around, flowing over stones and singing, softly, quietly like a muffled thing that cannot breathe. Like the world out here. Trees too short, browned too soon, never growing or thriving upward. Like death, creeping in slowly like it did in the villages back home. Sticks crumble beneath my feet, and I move around a tree, and another, and there is a boulder, on the earth, and the tree where I hid the eider flowers. There are only a few there, the ones I found in the days before I met the man with an axe and dropped the most that I had ever found in an afternoon. *Should I have looked for more, since then? The woods seem strange, after meeting someone in them. They are no longer just ours.*

A petal has blown off the nearest flower, out of the hole in the tree, caught in the leaves that litter the earth. A spot of color, dusty, pale, bleak pink in a world of nothingness. There is a fern beside it, half dead. *There must have been a frost last night. The last of the plants will be gone now, leaving just the dried blooms, scattered throughout a blank forest.*

It's not like the garden I left at home, full of color and life. A few dried, tiny flowers, crumbling on the ground. Nothing like the hundreds of dahlias, just about to bloom, nothing like the last of the fruit crops, bright and full of promise, nothing like the pumpkins and apples and shade crops that were all ready. It's a shadow, a passing shadow. That's all there is out here, only shadows of the things that are back home. A shadow of a home. Death. This is a death land, isn't it? Isn't that what winter is? Winter is death, death of all things beautiful, leaving only darkness, shadows and life without color, without light. Beauty was wrapped in all the colors, and there are none here. Only green and brown and gray, endless gray, in the shadows, in the sky and the trees.

I can't cope without warmth for so long, without color, without life. Five long years. Five long years with little that is beautiful, little that is bright and lovely and real. Only this harsh world. Only the bleakness of this wood, of the mountain off in the distance, alone, gray.

I step back, away from the tree and leaves crumble beneath my shoes, brown and empty, and the forest answers nothing back. *It's all just empty out here.* I turn.

"Child?" My heart stops in my throat. The voice is deep and full, a man's voice. I jerk backward, stumbling, eyes darting. Where is he? "Whoa, child," the voice again, through the trees, and it rumbles with a laugh, "I do not mean to frighten you."

A figure moves forward, and there is a man, taller than Yore by a yard, a horse beneath him, but there is no horse head visible, only the length of his cloak and the legs of the horse, moving with him. His hair is long, flowing, clinging and shifting with the gentleness of the breeze. I can't see the head of the horse.

A centaur. It's a centaur, taller than any man, his face hollow lines, and beard cut to a point on his face. *A centaur. I've never seen one before. They are not supposed to live in the north country. Are they? I've never seen one before.*

I swallow, my heart thudding. "I am sorry." *Centaur. Am I mistaken about them? Do they live up here? Do they dwell up here where no one lives, but the man and his hound and us?*

His eyebrow lifts, and his mouth twitches, upward. "What are you apologizing for? You have done nothing but jump at my sudden approach. I would have done the same."

I shift my shoulders, press them against the tree beside me. He's tall, and his voice is like that of a Dryland man that came through the village years ago, smooth and strange. I look up at him. "I did not mean to start, but I did not expect to find anyone here." There is silence, for a moment, and his eyes slip up toward the trees, and the wind brushes through. I swallow. What do you say to a stranger in the woods, to a centaur? I swallow again and fold my hands over my arms. "Do you have a name, cava?"

His eyes slip back to me, and they feel like deep pools, seeing more than I want them too. "Ovior. And I see that you are no child." He steps forward, calmly and gracefully, a stride that I could never match. "My tribe is merely passing through. Do you live in these parts?"

I shake my head. "Nie..." That's not true. I swallow. "Va. We do."

He smiles, bright and slow. "But not for long, I take it."

I shake my head. "Nie. Only a fortnight and a half. Where are you bound for, cava?"

He shakes his head, shifting his feet. "Not for, but from. We have spent the summer months in the heart of the frost world and are on our way back to the warmer places, before the cold comes." His eyes flicker to me, a brow lifting. "This is a strange place to come to winter, child."

I swallow, shake my head. "It's to settle a debt." I shouldn't have told him that. My jaw tightens. *There is no need for him not to know. We are not like to see him again.*

He nods, and his eyes soften, deepen, like he can see something that I don't know. "Be careful of bitterness out here, child. It can creep in quietly, if you are not looking. Find something that you enjoy." He moves, as if to walk away.

I shove off the tree, force my feet under me. "What if there is nothing that you enjoy here?"

His steps pause, and he turns back. His tail swishes, moving the fabric of his cloak. The wind brushes again, throwing hair across my face. "How could there possibly be nothing to enjoy?" His eyes find mine. "What have you left behind that could be so important? A man? A friend?"

My eyes feel damp. "Beauty. I left beauty. And life. There is no man." *Why am I telling him this?* "Yore and Alvea left other things, but I think they will find them again out here, but mine doesn't exist in this empty, frozen place. It's just so barren. There is so little of life here."

His brow lifts. "Life?" His head shakes. "No, kif. This land isn't empty of life, or empty of beauty. It is there, and you had best find it, or with that thought in your head, you will lose your mind to this place with the empty months of winter."

My heart sinks. "Find beauty?" He can't help. There will be no answers. Only endless months. Only the cold, on and on and the emptiness. "How... how can you find beauty? Or find life?"

His mouth lifts again, that soft smile, and he laughs, breathy and short. "Why, look for it, kif. How do you find anything? You will find what you look for in a place like this."

My heart drops lower. "But..." my throat feels empty, hollow, "how can you find something that isn't there? There is nothing out here."

"Isn't there?" He laughs again. "Kif, Elainai wove beauty into all that He made." I swallow, wrap my hands in my skirts, and he laughs. "Did He not make this place too? If you value beauty and life so much, then you will not find it lacking here. Look for it. You are blinded by a pathetic idea of what it is that will not help you. Look, kif. Take it in. Take time to seek it and you will not find it lacking" His eyes lift, off to the trees, and his legs shift beneath him again. "I must go." He nods, a slight movement and the wind brushes, throwing the cloak across his legs. He nods again and turns. "Look for the small things, kif. Look to what is small." He steps behind the trees, moving through the trunks and he is gone, behind a cluster of rocks stacked upon each other, barren in the woods. There are steps, crunching in the forest off somewhere, the sound greater than one landlot could make alone. *His tribe.*

I bolt forward, around the tree boulders, and there is something moving off, in the distance, in the trees. *Centaurs.* There must be fifteen of them, moving through the trees, off down along the ridge. The wind catches my skirts, throwing hair across my face, and the last of them are vanishing through the trees. *Will we see them back, in the future, or have the last of them gone now? Will they be brave enough to come back next year, to this lonely world?*

I flick my eyes to my fingers, gripping the edge of my cloak. *Find beauty. He says it can be found. 'Or with that mind, you'll lose your mind in the endless months.'* *There must be a trace of it somewhere, in the brown upon brown upon brown. But where, in this endless forest?*

Trees stretch out everywhere, and the pale, vacant shadows barely visible on the leaves below rustling in the wind below the gray of the clouds. *There is nothing beautiful here. There never has been beauty in winter before, back home when the long months came, with snow, and with silence and with pain, and chapped feet and cracked lips. I would have seen it. I would have seen it, back home, when the gray months came with nothing but the aching in your chest and the days that won't end.* I turn, and my steps crunch on the leaves left over from a season already gone. *Find beauty. The stag, and ferns, they were a trace, a little of what is beautiful out here. But the ferns are lost to cold, and the stag to the forest. There must be something else, more real, more bright out here, somewhere. 'In the small things...'*

The stream gurgles in front of me, quiet, and I pause. The cabin is all shadow, clouds across the sky leaving no light to stream upon it over the trees, and the light inside is barely visible behind the one open window. There is etching, thick on the posts, wild, like an old story of banishment and monsters and forests. *Who carved those images, on the post? Did the man in the woods know them, or was he here when they left?* I shake my head, leaves rustling, branches tapping hollow against each other over my head. *Where do you look for something not tangible? Something not present in plain, obvious ways? Something seen best in life where green things grow? That is where it has always been, in the dirt, in watering the soil, and watching the life spring from it, blooms and leaves and bulbs, all leading to something better, with a hundred flowers all sprung at once to life.*

My steps tap against the rocks, and then are silent on the earth beside the stream. The water is gray beneath, the same in the sky, and the world feels darker. *Small things? Like rocks or moles? What small things are there out here, in this broken, vacant place, with only a harsh man and his hounds and us for company? With only people who come through only to leave again, when their time is done, like us and the centaur? What else could there be, in this place?*

Chapter V

The air feels cooler today, licking at my skin, a breath of autumn on the wind, and there are clouds rolling overhead. I drop the buckets to the side, and my hands ache, marks white in my palms from the handles. I grimace and press them together.

The calli are standing beside the fence, their heads dipped into the water trough, mouths gulping up the water I just filled it with. One of them lifts her head, and bleats, just once, toward the shed. I grimace and brush a strand of hair out of my face. I pull the door open, and duck inside. Yore had better be back before they need water again. He didn't tell me when we brought them that I would have to tend them.

Alvea is on her seat, the waft in her hand, slipping between the strands of the fabric, a pale, soft orange. She looks up, and back down again. I slip my shoes off and toss the shawl over the rack. Her hands are still moving. "You look disgusted."

I scoff. "They are foul."

She shifts the bar, and back up again. "They?"

I scowl. "The calli. I was watering them like Yore asked." *I should be out, like the centaur said, looking for beauty before it gets cold, not doing this, but I cannot today, because Yore is gone hunting.*

She looks up, sharply, her nose lifting. "I know what you were doing," she says, her voice is curt. "I just didn't know what you were talking about when you just say 'them.' You should have started with that." She looks back down, and her hands are moving again as if I never walked in.

I shake my head and move toward the water bucket in the kitchen. "I thought you would have been able to put it together. It is not like there are many things out here that I could be referring to." I grit my teeth and dunk my hands into the bucket. The water is cold, still not much warmer than when I hauled it in from the creek. "They smell horrible, and they lay down in their own filth. It's repulsive." *It's no wonder Pakem always said that he would never be a farmer again, after we left the farm. I wouldn't want to be either, if it involved calli. Or sheep.*

She scoffs, a breathy, harsh sound. "Well then why don't you wash them? That would give you something to do for the rest of the day, wouldn't it? Then you wouldn't have to wander around anymore."

I spin toward her, fold my arms, my hands jutted awkwardly out to keep the water from dripping on my skirts. "I won't be in your way, if that is what you are worried about." *Give them a bath? That's absurd. No one bathes animals, aside from shows.* Water drips to the floor from my outstretched hands. I turn, dunk them back into the bucket.

Hers are still moving, busy, weaving. "I'm not worried that you'll be in my way. I just don't want you pacing. 'Pacers never profit anything.' And you said yourself that they smell bad. 'That which smells bad should be cleaned.'"

I purse my lips and shake my head. "I don't want any of your sayings today. And I'm doing the laundry, so you won't have to worry about where I am. And if I did wash them, they would just be filthy again in an hour, way faster than the time it would take me to even get one clean."

She looks up, sharply and her eyes are wide. "It's laundry day?" Her voice is startled, soft and loud at once.

I nod, lifting a cup from the shelf. I plunge it into the bucket. "Va. Yesterday was, actually, but I forgot it, so I am doing it today." Her hands are motionless on the loom, and her face is pale, eyes wide and dark.

She stands, spinning toward the back room. "I didn't realize we were off days. I thought we were doing well." Her voice is off, almost trembling, and she is gone through the doorway into Yore's room.

I shake my head and bring the cup to my lips. The water is cool, and I swallow, swallow again. *I am used to being the one who worried about doing things on the correct days. Where are all her sayings about taking time to do each thing that needs to be done? She hasn't quoted that in weeks.*

Alvea steps through the doorway, Yore's second set of clothes under her arm, a wad of dirty stockings in her other hand by her side. She steps forward. "Are you doing these outside?"

I shake my head, sharply, and the water catches in my throat. "What? Nie. It's cold out there."

She lifts a brow. "We live in the Frostlands, Oanéka. It's going to be cold, and it's less messy doing it out there, and it's less cold now than it will be when winter truly sets in."

I shake my head again and turn toward the ladder. "I can't use my fingers if they are numb, and that will make it far more messy than a few spots on the floor to mop up after.

I'm doing it in the kitchen." I grip the ladder, and start up. She is still standing in the middle of the floor, Yore's dirty clothes in her hands, and her shoulders tight, irritated.

I shake my head and pull myself up into the loft.

* * * * * * * *

The door swings open and Yore steps in through it. There is a smear on his cheek, bright red. *Blood.* His sleeves are rolled up, a strangely stained bag clasped in his hand, and his hair bound back tightly.

I jump up, bolt around him and push the door shut. Cold air swirls in the room, cutting through the sleeves of my dress. I press my hands against my arms, and stare at him, shiver. He is moving toward the table. Alvea stiff in her chair, her hands holding the waft awkwardly out beside the fireplace.

I step forward, press my hands into my skirts. "What did you catch?" I say.

Yore grins, turning toward me. It's a halfhearted thing, as if he can't help it. "A deer. Big one. Shot it through the heart before it knew I was there." He slips his bow from his shoulder and sets it against the wall. There is another bag on his back, lumpy and strange, stained like the first one. *The stag. Surely it wasn't the stag. There has to be more than one large deer out in this forest. It cannot have been the stag. Though this one must surely have been large.*

I swallow and point toward the bag on his back. "What is in there?"

He slips it from his shoulder, and steps forward, dropping the one from his hand onto the table. "It's the hide. I'll take it back out to the shed now, so that you don't have to worry with it being in here." He turns toward the door, glancing over his shoulder at me again. "Get the salt." He pulls the door open, and steps through again into the fading light.

I spin and move back toward the barrels at the back of the room. *Which one was the salt in? I didn't pack any of these.* I slip my fingers under the lid of the first one and pry it up. It comes free, slowly, wooden slab popping off into my hand. I shove the bag inside open. *Oats. Thank the stars we didn't bring that much salt.* I press the lid back down, and slip my fingers beneath the next one, pry it open slowly. It pops up, and there is a single bag again, large and wadded together. I shove it open, wheat grains scattering over the bucket space. *Not the salt.* I shove the lid shut, and the door is creaking open again behind me, cold air swirling for a moment into the room. I shiver, stretch my body over the barrels toward the other ones.

My fingers slip under the lid of the third barrel, and I pry it off. There are several bag mouths, wadded together at the top. I lean forward, over the other barrel and slip my hand into the first bag. Rose hips. A small bag. I shove it closed. Yore's steps are heavy across the room, moving toward the table. "Do you have the salt?"

I shake my head and shove my hand into the next bag. Coarse grains brush my skin, clinging to it. I grip the bag and jerk it out. It's heavy, and small, and definitely salt. I drag it across the other buckets and turn back to Yore. He reaches forward, and takes it, sets it on the table beside him, and flings open the meat bag. His eyes glance at me, his face almost light, like I haven't seen it in weeks. He seems calmer, as though there is now less weight on him. "Get a small barrel, to store these in. There are some empty ones in my room." I nod, and turn, back toward his room. There is the damp sound of raw meat slapping wood behind me. I step through his doorway.

His bed is made, neat and plain, a nightshirt tossed across his pillow. At the foot of the bed, barrels are stacked beside his tiny wooden chest. I grip one and pull it. *Empty.* I grab it and turn back toward the other room. Yore is moving strips of meat around, setting them in piles of strips of sizes that are alike. *I should have grabbed two of these. This one little barrel won't be enough, thank heavens, for all of it.* I set the barrel on the table beside him, and shove back the sleeves of my dress.

His movements slow, and he looks over at me, his back stooped a little over the table, hands still moving the meat. He lifts another strip, setting it on a pile of others. "I met your red hound today."

My heart stops. "You met Gyaith?" That was her name, wasn't it?

He nods, setting another chunk of meat on the stack. "She was out with her master, and two other hounds. He seemed to have had the same idea I did for the day."

"Did he mention any others?" Alvea's voice is soft and eager. She is leaning forward, her hands no longer busy.

"Other hounds?" She gives him a look. Yore shakes his head, a grin pulling at his lips. "I believe he is alone, with his hounds. He didn't mention anyone else." He glances at me. "They are impressive. I have not seen their like."

I grimace and lift a chunk of meat. "They are large." I lift another piece, and my lips twist down. It feels disgusting. *This won't feel so awful salted and stored.* I nudge the bag of salt with my elbow, and tip it. Salt pours sideways, onto the table space. I shove the bag away with the side of my arm and drop the piece of meat into the pool of salt on the table, rolling it. "Did you get his name?" I look up at him.

He shrugs, shoving the empty meat bag to the side. There are four piles of meat now, of varying sizes, some with bones still in it, other in tiny strips. "Wasn't important." He rolls another strip in the salt, folding it over and over.

Alvea's back straightens, her eyes snapping to him. "Yore." Her voice is sharp, exhasperated. "He's the only person we know of for miles. Names are important." She shakes her head, her hands gripping the waft.

He shifts, lifting a chunk of meat, and cuts it from the bone. "I know plenty of folk at the docks—" his voice cuts off, and he stiffens, freezing. He turns his face down, his shoulders tight, hands gripping the meat tightly. The room is dead quiet, with only the slap of the meat and the roll of the grains of salt beneath it. His back is stiff, hands busy, moving fast. *He won't say anything more now. He never does. He won't talk about them, won't talk about what he did there, the things we never saw, but the whole village spoke of, when they spoke of the vagabonds and the useless men. Those who wasted their lives, like pakem, and Yore, both wasting theirs with useless men.* I swallow hard, and lift another chunk of meat, drop it in the salt, and rub my hand over it, the grains rough and grinding against my skin and to the liquid that still clings to it. *Does he assume we knew it all, from those who talked about what those boys—men—did night after night? Is that what the shame in his eyes is from? He must have seen it on the faces of the villagers, or perhaps known it when we didn't go look for him when he stopped coming home. Perhaps I should have looked for him, gone to find him. But we already knew then, where he was. Would it have made it better or worse, to have seen him there?*

I flick my eyes toward Alvea. *What is she thinking of? Her days spent by the loom, never leaving it?* Her face is drawn, lips tight, eyes focused on her work again, a shadow cast from the fire across her eyes. *She didn't offer to help.* I frown. She always offers to help. My fingers flip the chunk of meat, and I toss it into the barrel, salt coating it over. Her hands are moving slowly, fingers parting the threads to slip through.

Chapter VI

Find beauty.

This is foolishness. Beauty is found in the bright things, the colorful, the wonderful things. There are none of those here. Not one of them, in this place.

The board of the porch step presses against my leg, skirts heavy on the one below. I fold my hands together and drop them between my legs resting on the skirts. The woods are dull. Hopelessly dull, dead and barren. *Beauty? 'Seek it'? You can't just find something simply because you have sought for it. It does not make it there to be found.*

I drop my head against my hands. *This is useless. It's been two weeks, and there is nothing. Maybe I am just looking at it at the wrong angle. There has to be something I am missing. What all did he say, anyway? 'Elnial wove beauty into everything that He made. You will not find it lacking here.'*

'Not find it lacking.' The trees are barren, skeletons, like death all around, and the ground is empty and plain, barren. *There isn't any beauty. It's all just brown and dull, dead.*

I press my hands against the steps, and push up, dusting off my skirts. My shawl slips off my arms, tangling in my skirts. I grimace, gripping it, and pull it back over my arms. *There must be something out there. There is nothing more to be done today. I can find it.*

My feet tap a rock, and I hop over it, knees jarring as the ground collides with my feet again. The stream runs in front of me, water trickling down, around stones, quiet and deep. I still. *Shouldn't I go some other way? This way, I have found nothing but eider flowers. And stags. And centaur. And wild men with hounds.* I shake my head. *All of those things I have found, but it is time to try another direction.*

I turn, and step around the rocks, skirts swishing around my feet. Boots tap the earth, and I hop over a rock, step around a log. *I can find it. There has to be something, somewhere. One thing out here. Doesn't there?* Trees reach out, at the edge of the tiny field, their branches bare to the sky. *They all look the same, trees after trees after trees. On the wagon, on the way up, it was the same. Trees after trees after trees, endless and the same, the endless dull browns, the endless plain, harsh greens. No beauty, just barrenness. The centaur was wrong. It's not here. Maybe to the studied mind there is something worth admiring here, but not to us, not to real people who just live. Not to the normal folk.*

He said Elnial wove beauty into all that He made. But surely He didn't weave it into this place, on the edge of nowhere where man doesn't go. Except those that are banished. This is foolishness. 'You'll lose your mind...' I'm already losing it. And we've not even been here three months.

* * * * * * * *

Alvea's breaths are soft, across the room on her cot. Something thuds downstairs, soft and heavy on the floor. *Steps. It must be dawn.* A yawn cracks through my chest, and I pull myself upward. The blankets roll off my arms, and I shiver, pulling them back up. *It's cold. The fire must have gone down over night.* I slip my feet over the side of my cot, and my stockings are soft against the floor, eyes heavy. Cold creeps against my legs. I shiver again—the air tastes stale, darkness heavy over the room. I stumble, and my hand fumbles with something. *Fabric. My day dress.* I jerk it over my head, and fumble, fingers slipping and sliding in the garment. I grip the ties, and pull them into place, and turn. I slide my foot forward, where the opening for the ladder should be.

My foot collides with a wall. I grimace, dropping to my knees and press my fingers along the wall. There is air, an empty place where the wall isn't. *At last.* I shuffle forward, hands and knees against the floor, and turn, backing down the ladder. The faint glow of light brushes the walls, orange and pale, and someone yawns across the room, long, slow and low.

I drop to the floor and rub my hands against my eyes. Yore is kneeling by the rack, tying his boots on. My eyes flicker to the window. It's barely gray out, dawn not here yet. I frown, press a hand against my eyes. "Where are you going?" My voice is a frog in my throat, harsh and low. My face warms.

He doesn't look up, brushes hair from his face as if it could reach his eyes. *It can almost now. It's grown a lot since we've been out here.* "Outside." There is silence in the room, only the popping of the fire and the shifting of his fingers on the boot laces. *Like the shifting of mice back home in the farmhouse walls.*

My arms are cold. I rub my hands over them and turn toward the kitchen. The buckets are by the washbasin, one empty, and one full of dishwater, grimy and cloudy. *They'll have to go out.* I stumble, and grip a bucket, and pull. It thuds against my shin, and my skin throbs. I grimace, rub my leg. *Foolish.* I snatch up the other and turn toward the door. Yore's figure is vanishing through it, and there is a gust of cold air, the clicking of the door closing. I scowl. *It's cold. Too cold out there.* I shudder.

I slip my feet into my walking clogs. I lift my shawl from the hook, and my hands barely get it over my arms, fabric slipping and sliding between my fingers, clumsy. I hook it into place, and turn, the bucket handles coarse beneath my fingers, and grip the door, dragging it open.

The air hits my face, chilled, frozen, and the world is all gray, coated with something, the ground gleams barely with the growing light of the dawn.

Frost. It frosted. And the air is deathly silent, not a sound of the world beyond.

My breath is a cloud before my face, misting in the chill of the air, and I step forward, drag the door shut behind me. The creek is singing quietly, its voice blending with the silence of the morning, as if a hum, as if the voice of the forest.

Frost. It's like silver, covering each blade of grass, each stone, and the steps of the porch, scuffed where Yore stepped down. *Frost. It isn't supposed to be beautiful. But it is. It kills all the things of summer—flowers, plants and grass. Back home it always meant the end of the garden, the end of warmth and harvest, death to all that wasn't gathered in before it came. But it is beautiful.* Light, pale and thin, trickles through the tree branches, and the grass is like a thousand tiny stones, caught with the rising of the sun.

My breath is caught in my chest, throat tight. *Frost. There is beauty, in winter. Beauty here. The centaur was right.* I laugh, and my breath is a cloud in the air. *This means the last of life is gone, leaving only endless winter, endless cold, endless pain, death. I was wrong. I was wrong about this. Is there more out here, or only this? Is this the end of the beauty, with the coming of the real breath of winter's dawn, or is it the beginning, with the long months and the aching gray ahead?*

I move down the steps, my clog half sliding on the frost that covers them. The sun is rising, the color growing with morning, and the tree branches are black against the sky, against the pink-gray hue. The world is brighter with the blue of the grass, the tiny ice that coats each blade.

It's stunning. And cold. Like a flower garden never could be. Frost. It's beautiful, in the light of the rising morning, a thousand tiny blades caught like stars spread over each one, a thousand tiny glimmers of silver. The tree branches are caught in it too, tiny slivers of silver ice brushing each beautiful branch.

I stoop and brush my fingers against the tiny grass. Cold bites my fingers, and it is lovely, a blanket over each blade, etching so small, so elegant that the finest of jewelers could not do the like, or match the simplicity. The brown of it is no longer separate, no longer alone and dead, but woven together in the gray-silver of winter dawn. *Beauty in the darkness, beauty in the light of winter.*

I lift my head, and my eyes are burning, throat tight. Light is blushed through the forest, pale and gray, cutting through the endless trees, caught up in shadows and frost, and their branches are light, bright and beautiful over the evergreen and the endless brown. And everything is the same, and different. We still can't go home. And this is enough and not, in the icy fingers of dawn. There has to be something else. Something more out here.

Light hits the ground, and there is gold, blending with the silver, and casting blue shadows across the ground, so few colors, and so many hues in the morning of winter. And it's beautiful, cutting across the ground.

Chapter VII

There are patterns on the windowpanes, only visible from this side of the panes with the shutters closed, as they always are. The detail is thin, finer than the most careful stitches that I've seen done by the women back south. *It's so beautiful, delicate, the frost on the glass of the window.* My fingers are clumsy, cold. *The shawl is too thin today.* I swallow, and step forward, looking closer at the lacework of the frost strands. *Like flowers, frozen into glass, colorless, pale and beautiful. People often spoke of snow as a beautiful thing, when it first comes down, but they never spoke of frost this way. No one speaks of frost this way.*

I lift the buckets and turn back to the house. My breath is a cloud in front of me, misty and white, and the frost is still coating all the grass and the tree branches under the clouds of the sky. *Without the sun, will the frost last longer today? Yesterday, it was gone in an hour. But today? It might last longer with the sky covered over. I've never noticed how frost fared. Back home, it was a plague. But here, there was little to die, only the ferns that were already half gone. They'll all have been touched today. The frost was thicker, coating every branch in silver beneath the gray of the sky.*

I shake my head and set down the buckets on the porch; it creaks beneath them. My hand fumbles with the doorknob. I pull it open, and the air is warm, hitting my face. The fire crackles, around the corner where the kitchen space is, and Alvea's seat is empty. I tip my foot back, knocking the door shut, and the bucket in my hand sloshes, dangerously close to the edge. I freeze, and swallow. The water slows. I turn, steps sounding on the floor. *Alvea must have gone upstairs, or to the loo.*

I set the buckets down and lift my hands. They are white, crinkled with cold and I can't feel the skin as I press my fingers against it. *Cold. It's getting colder out there.*

A step taps, door opening at the back of the room where the loo is, and I turn. Alvea steps in, dusting her hands on her skirts. Her eyes lift. I turn back toward the fireplace, rub my hands together in the ring of heat.

Her steps pause by the chairs. "Did you get your hands wet?"

I shake my head, and slow the rubbing, my skin tingling a little before the fire. "Nie. It's just colder today than it was yesterday. I am glad the dwarves who built this place knew a little about plumbing for the loo, but it would have been nice if they'd known something about kitchen plumbing as well."

Alvea shakes her head—there is a smile, at the edges of her mouth. "Hauling water isn't so bad." She drops into her chair, tilting her bad leg to the side. She lifts her work. "It's good to have something to do first thing in the mornings."

I nod and press my thumbnail against my fingertip. *I still can't feel it.* I rub a little faster. "It's beautiful out there, with the frost on the ground." I fold my hands under my arms. "The creek was half frozen today."

Her head jerks up, eyes startled. "Already?"

I nod, and the fire crackles, flames licking too close to my fingers. I hiss, and jerk my hands back, pain spiraling through my them. I shove them under my armpits. "Va. I guess we'll have to start breaking it soon." I turn toward her. "Do you think that is what people do? Just break the ice when it freezes?"

She shrugs, and picks up the waft, but her hands are slower. "I don't know. I didn't ask many questions about living away from a village. I didn't think to." She shakes her head, turning the waft over in her hands. "I'd assumed that there would have been others out here, at least someone who would give us the information that we needed..." Her voice trails off, and she looks up at me. "Do you think there is much that we don't know? Surely it must be like preparing for winter back home. It cannot be that different. Wood and food stores and things. Barrels of water indoors in case of ice storms?"

I shake my head and turn toward the fire again. My hands are tingling all over, skin turning bright red. They are aching, skin still stiff and strange. I grimace. "I don't know. It at least can't be that different. Winter is winter, isn't it?" I tuck my hands under my arms again.

She slides the bar down on the loom, plucking a string. "Yore may know more." She looks up, sharply, and her eyes set. "Someone needs to find that man from the woods and ask him some questions. He must know more than we do about the world out here. You should ask him."

I freeze. "Me?" *There are hounds. Yore said he had three of them, and I didn't like the only one I met. There are two more.*

She nods, hands moving faster now. "You are the only one who knows where he lives, and Yore will never go ask him. You should. If he sent you home with directions, then he must at least be somewhat reasonable. A halfway decent man."

I swallow, and my hands are burning, the ache gone now. Her face is bright, lit up. She's excited about this. I swallow again. "Are you sure that's really necessary? Shouldn't we just... wait until we know what questions to ask? I don't want to visit a halfway decent man in the woods by myself."

She shakes her head. "What if it gets colder? Just ask him what things he thinks we should know about winter out here before it gets any worse, and then you won't need to go later. He surely won't mind you coming and asking a few questions of him. You can go today. There is nothing to do here, and you could find him and easily be back before it is even thinking about getting dark, if it is not too far to his cottage?"

I swallow and shift my hands up under my armpits. They are burning, aching down to the bones. I shake my head. "I'll go tomorrow, when I have time to think about it."

She looks up, a brow lifting and her hands slow for a second. "Tomorrow is bread day. And we said we weren't going to get off schedule again. You can take him some of the pastries I made this morning if you go now." She inclines her head toward the counter, a trace of excitement in her eyes.

I swallow, and turn away, toward the fire and the buckets beside it. *This is foolish. He didn't like me showing up last time. He's not going to like some random kiv showing up again at his place in the middle of nowhere, asking questions with a bundle of pastries.* I press my hands tighter under my arms. *My hands have not fully thawed yet from last time I was out there.* I glance back at my sister.

Alvea's back is straight, her face lit with that excitement and with contentment. *She thinks it is settled, that I am going. Because it makes sense.* I purse my lips, and turn away, my hands burning. *I don't want to go out there and talk with him. What if he does not like seeing me by his home again? What if he doesn't take it well?*

But we do need to know more, more about winter out here. It is not the same as home.

I shake my head, press my hands further under my arms. "Alright." Her face brightens, and her hands are moving faster again, flying through the strands of the loom.

I grimace, look away. *What am I going to say to him? How do you ask for information, from a half-stranger? I don't even know what his name is. What if he sets the hounds on me? I cannot outrun them. I could not have outrun even the one.*

He did not seem like he would set them loose on me, but that was an accident, showing up there. This time will not be one.

* * * * * * * *

Wind cuts through the trees, cold and sharp, and my breaths hurt, lungs heave. *This is foolish.* The bare patch of trees stretches out, the last leaves rattle in the wind, clinging to the branches. The clouds overhead are high and gray, dull and rolling over the trees. I shift the heavy shawl, and adjust my skirts, tangled in my legs and boots. I huff out a breath; my nose is tingling, chilled. A branch snaps under my boot, crackling through the forest. I grimace. *So much for being quiet.* I straighten, and grimace again. *Maybe*

I don't want to be quiet anyway. It will be better if he knows that I am coming. Then he can call back the hounds. What if they are outside, and he is not?

I shiver, pull the shawl over my shoulders. *This is foolishness. He doesn't want us poking around. No man with half a pack of hounds in the middle of nowhere is inviting visitors, or even desires them. Especially not random women who only come to ask questions.* My feet crunch on the ground, and the patch without evergreens ends. There is a trail, small and slender, curling through the trees. I step onto it and pause. *Which way? Was it left or right?* I bite my lip, folding my arms over my stomach—the bundle of pastries bumps against my hip, hanging from my fist.

Which way? Both ways look nearly the same, trees stretching toward the sky. I turn right and start down the path. Bushes poke out over the road, licking toward the center more with each step, crowding in, and there is a tree over the path, down and dead. I frown. *This cannot be the right way.* I turn and move back up the path. I press a branch back from my face, ducking. It slips from my fingers, and slaps against my face, stinging.

I grimace, pressing a hand against my cheek and sidestep, face stinging.

I move forward again, and shove past the next branch. *They shouldn't be over the path like this, should they?* I step forward again.

The path opens ahead, curving back away from the mountain, and there is no more brush, only slender trees bare to the sky. I pick up my pace. *This is the right path.* I grimace. There is a bark, somewhere off in the forest, and it echoes, bouncing off the trees and is gone. I freeze. A shiver runs up my spine. *What if he is gone and the hounds are here alone? What if there are more than three of them? Six? Seven? Could one man hold off seven hounds?*

I swallow hard and move up the path. There is a clearing, the cabin in the middle with a small cloud of smoke curling out of the chimney toward the colorless sky. My throat bobs, and I step forward again. *If he isn't here, and they are, what should I do?*

A door opens, and there is a bark, followed by another, and something is flying off the porch, barks echoing through the forest. *A hound, shaggy and huge.* I gasp, and jerk backward, throwing my hand out in front of me, and squeeze my eyes shut. *I'm going to die, I'm going to die, I'm going to die!*

The steps stop, a few feet from me, and there is a sniffing sound, the bundle in my hand shoved sideways. I jerk my eyes open, and the air leaves my lungs.

The hound is standing in front of me, its head only a little lower than mine, smelling at the bundle of pastries in my hand. It barks. I jump, jerking the hand back toward me. The hound's tail wags, its head turning to look at something standing on the porch.

The man. His brows are drawn together, and in full daylight, he looks younger than before, not more than a few years older than Yore, if any. His eyes are on me, arms filled with cut logs. "Why are you here?" His voice is still gruff, eyes watching. *Why am I here?*

I swallow, and my heart sinks. "I..." I straighten, clutching the bundle to my chest. "Alvea sent me to ask you some things and give you pastries."

He shifts his weight, just slightly, brows lowering. "Who is Alvea?"

The hound turns toward me, taking a step closer. I lift my chin, and flick my eyes toward the man, and back to the hound. "She..." The hound steps forward again, and snaps at the bundle in my arms. I gasp, jerking backward. The hound steps closer, his eyes on mine, watching, head lower now, stalking. My eyes widen, heart pounding in my chest. "She's my sister!" The words spit out of my mouth, and the man snaps out a word—the hound pauses and drops back on his haunches, like he has been there all along. His eyes are still on my face, watching. I swallow and tighten my arms. "Does he bite?"

"Va." I glance up. He is leaning against the pillar on the porch now, closer by a few feet, arms still filled with logs.

I swallow again. *Curses.* "Oh." I press my arm harder against my chest. "I should not have bothered you. I am sorry." I step backward, slowly, eyes watching the hound.

The man straightens, and looks down for a moment, shoulders moving like a breath heaved behind the logs. He looks up and nods his head toward the porch. "Come over here. She won't hurt you." He stoops, setting the logs on the porch floor, "Unless I say so." My heart drops, and I look down, at the hound. She is sitting, her eyes unnerving on me, twitching with every move I make. I swallow again, and inch forward, toward the porch. The hound follows my movement, hers mirroring mine with the grace of a forgotten thing, her movements like the wind, and the growl is silenced in her throat now. My heart pounds in my chest, and I stumble, my leg collides with something, pain spiking up my leg.

The steps. I swallow, and turn, toward the man. *The hound won't attack unless he says. Is that a comfort or a threat?* I swallow hard, my throat catching. "I am sorry to intrude again, but my sister wanted advice, and you are the only person we know of for miles in any direction, so I came here. You would know the land better than anyone else anyway. We won't intrude again after this, and you have my apologies, and those of my family."

He moves slightly, and his eyes shift to the hound. "Marin, back." I turn, and the hound is stepping away from me. *She'd moved closer, when my back was turned.* I swallow. Her head low, eyes still watching, like I might run at any moment. I turn back to him. He is looking at me. "What sort of advice?"

What sort? I swallow. "Just... we wanted to know what kind of things we should be aware of, out here in the winter. The winters at home were much shorter and they will be milder... and we lived in a town. We wanted to make sure that we are prepared, and wanted any insight you are willing to give. And Alvea wanted you to have these pastries. They were made this morning, by her. She thought you might enjoy them." Wind cuts across the ground, throwing my skirts against my legs. I shiver and wrap my arms tighter around my chest.

His eyes are watching me, closely, like the hound that he called off. "The pastries you let the hound sniff."

My eyes widen, face warms. "I didn't mean to. I thought she was going to rip out my stomach."

His brow shifts, just slightly. "They go for throats first." My eyes widen, and something flashes across his face, almost a smile in his eyes, and it's gone again. He shifts, moving toward the wall. "You want to know what you should be prepared for." He nods toward a chair. "Sit. There is no reason for you to stand down there."

I swallow and step up onto the porch. He hasn't moved, and neither has the hound behind me. She is just standing there, staring, watching. There are two chairs on the porch, a little apart, wood carefully carved, though there are no markings in them, nothing to make them unique. They are just chairs. I slip into the smaller one, fold my arms over my chest.

The man moves, setting the load of logs down on the porch. He pulls the chair a few feet further away from me, and sits, sharply, gracefully, like the hounds that follow him. He turns toward the edge of the porch, where the blue hound is still sitting, and whistles, sharp and clear. The hound stands, and moves over, her head still low, eyes on me. She drops down next to him and settles her head between her paws. "All you want to know is what you should prepare for?"

My head snaps up, and my eyes meet his. "Va. That's everything." He is watching me, his face dry, unamused. The words are out of my mouth, before I can think. His brow shifts, hands now resting between his legs. I swallow hard. *The pastries.* "These are for you." I reach them out toward him, my arm jutting awkwardly between us.

He looks back, toward me, and reaches his hand out, his arm stiff, and his fingers lift the bundle from mine. He drops his hands between his knees, and his shoulders tense. He looks awkward, unsure. "Out here," his voice is steady though, "storms come up faster than you think, and they are deadly." He turns back toward me. "Make sure that you don't stray far from shelter. Water is more deadly than storms, especially frozen water. It's not always as frozen as you think. Winter is long and meat is scarce, so store what you can before it's here in force." *Perhaps it is better than I thought that Yore has been hunting.* He pauses. "Do you all have animals?" He glances at me.

I nod. "We have a few calli. Not many."

His brow lifts, and his face goes back to what it was, dry and unamused. He looks away. "Tie a rope from the shed to your porch and don't ever let the fire go out."

I swallow. "Why not?"

He looks back at me. "Why? Because cold hands don't start fires well. If your house goes cold, you're as good as dead, and there won't be anyone to bail you out around here. Keep it going."

I shiver, and my heart chills. "Are you the only one here?"

He looks at me, and his eyes are guarded again, hard and I can't read them. "Most people who come this far from civilization are either looking to prove something and make a name for themselves, or to get away from something. This is a land of hermits who prefer to be alone. Not for those looking to build community. I don't know which you are, but there won't be others around here to bail you if you are unsure about being here."

My heart drops. *I've overstayed. Curses.* I stand, brushing out the wrinkles in my skirts. "Thank you." I bow, slightly. "I am sorry again, for intruding. We won't do it again and I appreciate your help..." I pause, press my hands against my skirts. "I don't know your name. I'm sorry."

He nods, and stands, the hound moving with him; her eyes are on me again, watching, waiting. "I know. I don't know yours either."

My lips tighten. "I told you mine when I met you the first time." He doesn't move, still watching the ground. My lips twitch. "Fine. I will just refer to you as the wolf man."

He frowns, the movement barely visible beneath his beard, with his face turned away. "They are hounds. And I didn't figure you would be back."

I nod, and my lips twitch. "My name is Oanéka. And I hadn't planned to be back. But it seems like you might have expected to run into us again. It is not far between our cabins, so even if we try, we are still likely to see you at some point, sometime. I would make sense to at least know each other's names." He is not looking at me, still standing beside his chair. *He's not going to tell me. Alright then.*

I turn, and his voice cuts out. "Some advice for you, Oanéka?" I turn back toward him, and he is kneeling, petting the ears of the hound. "Go back to where you came from. This isn't a world for women from towns. No matter how strong. Your brother should never have brought you out here. This place kills those who don't know what they are doing. It is not a place for the soft, or the unsure." He stands, eyes meeting mine. "And my name is Goran."

I lift my chin, and my jaw clamps. "We are staying." His eyes flicker with surprise. I shake my head. "We made this choice carefully, and it wasn't some foolish hope for fame or to get away, or anything of the kind, and we will be staying." I step off the porch, and there is the bark of a hound, far away.

His voice cuts out, low and harsh. "No one makes the choice lightly, but that doesn't mean it's the right choice. This place isn't for those who have no wish to be here. Tell your brother to take you home, back where you came from. Too many come who aren't prepared, and they don't last long here. Go back home."

I turn, and he is opening the door to his cabin. He vanishes through it, clicking it shut behind him, the hound gone with him. I pull my shawl up, over my arms. *We'll be fine. It's for Yore. We'll be just fine out here. We have to be. We chose this, and we'll be fine. We'll all be fine out here. I'm not telling Yore this, any of this. We'll be fine. We will be.*

Chapter VIII

“He didn’t mention anything else we should be aware of? I knew about water, from back home.” Alvea’s hand goes slack on the waft in her fingers and the cord is idle in her lap.

I shake my head, and splash water over my face. “Va. Nothing else.” *He said we shouldn’t be here, that we should go home, but she does not need to know that, not from him. We heard it enough before we came here.*

She tosses her hand, lifting the cord. “Did you find out his name, then?”

I nod, and lift the towel, touching it across my forehead. “His name is Goran. I did not ask his surname.”

The door opens across the room and there is a gust of cold air. I shiver and pull my arms around myself. Yore kicks the door shut, and sets down a fire of wood, beside the fireplace. He straightens, rolls his shoulders, as though they ache. *Do they, from all the wood he has been hauling? Is that what he has been tending all these afternoons, when he’s not repairing the shed?*

His eyes flicker to me. “Why is your face wet?

My head nods, and I press the towel against my cheeks again. “I washed it.” I drag the towel back, and toss it over the rack where it goes.

He has straightened, his eyes unimpressed, scanning my face. "Where did you go, in the woods? I saw you coming in."

My lips pull down. I turn away, toward the stove and the soup that is steaming over it. "You never asked where I went before. Why do you want to know now?"

He folds his arms over his chest, eyes watching me. "You never left with a bundle and came back without one. You usually come back with more than you left with out here, not less."

I shrug and lift the spoon from the stove. "Alvea asked me to take pastries to the hound-man and see if he had any useful things to know about living out here in the winter."

His brow barely twitches. "And did he?"

I nod, and set the spoon down and straighten. "He had a few things. One of them was a little strange. He said that we should tie a rope from the porch to the shed?"

Yore scowls. "Why?"

I shake my head and turn back to the soup. "I don't know. I didn't think to ask." He frowns, and turns away, his back sharp and hunched at once. *Yore's shoulders are never hunched. Not even once since he stopped taking to the pub. He can't be that tired, surely. Is he? Has he been trying too hard out here?* I swallow and set the spoon down. "Yore." He turns toward me. "Are you alright?"

He shakes his head and straightens sharply. "I am perfectly alright. I have work to tend. You can tell me the rest of what he said later." He turns toward the door and is there in two steps.

"Yore!" I step across the way, stocking-skating on the wood of the floor. I press my hand against the chair. "You've been working nonstop since we got here. You can take a break for a minute."

His hand grips the door. "Nie. I can't. I have things to tend."

I throw my hands in the air. "What things?! You have time to sit down for a moment. You have time to sit and talk with us."

He snorts. "You two have better things to do than talk to me in the middle of the day. I'm going out to work on the shed." He pulls the door.

I press my hand against it, shoving it shut. "No, we don't! Sit down."

The light goes out of his eyes, and his shoulders slump down, like I struck him. His hand shifts on the doorknob, his jaw twitching with pain. His throat bobs, a smile wry and horrible on his lips. "You are right. You don't. Because I brought you out here to the middle of nowhere. You don't have anything to do." He jerks the door open, and it clicks shut behind him.

I swallow, and my eyes are burning, swimming. *I never said that I blamed him.* I turn back toward the kitchen, and my arms are chilled with the cold, with the wind that blew in when Yore went out. Alvea's face is drawn, her hands still on the waft. She looks down, away.

I turn toward the kitchen again. *He blames himself. He blames himself for bringing us out here. And I thought that he didn't think of us at all. But he blames himself. Did he feel trapped, when the cregf gave him the choice between the war and the settling lands?*

But he still valued his own life over ours, and he didn't ask, before the choice was made. There is no choice there, not for him. We would have told him to choose this if he had asked. We would have told him that we would rather face the five years alone, out here, than send him to the front to be killed in a worthless war.

I swallow, and my eyes are still burning. Alvea's hands are busy again, working at the cloth that is never done, her eyes on the shuttered window across the way. *She didn't see the look in his eyes. She didn't see the emptiness of them. Does she know that he blames himself? Have they talked, in the weeks leading up to this, to coming here? Have they spoken since we came, when I was not around?*

I purse my lips, and press my hands against my skirts, and my throat is tight, the world too small.

* * * * * * *

I step down the ladder, and the world is blurry in the darkness. I frown and press a hand against my eyes. The lantern is gone, and the fire is burning, leaving a glow on the floor in front of it. The light from the one open shutter is strange and white, glowing bright. *Surely, it's not that late in the morning. Did I sleep through the morning?* I move forward, and something thuds against my leg. I gasp, falling against a chair, and pain spirals up my shin, colliding with my foggy brain. *Figs and harvest-moles, that hurt! Curses. Just a chair.* I limp forward, grip the buckets from the floor, and my shin is throbbing, pain curling off it in waves. *Cursed chair. Why was it sitting there?* I step up to the door, and jerk it open, and there is white, everywhere, blinding, cutting into my eyes, pure white.

Snow.

I stumble, and the door creaks behind me, hitting my heel. The snow is coating everything, a blanket of white across the earth. Each branch is lined with it, and it flows up onto the porch where it was blown with the dawn. *It's early morning yet. Snow.* Cold licks into my toes. I look down sharply, and there are stockings over my feet and nothing more. *I forgot to put my boots on. And my shawl. I didn't put on anything against the cold.* I step backward, and press the door shut again, buckets tapping against my leg. *It snowed. So early. It's too early for snow. It never comes this early. We didn't expect it this early. Does it always come so soon?*

My eyes trail to the window, and I shove my toes into my shoes. *How can it have happened so soon?* My toes stick in the ends of my walking shoes, and one of them throbs. *Walking shoes. I can't wear them in the snow. They are too short, and it will all come inside them.* I shake my head and slip my foot into my boot. They are still stiff, barely ever worn since I got them. *Snow. It's beautiful. And too early. But Yore must have expected it. He's been storing things, had everything ready weeks ago. He must have known, before we left that this was likely, that there was a chance it would be this soon. He must have known, when he spent those days hunting back home, before we came up here.*

My hand grips the doorknob, and I jerk it open again. There is the whiteness, vast and pale in the bare dawn, ending only where the tree trunks stand out above the blown snowflakes. I step down the porch, and it clings to my boots, smooth and powdered, and it tosses ahead of me with each step, a clump rolling into the snow. There are footprints, stamped in it, larger than mine and impressed deep in the powdery white, one after the other out toward the shed where they end by the shut door. *Yore's steps.*

One of the calli is standing outside the shed, in the fence, its wool dirty gray against the clean, even white of the snow in the morning light. It is chewing something. *Always chewing.* She looks like she belongs here, some kind of snow beast, penned at the end of the little shed. *How do they always chew? My jaw would wear out. And then I would only be fit to swallow soup like an aged women.*

Wind blows, and there is cold, snow cutting across the earth and it slices at my skin. I gasp, and lift my hands, and there is only whiteness for a moment, and the wind, and it's settled again.

My heart thuds in my chest. *Snow swirls. The wind in the loose snow.* I move forward, and the snow continues to flick out in front of my boots, small clumps of it flipping out with each step toward the stream, which is curling, a dark line through the white world around it. The stream of midnight water, stones stark and brown within it in a world of white. *How long until it all freezes over? How do you break ice in the winter? We never had to do it at home. It was done for the village, by the lake. I didn't think to ask Goran, didn't think to ask him how to do anything, though this was the thing that I went to ask him for.*

And now snow is here. It can't be here yet. No more frost in the mornings. No more of studying the frost lit grasses and leaves. Only snow, endless, boundless snow. Only white from the earth to the treetops and the gray skies.

My eyes flicker upward, and there is the lone mountain, white against the gray of the sky, coated to its tip with white.

It's stunning. Beautiful, like nothing at home, and my heart aches strangely in my chest. *How can so much beauty come with so much bleakness? And so much death? With so many gray clouds and empty days?*

The mountain is stark over the treetops and somehow, the trees are no longer dull beneath the blanket of whiteness. Each line of the tree is lit, beautifully, as if ready for a dance, or a celebration in the quietness of the morning, lined like the frost, and yet its fuller, more gracious than the frost. *This lasts past the first light into day. It's beautiful.*

That's not what Pakem always said. He said there is no life in the colorless things. And there isn't. Nothing is moving in this beautiful, haunting stillness of the earth beneath the white that has fallen. It's more still than death, a ghost of daylight, beautiful and strange, and I could stand here for hours, watching that still, lifeless joy.

Winter has come like a breath in the night.

Something creaks, off toward the shed. *Yore.* I turn, and move toward the creek, buckets in hand, and dunk them into the water. My arms strain, and I lift them, stand. Yore is walking around back of the shed, his back already to me again, and the world of beautiful nothingness between us. *White. Like a bride. Nie. Brides come in joy. Winter comes in sadness, in death through a blanket of cold and white. And yet there is something achingly joyful in the coated world.*

I step up the slope, and the snow skids beneath my boots, water splashes, sloshing in the buckets. *This is harder in the snow.* My teeth clench, and I set one bucket, and then the other on the bank. I grip the ground, dragging myself up, my fingers burning with the cold. *I should have worn my gloves.* I stand, dust off my skirts, and grip the buckets again. The calli is still standing there, chewing the everlasting nothingness. I stamp up the porch steps and set a bucket down. I pull open the door handle and stomp out my boots out of the door. There is a gasp, and something clatters to the floor.

"Snow!" Alvea's voice is high, startled and she is stooping to pick something up off the floor in the kitchen, her leg bent awkwardly beneath her skirts.

I shake my boots off, and kick the door shut. Her hands shoot out, and she steps forward sharply, a step and a limp. "Don't come any further in! You'll get snow over all of the floor. I'll take those from you." She reaches her hands out to take the buckets.

My face is hot, the air of the cottage clinging to it, burning my cheeks, my nose, my ears. I shake my head, shuffle my feet before the door. "I can get them. I'll just take off my boots here." I stoop to grab my laces. She shakes her head at me, and grabs the buckets, lifting them. I fold my arms, straightening. "I thought you said you couldn't lift them."

She glances back at me, and her back straightens again, sharp, perfect beneath the weight. "I was sore from our journey. But I'm not anymore. I said I couldn't lift them that day." She sets the buckets down and turns back to me. She shouldn't carry buckets, with that leg. They are heavy.

"It snowed?" She lifts a brow at me.

I nod, and my eyes flicker to the window. *The world is enchanting out there, snow on every branch and twig, like something Yore would have talked about in one of his old poems. I should have stayed out for longer.* I laugh, and it feels strange and tight. "It snowed, Alvea. It's all white out there, like a forest in an old poem or tale."

Her lips tug upward, eyes glancing at me. "They don't describe forests in poems, Néka." She steps beside me, and her eyes turn out the window, toward the white world. Her eyes flicker—they are taking in everything, dark eyes caught and brighter in the light of the window.

She nods, still staring out at the world beyond. "We should bake something." I look up at her, and her eyes are only barely above mine. *We never stand this close.* She nods again, eyes still out the window. "For the first snow, Yore's favorite. We are ready enough for it, for the snow. Everything is already put away, stored for it, so we should bake." She smiles, a half thing, and her eyes are brighter again. She spins, turning toward the kitchen. "We'll use some nuts and a little of the syrup. Yore will be befuddled when he comes in and finds us baking sweets. We'll give him a shock." She grins, as if to herself.

I laugh, and it bursts from my throat, loud. Her laugh curls off mine, and she is grinning, tying back her hair and rolling up her sleeves like she hasn't done in weeks. *She didn't even put up her hair in a bun first.* I grin, and step across the floor, a curl in my eyes, and kneel, fingers twisting in my bootlaces. They are damp, cold and Alvea is picking up mixing bowls, her face set again, but it's not tense anymore, and her eyes are alight, with the glow from the snow coming through the window. *Maybe snow can cause small, beautiful things indoors too, if you look for them.*

Chapter IX

Yore's shoulders are tight, his mouth set in a thin line, jaw tense. He tugs at his shoelaces, and drops his heavy boots into place beside the door. My back straightens. *What is wrong with him? Does the first snow not brighten his moods, as it did Alvea's? Does he not care for snow? Did he care for it back home? I don't remember, don't know. Are we not ready for it yet? I thought we were ready, weeks ago.*

Alvea turns, stepping, her movement uneven toward the table. "Yore," her voice is careful, bright and she lifts her eyes, and they are brighter than they've been in weeks. *Can't he brighten too? Can he not match her for just a second and let this be?* She looks at him. "How are the calli? Are they alright?" Her eyes flicker to him again, and back to what she is doing, setting the pan on the table.

He nods his head, and moves toward the washbasin, mouth still in that line. "They are fine. What are you doing?"

I lift my head, brush hair from my face with the side of my hand. "Baking."

He looks at me, and his eyes are dry. "Sweet breads?"

Alvea laughs, halfhearted and short, the light fading in her eyes. "Nie. We made pastries, amirif non, for the first snow. It is a tradition. We have missed a few years, but not this one." She raises her chin, turning to him, as if defiant.

His brow lifts and he turns back toward his room. He runs a hand through his cropped hair, his jaw tight, and he is gone through the frame, the door clicking shut behind him.

Alvea shakes her head, turning toward the kitchen again. She whispers something, under her breath, a murmur, and her eyes flicker to his door. She shakes her head, and steps away, moving back toward the loom. "Well, they are there if he wants one. He might have at least smiled. He always liked them, back home, for the first snow. He might have at least smiled." She shakes her head, and her lips are tighter, the last crumbs of the amirif non on them. She shakes her head, and lifts the waft, her jaw tight like his, eyes set again.

I look down. There is flour, caked to my fingers, turning my skin pale brown. *That was it. A moment gone.* I turn away, back toward the mixing bowls, stacked and clean beside the wash bucket. *She's retreated back into the everlasting weaving and silence. What did she expect from him? He has barely smiled in weeks. Did she think that he would come back out again, and undo years of leaving us, years of frustration after a few pastries?* I press my fingers against each other, the flour caked and rolling between them, dried and crumbling, flaking away and useless.

* * * * * * *

I press the door shut; hands chilled over the handle. My fingers ache, nose throbs. *It's colder.* My face stings with a thousand tiny snowflakes, thrown like shards into the breeze. Alvea lifts her head, not moving from the sink. "Is Yore in?"

I shake my head, set the buckets down. They thud against the floor, water swirling, nearly splashing over the lip of the one on the right. "I don't know. Did you not see him in his room?"

She shrugs. "I don't keep track of him."

I frown. *But you expect me to?* I jerk the laces of my boots, fingers fumbling with the laces. I purse my lips and turn away. "I think it may be a little colder now than this morning was. My skin is burning." I lift my eyes. She isn't looking, eyes fixed on the sink, on the bowls she is washing. I bite my lip. "Do you think there will be a new coat of snow tonight?"

Her eyes flicker to me. "I hope not. It was a hard enough battle for you to get out today, was it not?" She looks away again, back toward the dishes. I grit my teeth, jerk the laces free and the boots from my feet.

"It's been perfectly alright. It's barely even a walk to the creek, or the barn."

The door at the back creeks open, Yore stepping into the room. His hat is in his hand, hair mussed on his head, eyes dark. He glances at me, and crosses in two strides, taking the buckets from the floor. I drop back on my heels, and he is across the room already, setting the buckets beside the stove. He turns, eyes half on Alvea, half on me, on the floor. "Is it dinner time?"

Alvea nods, her head still high. "Va. As soon as you are ready, that is." Her voice is curt, sharp. Yore grimaces, turning his head toward the floor, his feet padding softly, stockinged against the wood of it. *He should have taken her pastries yesterday. It would made things smoother for him today.*

* * * * * * * *

My eyes flicker toward the window, steam clinging to my skin above the stew. Shadows are getting long. The third day with snow is nearly over, nearly gone, and I've missed all the blue sky against that beautiful white, all of the snow drifts coming off of the trees. *I've missed all the soaking up of the beauty that is here.* I swallow, shoving my sleeves back down my arms. "I'm going outside."

Alvea looks up, her hands still moving on the loom. "Don't go far."

I shake my head. "I won't." *I just need air, maybe to catch a glimpse of the sunset.*

I reach down, and grip my stockings, pulling them up on my legs again, and shove my feet into the boots by the door. Alvea isn't looking, her hands and mind busy with something. I shake my head and turn toward the window. The sky is barely visible between the porch and the trees through the windowpanes of the one open window, and the snow light is still bright.

My fingers grip the door, and I pull it open, grabbing my shawl from the hook beside it. The air is cool, and it nips at my face, at my fingers, and cuts at my skirts. The snow is bright, shadows moving long, almost blue-black across the white, and the sky above is tinting toward rose, blue and purple together with another tone. *How many shades of blue can be in one sky? It will be sunset soon, all the colors blending together in the open sky. I can't see it from here, with the trees too close beyond the creek.*

I purse my lips, grip my hands. The ground is not even here in the forests. *Surely there must be some kind of overlook where the sunset will be well visible out there.* My hands clench my shawl, and I turn, into the wind. The ground rises, off in the trees, but closer to them it is no longer plain, the rising trunks block it from sight. *It shouldn't take long to find, and the sunset will be worth it, this evening. It is already tinging another color in the blue of the sky.*

There is a hill, rising from the ground through the trees, off somewhere to the right, where the sky is still so blue. It's off, through the forest, but it cannot be that far. I start up the creek, and the snow packs beneath my boots, crunches and moves. Beneath the trees, the snow is lighter, only a dusting of it down beneath the evergreen branches where the earth is still dark. I duck under one, and press another out of the way. My hands sting, the cold cutting in the wind through the trees. It looks warmer out here than it is, even with the snow upon the ground.

I tighten my arms, and step around another tree, and there is the stream, cutting across the earth, away from the sunset. I always thought that it went toward the mountain. I hop, onto a rock, and another, and there is the bank, beneath my feet again. Snow crunches, thick under the bare branches of the skeletons of the trees beside the creek.

The light from the sky is beginning to change. I'm not going to miss that sunset.

I bolt, weaving through the trees, and clutch my skirts in my hands. The air is sharp on my face, tree branches reaching toward my skin and my breaths are heavy in my chest. It's going to be beautiful, up there, if I can just find it, if

I can get up there on time. My steps pound on the snow, and there is a break in the trees and there are rocks, leading upward toward a small hill. I grin, and move toward it, shawl flapping and skirts clutched in my hands.

The rocks are huge, snow across their surfaces, and they are all jumbled together at the bottom of a hill. Behind them, the ground is rough-hewn, upward on the hillside until there is a little pocket of trees up there. I start up it, skirts still in my hand, and the slope is steep. The sky is turning orange and yellow, blending in with the brightness of the blue over the snow coated world. My breaths rip at my throat, and there is the hilltop ahead, with rock and trees, and an abrupt ending. *A cliff.* I step up to it, and there is the sunset, bright and glorious over the tops of the trees, off toward the mountain. *It's beautiful. Color. There is color again.*

My breaths rag in my throat, and my eyes are burning. *It's simple out here, just the sky and the bare trees and the ground, with snow across it. And it's beautiful, just beautiful with the fire of the setting sun across the whitened world, every blemish ironed over for just a second. Not complicated like frost is. Snow is a quiet, softened beauty, and the world is still beneath it.* I lean against the rock beside me and fold my arms. The wind is sharp, and my cheeks are hot from the walk, neck slick beneath the wind. *But I made it. I found a spot. A smile tugs at my lips. And it's perfect for viewing the setting of the sun, the colors lit behind the lonely mountain.*

The colors brighten, orange pushed to the center now, where the sun is setting in a cloud of yellow, and there is red, along the edges, and pinks and purples like no tapestry can show. The sky above it blue, darkening by the moment, turning the colors darker, as the sky turns toward night.

It's almost purple, like crocuses. Pink is drifting along the mountain, the faint of primroses, clouds low, light and thin brushing the horizon like feathers. *Oh, it's beautiful. And not the garden I left behind. It's beautiful in a different way, more full, and empty.* There is sweat, clinging to the side of my face. I swipe it off, my sleeves pulled down over my hands. My nose is burning, cold clinging to it.

You can see so far. Out over the trees. The tallest evergreen only barely reaches the top of the rock face beneath me, and the mountain is plain in the distance, beyond that the never-ending trees beneath the sunlit sky.

The air shifts, cooler. And the clouds are moving, colors and colors. Pinks, in the clouds, purple in the sky, stunning, and the textures look like a thousand giant feathers, brushing across the horizon line into the never-ending sky.

It is fading to orange like the end of coals, darkness stretching out overhead. *It will be dark soon. I should turn back.* I rub my hands along my arm, the last of the colors faint on the horizon. *I should go back now.* My heart aches. *It wasn't long enough, none of it, and it's gone again. But it was beautiful.*

I step down. The trees up here are all evergreens, and their branches are shaking slightly in the coming breeze. I clutch my skirts and pull my shawl tighter about my shoulders. *It's colder than it was a minute ago. Or maybe I am imagining that, with the end of the colors in the sky.*

The snow skids beneath my feet, packing, crunching on the hillside, and my steps are a dark trail—step after step down the hill to the boulders below. The trees are swaying gently, and my face stings in the coming wind. *It's getting a lot colder.* My hands drop the skirts, and I tug my shawl about my arms, pull down my dress sleeves over my wrists.

Back this way, toward the creek, then over it, down a little and home. The snow crunches beneath my feet, loud in the forest, and birds are calling faintly, shadows getting longer. *Thank Elnial for the snow. The light from it makes the world brighter, surely. It is at least easier to traverse in the dusk.*

I step around a tree, and there is a fallen log, large, and the earth is ripped up around it, creating a bowl in the ground where the roots have taken the earth with them. *I didn't pass this on the way here.* I swallow, and turn, right, and duck around a tree. The wind brushes through the branches, and rips at my hair, pulling it from its place and branches knock together, creaking and clattering in the air. I tighten my arms. *It can't be far. It must be this way.*

Snow crunches and branches knock together, and my breaths heave in my chest, hissing. There are rocks—more boulders—under an evergreen. *Those must be the ones I passed on the way to the hilltop.* I step around them, and the shadows are getting longer, light gone from the sky, and there is nothing but shadows now in the forest. *This has to be the right way.*

Snow crunches, and branches knock together in the treetops above, and there is a call, a hooting in the trees. My heart stutters. *A bird. It can't be far to the cottage now. The creek, and then down to the crossing, and the porch.* I step through the trees and pause. There is silence, but for the brushing of the wind in the trees. No sound of water, no stream cutting through the pale white of the earth. *It can't be far to it. I didn't go far.* My lips tighten, and I pick up my skirts, step through the trees. The trees are only shadows now, clinging to each other, shapes barely there between the churning of the snow. *If they are familiar, I don't know them. But it was an easy walk. It wasn't far. I didn't go far. I should be able to find it even in the dusk.*

Snow crunches, and branches knock together in the treetops, and there is the brush of the wind. *I should have passed the creek by now. I'm going the wrong way.* I lick my lips, press my arms tighter about me, and the wind cuts through the trees. They rattle together, cold thicker. *The stream must be to the right, toward the last of the setting sun. Isn't that the way I came from? Va. it was. Toward where the sun sets. That must be home from here.* My throat is tight, and the wind cuts at my cheeks. My nose is running. *What if it's not? What if I am wrong?* It's getting dark. The shadows are long between the trees, melded together into one.

Something slides beneath my feet, a rock rolling, and my ankle jerks, protests. Snow crunches, beneath my boots, and there are more trees, onward and onward like shadows, and a clearing. *I walked through a clearing, didn't I?* I pick up my skirts, and bolt across it. *This is the right direction; it has to be. The creek will be right there, and then the cabin.* Snow crunches, branches knock together in the wind, and my breaths hiss, a faint cloud in the darkness before my face. *It can't be far. It will be right there.*

I move around a tree, and there is something slipping through the trees, a shadow in the darkness, shifting from one tree to the next. I freeze—a stick snaps beneath my foot. The shape pauses, and I can't see it anymore, between the trunks, tall and dark. My heart pounds in my chest, throat tight. *Curse it. Call out. Just call out. It'll leave.* "Is..." My voice shakes, I can't make it loud enough. "Is something there?" *Oh stars, let nothing be there. I didn't bring anything. I have nothing to fight it off with. Not even a stick. Oh stars.*

Someone grunts, almost like a curse beneath their breath. My heart sinks. *A man's voice.* I swallow, and step backward, stick snapping again. *Is it Goran, or another hermit in the darkness? Another traveler we don't know? I should run. I need to run.* My throat is thick, and the shadow moves a step toward me. *It can't see in the dark. He can't see in the dark, surely he can't see.* I turn, and it moves toward me again. *He isn't speaking. It isn't speaking. What if it's not a man? What if it's something else?* Something moves beside my face, sharply. I scream throw my hands up into the air. Wings flap around my head, loud, and they are gone, with the sound of rushing wind. *I need to run.* I turn.

"Stop." It's a sharp order, and the voice is familiar. *Goran.* My heart slows in my chest. *It is Goran. Praise Elnial.*

I press my back against the tree and tilt my head back against it. "Is that you?" *Where are the hounds?*

Something growls, off in the underbrush. A shiver climbs up my skin, and he is speaking. "Va. Are you lost?" His voice is cold. There is a growl again, on the other side now. *The hounds are with him. That must be what spooked the bird.* I step to the side, and shiver, pull my shawl over my arms. *Am I lost?*

I swallow and shake my head. *He can't see me nod in the darkness.* "Nie. I just..." I swallow again. "I was walking, and I misplaced the path home, and then it was darker than I thought..." My throat is thick, and it's hard to speak, and I can't make out his figure in the darkness anymore. *What if I am only speaking to myself? What if he left? What if I am alone out here again?*

He grunts, and there is the crunch of his footsteps in the snow, moving toward me, and he is only a few feet from away, tall, a shape between the glow of the night snow, and the shadows of the trees. "Come along. I'll show you the path home." There is the crunching of steps again, moving away this time. *I shouldn't have been anywhere near him. I should have been in the wrong direction, shouldn't I? Wasn't the cliff on the wrong side, from him?* My steps crunch, and I start after him, the air cold upon my face, and the world all shadows around us but for the glimpses of snowlight between the trees.

He ducks under a branch, and there is something large and dark ahead. *Evergreens.* The scent is heavy in the air, and they are packed tightly together, branches waving in the wind. He steps around them, his shadow blending with theirs for a moment, and he is gone. Panic churns in my chest, shoving in my throat. I bolt after him, legs jerking with each loud step. Snow crunches loudly, thud after thud pounding in my ears. A branch brushes my skin, and I duck under it, and straighten. He is ahead, moving toward something large and dark, moving around it in the strange gray of the snow. I dart after him, and the snow clings to my feet, each step harder. My legs ache, breaths heaving.

He turns, around the dark thing, like a cluster of evergreens, and there is a light, through something square. *A window.* I pause. *His cabin.* His steps sound on the porch, strange and hollow after the crunch of the snow. Mine tap, quiet after his, and the hounds' nails clatter against the frozen wood. I pause on the porch. He is stepping through the door. "Come in. I need to get something before I can take you home." His voice is dull, not an invitation or a command, just there, plain and dry.

I shake my head and fold my arms around my chest. The wind cuts through the porch, cold, and I shiver, wrapping my arms tighter. My teeth chatter. *Is he not going to just show me the trail?* "I'm alright. I need to go home." *It wouldn't be appropriate to go in there with only him. Why are we at his cabin?* I glance back toward the woods. *I can find my way from here, even in the dark. It's just through the trees there. I know the path.*

He turns away, the door creaking and the light shifting, and the door still open in his hand. "There is no reason for you to freeze on the porch. I have to get the lantern before I can take you home." He steps inside, leaving the door, letting all the warm air out. A shiver runs up my spine, brushing through my scalp. *It's cold, so cold.* My lips tremble. *He is just grabbing a lantern. I can step inside, and back out. I shouldn't leave the door open, in any case.* I step through the door and press my back against it. It clicks closed, and there is warmth, the sound of the wind clattering in the trees is gone. I shiver. *Everything is cold now.*

Goran is across the room, his back toward me, working on something and there is the clatter of metal. *The lantern, undoubtedly.* I swallow, and fold my arms tighter, rubbing my hands up and down on them. The room is not large, just one room that joins sitting space, kitchen and eating place in one. There is a door, at the back, and seats, large and comfortable, furs hanging over them beside the fire. His table is small, tucked right next to the kitchen, which is on the wrong side of the house, across from ours. It is small, and the shadows it casts are long under the chairs, tables and the legs of the hounds.

There is a hound on the floor beside the fire, in the sitting room. Gyaith, the great red one who tried to attack me the first day. There are two others beside her, the great gray-blue one, and another, brown and shaggy. It lifts its head and sniffs the air, and growls, setting its head back down on its huge paws. Its teeth still bared at me, eyes yellow in the shadows of the fire. I step to the side. My heart shudders. *The red one, who was so large beside Goran, it is the smallest of the three. The* brown one must be the largest, and it is shaggy, its great head on the floor, eyes watching me. It growls again.

Goran shifts, and there is the spark of fire against the wick, just barely visible over his arm. "Be silent, Crith." The hound lifts its head and looks over, toward Goran. Its eyes flicker back to me, and it growls again, head staying upright, eyes narrowed, teeth bared. It looks older, hair rough and gnarly around its ears. I swallow, and tighten my arms, glance toward the door. *I should have stayed against the door.* Goran turns, and there is the lantern, lit in his hands. His eyes flicker to me, and he shifts his coat, putting it back into place. It's fur-lined, thick and made of tanned hide and cut to him. His eyes flicker toward me again and pause. "What were you doing out there, dressed like that? You were not lost?" *There is something in his voice, like cynicism.*

I tighten my arms, and shiver. "Dressed like what?" My voice trips. "Nie. I'm not fully lost. I went for a walk and got sidetracked, like I explained to you. It was dark..." I tighten my arms, and heat rises to my face. "I was just finding the creek, and then I would have been home again once I did."

He frowns, mouth barely traceable beneath his beard. "The creek? Where were you coming from?"

I swallow, grip my arms beneath my fingers. "You may not know it, it was a hill, with a cliffside on it."

His eyes narrow again. "The cliffside? What were you doing up there?"

I swallow again. "I went up to see if there was a view and I was heading home again."

His hand with the lantern lowers, and his brows raise, surprised. “You went up on the cliff, without a light, alone, near dark?”

I shake my head. “I knew where I was going, I just find the creek, and head home. I was fine!”

His face goes dry. “The creek is south of the cliff. You were going northeast. You could have been lost out there, in the cold, and there is more snow coming tonight. What were you doing?” His voice is sharp. *What right does he have to lecture me?*

My eyes burn. I purse my lips, shift my hands. “I was watching the sunset. It was beautiful tonight, and I wanted to see something real again after all the brownness out here for all these weeks. I was just trying to find the sky.”

His mouth tightens, hand shifting the lantern. “You came out to this land of your own choice. You cannot have been expecting beauty around every corner and risking your life for a sunset is foolish. Next time, bring someone with you. And bring a lantern. Going out there like that will get you killed.”

I clench my teeth. “I didn’t think it would get dark so fast, and there isn’t anyone to bring with me!” I turn, and pull the door open, stepping out into the darkness.

The air is sharp, and it bites my skin, and I am shivering, arms trembling around me with the sudden cold racing down my spine. There is a thud of a door shutting and steps on the porch beside me, sharp and hard. The lantern light is glowing orange upon the snow off the edges of the porch, and he is steps off, into the night. My steps are hollow on the porch behind him. I hop off, into his prints that are already packed into the snow from the last few days, and they crunch with the new cold of night.

His stride is long, the circle of light before him, and the wind is sharp on my skin. My chest is shivering, arms shaking around me, and my shawl is snapping in the air, the sound of it loud, mixing with the crunch of each step of our feet.

He winds to the left, then he fades right again, and we are in the patch with no evergreens. The creek is just ahead. I swallow. My voice stutters, chest cold, "You don't have to take me home. I can find my way home from here."

"I know." His steps don't slow, the light of the lantern a glow before him casting strange shadows on the trees, and it's eerie and too quiet in the wind and the snapping of the shawl, and the crunch of each step.

He pauses by the creek and waits for a moment. I step up beside him. He doesn't move, waiting. *For me, like Yore did last time.* I hop onto the middle rock, and over to the other side, and he steps over, movements even and clean. I grip my shawl, jerk it back over my arms. He is walking ahead again, steps crunching in the unbroken snow, each one a jerk. My legs ache, and I stretch them, stepping into his footprints. His foot slides, stumbling. Snow skids off the creek bank, splashing into the water below, and he is already moving forward again, balance won back. I purse my lips, and my arms are still shaking around me, his steps too long for my legs.

He turns, and there is the shed, beside us, and the light from the one unshuttered window. Someone is walking across the porch, steps loud, toward the door. *Yore.* He pauses and turns, and his eyes widen for a second in the faint glow of the window. His gaze flickers to Goran, and back to me. "Oanéka, what are you doing out here?" He glances at Goran again. "Where did you find her?" I shiver, and open my mouth—Yore shakes his head, shoving the door open, and his brow lowers. "Get inside. It's too cold to be out here."

I move past Goran, and he is still following me, the glow of the lantern hitting the snow and mixing with the glow through the door. I step onto the porch, and my foot slips. I grimace, and step again, slowly, and onto the next step. My boots thud on the porch. Yore is holding the door open behind him, stepping through into the glow of the room.

"Yore..." Alvea's voice is tight, her eyes wide. They flicker toward me, and she stops, steps forward, a limp, and she freezes again, eyes going wider. "Who is this?" She gestures toward Goran. I step through the door, and Goran moves in behind me. I press the door shut, shivering. He steps to the side, as though moving out of the way of the door. His fingers grip the dial on the side of the lantern, turning the wick down, the glow tiny and drowned in the light of the room.

I swallow, and my jaw aches from clenching, shaking. "This is Goran." I nod toward Alvea. "Goran, this is Alvea. She is—" my teeth clatter for a moment. "She is our sister, the one that sent you the pastries." I grimace. *She's our only sister, and he likely knows that by now.*

Alvea's eyes flicker from him to me, and she steps forward sharply. "You are frozen." She starts forward again, and pauses, leaning backward onto her bad leg, and folding her hands. Her lips are tight. "Go sit by the fire, Oanéka."

Yore is standing beside it already, his arms folded, eyes flashing bright gold in the light of the flames. *Angry.* "Where were you?"

I swallow, and step forward, and I am small beside him. A shiver creeps up my spine, catching my neck. I hunch my shoulders, shudder. "I went walking and got lost."

Yore swears, spinning toward the man still standing beside the door. "How did you find her? Did your hounds find her?" Yore's voice is strained, sharp and high.

Goran shakes his head, and his hand shifts with the lantern. "Nie. I came upon her in the woods." His eyes flicker to Alvea. "Do you all have warmer wraps?"

She nods. "Va. We just did not think to bring them down yet. I did not think it was cold enough yet."

He shifts the lantern. "Bring them down. It is almost always colder than you think it is. You should not be wearing things that flimsy." He nods, toward me.

I shake my head, and another shiver runs up my spine, sharp and cold. "It was fine until the sun went down."

His eyes narrow. "It's getting colder. This is winter. If you are not prepared for it, you won't make it back home next time, if you can find your way."

Alvea shakes her head, her face glowing, flushed. "We'll get them out." She nods toward the kitchen, her back straight, perfect, her hair piled high. "Thank you for helping Oanéka back home. Would you care to stay for dinner?"

He shakes his head, one short movement. "I cannot. If I am gone too long the hounds will eat what I already have cooking. Get her something warm." He nods toward me.

I purse my lips and shake my head. "I can get it myself. It was my mistake, and I can take care of my own faults. Thank you." I straighten. "And thank you for bringing me home."

His eyes shift to me again, and his brows narrow. He half bows at the room in general. "Goodeven." He moves for the door.

Yore steps forward, movement sharp. "Hold on, Goran." He nods and runs a hand through his hair. "Thank you for getting her home, and for last time, when you sent her back. I meant to thank you when I saw you before but it slipped my mind." Goran nods, and Yore shifts his stance. "Oanéka told me something the other day, and I've been meaning to ask you about it, if you can stay a moment." Goran pauses, and shifts, his brows lifted, eyes watching Yore. Yore shifts his stance, folding his arms. "You said to tie a rope from the shed to the house. Why? I've never heard of anyone doing that for anything."

Goran straightens, and he nods, just barely, eye to eye with Yore. "It will save your life if you need to get from the cabin to the shed or back again in a snowstorm. There's one coming tonight. Put the rope up. Men get lost in the space to their home when the storms hit."

Yore nods, like he understands something I don't, and he is stepping toward the door.

Alvea shakes her head, one sharp movement. "Wait, Goran, you can at least take some bread for your trouble. It was made yesterday and is still fresh." She turns, and steps toward the kitchen, her head high, back straight, and her steps uneven as always, one step and one limp. She grabs a loaf of bread, and turns, moving across the floor toward him again. Her movements are smooth and awkward at once, sharper than normal, head higher than normal. Like a bird with a damaged wing.

He takes the loaf, and nods toward her. "Thank you." His eyes flicker to Yore. "I'll show you where to hook the rope, if you can come outside now."

Yore is lighting our lantern. His eyes flicker toward the other man, and he nods. He lifts the light, turning toward the door, and together they vanish out into the darkness.

I swallow, shivers grabbing my spine, my toes curling in my boots. *Boots.* I shiver again and sink into the chair. My eyes flicker down to the shoes, still on my feet. There is already a pool of muddy water around them, snow slipping off the top and sliding to the floor. I groan. "Now we have to scrub the floor again tomorrow."

Alvea's eyes flicker to mine. She steps around the chair, over to me. "You should have taken them off earlier. She glances at me, eyes scanning me over, worried. "Where did you go that you got lost? I told you not to go far, didn't I?"

I jerk my boot off, set it on the floor beside the chair. *My hands are trembling.* I shake my head teeth chattering together now. "I w-went walking. And it wasn't far. It just... it looks different in the dark. But I didn't go far."

She looks down at me, eyes dry, face unimpressed. "Well, next time don't go out. Sunset is too late to go out walking out here." I tug at the laces of my boots, hands trembling, fingers only half, working. She stoops in front of me, pulling one of the laces free from my fingers. Her eyes flicker to mine and soften. "Is it really so cold outside?" She grips the knot, pulling it free where my hands were failing.

I shiver, and nod. "It wasn't earlier. He said it is going-ing to snow-w tonight. The temp-perture must be d-dropping."

She turns away, her eyes brighter, head shaking. She pauses by the chair by the end of the table, her head still high. "A person... out here..." Her eyes flicker toward the window. "They said there wouldn't be anyone."

Did she not believe when we told her he was out here? I turn toward the fire, and the flames are dancing, bright and cheerful. The wind howls outside, and the house shudders around us, shaking for a moment. I swallow, and my eyes dart up. *The storm must be getting close.* He was right. I stand, and move across the room, arms about my shoulders, and everything is shaking. The air by the window is cooler, and my teeth chatter. There is only one light visible through the panes, moving off into the woods, and a glow in the barn between the dancing reflections of the fire on the window panes. *Goran must be leaving. Good. He needs to make it back before the snow starts.* I lift my head. *Elnial, let him make it home safely.* My teeth clatter together. *He doesn't need to be unsafe, for bringing me home. I shouldn't have gotten lost, should have paid more attention out there. Foolish. And I thought I did so well, finding that cliff so quickly for the first time.* I swallow hard. *Let him make it home.*

Alvea is by the stove, her face white and flushed at once, her hands pouring soup from the pot to the bowls, one by one, until there are three. She turns, and her eyes are lost, looking for something else, somewhere else.

Chapter X

There is a whirring sound and tapping somewhere. I drag my feet out of my blankets and push them against the floorboards. Cold slips up my toes, crawling up my legs. I shiver, glance over my shoulder, my vision blurry from sleep. *Alvea's bed is empty already.*

I shove my hands against my eyes, and frown. My feet are chilled on the bare boards, blankets warm on my side. I shiver and throw them off. *Alvea isn't usually up before me.* I force myself from my bed, wrapping my arms around my shoulders. *It's cold up here.* My teeth clatter. I grip my dress and jerk it over my head. I scowl. *Why is Alvea up already? Could she not sleep?*

I grab a pair of stockings from my chest and jerk them over my other pair. My foot shuffles, I am wavering, stumbling sideways, one foot half in the stocking. I grimace, and shove my foot into it. *Getting on stockings shouldn't be so hard.* I press a hand against my eyes, blurry, and kneel, slip down the ladder. The whirring and tapping sound is louder, firelight licking around the room, bright. Alvea's loom is to the side of the room, pushed against the wall from where it has been since we arrived. I frown, and rub my eyes again, stepping around the corner. She is in her chair, hands working wool and a thread.

The spinning wheel is out. I rub my eyes again, and fold my arms, shivering. *It's chilly.* "Alvea?"

She glances up, and back toward the thread she is spinning, and the whirring tapping goes on, the whirring of the wheel, the tapping of her shoe, back and forth and back and forth. "Gooddawn, Oanéka."

I shake my head. "What are you doing? Aren't you working on a tapestry?"

Her lips tighten, and the spinning wheel moves faster, the foot going back and forth and back and forth a little more. "I am out of thread." My mouth rounds, and I nod, turning away. She shifts. "There is toast for you, over there, and a bundle of fresh oat cookies."

I frown, and step over to the counter space. There is toasted bread, nuts beside it, and a bundle beside that, steaming slightly. I pick up the toast. "You made oat cookies this morning?" My eyes flicker to the window. *Light is barely on the trees. It can't be much past dawn.* I look back at her. "How long have you been up?"

The whirring continues, foot tapping. Her mouth is tight. "You are going to take them over to that man to thank him for saving you."

I freeze. "Alvea..." She doesn't look up. I move toward her. "Alvea. He doesn't want me to thank him. I think he would rather be left alone. That's why he's out here."

The whirring continues, her eyes still fixated on the wool between her fingers and the wheel. "No one wants to be left alone." Her foot keeps tapping, fingers slipping along the thread. "You are going to bring him those cookies."

I shake my head; my fingers shift on the bread in my hand. "I haven't even hauled the water yet. It's too early to talk about this." I turn away, and the whirring picks up.

"I'll haul the water." Her voice is hard. "You take those over to him, this morning, while the snow is soft. It's beautiful out there this morning."

My lips tighten. I turn. Her face is set, hands steady and perfect on the thread, focused. I shake my head. "I'm not going. He doesn't want to be bothered and you aren't hauling the water in."

Her eyes snap toward me, head whipping around. "Because I can't?" She shakes her head, sharply, face set, hands folded in her lap. "I can haul the water, and you are taking those to him this morning, or I will go. It does not do to sit on gratitude. So, take them. Now." She turns back, and the whirring starts again, foot tapping, tapping. "'He who sits on gratitude may find himself friendless.'"

I grit my teeth, and I clasp my arms about my shoulders. *I just woke up. This is folly. He doesn't want to be thanked and I don't want to go. This is just foolishness. He didn't appreciate finding me last night, and he isn't going to appreciate finding me on his doorstep today.* I drop my arms, move away from the counter. "I don't want to be friends with him. He's a man. And too close to our own age, Alvea. Besides. I have already shown up on his doorstep twice and he made it clear that he wasn't impressed by my presence there either time. He doesn't want us bothering him. I think he came here to be alone, and us disturbing his quiet isn't going to make him like us being here." *She isn't looking at me, the wheel whirring. This is ridiculous. It's way too early for this. Any of it. Why does she have to get ideas?* I shake my head. "I'm not going, Alvea."

She looks up at me, eyes sharp. "Then I am." Her jaw sets, eyes sharp. "It does not do to sit on gratitude."

I grit my teeth. *Curse it.* I spin, snatching the cookie bundle off the countertop, and sulk across the room. My feet slide into my boots and I snatch the toast into the hand with the bundle, jerk the laces tight of my boots tight with my other hand. The whirring and tapping has started again, faster now. *This is foolish, at this hour in the morning. No one wants visitors this early. Isn't there a saying about that?*

I grip the doorknob, snatch my shawl off the hook and jerk the door open, and there is white, all around. I grimace, and jerk my hand up, shielding my eyes with the bundle. My breaths hiss. *Why is the world so bright?* My eyes water, burning, swimming. I grimace, wrapping the shawl around my shoulders. *It's too heavy. The winter shawl. When did she have time to pull that out upstairs? How did I not wake, when she did?* I glance back toward the door and shake my head. I turn, stepping out into the snow.

My foot sinks down into it, and there is a strange crunch as my knee jars. I grimace. *The layer from before.* My eyes widen. *This is going to be a long walk, if every step is like that one.* I shake my head, and step again. My foot sinks, and crunches through, sinking further to the ground and my knee jars again. *This is ridiculous. Just because she is excited doesn't mean that I need to march out to give someone pastries first thing in the morning. I could do it some other time, when the snow is not so deep. He probably doesn't even want to be thanked. He probably just wants to be left alone. Why else would someone move out into the middle of nowhere? To be left alone.*

We didn't move for that reason. And we live in the middle of the forest, in the middle of nowhere. None of us wanted to be alone. We came because we had to, at the will of another, and necessity. Maybe she is right. "But not at this hour in the morning." My voice is awkward in the stillness of the forest. I snort, shaking my head, and step again. The snow sinks, and then crunches, same as each and every step before, jarring through my neck, through my shoulders and head.

The branches are lined again, snow upon each finger, upon each twig, and it's lovely. *Beautiful. Like the centaur said. I never told any of them about the centaur.* I swallow. *Would they have been curious about it, or have they seen more of them than I have?* I shake my head, stepping again, and look up. *The evergreens are enchanting, their branches heavy, green stark and beautiful against the world of pure, bright white in the morning sunlight, coming over the trees. It is beautiful, like Alvea said.* My heart sinks. *Did she see the beauty out here before I did out in the middle of nowhere, where we went without a choice? Am I not better at seeing than her, after all these weeks of looking, or does she see it easily where I cannot?*

I move around the thick evergreens, and there are only bare trees, stretching up toward the blue of the sky. *Beautiful.* White against blue. *It's beautiful, stunning, the brown of the trunks beneath the white of the snow, with the perfect sky above, crystal and clear.* My throat catches. *The world is calmer like this, when the winter cold creeps in.*

My skirts shift, wind cutting through them, throwing them around the trunk of the tree beside me, bare to the sky. I grip a handful of fabric in them, and step again—soft and then crunch, soft and then crunch. The air is crisp, cool with only a little wind, throwing my skirts to and fro with the chill of morning. I stumble, snow crunching, thudding. My legs ache, but the air is perfectly silent, nothing is making a sound in the forest, not a single sound. *The world is muffled beneath the snow, as though something has fallen upon it. Something peaceful, quieter than dawn.*

I step again, and there is the crunch of my feet, each step a muffle and a crunch, and there is the trail, winding up to the cottage. Smoke is curling up from the chimney, into the blue of the sky, just a puff of gray, and then gone with the breeze, curling off. I swallow, steps loud on the ground.

The porch stretches in front of me. I stop and lift my chin. *I can just give these to him and leave.* My legs ache, sore and heavy, snow clinging to my boots. I grimace, and step onto the porch. My steps are too loud, thudding with each step. *Cumbersome and huge.* I grimace, and lift my hand, tap my fist against the door. The knock rings out, and there is a bark, and another. A voice speaks, muffled by the wood, and maybe there are steps. I swallow hard. *He is coming.*

The door swings open.

Goran. He is dressed in a simple shirt, his hair down over his shoulders rather than pulled back like it always is. I swallow and jerk up the bundle. "Alvea ord—asked. She asked me to bring these to you, as a thank you. For saving me last night when I got lost."

He reaches out and takes the bundle. His brow lifts. "It was better than finding your body this morning."

I flush, and look back down, toward the steps. *My legs ache.* I grimace. "I'll leave you alone now. I apologize for any intrusion. Goodmorn."

A dog barks, and he shifts, just barely. "Oanéka." He half nods, back over his shoulder, barely a movement, and his jaw sets, like he's made a choice and he isn't certain of what it will mean. "I made tea. You can have some. If you will pet the hounds." There is no trace of a smile beneath his beard, his eyes hard to read above it.

Pet the hounds? I flinch and look up at him. *Tea will mean not having to go back to Alvea so soon. And I won't have to start back through the snow now. But what will I say to him?* I shift, and my legs ache. *I can pet the hounds for a minute, and then leave, quickly, speak only a few words to him, as not to trouble him.* I nod, gripping my skirts. He gestures back, into the hut and I step past him. *This isn't supposed to be appropriate, not supposed to be how this is done. But that seems foolish when you live in a world of nothing, to worry about what is appropriate with things like this, the little things. There is no one here to see that things are appropriate, no one to care. Curse it.*

The door shuts, and there is a hound growling beside me. I jump. The brown hound is beside me, eyes on mine from the same level as my elbow, fur raised on his neck, teeth bared. *There is gray on his muzzle, like I thought.* His eyes are narrowed.

"Crith." Goran says. His voice is sharp, and the hound lowers his head. His eyes don't leave mine, and he growls again, lowering his muzzle a little more toward the ground. I swallow, grip my skirts. Goran's eyes flicker toward him. "Crith. Lay down." The hound drops to the ground, and his teeth are still bared, eyes not leaving mine. I swallow, twisting my fingers a little. Goran nods toward a chair. "You can sit there. If you call her, Marin will come over to you. She minds strangers a little less than Crith."

I glance around the room. *If the red one is Gyaith, and the brown one is Crith. The blue one must be Marin.* I swallow and tap my leg. "Marin. Come here." The blue hound lifts her head, and stretches, long and lean. Her tongue lolls out for a moment, thin and purple, and she is walking toward me, steps light and even. I sit down, in the chair he gestured to. She drops down beside me, face even with mine in the seat. I lift my hand. *Will she growl at me, if I am petting her?* I lift my hand, and set it against her muzzle, slowly. She blinks, watching me, waiting, mouth closed now. I smile. *No growling.*

There is a growl, across the room. My head whips around. *The brown hound.* He is still watching me, like an old man who did not care to be disturbed. I swallow and stroke my hand down Marin's neck. Her tongue lolls out again, and she lifts her head, pointing her nose toward the ceiling, tongue lolling further. *Is it this easy to make a hound content?* I swallow and stroke my hand down her head again. Her face turns toward me, and a puff of warm air brushes across my face, and everything smells like death and something rotten.

I gag, and turn away, hand still stroking her head. *That is awful.*

I keep my head turned to the side. Her awful breath is still fanning across my face, hot and muggy. I swallow, turn my head half away from the hound. *I should say something, should break the silence.* "Does it usually snow this early in the year?" My eyes flicker toward Goran. He is pouring a pot of water into cups, steam curling up in a cloud above them in the light of the window.

He sets the pot down on the table. "Were you not expecting it?"

I shake my head. "Nie, we were. But I had hoped that it would be a wrong expectation." I run my hand down the hound's head again. Her damp nose nuzzles my arm, damp through my sleeve. "It seems hard to have so little blatant beauty for so long every year, with all the winter. Only snow."

His hand reaches out toward me, a cup within it. I take it, my other hand still stroking Marin's head. He moves away, toward another chair. "Is snow such an ugly thing then?"

My eyes snap up. "Nie. It's not. It can be beautiful. But it seems to be the only thing that is of any real beauty out here, I suppose." *Why did I choose this subject?*

He drops into the chair, and his hair is now bound back, not down like it was before. *When did he put it up?* His eyes look dry. "Snow is half of winter out here, snow upon snow. If you are calling it beautiful, then why are you complaining about the beauty of it? There is enough of it to keep your eyes busy." His brows are low, tea steaming in the cup in his hand.

I swallow, and scratch behind the hound's ear. "I wasn't... I didn't intend to complain. I just... There doesn't seem to be much out here other than snow that is beautiful, and that cannot last. Does it not grow uglier, as the months go on, snow upon snow upon snow, like you said?"

He looks down, shifting his legs so his knees are apart. "It sounds more like you are saying it isn't 'pretty.' I cannot say if it gets less beautiful. I have not paid much heed to that sort of thing out here."

I scowl, nose scrunching. "Nie. I meant beautiful. And there is not a difference in any case."

He shakes his head and clicks his tongue. The brown and red hounds both stand, moving toward him. They drop to the ground beside his feet, and he takes a sip of his tea, running a hand over the brown one's head. "I thought beauty was deeper than surface and skin. Isn't that what the writers and sages say? What you have described sounds entirely surface."

My lips turn down. *Writers and sages? He cannot have been out here forever.* I turn toward Marin. She is looking over her shoulder now, eyes on the window. I swallow. "I don't know. Maybe beauty is, but I have never thought of it that way. It seems that there are a lot of things out here in the world that are beautiful and skin deep, colors and life and things." I shake my head and look back at him. "And are prettiness and beauty woven together?"

He shakes his head, rubbing the neck of the red hound beside him. "I don't think those things are only surface things. If Elnial made them, then there is a beauty that goes further than that, in my mind, which makes them more beautiful for it. But I'm no scholar. You'll have to take up those questions elsewhere. I've seen things that were stunningly beautiful, without a trace of prettiness in them in the world. The beauty of winter is not pretty, in the ways that I've seen beauty in it." My lips pull down further. *But doesn't it have to be pretty to be beautiful, as I said?* I turn back to the hound and stroke her head again. The teacup hot beneath my fingers, steam curling toward my face and fanning across it, like the hot breath of the hound before. She turns, and her breath brushes my face again, joining the steam. I gag, and turn away sharply, lift the tea beneath my nose. The steam smelled like lavender, and something else, fresh and bright, like spring. I swallow. My eyes burn.

"Did you lose your tracks last night?" He says. His eyes are on the hound next to me, watching her.

I frown. *Tracks?* "What tracks?" I drop my eyes. *What tracks did I lose last night?*

His mouth twitches beneath his beard. "Your foot tracks."

I scowl. "I wasn't following them. How could I have lost them?"

His mouth flattens beneath the beard. "Because you can follow your tracks back where you came from." *Tracks in the snow.* My mouth falls open. *I could have followed them home, even in the dark, with all the light coming off the snow with the brightness of last night's sky. I could have seen them. Foolish, foolish, foolish. I never thought of following my own tracks back. I could have made it home without him. I could have made it back without dragging him out in the snow last night, without coming out here to bother him this morning.* My face heats.

I swallow, turn back toward the hound. I lift my chin. *Change the subject, ask him something, something other than that.* "How long have you been out here?"

His eyes flicker to me, and back to the hound and the firelight dances in his eyes. *They are dark, unlike Yore's. Nothing about him is like Yore. Nothing but their height.* His eyes flicker down to the hound again. "Years."

My eyes widen. *Years? Why would anyone live out here for years? Was he forced out here?* My eyes flicker to him. His gaze is still on the hounds, hand still fondling their heads. *I can't see his face* .I look down, take a sip of my tea. The liquid splashes into my mouth, hot and air catches in my throat. I cough, and set the cup hard against my knee, a cough grating my throat. *Pet the hound. Tend the hound.* I stroke her head, faster. *Air is still caught in my lungs.* "Years?" My voice is too high. *Foolish. I should not have tried to speak so soon after choking.* I glance at him. *He didn't struggle with drinking it. Does his mouth not get burnt? It was boiling hot.*

He nods, and his eyes flicker toward me. "Va. Four or so."

Or so? He doesn't know how many years he's been out here? I lift the teacup to my lips, and freeze, pulling it back. *Not burning my throat again. Not choking again.* I look up. "Are you a..." *What would someone do in the forest?* "Woodcutter?" *All of the furniture in the room looks like it was carved by the same person, the patterns neat and similar, the wood the same tone, the marks the same. But there are animal hides, over many of the pieces.*

"Hunter." His voice is curt, and his teacup is empty on his knee. *He finished it? How did he drink that? How can he still speak after that? Can he taste anything?*

Hunter. I frown, and swirl the teacup, and brush my hand down the hound's head again. *If he is a hunter, did he come here of his own volition?* "Who do you sell the meat to?"

He shifts, arms resting on his knees, cup empty between his fingers. "The furs."

My mouth shapes an 'oh,' and I lift the tea, and take a sip, turning my head away. *Who does he sell them to?* I swallow, and I can barely feel the heat of the tea. *I will have scalded my tongue.* I grimace. "Who do you sell furs to? Are there others crazy enough..." I grimace. *I shouldn't have said that. But the words are already out of my mouth.* "...to live out here?"

His eyebrow quirks, and his eyes flicker to me. "Do you dislike it out here so much?"

My face flushes, warms. I look away, toward the hound beside me. She is staring at the window still, eyes half-closed. "We left a lot behind, and I miss it, though I know that we have not been here long yet." I swallow, slide my hand down the hound's neck. "Are there others out here?" I lift my eyes.

He is shaking his head. "Nie. There are not." His eyes flicker back to me, sharply. "If you miss home so much, it seems strange you would choose to come out here, or choose to stay, once you have arrived."

"It wasn't a choice." I bite my lip. *I should not have said that.* I shake my head and take a long sip of the tea. I look down, the tea too hot again in my throat. My hand rubs Marin's head. I lower the cup. "I should go. You probably have a hundred things to do today, it's early." I look down at the teacup. *I'm not leaving a half-drunk cup of tea.* I lift it to my lips, and tilt my head back, and the liquid hot and bland over my tongue. I bite back a grimace, set the cup down on my knee.

He stands before I can, moving to take the cup from me. "It is winter. There are only so many things to be done in a day." He lifts a brow at me.

I frown. "Then what does Yore do all day?"

He glances back at me, and turns away, taking the empty cups toward the table. "Only he would know that, if you and your sister don't. Though he likely has preparations to make for the outdoors with the coming of shorter days. You all did not have the summer out here to make everything ready."

I had not thought much of that. I turn my head away, and stand, hand still brushing Marin's head. *What will she do if I stop?* She looks up at me, her tongue no longer lolling. I swallow, and blink. *Can I get away?*

Goran's footsteps are loud on the floor. "You can step away from her."

I look up, sharply. "Are you certain?" *Of course, he is certain.*

He lifts a brow. "Did you not have hounds at home?"

I swallow again, brushing my hand down Marin's head. Her eyes close, happy, and her tongue lolls out again. I shake my head. "I avoided them. The men who owned most of them back home were unsavory fellows."

He looks away. "Well, you can step away from her. They will not hurt you." I look up sharply. *There is no, 'unless I tell them to.' Only 'they will not hurt you.'* I swallow, and step away from Marin. Her tongue snaps back in, and she stretches, moving over toward her master, where he stands across the room.

I move toward the door. "Thank you, for the tea, Goran." I swallow. His name feels weird on my tongue. "And for saving me last night. I was lost, and I'm sorry for your trouble."

He turns back toward me, stretching his arms into his coat. "Don't get lost again. It wasn't trouble, but winter is harsh. You need to be aware of where you are at all times."

I nod. "Tracks."

His eyes move to mine. "Nie. Don't go out so close to dark." He slides his other arm into his coat. "Or take someone else. And a lantern. You cannot find tracks well in the dark, even if you have trained at it. And your hair will not help anyone find you after the sun has sunk."

I scowl. "I'm hoping they won't need to find me. Isn't that the point of taking precautions?" *Why did he have to bring up my hair? Is it bad, today? Does red bother him? Is it bothersome?*

He nods, and shifts. "Va. It is the point. But it would be better if you didn't go out." He drops his hands into his pockets. "This place is not friendly to lots who wander idly."

A shiver runs up my spine. I nod and turn toward the door. My hand pauses on the handle. *Alvea would want me to invite him over. He invited me in. Maybe he wouldn't mind if we asked him back?* I swallow and turn toward him. He is picking up his axe from the corner, a hat on his head now. "You should come over, for dinner sometime. You and Yore could talk."

He nods, and straightens, slinging the axe over his shoulder. His eyes drop to me. "Are you speaking for yourself, or for your sister?"

I nod my head. "Both of us. All of us. It would be an honor if you came over, Goran. To all of us." *I shouldn't be calling him by his first name. It's too forward for new acquaintances.* I swallow. "What is your family name?"

His brow lifts. "Goran is fine."

I shake my head. "It's forward."

He lifts a brow. "I'm the only person for thirty miles in any direction. Goran is fine." *So there truly are no others, out here. It's just him, just us, and vast emptiness. He'd said before there might have been hermits. Are there truly not any that far in any direction?*

I swallow, turning toward the door. "Alright then." I nod at him. "Thank you. You are welcome any night. It would be an honor, if you came." I move through the doorway, and he is following me, moving behind me without the hounds. The door clicks shut, and my steps pound on the porch, until the snow muffles them, and then there is the crunch of it beneath my feet. I tilt my head and look up. *'Beauty is deeper than skin.'* I shiver, and wrap my shawl tighter, about my shoulders, Goran's step loud behind me, turning away.

Chapter XI

The snow is crunchy, three days of freezing, with no fresh snow, and my breaths are heavy in my chest, loud in the air. I step forward, foot crunching through the crust, and my heel thuds against the ground, again and again. Sweat trickles down my neck, warm, the air frozen, sharp against my nose, sharp in my throat, sharp on my eyes.

I step around a tree, pressing my hand against it. The cottage is just over the creek, close now. I swallow and press my fingers against my cheeks. *Cold. My fingers are frozen.* I jerk them back, and huff out a breath. It puffs, a white cloud before my face. *It doesn't seem beautiful out here, not today. It's just cold and stale. Gray nothing in the clouds, over the snow that is only white in patches now 'Beauty is deeper than surface.' It's just cold, bone deep cold, biting into your fingers, biting through your flesh and creeping in where warmth should have kept it back. It's all gray, and all sameness. If there is something more out here, I don't see it. Today there is only gray, and frozen earth beneath hard packed snow.*

"Oanéka." My head snaps up; Yore is there, across the creek. He is coming across the way, back from the calli shed. There is dirt, caked to his coat that is only half on and his face is set. He nods his head back toward the shed behind him. "I was coming to look for you. I need your help with a calli." My breaths puff out, stomach sinking. He shakes his head. "It's not a birth. And I'm not asking Alvea because I don't want her kneeling in there right now."

Oh. My face warms. I nod, and step away from the tree, move across the creek. My boots tap against the stones, and the snow on the other side is slick with ice, hard packed snow, slicker now. Yore's hand grips my arm, pulling me up the bank. He is turning, back toward the shed. I move up beside him, look up. His jaw is not tense today, like I thought it was. He has let his beard grow out again. It's scraggly, on his cheeks and chin, and I hardly noticed before now.

He glances down at me, and away. "One of the calli got a large thorn branch caught in her wool. I need you to cut it out." He shuffles his shoulders, steps slowing to match mine. "She won't hold still for me." I lift a brow. He grabs the door, pulling it open. "I'm going to hold her down."

Oh. I nod, and step through the door ahead of him. I pause. He steps past me, his chest brushing my shoulder in the small space. He is moving up to a small gray calli. Her eyes are wide and large. She bares her teeth and bleats loudly, bolting to the side. I slap my hands around my ears, grimacing. They are ringing, the noise too loud. Yore steps forward, his hands looping around her, and he grunts, lifting her easily from the hay scattered floor. The calli struggles for a second, and calls again, louder, panicked. Yore grimaces, and turns toward me, his face still pinched. I swallow. *There is something dark, tangled in her wool, twisted in it. The thorn branch.*

I shuffle my feet and drop my hands from my ears. He is shifting the calli in his arms. I fold my arms around my waist. "How do you want me to get it out of there?"

He nods down, toward his belt. "My knife." The calli kicks, and he grunts, straining to keep the creature in his arms. I grimace, lick my lips. *Knife. I use knives all the time. I can cut this out easily and be done.* I step forward, and Yore is kneeling, lowering himself to the floor, the calli still in his arms, her eyes wide. I kneel beside him, by the back legs of the calli. I reach my fingers out. Her leg twitches, just barely. I flinch. *It's fine.* The tip of his knife sheath is poking out beneath his coat, hardly visible beneath the puff of wool and teeth in his arms. I press his coat to the side, and the calli half shifts, and stops. I flinch, and puff out a breath. My hand grips the handle, pulling it free, and there is the knife, a short, a stubby thing, within a pale tan sheath. I grip it and turn to Yore.

His eyes are on the calli's head, his voice soft and smooth, breathing out something that I can't hear, a whisper. I swallow. "How do you want this done?"

His eyes flicker to me, and his voice goes on, for a moment, speaking softly to the ewe. He nods, his arms still around her. "Just cut carefully. Try not to tug her wool, and try not to cut it if you don't have to. It may just be tangled in there; in which case you can pull it all free." I nod and lift the knife. *There is only an edge on one side of the blade. That is good.* I swallow, tilting my head to the side. The calli is still, her eye yellow-brown like all of theirs are, with tiny slits where irises should be, and it's watching me.

I lick my lips, grip the knife handle. I lift my eyes. "Does this one have a name?"

Yore glances at me, speaking softly to the creature again. His brow lifts, an expression like Alvea's. "Coriander."

Coriander? My brow lifts. I scowl and turn back toward her. *A plant name?* "It's pretty." I glance at him, and shift toward the calli. "Why did you choose it? Why a plant name?"

He moves his head, somewhere between a shake and a shrug. "I'd heard you mention it, and it seemed to fit her. A little dainty."

A smile curls at my lips. I lift a brow, brushing my hand against her wool. It's soft, thick and grainy, like sea sponge. She doesn't pull away, doesn't move, eyes still too wide. I shift my hand. "You know it's a plant?"

He tilts his head again, like a shrug, and his face colors a little beneath his beard. "It seemed to fit. And I'd heard of the color." A laugh bubbles up in my throat, and I purse my lips, shutting them tightly. *Don't laugh.* I swallow, and lift the knife, cutting a little into the wool. The calli shifts sideways sharply. I jerk the knife back. She stares at me, eyes looking to pop out of her head, face pressed against Yore.

"It's an herb." I say. "Small seeds. It smells sharp." I move my hand forward again. Yore is quiet, his arms around Coriander. I lick my lips. "The flowers are often yellowed, which is I think where the name came from." His knife in my hand cuts a little through the wool, and there is something brown, large and twisted deep within the wool. The thorn branch. *It is no wonder he could not get her to hold still for long enough.* I grab the branch and tug a little.

The calli bleats, jerking sharply, her head flying toward Yore's. Yore jerks his head back, his breath rushing out in a grunt. His eyes snap to me, and narrow, his arms straining around the thrashing creature. "I said—" the calli thrashes again, and he grunts. His eyes flash to mine, calli stilling for a moment. His teeth grit. "—don't tug."

I frown. "You also said try not to cut it." I lift a brow. "I can't do both very well without trying a little of each to see which is the better option."

He shakes his head. "Don't cut, if you don't have to but don't pull. She doesn't like this and I want to keep my face."

I nod, and then half shake my head. *Of course she doesn't like this.* I turn back and tug a little at the wool around the branch. The calli doesn't jerk this time, her eyes still wide, staring back at me. *That strand must not be connected anymore.* I jerk it, and it comes free in my fingers, greasy with the calli wool. *Eww.* I set the knife down, and purse my lips, twisting my fingers into the wool around the branch. *There has to be a way to do this without cutting it anymore.* A strand of wool comes free when I tug it slightly. The calli doesn't jerk, her eyes not moving, head still. *Move slowly, work gently.*

I swallow and work my fingers further into her wool. I flick my eyes up, toward Yore. His eyes are on my hands, his voice no longer speaking in breaths to the calli. His arms are still taut around her. I look down at my fingers, and swallow. "Yore..." he glances up at my face, brow creased. I look down. "Do you think that there can be any beauty in winter out here?" I look up at him. His eyes are a little wide, startled. *Why does he look so surprised?* I swallow and pull at the wool again. The calli jerks, and Yore strains, tensing his arms around it. I swallow again. "Sorry. I mean, if any part of it will be? And not just darkness, when the days grow shorter?" *What happens when there is less light, and only the short days? Will they be much shorter further north, as we are now?*

His eyes flicker away, and he is still. I frown. *Maybe I am asking too much. I shouldn't have asked. Maybe he doesn't want to think about the shorter days, and what they will look like, when the shadows grow longer with time, and the months stretch on.* My lips pull down, and my heart shivers. *The long months. The short days. I had not thought about them. Oh stars. Will the gray last forever?* I tug at the wool, and there is more of the branch visible, thorns large and jutting through it, their tips barely away from Coriander's skin. *That will be why she was so antsy about it.*

I tug again, and the end of the branch is visible, tucked away beneath another strand. I slip my fingers beneath is, and tug, fingers weaving around the enormous thorn beside them. They are big enough to impale. I pull, and there is the branch, free. Thorns prick my fingers, and I grimace. I gingerly shift my fingers around the thorns, scooting back.

Yore's arms release Coriander, and she jumps up, bleating, that loud, high, strange call, her hooves pressing against Yore's legs leaving footprints of dust behind on them, and she springs off, out the open door into the pen beyond. Her call rings again, and is answered, a lower call, another calli, out in the pen.

I press my feet under me, and stand, slowly. The branch catches my skirts, tugs at them, and I grimace, pulling it away. Something thuds to the floor, tapping the edge of my foot as it falls sideways. *Yore's knife.* My heart thuds, hard in my chest, and I swallow. I stoop, grabbing it from the straw. *It barely missed my foot.* Yore is by the doorway, watching the calli in the pen. He turns back, and reaches out, his hands grip the branch, pulling it from my fingers, and he is gone, to the door. He shoves the door open with his shoulder, and steps out, casting the branch to the side, out over the stream somewhere beyond where the calli won't get it again.

I step out after him, and press my hip against the door, nudging it shut. The knife is still clutched in my hand, handle warm and small. I turn, and he is still standing where he was, his figure stilled, shoulders straight and hunched at once. He lifts his eyes, toward the sky, and there is silence. "'Truly, the light is sweet.'" His voice is low, simple and soothing, like a verse, like a song. *Like it used to be, before the world crashed down, before he made choices on his own. Before mamé left us, and Yore walked out the door toward the docks stayed out later with each passing night, not coming home until the early mornings, if at all.*

I swallow. My throat is tight. He turns, and his eyes are quiet. "We should go inside." He turns, and moves back toward the cottage, and I am still holding his knife. *That will be his answer, to my question. To beauty, out here. 'Truly, the light is sweet.'* I swallow, the branches of the trees are lit by only the gray light of a pale sky, covered with clouds and darkness, and the barest traces of snow. *Is the light sweet here? It seems all dark, faint if it is there at all, covered with clouds, with shadows and the gray of everywhere.*

Chapter XII

Yore's voice rises and falls, a poem on his lips again, dark and deep, and his eyes are lost, scanning the fire where it flickers in the hearth.

"The nights flow into days, and the skies fill with hope,
Stars, moons, clouds, and light falling down upon the slope,
Here in the valley, low in the north,
The sky."

Alvea's wheel is spinning, spinning beneath her foot. Her head is high, eyes on the window, shuttered across the way. *Do they not see each other?* Yore's voice is clear, it's always clear, continuing with the verse.

"We call when we know not, ache with a hope that fails,
Man calls, he cries, and to the hills, he rails,
'What is the creed, we've taken up?'
When will the hills cry out 'enough'?
But here, the sky, still filled with hope,
And here, the light shines down these slopes."

Alvea moves sideways, and her leg shifts awkwardly. Her hands shift on the thread, moving it over on the wheel, whirling, whirling. She turns her head, back toward Yore, eyes lifting to his. *His eyes are on something in the fire, haven't moved from where they've sat the last hour.* His brow twitches. "What is it, Alvea?" He doesn't look at her.

She shakes her head. "I was only wondering, that you chose that one." She pulls the needle through again. "I've never heard it, but it sounds like one of the ones you would have learned first, at the school. The early ones." *The ones he often told her in the evenings, when they were young.*

He folds his hands between his knees, eyes still on the fire. "Paun taught it to me." I grimace and pull my needle through my needlework—the purple thread jerks tight, needle stabbing my skin. I flinch. *I thought the thread was longer.* Alvea glances at me, and rolls her eyes, shifting her hands again on the surface of the wheel. I push the needle through again, pursing my lips. *Paun. I haven't thought of him in weeks. Ugly old fisherman. All he ever spoke about was death, with all those black teeth in his mouth. And he always reeked of fish, and something sweet and sour. His hat never straight on his head, the man Yore sat by, day by day, when he quit the pubs and the taverns. The man who sat with him when he wasn't at home with us.*

Yore lifts his head, shifting in his chair. "It never seemed appropriate at home. And you two never cared for that kind of verse there."

Alvea shakes her head. "I did. You just never liked to speak of it." Her eyes are lifted, chin tilted slightly back.

Yore drops back in his chair, sharply. His eyes are narrowed, irritated, lips pursed. "Only after Korta left you." My heart slows. *Oh, curse it.*

Alvea's eyes are flashing. She jerks her hands away from the wheel, feet snapping under her. "I cared for real things before he ran off and married that girl." Her voice is sharp, loud. "Don't throw him in my face. I don't think you want to talk about faults, Yore. I don't think you want to talk about things of the past, do you?" The thread scrunches in her fist, his eyes are on the floor, head down, shoulders drooping. "Nie. You don't. You run whenever we mention it. Don't you bring him up to me. Don't you bring him up, not when you could have done something just by speaking, just by saying a word." She turns, and her hands are shaking by her sides. She moves for the ladder, steps loud and unstable, the limp tap limp tap, and she is gone, into the room above, her steps loud upon the floor.

Yore jerks up, the chair crashing to the ground behind him.

I stand, slowly. My heart shakes. "Yore..."

He turns, and his eyes flash at me. "You want to add something to it? You want to remind me what I did? You want to remind me what I didn't do? I didn't make his choice for him; didn't know he was going to leave her. I never saw him with that other girl." He shakes his head, and turns away, toward the door. His hands are shaking, like hers. "You don't even know what I've done, don't know the half of it. And she doesn't either. She doesn't know what went on at the docks, all the things we did." His hand grabs his coat, and he is jerking it on. "She doesn't need to bring up what I've done. As if I could forget it. We all know she's a hundred times better than everyone else, and I'm a hundred times worse." His hand is on the doorknob, and he jerks it open, lost to the outside.

I swallow, and my heart is pounding. Cold air swirls into the room, cutting into the warmth of the fire. *Cold air. He can't go out there, it's after dark and it's cold, too cold to be out there. And he didn't take his gloves.*

I bolt across the room and snatch his gloves from the floor, and spin, jerking the door open. Cold blasts my face, sharp, and the wind is brushes, whistling on the porch beams and swirling over the frozen snow. I swallow hard, and jerk the door shut behind me. The wind rips at my dress, cutting through the stockings on my feet, and my nose is burning, cold, the snow flat and frozen beneath the wind, trees bending in it. I wrap my arms around my waist, lift my voice. "Yore!" It whips off in the darkness, and there is nothing, but a light off in the shed. *He grabbed the lantern.*

My teeth chatter, hard against each other, just once and I shake my head, stamp my feet and turn, skirts catching in the wind, jerking hard. I stumble, jerk them back against my legs. *I can't get to the shed. He'll come back when he is ready. And the shed may be warm enough, with the calli in there...* I swallow hard.

Could they not have been civil tonight? One night. One night when Yore was himself again, before the pubs, before the docks, before mamé and pakem left, before we were sentenced to this or death, for Yore's sake? Could they not have lasted one night? One night of simplicity? True simplicity? Not just idle staring at the fire, not just the spinning, the foolish spinning of that wheel or the tapping of the loom?

My eyes burn, and my teeth knock together, cold cutting into my skin. My hand fumbles with the doorknob, stiff and cold, and it slams shut behind me, jerked by something. *By the wind.* I shiver, my teeth chatter, and my arms are shaking, shaking. *Curse it.* I swallow, and my eyes are burning with night, and something else. *This wasn't how it was supposed to be. None of this. We were supposed to settle, with gardens and future and hope. Not this, not this emptiness, not this pain, never this. This wasn't how it was supposed to be. This wasn't how life was supposed to be, none of it. It isn't right. We shouldn't be out here.* I step forward, and the wood of the floor echoes, hollow.

The firelight crackles, snapping and leaping, and there is nothing to any of it. *Only pain. Because that's all that can be out here. Pain, and the empty, echoing nothing of the woods that roll on endlessly toward nothing but ice and snow.*

Chapter XIII

There is a knocking sound on the door.

I freeze, hands in the dough and flour. My eyes widen, and flicker across the room. *Probably a trick of the wind over the porch.* Alvea is staring at the door, her hands slowing from their furious pace. She stands, slowly, her eyes flickering to mine. "Are we expecting Goran?" She lifts a brow, and sets down the thread she was spinning, moves toward the door.

I shake my head. "Not now."

She straightens her skirts, brushes back her hair, as if readying for a guest, and glances at me. I swallow. *He isn't like to be there. If Goran has not come by this point, he isn't likely to come at all. It's been a week or more.* I shake my head and look down. The dough is sticky and wild on my skin, clinging to it. *More likely a trick of the wind.*

Alvea pulls the door open, and cold swirls into the room. She straightens. "Goran." My eyes snap up. *Goran?! He came?* She is moving out of the way to let him in, into the room. "It's cold out, please come in."

My eyes snap down. There is dough, thick, sticky and messy caked up to my elbows, flour over my arms, over my skirts. Hair is in my face, wild strands of red, in my eyes, curling across my cheeks. Oh curses. Be calm, be calm. It's...

Alvea steps to the side, and there is Goran, stepping through the door, the blue hound by his side. Alvea folds her hands, neatly in front of her, and she nods. She is poised, eyes kind, smile soft, nod gentle, like a lady. "Yore is out, but you are welcome to come sit." She gestures, to the chairs, across the room. *She looks like a lady, and I look like a wild thing that fell in a pastry dough. Oh curses. Oh curses. Maybe he did come for Yore.*

He nods. "I'm actually here because Oanéka invited me. I brought meat." He lifts a bundle, and Marin's head lifts beside him, her nose following it. My heart sinks. *Oh curses. I never told Alvea.*

Alvea's eyes flicker toward me. I smile, and it sticks to my lips, small, brittle. *I didn't think he would actually come. He didn't seem to care much for company. I thought he came to get away from people, to be a hermit. Curses. I should have told her. I didn't think he would come. It's been so long.*

Alvea smiles at me, and there is a slight glint in her eyes. She turns back to Goran, pushing the door shut. "I'm glad she did. Come, sit. Oanéka is making bread, but I believe she already has a stew on that will be ready soon. You are a thousand times welcome." She nods at him, the welcoming nod, and half bows, curtesy.

He nods, returning the bow, and steps forward into the room. His movements are strangely graceful and wary at once, as though the space is his, and he fears it. *Like a hunter. Like a hound.* He steps toward me and sets the bundle down on the counter beside me. His eyes don't look for mine. I swallow, and my face is hot. *Am I a post?* I shift my hands. "I didn't think you were going to come."

His eyes turn toward me, and he slips a finger into his coat, slipping the buttons open. He loses the scarf from around his neck. "It's the last of hunting season. I was busy, until now." His eyes are on his hands.

I nod, and swallow. *I'm not going to be awkward. I'm not going to be awkward. I invited him here.* I nod my head toward the rack, where our cloaks hang on the wall. "You can hang your coat over there, on the empty peg." He nods, moving toward it. I swallow again and roll my fingers in the dough. It smushes between my fingers, swirling around them. I look up, pull my hands from the dough. *I should offer something. I invited him.* "Would you like something hot to drink?" He glances back, hands looping his coat onto the hook. His eyes flicker down to my hands. My face warms. I lift my chin. "I can put a kettle on in a minute. This won't take long to bind together." A strand of hair slides into my face, over my eyes. I look down. *Just knead the bread.*

Alvea shakes her head, moving from her place by the door. "I will put it on." Her steps tap the floor, step, tap, step, tap, and she lifts the kettle, her chin up like mine was a moment ago. *Maybe it runs in our family. But her movements are graceful, clean and even, as they always are. Except for last night.* I flinch, and press my hands into the dough, harder.

I glance at Alvea, as she lifts the kettle. *He never said he wanted tea.* A laugh breaks from my throat, and I sag backward, hands still in the dough. Alvea's eyes snap to me, and narrow, face dry. I shake my head and turn toward Goran. His eyes are on me, expression almost wary. I nod. "I'm sorry." I shake my head and laugh again. "We aren't used to having guests anymore. Please, make yourself at home, and you don't have to have tea if you do not want it."

Alvea straightens, a strange expression crossing her face. She half laughs, like something remembered. "I am sorry. She is right." She nods at me. "We neglected to wait for your answer. We have gotten out of the custom of having guests."

Goran steps across the room, dropping into the chair across from Alvea's. "I wouldn't mind tea." His mouth half quirks, almost a smile. *He didn't mind. Thank the stars.* I puff out a breath, and turn away, back to the bread. I jerk my hand from the dough and take a handful of flour. It puffs into the bowl, clinging to my fingers and dropping in clumps onto the counter.

There is the splatter of water, and Alvea sets the kettle on the stove. She turns, graceful, moving slowly back toward her chair. Her head is high, limp almost hidden now. She glances at Goran. "I've been thankful for these last few days without new snow." She takes her seat, picking up her needlework from the bin behind her chair, leaving the spinning wheel idle in front of her. I smile. *She's inviting him to talk. Good, then I won't have to worry about it.* My heart twists. She lifts her needle. "It's let Yore work in the woods. I imagine it's been the same for you."

Goran is brushing a hand over Marin's head, stroking his fingers through her fur. Her head is up, nose lifted, eyes taking in every part of the room, flickering across everything. He nods. "It's made for good hunting. The beavers and like have been out in force."

Alvea looks up from her needlework, pressing the needle through again. "Beaver?" She looks down, and back up, slipping the needle through with her fingertips. "I thought they lived in rivers."

His hand is still stroking the hound's head. "They do. There is a river, an hour or so from my hut, a little more from yours. They are plentiful on it, in the summer months. The river has shifted several times as a result of their homes clogging the flow."

I thrust at the dough under my hands. It is coming together, sticking to itself and not to me anymore, a ball, thick and soft, firm. Alvea lifts a brow at him. "They can do that, with their homes? Change the course of a river?"

He nods. "Va. And do, frequently."

Her eyes widen, just slightly. "I hadn't realized they could do that. At home, they just built in the corners of the lake, and caused trouble to only fishermen, I believe. Though, I confess, I rarely conversed with those who would know. Those who owned boats mostly lived on the outskirts of the village."

A ghost of a smile brushes across Goran's face and is gone again. "They do that. Did you all live near a lake?"

Alvea nods. "Va. We are from a lake village, Carvi, beside Volah, or Swiftcurrent. It's a tiny little town, but the lake was stunning. Is stunning. Especially in the summer months, with all the greenery around it. It was a lush valley, though it still had many of the same trees that I imagine grow here in the summer months." She turns her head back toward her work, fingers moving swiftly. "What is your hound's name?"

Goran's brow twitches, watching her. "This one is Marin." I turn back toward the dough.

She nods, lifting her head. "And you have three?" He nods. She lifts a brow. "How did you come to have them, and what are they like?"

He shifts, calmly. My eyes flicker from him, back to the dough in my hands. "This one was from settlers who did not stay long. They did not want to bring her back to the village they were returning to." Goran's voice is even, low, as though that were not an echo of his warning to me on the porch, weeks ago, when he told us not to stay. "I brought Gyaith with me when I came, she is red, and smaller than this one." I frown. *Not by much.* "Crith is older, brown, and he doesn't care much for strangers."

Or visitors, it seemed. I swallow and set the bread in the bowl. I turn toward the wash bucket, cupping my hands together to keep the flour from the floor. My eyes flicker to Goran. "How did you come to have Crith?"

He glances at me, hand still brushing Marin's head. "An elderly woman. She used to live up by the mountain."

I shove my hands into the water and flinch. *It's cold.* A shudder runs up my spine. I scrub at the dough, caked and hardening on my skin, stuck to the thin hairs on my forearms, clinging to the creases in my skin. I tilt my head over my shoulder. "She gave him to you?" I lift a brow, scrubbing.

"She died, and did not want her son to take him south again."

My eyes snap up. *Oh.* The blood drains from my face. I turn away, and my face is hot. I scrub harder at the dough on my skin. It's clinging, messy and gooey now, floating in chunks and drifts in the cold water.

Alvea clears her throat. "I'm sorry."

I jerk my hands from the water, and lift the towel, pressing my hands into it, and I glance at the pot on the stove. The stew looks thick, hot and ready. *Ready enough.* I swallow. "The stew is done. I'll let Yore know."

Goran shakes his head, his hand working behind the hound's ears. Her tongue lolls out, eyes half shutting, happy. "He said he would be in in a moment," he says.

I pause, hands scrunched in my skirts. "Oh." *Then should I tell him anyway?* I purse my lips. I should set the table. I turn lifting the bowls from their place on the shelves. I pause by the table, eyes scanning it. *The table is not large. We should eat by the fire tonight. I do not know that any of us want to be that close together.* I set the bowls on the counter.

I snatch the ladle from its place, and the door is opening across the room, and Yore steps in, pulling his hat from his head. He shoves the door shut, tapping out his boots on the floor. Alvea stands. "Perfect. Oanéka just said the stew is done, so we can eat as soon as you are washed up."

He nods, and glances at Goran and the hound. "Have my sisters talked your ears off your head yet?" He stoops, slipping his fingers into his boot buckles.

Alvea's eyes snap to him. "You know we have done nothing of the kind." Her voice is almost sharp. Yore grins, a halfhearted thing hid beneath his hair, and slips his boots off. He moves across the room in four steps, and is gone through his doorframe. *He didn't take his coat off.* I drop the ladle in the stew and grip the last bit of last week's bread from the shelf.

Goran stands, and the hound drops to the floor, resting her head against her great paws. Alvea gestures toward Yore's room. "You are welcome to wash up in there. That water will be cleaner than the washbasin in here right now, since it's bread day."

He glances at her. "Do you need more water hauled?"

She shakes her head, brushing him off, and my heart drops, relieved. *I can haul it in the morning. We have enough in the bucket for dish washing tonight.* "We'll get it later. Wash up, before the stew gets cold." She says. He turns, and is through the doorway, gone. There is the low rumble of voices, Yore's voice a little higher than his, but only barely, and I can't hear their words, only the sound of their voices mixing together,

Alvea's eyes flicker to the bowls on the counter. "Why did you put them over there?"

I glance at her and churn the ladle in the stew again. It is thick, brown and beautiful. It will do. "I thought it would be more comfortable to sit around the fireplace this evening."

She half smiles at me. "That is a good thought, Néka. It will be lovely to be around the fire. Plus..." she glances toward the door that the men went through. "I am not sure that their legs will both fit under that table. He is equally as tall as Yore. That table was made small." I laugh, and she glances at me. She shakes her head, a smile playing at her lips. "It would be our luck that we would end up with a tall guest as our only one out here. Yore's legs barely fit under the table on their own." She shakes her head, and half shudders, laughing again.

I laugh. Yore is stepping through the door. His eyes flicker toward me. "I heard my name?"

Alvea spins, turning away from him. She is lifting the stew pot from the back of the wood stove, moving toward the table. There is a doily on the table, white and waiting for her. I didn't see her put it there. She sets it down. "I was wondering if you would mind sitting by the fire tonight, since it is more pleasant by it on a night like tonight."

His eyes snap to her. "Is your leg troubling you?" His brows are knit, close together. *Concerned.*

She straightens, and lifts the ladle, serving up a bowl. "It is not. It's never been better." Her lips tighten. She turns toward the stove again, "But it is nice sitting around the fireplace with company."

There are steps, across the room, and the tapping of hound nails against the wood floors. Yore glances up at Goran, and steps forward, next to Alvea. He nudges her with his shoulder, gently. "I'll serve myself. Go take your seat." She pauses, and drops the ladle back in the pot, nodding. *He is letting her not have to take her seat last.* I swallow. *I should have thought of doing that.*

She lifts her bowl, and nods to the one on the table. "You can take that one, Goran. There are spoons there." She points toward the spoons in the jar on the table. He nods. His sleeves are still rolled up, forearms bare. I lift a cup from the shelf, and another, and fumble. One of them slips, colliding with my hip. I grab it, and grimace. *Move slowly.* I lick my lips. *I was not this awkward with guests back home. It's just a woodsman.* I set the cups down, and lift the water bucket, pouring it, slowly into each one.

Yore cradles his bowl in the crook of his arm, against his body, and lifts a cup in each hand, nodding at me. "Thanks, Néka." He turns, and steps across the room. I lift my cup and turn to the table. Goran is stepping around me, lifting a cup, and Marin is following where he goes, her head against his hip, protecting him from nothing.

My fingers grip the ladle, and I dump the strew into the last bowl, and grab a spoon from the jar, shoving it into my bowl, and lift the cup again. Yore is handing the second cup to Alvea. She looks up at him, and takes it, her cheeks paling a little. *She doesn't like being cared for. He knows that.* He turns, stepping over to the chair. He takes the one furthest from the fire.

I step across the room and take the seat closest to me, beside Alvea. Goran is moving to the one across the way, Marin's nails tapping loudly on the floor, blending with the cracking of the fire. *Like a breath of some evening that I don't know.* Yore is already eating, Alvea chewing thoughtfully, the cup held between her knees. Goran sets his cup on the floor, on the side away from the hound and takes a bite of the stew. *I'm staring.* My face warms. I look down, taking a bite. The stew is thick, hot, and tastes of potatoes and venison, and a hint of onion, herbs. Not bad. I swallow. *I could not have made better.*

"Good stew, Oanéka." Yore says. I glance at him, and my face is still warm. I nod and look back down at my stew. A strand of hair falls in my face, curled and long. *And white.* I frown, and my eyes widen. *There is dried bread dough in my hair.* My fingers inch upward, slowly. I glance around the room. They are all looking at their food. *No one is looking.* I grip the strand, and grind my nails into it, run them down it, and there are white flakes, floating over my eyes, into my lap. *Why didn't Alvea tell me that was there?* My heart sinks. I grimace. *It doesn't matter. It's just a little bit. No one will likely have noticed. And it would not matter greatly if they did.* I grab my spoon, take another bite.

Alvea is wiping her mouth carefully on a napkin. *I forgot to get one.* She glances across the room, at our guest and his hound. "Goran." He looks up at her, and she folds her hands neatly around her bowl. "How did you come to be in the settling lands?" Yore's brows tighten, but she isn't looking at him.

Goran shifts in his chair and sets his spoon down. He rolls his shoulders back, lifting his bowl a little higher out of the reach of his hound's nose that is turning toward it, seeking. "I was told there was free land, and not many people."

Her neck straightens, sharply. "You came here alone?"

He nods, and lifts a brow, in that almost arrogant way that he did when we met. "Va. Not everyone has family to follow them around."

Alvea nods her head. "Of course. I only meant that I was surprised anyone would have the courage to come this far above the Wan Core alone. It is..." She bobbles her head, uncertainly, looking down. "Bitterly cold."

He leans back in his chair, further away from the nose of the hound that is over his lap. "But it is also quiet." He glances at Yore. "I take it you all are from within the Wan Core?"

Yore nods. "Va. It was still harvest time when we left. It wasn't even half done."

Goran's brows shift, something flashing through his eyes, and he moves—just slightly—hands shifting. Alvea's eyes flicker to Yore. Her lips tighten, and she moves her gaze back to Goran, moving a little in her chair. "We collected Oanéka's crops, and then came. It was a pleasant journey on the whole." *She is changing the subject again.* "It's strange though, seeing the differences in seasons up here, without the Wan Core to warm it. I always thought it was funny, the stories you hear of what people think of our land until we came. Now I understand a little more. Are you from above it?"

He glances at her, and back toward his food. "Va. I'm from the coastland." he glances at me. "What crops did she raise?"

He changed the subject. My face warms. I lift my chin, pursing my lips. *I don't want the subject to be on me either.* My face warms further. "She is using the word 'crop' loosely," I force a laugh, breathy and too high, "I raised flowers, for their own sake, and little more. Occasionally for dyes, or seed. When we came, we'd collected the ones that I was to sell, and left the rest standing where they were." I look down. *Many of them were still in bloom, or about to come to bloom.* My throat is thick. *There was little point in all that work. No one was likely to tend them, after we'd gone, or even to see them.*

There is a cry, high and mewling from somewhere outside. *Calli. Praise Elnial.* I snap my feet under me, and bolt across the room. My stockings slide on the smoothness of the floor, and I press my hands against the wall beside the window, slowing. The calli are crossing the space in front of the cottage, the large one leading, her head in the air. She calls out again, moving beyond the sight of the window.

I turn back, and Yore is moving, standing. I swallow. *He just got inside.* He lifts a brow at me, a question. I nod toward the window, strands of hair falling into my face. "They are out, moving for the tree line," I say.

Yore nods and he is moving for the door, his hand snatching up his coat. He slides his arm into the first sleeve. "All of them?"

I nod, and glance back out the window. The last two are crossing in front of the house, their tails lifted behind them, feet held high with each step in the snow. "Va. I'll grab my boots." I turn, and snatch my shoes from the floor.

Goran is moving across the room, four easy strides and he is by the coat hooks, lifting his. Marin is by his heels, her eyes sharp, watching. He glances down at her, and lifts his arm, pointing toward the fire, by Alvea's feet. "Go. Stay." The hound drops her head, moving slowly away, and her eyes still watch him as she moves across the floor, head low to the ground.

I shove my feet into my boots and jerk the laces. *I don't need to tie them. We'll just be out for a second.* I twist them together, shove them down into my boots stomping forward.

Yore pulls the door open, cold air flooding into the room, and he steps through, Goran behind him, moving through the open doorway. I jerk my shawl over my arms and bolt out after them. My untied boots slap against my legs, skin stinging through my stockings. I jerk the door shut, and spin. The cold bites at my skin, exposed face burning. *I should have put on a scarf.*

Yore is moving across the ground, his steps crunching loudly in the ice-covered snow, his movements jerky with the force of the ice breaks with each one of them. He pauses by the creek, glancing down, and he slides sideways, foot skidding on something buried beneath the snow. It's treacherous, walking in this half-frozen snow. *At least I am shorter than them. It should be easier for me than them, closer to the ice.*

I step off the porch, after Goran. He is moving through the snow, stretching his legs long. Each of his steps is two of mine. *I can't walk in his tracks.* I swallow, and step, snow crunching, force jolting through me. I grimace, my head pulses. The calli are by the forest, where the creek turns and angles off toward the east, where the sun rises every morning. One of them is up on its hind legs, ripping at a cedar tree. Its movements are slow, bored, the branch jutting awkwardly from its lazy mouth.

I step again, snow crunching, breaths heavier, and brush a strand of hair from my face. Yore is nearly to them, angling to the side, getting around behind the group of them. I swallow. The cold is sharp against my throat. *It stings.*

One of the calli mewls and lifts her head. She is moving off, across the snow, her steps jerky like ours, and the others are not following her like they usually do when one leaves but staring at the one chewing on the cedar tree. I glance at Yore. "I'll get her."

Yore nods. He is behind them now, between them and the stream, herding them back toward the shed, his arms in the air. Goran is across from him, stepping slowly up toward the calli, his movements fluid and cautious. One of them looks up, sharply at him, and mewls, showing its dagger-like teeth. *They don't look white against the snow.* I step again and it step jolts through me, crunching. Goran says something, under his breath, and I can't hear it. I turn, and hop forward, into the footprint he cut in the snow on his way here, and step again, crunching into the unbroken ice. The calli is still ahead, walking straight, her tail stretched out behind her, and her breath is a cloud, brushing back from her nose as she moves.

I hop forward again, and the air cuts my throat, sharp. *I just need to move around in front of her.* I step forward again, and shuffle. Something catches my foot, jerking, and I gasp, pull my leg forward sharply, and the ice crunches; breaking, crashing. I grit my teeth, jerk my skirt from under my boot. I force my jaw, loosen it, step again, gripping my skirts in a fist. The calli stops, and turns her head toward me, the cloud of breath still puffing out from her mouth. I move closer, clutching my skirts in my fist. She blinks at me, her eyes that stale blank of sheep and goats and calli. I swallow, and point, back toward the others. "Come on, back. Come on." I lift my hands, and wave them, gesturing back toward the rest.

She blinks, and mewls, long and loud. My ears ring, and I grimace. I wave again, arms half flailing. "Come on. Come on..." I wave. She turns, walking slowly back toward the others, her tail swishing, steps crunching through the ice coated snow. Why doesn't Yore usually use hand gestures to get them back in? I hop after her, steps jerking. My neck hurts aches with the force of them.

The calli is strutting, her head high, and her steps crashing through the snow. Her eyes flicker back, toward me, and she flicks her tail, and mewls again, low and lazy. Another calli calls back to her, its call echoing in the wood. Snow crashes down from a tree, beside the creek. I shiver, wave my arm. She doesn't move.

Yore's voice is drifting softly over the ground, mixing with the breeze, short, even words to only the calli, and his hands are waving ushering them back toward the shed. I step forward again, and something jerks on my foot. I gasp, flailing, and there is cold, all up my foot. I flail and jerk backward, swaying on one leg, my other foot coated in cold air. *My boot came off. Curses. I should have tied them on.* I stoop and my fingers fumble with it, caught in the ice of the snow. I pull, and sway, balance off, foot shifting in my one good boot. My foot is stiff, wind cutting through the stocking in the air. I shove my foot back into the boot. Ice crunches at the end of my toes, shoving against the end of the boot, and grinds against them. I flinch, falling sideways.

I shove my foot back into the boot and wrap my arms around myself. *It feels colder out here now.*

The calli is standing there, eyes on me, idly chewing something. *Always chewing.* I grit my teeth and stoop, jerking the laces tight. Wind cuts across my back, throwing my shawl sideways. I waver with it; a shiver runs up my spine. My leg is cold, the woolen pants under my skirts not thick enough anymore. I grimace, and run my hands down my shawl, straightening.

The calli flicks her tail, lazy, and her eyes are watching me, her mouth working at whatever is in her mouth. Strange animals. I step forward and wave my arms again. "Go on. Go..." She flicks her tail, and steps forward, her movements slow and lazy, steps sliding on the ice ahead where the snow has been packed low toward the shed. Yore is gone, within the building, Goran by the door, herding in the last of the four they brought over. Mine moves up beside him. He steps back, and she walks in, casual and he steps through the door, after her, pulling it closed behind him.

I cross my arms, and a shiver running over my scalp. *I am not needed here anymore.* I purse my lips and turn back toward the cottage. The shadows are long across the snow, bluish on the white of it. *Dark is coming on.* And my foot is wet in my stocking, squishing. *Horrible.* I step onto the porch, and my toes feel numb and awkward, strange against the leather and half frozen stocking.

I pull the door open, and hobble inside, pulling it shut. Alvea is beside the fire, and the hound is beside her, the large blue head settled in her lap. Her eyes flicker toward me. "Are they back in?" Her hand runs over the hound's head again, sliding down the fur, and Marin's eyes are shut, her tongue lolling out.

I nod, and slip my fingers into my boots, tugging them off. My stocking slaps the floor, wet, and there is a chunk of snow wedged in my toes, clinging to the fabric. I scowl. *I should have tied my boots.*

"Is your stocking wet?" Alvea is looking at me, her hand working over Marin's head.

I tug the stocking off, and pull the door open, tossing the chunk of snow out. "Va. I got ice on it."

Her brows knit together—I pull the door shut. "Were you not wearing your boots? Aren't those your new ones from the spring?"

I nod, and hobble across the room, my single bare foot slapping the wood, strange and awkward. I grip my skirts. "Of course I was. But thick boots aren't much help when the snow comes in the top."

Laughter bubbles in her eyes, and the door is swinging open behind me, the heavy steps of feet. Yore's eyes trail down to my bare foot, sticking out of my skirts, and his brow lifts, but his mouth stays shut, hand pulling the coat from his back. He drops it on the rack.

Goran tugs off his coat, and he is across the room in two steps, taking up his bowl and his chair. *I can go get another sock in a few minutes. He won't be here for much longer.*

Alvea looks up, and her eyes trail the room, watching me. I drop into my seat and lift my bowl from where I left it. I press my skirts around my knees. *My bare toes are numb.* Her eyes flicker over to Yore, and to Goran, her hand still gently stroking Marin's head. I tuck my feet under my skirts. My feet seem awkward, and I can't feel them still.

Alvea's eyes flicker back toward Goran. "Goran, do you care for stories?"

His brow lifts, that skeptical look again. He shifts in his chair—his eyes flicker down to the hound beside Alvea. "If they have a purpose. Va." He lifts his spoon, cautiously. "I don't care much for the Dryland epics or the tales that seem to go on forever with no reason."

She laughs, gentle and breathy. "What I have in mind is neither of those, if you care for it." Her eyes flicker to Yore. "Yore, would you favor us with a tale tonight?"

Yore's face relaxes, his shoulders rolling backward. He nods, and his eyes drift toward the fire, thoughts churning behind them, swirling together. I swallow hard, tuck my hands around my bowl. *I guess we will be here for a while. Curses. I can't get up now. We're all already seated.* I swallow hard and fold my feet tighter against each other. My toes feel strange against the woolen sock of the foot beneath them, and my face is hot. I fix my eyes on the soup bowl. Yore's voice has not begun, firelight flickering across his face.

Chapter XIV

Snowflakes flicker over my nose, drifting from the sky in sheets. Each flake is outlined so sharply against the forest, the dark of the wood. The drifting of the flakes strange, beautiful, churning together, like a dance. My lashes are thick, white catching on them, catching on my nose and drifting over the stream. They swirl together, mixing, each one caught in my sight for only a moment, drifting along in the wind, drifting along in the breeze and I can't track them all, can't follow where they are going, drifting to join the rest on the earth. A smile pulls at my lips.

The creek-bed is slick, my steps sliding, skidding across the surface. A snowflake drifts into my eye, gone in a moment, and it stings. I blink hard, squint. The flakes swirl. The snow is not yet deep enough to help with the slickness of the creek-bed, only dusting the ground, new over the ice. I step up—my ankle twists, knee bending sharply with the weight of the buckets on them. I grimace. *Curse it.* I heave the buckets up, over the lip around the creek, and drag my body upward. The water sloshes, dangerously close to the edge, swishing in the buckets. I purse my lips, the water still sloshing, slowing. I grip the handles and move across the frozen earth. Flakes cut across my vision. My arms are white, snow piling atop of them, piling up and sliding off with each movement in clumps all pressed together.

Something calls from the barn, that high, strange sound of a calli. I shake my head, and step again, my foot skids on the porch step. *Slick. Everything is slick with this ice.* I plant my foot. The next porch step is cleaner, harder, barely any ice upon it, only the brown of the wood. I move across the porch, set the buckets down, and pull the door open. I grab them, and step through.

Alvea is kneeling on the floor, a vat before her, steam curling up from it. *The dyeing vat.* "Vea." I shove the door shut with my boot. A breath puffs out of my lungs, the water buckets nearly sloshing. "What are you doing with that?" I move toward the counter.

She looks up at me. Her face is calm, hands shoving the sleeves of her dress back up. "I'm going to dye some thread. We can function out here, and live well, even if there are no people here. And I am not going to do it without good thread." A smile twitches at my lips, and I turn away. *She's trying something again. And not just because she is angry.* My heart is lighter. She lifts a chunk of thick wool, dropping it into the vat. It slaps the surface, sinking. "I'm not going to sit on my hands anymore. We have this place, and I am going to make the most of it. We don't need other folk around in order to do well out here." Her eyes flicker to me. "And you don't have to grin." She shoves her hands into the water, chasing the wool.

I shake my head, tuck the smile back on my face, and stoop, setting the buckets down in their places. I straighten, and press my fingers into my skirts, drying the water off of them. "What color will you dye them?"

Her head bobbles uncertainly, and she drops another puff of wool into the vat. “A blend of red.” Her eyes flicker up, to mine. “Perhaps one to rival that puff of hair of yours.” She grins.

I laugh, and pull my hair cord from my pocket, tying the puff back into place. *She took up a task, for real.* My throat is tight, smile across my lips. *Praise be to Elnial. She’s trying for real. She’s doing it.*

I drag my hands from my skirts and move toward the kitchen. “Are you planning a piece, or just dyeing to have on hand?”

She pauses, her hands on the rim of the vat. “I don’t have one project yet, but I need red to finish the cross stitch. You do as well, I think, from looking at yours. Why did you come in so late from getting water?”

I glance at her, shove my sleeves up on my arms. “I went for a walk before I brought it in.” I glance back at the bucket on the counter. The dish water is murky, dark. *I do not want to wash my hands in that.* I shake my head and grab that bucket. “It started snowing out there again,” I say.

She shoves her sleeves back further, twisting them tightly into place. “It has?” I nod, and grip the door, pulling it open. Wind brushes in, cold, throwing my skirts back. I shiver, and shuffle out, jerking the door shut behind me. My steps thud on the porch, hollow, empty, and the ice crunches near the edge. I lift the bucket, dump it off the side. The wind whips, throwing my skirts sideways, flakes pelting my face. I grimace, duck my head against my shoulder. *It’s getting a little sharper.* I turn, jerking the door open. The wind pushes me through, hair whipping around my shoulders. I press the door shut.

Alvea glances up, a brow raised. “Is there much wind?”

I nod, set the bucket on the counter. "Va. I think it may be getting colder already." I rub my hands up my arms, and down again. "Though it's hard to tell, once it gets this cold. You would think the evergreens might lose their needles from it."

She grins, laughing breathy and short. "It does seem like this place might kill them too, but I'm glad it hasn't." She half smiles. "And that it hasn't defeated us."

I smile. "Nie. It hasn't." She shoves her arms into the vat. A grin tugs at my face, pulling at the edges of my mouth. "You are going to turn your arms red, like my hair that way."

She laughs, her arms deeper in the vat now. She flicks her head, throwing a strand of hair back from her face. "I know. But I never have liked doing it with a stick, and this way is more fun anyway." She grins, twisting her hands in the steaming vat, "Besides, there is no one to impress out here, and this will be gone long before spring ever sets in."

I laugh, shake my head. "When the only other person who lives here comes over the next time and gives your hands a strange look and never asks why, then you may rethink that. I would think it would be awkward. He doesn't seem like he would ever actually ask the question, just give them a weird look, and then you couldn't explain them. They would just be there. Off red like a bad burn."

She laughs, throwing her head back. "He won't be staring at my hands. I would be more concerned about the confusion of his hounds." I shake my head, pouring water back into the wash bucket. Alvea hums, a single low note, her arms deeper in the dark liquid of the vat, steam curling up through her hair. I shake my head and breathe out a laugh. *She is trying something, finally. After all these months. No more of that constant wheel and loom.*

* * * * * * *

I drop the spoon and steam is curling upward, pleasant and thin over the pot. My lips twist, a smile tugging at them, a song humming on the edges of my mind. I press my hands against my apron, glancing toward the one window. The light is bright, snow light reflected back on the window with afternoon. I turn toward the counter. *The stew will need time to thicken.* It's watery now. My eyes flicker toward it. *It should be good when it is time.* I hum again, and it sounds funny, off key. I grimace and roll my shoulders. *Maybe not that song.*

Something thuds across the room, slapping against the floor and Alvea drops into her chair sharply. Her boots are beside her, one of them sideways. She grabs one and slips her foot into it. I frown, and she grabs the other, slipping her foot into it. She grips the laces, jerking them upward. "Well." Her voice is solid, like she has decided something; like she knows something.

I frown. "Well, what?"

She looks up at me. "We should go for a walk." She ties off the laces of the one a bow neat and simple and grabs the others.

My heart plummets. "No, we aren't! There is a whole blanket of new snow." *She can't go out there. She can't. It will be too thick for her to walk in well, with the ice underneath.*

She looks up at me. "'She who does not get out can do nothing.' And I want to see the snow in the forest. I've not gone out when it's fresh and bright since we got here." She twists the laces. "We can go out for a minute, and your stew will be fine until we get back."

I blink. *Stew? What about her leg? What about her? What happens if she stumbles out there? There is no doctor to help with pain out here. Only the last of the salves.* I curl my hands into my skirts, and they twitch. *She'll go alone if I don't go with her.* I swallow, and my throat is tight. *She'll be perfectly fine. The snow is thick and new, so it will be softer. Perhaps it won't even break underneath. It could be good to go out there.* I nod, and step across the room, gripping my cloak. She is standing, moving over toward me, the sound of her boots strange on the floor. When was the last time she went out? Her eyes are bright, alert. *I didn't think she would want to go outside this late in the year, with the snow being hard. Not for a walk. It's hard for me to walk in the woods now.*

I shove my foot into my boot and twist the laces. She is pulling on her cloak, her back straight and her head high, eager. *Curse it. We can't be out there long. It's cold, and she can't slip. We won't be out there long. We have to get back for the stew anyway, to keep it from burning. She knows that. She'll know that. And she knows how to watch her own leg. She'll be fine. There isn't anything to worry about.*

She glances at me, and her eyes narrow. "Come along, and stop thinking like that. We will be just fine, and it's good to go out for a walk." She folds her shawl over her shoulders and tucks it into her skirt waist. I twist the laces into a knot and stand, gripping the doorknob. *This is fine. It'll be good for her.* My eyes flicker back to her, and my heart twists. *She's fine. The snow is not that hard today. She knows how to watch her step. She's been doing it nearly all her life, all of mine.*

She steps outside, pulling the door shut behind us. Her face is pale and flushed at once, and her eyes are bright, excited like they were all day yesterday with the dyed wool, with the newness. I grimace and wrap my shawl tighter, tuck it into my waist. She pulls her gloves over her fingers, glancing up at me. "Which way is your favorite walk?"

I blink. *My favorite walk?* I blink again and flick my gaze out. The wind brushes gently, cold and sharp, and the trees are coated with snow. Some of it flutters to the ground, a white cloud among the trees, drifting downward. I tighten my arms. "I love the one across the stream, but the ice is hard for me to get over now." I glance backward. "The one around back, the way we came from when we came out here is beautiful too, though I've been that way less." I nod toward the back of the cottage, and she nods at me. She grips her skirts in her gloved hands, stepping off the porch easily and cleanly. I shove my fingers into my skirts and scowl, stepping after her. *I forgot my gloves again. I always forget them. Curses.*

She is stepping through the snow, her steps awkward and bright at once, and I grimace, stepping past her. *I can break a path in front of her, if I am ahead.* "I'll lead." I say. She nods, and her eyes are bright, excited. She glances at me, but doesn't say anything, breaths a puff of air before her. The snow is thick, soft, and it doesn't stick to my skirts today, powdery and dry. The wind brushes again, and tosses it up, a small dusting in the air, swirling, strange and beautiful. A smile twists at my lips.

The trees rise, short and tall and green and brown, made alike beneath a blanket of white, and Alvea's breaths are even and easy behind me. I move around the first tree, feet breaking a path in the powdered ice and snow. Alvea's steps are even behind me. She glances up at me, and smiles, and her dark hair is caught beneath the hood of her shawl, dark against the pattern. Her eyes are wide, brighter than they have been since we came, flickering through the trees. "Is it like this every time?"

I nod. "It gets better. Come on. Further in the forest it's more beautiful, with all the trees, and the quiet and the breeze." She looks at me and doesn't say anything. Her face is flushed, and pale at once, her eyes drinking in everything, searching. *She should have come out here before now. A lot more before now. Why didn't she ever try to?*

I move forward, snow packing and shifting under my feet. Her breaths still sound as even as mine do, with the pushing through the snow. I glance back. Her eyes are still skyward, flickering through the branches. She grins. "No wonder you spent so much time out here the first few snows." A smile pulls against my lips, and I laugh, and shake my head. I turn back, lift my skirts a little higher and step into a hole made by a large rock in the snow. *I didn't realize back then how beautiful it was. Maybe she appreciates it more than I do.*

The trees are thicker out here, further in the forest and they are coated in white, flakes blowing off with each breath of wind. Tiny dustings swirl through the shadows of the trees, like fog that settles and blows in a way that the lake mists never did. My throat tightens. *The lake mist. We won't see that again, not for years.*

But that's alright for today. I don't want to think about it. I shake my head, toss my braid over my shoulder. Alvea's face is lit, her eyes bold and glinting, like they used to do when she would talk at home, when Elima would come, and sit with her. *Elima. What became of her, after she stopped coming around? After she taught Alvea how to weave, how to spin, after mamé left and never came back?*

Alvea steps up beside me, eyes on the branches overhead, flickering toward the sky. "Let's go a little further." She breathes. *I hadn't realized I'd stopped.* I nod, step forward again, and the snow shifts and crunches loud in the quiet of the forest. Alvea is right behind me, her steps shuffling in the path of my steps.

There is a hill ahead, one we traveled around in coming out to this place with a wagon and a driver who left so quickly. Alvea has a smile stretched across her face, her eyes bright and they are on the trees now, on the snow and the prints impressed in them. Her cheeks are red with the cold. *Mine will be too.* I press my fingers against them and flinch, jerking my hands back. *My fingers are cold. Frightfully cold.* Alvea's are within her gloves. *I should have brought mine.*

She half gestures, and points ahead. "Let's sit on that rock over there for a minute. It looks a good place to watch the snow fall, from the trees." She grins at me. "I never thought I'd want to sit and watch the snow fall with you." She laughs, and steps around me, moving for a boulder that the snow has blown clean from. I laugh, and step after her, moving up beside her.

There is a curse, somewhere off in the forest, a voice I don't know. I freeze, hand on the rock. Alvea's glove brushes my arm. My eyes flicker to hers. She stares at me, eyes wide. "It might have been Yore." She breathes. *It didn't sound like Yore.* I swallow and lick my lips. They are dry, cracked a little. Alvea's hand grips my arm, tightens, and she breathes out, hard. My eyes flicker back to her. *It could have been Goran.*

She is staring, out through the trees, and her gloved hand tightens on my arm again, eyes widening. My gaze flickers out, through the trees. There is a figure. Leading a mule, toward us. A man. He is dressed in furs, his steps long and even. He lifts his eyes, and a bright smile flashes across his face, white against his midnight skin, and his eyes light with it, bright and bold. "Goodeven." He waves an arm, and the mule stops, jerking the rope sharply backward. The man grimaces, his arm pulling tight with the rope. His eyes are still on us, bright and surprised. I swallow, and Alvea's hand is too tight on my arm, grip tightening further. My arm is numb beneath it. *I cannot tell his height beneath the trees, cannot see much of his face beneath his scarf, beyond his eyes and his smile, whiter than the snow, and carefree.*

Alvea stands, pulling me up with her, her feet planting into the packed snow. "Goodeven." Her voice is soft, but her head is high, her posture sharp, like a challenge. "Are you lost?" I look up at her, and back to the man. *Lost? He doesn't look lost.*

His face flushes a little, barely visible across his skin. He is only a few paces in front of us now, and his coat is thickly fur lined, as if for long travel. "Is it that obvious?" He shifts his hands on the mule's lead, and glances at us again. "Va. I am quite lost. I cannot find the trail that I usually have taken getting up here, so, when I saw you, I thought I might ask for directions, if you have any to offer?" He smiles again, almost sheepishly.

"What trail are you trying to find?" Alvea says, stepping forward. "My sister may be able to help you." *What?!* My eyes snap to her, and my heart drops into my stomach. I nudge her leg with mine. Her eyes are fixed on the man, ignoring me, calm and put together. *She doesn't flinch, doesn't look at me.* I swallow hard.

He glances at me, and back to her. His hand stretches back, stroking the nose of the mule behind him, running his hand down it. The mule nudges his fingers, nipping at the skin. He winces. "Do you know the northward trail?"

I shake my head. "Nie." My heart sinks. "I haven't even heard of it. Are you sure this is the area you mean to be in?"

He grunts, and shakes his head, glancing back at us. "It may not be called that. It may have another name. I have only been out here once, and I confess that I paid little attention to the road names. As if it would help. They are not labelled and there is usually no one out here that I know of." He glances out toward the trees, shifting on his feet. "I was not expecting the snow to have come so early."

My sister lifts her head, searching for his eyes. "It's been here for weeks."

He laughs, breathy and loud at once, and shakes his head. "That's a fact? Odds what. I really didn't think it would be so cold so early. They warned me, but I did not believe it." He shakes his head again, eyes down.

Alvea laughs, and steps forward. "Well then, you must not have spent much time out here." She nods and drops her hands from my arm. "Come back to our cottage. We can offer you hot tea and a moment to orient yourself while you figure out your path, and we can ask our brother about the road you spoke of, to see if he knows more than we do of it." I rub my arm. It is numb, from her grip, sore.

His eyes brighten, and he checks himself, sharply, his eyes guarded again. "Are you certain? I do not want to be an imposition to you all, and it is getting late."

She nods, folding her hands neatly in front of her. "I am certain. If you do not mind our pace, then you are welcome. I am not fast at walking, but we may still be able to offer you aid back home, if you are willing to bear with us."

He nods, inclining his head toward her, and smiles again, and it is strange to see a man smiling, after weeks of only Goran and Yore, who rarely smile. "I would not begrudge someone their walking pace and will not complain against any hand that leads me out of these woods. Thank you. You are both kind."

My sister smiles, a brief, soft thing, and turns away, back onto the trail I broke for her. The man is following, his steps even and slow. I turn, walking beside my sister, and the snow is soft and crunchy beneath my feet, loud, where theirs are not. I grimace, and look down. My face is warm and cold. *We didn't ask the stranger in the woods his name. Again. Curse it. We don't know anything about him and Alvea has asked him back to our cottage, without even knowing why he is here, what he is doing wandering the woods, what he is trying to get back to other than a trail.*

The mule's steps are loud behind me, but the man's are quiet on the broken trail. Alvea's hands neatly clutch her skirts, her neck straight, her posture sharp, and she is leading around the trees, over the snow-coated earth, her steps only barely kept even, her head proudly high. Snow brushes across the ground, swirling through the trees. It stings at my skin, cutting at it in the wind. I shiver, shove my hands under my arms. *I still can't feel my fingers.* They are numb against the fabric, like carrot sticks on the ends of my hands.

Alvea steps out of the last of the forest, and into the open space behind the cottage. Smoke is curling up from the chimney into the sky, and there is a calli out in the paddock, nosing the snow around. Alvea is moving around the hut. She steps up, onto the porch and stops, stomping her boots out against the wood. I step up, and glance back at the man. His eyes are watchful, calm and waiting. I swallow and rub my hands against my ribs. My fingers are lumpy, awkward. "You can tie your mule to the porch." I wince. *My voice sounds forced.*

He nods, and his hands are already tying the lead to the pole, easy and quick, though his fingers fumble. *How can someone be graceful and fumbling at the same time?* He steps back, and whistles shortly, a tune and it sounds off key and on at once. *It's clean and bright, and I don't know the tune it carries.*

Alvea's hand grips the doorknob, pulling it open and she steps through, leaving the door open. I step in after her, the man behind me, slowly, watching, and he presses the door shut. I step over to the rack, and slip my cloak off, slinging it over the peg. I stoop, jerking my boot laces free. I nudge the shoes from my feet, and look up, rub my hands together. The man has not moved, he is holding his hat, turning it in his hands, his scarves still around his head and face. I frown. *How do we invite him in, welcome him as much as we can?* Alvea is sitting on her chair, slipping off her boots. *She hasn't noticed that he is still standing there.*

I swallow and tuck my hands under my arms again. He is wearing huge, chunky boots. They are coated with snow, caked to the fur and fabric. I nod toward them. "You are welcome to take your boots off and sit." I gesture to a chair. My hands are red, awkward and stiff. I grimace and tuck them under my arm again.

He glances at me, and laughs, his hand reaching to pull the scarf from his head. "I am not sure I can get them back on if I do. They are monstrous."

Alvea's gaze flicks to me, eyes unsure. *What do we do with a guest who can't take off their snow boots?* I swallow again, and turn, snatching a towel from the counter. The stew catches my eye. It is steaming, bubbling over the stove, nearly too thick. *I need to mind that after this.* I move toward a chair, towel in my hand. "You can set your feet on this. Come sit down."

He glances at me, and then Alvea. "Are you certain?" The scarf is off his face now, and his hair has sprung up, short, dark cords sticking out in every direction in a style that I don't know. He is young, not much older than Alvea or I, and his smile is easier now, big and bold against his dark skin. His eyes crinkle at the edges as he smiles, manner easy by habit, but he seems uncertain.

I nod and spread the towel by the foot of a chair near the fire, a little away from Alvea. Her boots are off, beside her chair now, hands folded. She moves to stand. I step forward and grip her boots. "I'll get them." She glances at me, and her eyes sharpen. Her face is a little flushed. I turn toward the door. "I'm going that way anyway."

I move toward the door, and offer my hand to the man, nod toward the scarf and hat in his hands. He offers the scarf to me, moving toward the chair, and half nods toward me, thanks. I throw the scarf over the peg, setting the boots beside mine on the floor beneath it. The man's steps are muffled, crunching with ice and packed snow beneath his boots. He turns, and drops into the chair, setting his feet cautiously upon the towel I laid down. He looks up. "Thank you both. It was getting a little long out there, hunting up the trail." I swallow, and turn toward the kitchen, fingers wet from the boots. I step over and slip my fingers into the wash bucket, and glance over my shoulder, at the man sitting by the fireplace.

He is shifting in his chair, hands awkward, legs easy, and his smile gentle. "I'm sorry. My name is Pevi Likloré-Morfonnen. I forgot to introduce myself outside. Thank you both for taking me into your home for a moment. I have never been turned around before. Or at least, that turned around. Not out here."

Alvea looks over at him. I pull my hands from the bucket, dry them against my skirts and grip the spoon, stirring the stew. Alvea nods her head respectfully at the man, Pevi. "I am Alvea Orien. And you are welcome. Do you live in these forests? I was not aware that there were others, more than the man we met."

He lifts a brow. "There is another?" His eyes are curious. The steam cuts at my hand. I hiss and jerk it back. *I should have moved it sooner.* I set the spoon on the lip of the pot and tuck my hand into my skirts. He shifts, moving his feet on the towel and looks up at Alvea again. "I was not aware there were others at all. And I do live within the forest, though, I confess... I haven't spent much time out here looking around. I mostly just stayed with my cottage, tending crops and the like. I have not been here much longer than the summer."

Alvea nods her head, shifting her skirts over her knees. "We haven't been here long, but Goran lives nearby. He is the other man. How..." her voice pauses. "How did you come to be out here? You do not seem like the sort to be out here, in this place."

His eyes flicker toward her, and he nods, eyes glancing at the fire. He runs a hand down his head, his gaze staying fixed on the flames for a moment longer, and he looks up. "I am not the kind to live out here. It's never been my way to hide away, in the sort of fashion that goes with this place. But, necessity compelled me, along with an offer from my uncle. I had little other choice, so I've taken up this place for a time."

and I lift the spoon again, and stick it into the pot, stirring. I swallow, glance at him. "Is it far back to your hut?"

He glances up at me, and pink flashes across his cheeks, barely visible, but it is there. "I am not certain. In truth, I have no idea where we are right now." He straightens in his chair. "But I do not think that it could be more than a couple hours' walk, so it should be achievable by nightfall."

My heart drops. Alvea's eyes flicker toward the one unshuttered window, and her eyes soften. "There are not a couple hours left before sunset." His gaze darts to the window, and he curses, nothing like the colorful words that Yore picked up from the docks. A laugh bubbles in my throat. I choke it back and press a hand against my throat. He jumps up, and is moving toward the door, steps fast. *He is going to set out, in the cold, the ice and into the darkness, without knowing his way. Goran said men have died for less.*

My heart sinks. I jump forward. "Wait!" He glances back at me. I shake my head and grab my shawl from its hook. "Let me speak with Yore. There has to be something better to be done then just sending you out into the woods this close to dark. Let me talk to my brother. Wait here." I wrap my shawl around my shoulders.

He shakes his head, grabbing the doorknob. "You are not sending me out. I appreciate your kindness, but I cannot impose upon you all, and as you said, it is late. Dark is coming on."

Alvea steps forward. *I never saw her stand.* "So, you would rather die than impose?"

His gaze flicks to her. She meets his gaze, head lifted, eyes steady and gentle. His lips purse, and he looks down. I take a breath. *He cannot go out there.* He looks up, and nods, slowly, a thousand thoughts playing across his face. "I would appreciate your help, though I do not understand what you will do by asking your brother. Does he know the trails anymore than you?"

I nod, and shove my feet into my boots. I slip past him, grip the doorknob, flicking my eyes to meet his. "He often has ideas. He will think of something. He always does, and we will not send you out to die in the snow." I glance at Alvea. "Please don't let the stew burn. It's thick." She is nodding. I pull the door open and step out. Snow swirls, caught in the wind, and it presses against the door. I jerk the door closed. The boards of the porch creak beneath my feet, ice crunching where it didn't seem to be earlier. I pause. *I just left my sister with a stranger I barely know. I don't even know where he came from, or what reason caused him to come beyond necessity.*

I glance back, toward the door. *I won't be long. And she would not appreciate me coming back now.* I step down, and the snow creaks beneath my untied boots. I move forward, and the path crunches, sunlight glinting faintly over the trees. *There is nowhere near enough time for him to find a lost trail and still make it home... what was he doing out? How did he lose his trail?*

I push the door of the shed open, and there is a calli, standing there. She looks up at me, her strange eyes lazy, and calls, that loud, grating noise. I grimace, and step backward. Yore isn't in the shed. *There is nothing in here but the mound of hay and the calli.* I frown. Steps crunch, somewhere behind me, loud against the snow. I jerk the door shut and turn.

Yore is hopping across the creek from rock to rock, movements easy and slow. His bow is slung across one shoulder, an axe on the other, and his feet are careful on the ice. He hops to the bank, and moves toward me, toward the shed. "Yore," I say. He glances at me and steps past, pulling the door of the shed open. He is gone inside. I step through after him. The calli is still standing there, chewing cud now, and staring, blankly. I swallow again, flick my eyes to Yore. He isn't looking at me, putting the bow down from his shoulder, isn't listening. I twist my hands. "Yore, there is a man in the cottage."

His head whips up and his eyes snap to mine, his hand stopped halfway with the bow. "What?"

I nod, back toward the door, and shove my hands under my arms. *They are cold.* "Alvea and I went for a walk and met him in the woods." I swallow. "He was lost, and Alvea invited him back to the cottage, so I came to get you."

Yore straightens, and his hand is still on the bow. "He is still there?" I nod. "And you left him with Alvea, alone?"

I swallow, and nod. "I came to talk to you. He was going to leave, and he said that he doesn't know where he is going, only that he—" Yore bolts past me, and he is walking across the yard, the axe still over his shoulder, steps furiously fast. I jerk the door of the shed shut, and bolt after him. My feet slide on the ice, throwing me sideways. I spin my arms out, flailing, and slow, planting my feet. Yore is already across the porch, moving for the door. I dart after him. He jerks the door open, freezing in the doorframe, axe in his hands, body lit by the light of the room. "Who are you?"

The man is across by the fire, standing next to the chair he was in earlier. *I can't see Alvea with Yore's body blocking the doorway, blocking almost all of the room.* The man's eyes are wide, cautious in his face. He straightens, stepping forward, and bows, a half bow, in the way of a wealthy man. "Goodeven." He straightens, folding his hands in a gesture that I don't know, precisely, carefully, like it matters in all that is right now. "I am Pevi Likloré-Morfonnen. I am sorry to have intruded into your home, but I got lost in the forest and your sisters offered assistance. We will leave at a word from you." He is watching Yore, his eyes steady, never wavering, wide and white in the shadows of his face.

I step into the room and jerk the door shut, bumping Yore's shoulder with it. I wince. He doesn't shift, doesn't even flinch, eyes studying the man across the room. I shove my hands under my arms. Alvea is by the stove, her eyes only on Yore, wide, watching, her body perfectly still.

My brother inclines his head, and steps forward again, lowering the axe until its handle is on the floor, quiet, simple. "I am Yorevali Orien. If my sisters offered you hospitality, then the offer stands. And you are welcome." Pevi's face relaxes, just a little and his arms droop. Yore nods toward the window, shifting the axe. "How did you come to be lost? Could you not use the mountain as a guide?"

Pevi shakes his head, stepping back to the chair. He sets his great, furry boots upon the towel again. A kindness, but he isn't sitting. He shakes his head again. "I came from a different direction than I have in the past, not from my old village, and it has been months since I was last here. I confess, that I did not get a good mind for my surroundings, and

I have never been here in the winter months. I got turned around completely. The world looks nothing like it did last time I was here, and I should have paid more attention to the landmarks along the road."

Alvea is watching at him. Her lips tighten. "Did you not say you live here?"

He nods, glancing at Yore, and back toward Alvea again. "I do. But I do not want to waste your time or mine with a long story if we have no time for it, and it is fairly long. The short of it is that I did not summer here, and that I had not been here for long enough before that to get my surroundings set in my mind. I have not the ability or gift of navigating as well as I think I do."

Yore folds his arms, and gestures with one hand towards the chair. "We have enough time for a tale. There will be no finding a road tonight. It is too late. Even if you knew the markings, there would not be much of a chance of finding it this late."

Pevi straightens sharply, inclining his head. "I appreciate your hospitality, but I do not wish to overstay myself. We have never met. I cannot impose. I will find my trail again tonight."

Yore shakes his head, turning toward the door. "This is winter in the wild, Pevi Liklore. I will not send a man out to die, lost in the cold. We have space enough here to see to your life and your mule's. If you leave here tonight, it will not be to make it back to your cottage. There is cloud cover, which would make it treacherous for a man who knew his way well." Yore grips the doorknob. "Let us hear your story after we tend to your animal. The air is getting colder with the sun dropping."

Pevi nods, moving past me. His steps are muffled on the floor under his great furred boots. He grabs his coat, and nods to me, stepping out into the air with Yore. Their voices are a faint murmur, and then gone.

I swallow and turn. *Yore was still carrying the axe.* Alvea's eyes are on the window, the spoon still in her hand, frozen above the pot. I swallow again, and pull my boots off my feet, their laces slapping my skin, cold and frozen where I didn't tie them, and my fingers fumble. I step across the room, over to Alvea, and grip the spoon. "I'll finish this."

She nods, and steps away. "Why was Yore carrying his axe with him?" She looks back at me. "That is not the right way to greet a lost man in your home, even in a place as wild and empty as this."

I shake my head. "He had just come from the forest when I caught him. At least he didn't bring the bow."

Her eyes fly to mine. "He had the bow too?" A smile breaks across her face. She laughs. "We thought we were so civilized." Another laugh breaks from her lips, ringing across the room. A smile breaks across my face, and she is leaning against the wall, breaths heavy. "Yore brought an axe to greet a guest in our house." I laugh, and she grins at me, a tear rolling down her cheek, smile stretched across her face. She wipes at the tear, and laughs, her head shaking. "He used to go around with the cregf's son, in his group of boys. And now he carries an axe to greet lost men in his home. We have only been here a little more than two moons." She does not move from the wall, her back still against it, eyes gazing across the room, at her loom, vacant, and there is a smile across her face.

Chapter XV

The door thuds open. I turn my head, the stack of bowls in my hands thumping against each other, against my chest. Pevi is stooping through the doorway, Yore right behind him, taller, his form like a shadow. *But he is smiling.* They both are, smiles easy on their faces. Pevi steps to the side and stoops, shoving his fingers into the mess of cords over his boots. I set the bowls on the table and turn back, lift the stew pot and set it on the doily waiting for it.

Yore is bending down, pulling his boots from his feet. He straightens, hanging his coat over the peg on the wall. His eyes meet mine, and he nods, golden eyes matching mine, but his glint in the light glowing from the lamp beside me. "It smells good, Néka." His voice is easy, and he steps back, moving toward his room.

I swallow, and glance at Alvea. She is standing, setting her handwork aside. Her face is calm, gentle, and her back is straight, posture sharp again. She moves past me and dips her hands into the water basin. She pauses, her hands cupped in the water, staring at it for just a moment, and nods, as if to herself. She pulls her hands from the bucket and turns toward the utensil jar, lifting it. She sets it down on the table, beside the stack of bowls. Her eyes flicker across the room, toward the man still kneeling on the floor, untying his great furry boots, caked with snow. *He meant what he said about getting them off. He has been working at them for several minutes now, and only one of them is off.*

Alvea glances at me, and her eyes scan mine, as if uncertain. I shrug, and lift the ladle, dropping it into the stew, and it rests on top of it, strange and awkward. *The stew is thick. Thicker than I thought.* I swallow, and grimace. *Hopefully not too thick. It shouldn't be too thick. I shouldn't have dropped so much flour and tallow in it.*

There is a step behind me, and Yore is in the room once more, moving toward the table. His sleeves are rolled up, and his gloves gone from his hands. *They look damp.* He nods to me, glancing across the room. Pevi straightens, his boots set aside, his hand drawing his coat off his arms. He sets it over a hook, and turns, stepping across the room evenly. He pauses, a few feet away. Yore glances at him. I grab a bowl from the table, and dump food into it. The stew glops into the bottom of the bowl, and slowly spreads, evening like stew is supposed to. I bite back a grimace. *It might be too thick.* I drop a spoon in it, and reach out, handing it toward Yore. Pevi is by the wash basin, drying his hands off.

I pour another bowl, and offer it toward him. He takes it, nodding at me. "Thank you..." His eyes meet mine. He laughs, short and easy. "I am afraid I do not know your name."

My face warms. I laugh, and it hurts my chest. *I didn't introduce myself.* I grab another bowl, and quickly dump stew into it. "Oanéka. Oanéka Orien."

He nods. "Thank you, Oanéka. It smells good."

I dump more of the stew into a bowl, and nod to him. I swallow, turning to hand it to Alvea. "It may be a little thick," I say.

She shakes her head, pressing the bowl back toward me, and dropping a spoon into it. "You take this one. Go sit. I'll serve myself." She lifts the last bowl from the counter, dumps the thick stew into it, the glop almost bobbing at the bottom of the bowl, steam curling off it. I wince. *It is too thick. How much thicker will it be, if any of it chills?*

I turn, and step across the room, toward the chairs by the fire. Pevi is sitting with his back to the front door, and Yore is in the seat closest to me, between me and Pevi. I step past him, over to the far side of the room to the chair beside a shuttered window. Alvea's steps trail behind me, and she turns, dropping into her chair. Yore is picking up his spoon. He takes a bite, and jerks back, coughing, choking, the spoon clutched in his fist and he pounds at his chest, coughing harder, a tear streaking down his cheek into his beard. My eyes widen. He jumps up grabbing a cup, dunking it into the water bucket, the wrong water bucket, his body half stooped over. *The dish water.*

I jump out of my chair. "Not that one!" He pauses, cup only barely above the water, another tear streaking down his cheek, his throat still choking and he turns, dunking his cup into the other bucket. He lifts it to his mouth, drinking hard, fast, eyes still watering down his face. He pulls the cup back, dropping against the counter, his breaths hard and too fast. I swallow. *I have never made a stew that poorly before. My stew almost killed him.* Yore looks up, and his eyes meet mine, red rimmed. There is another tear on his cheek. "Onion." He breathes, straightening from the counter. His voice is raspy, hoarse.

My head lightens. *Onion? Did I not cut it small enough, was it too big? It had been cooked in there for hours. It should never had been that strong or big enough to do that. I charred it first, in the pan.*

Yore shakes his head. "It was just a chunk on the first bite. The stew tastes good, Oanéka."

I narrow my eyes. *Does it? He just choked on it.* I step forward and move toward the shelf with the last loaf of bread on it. "This may help." I snatch the loaf from the shelf. I turn, ripping off a chunk, and hand it to Yore.

He nods, and half smiles, the tears gone into his beard, his eyes still slightly red, face amused. "Thanks." His voice is hoarse, not clean, smooth, and even like it always is. "It was the top of the onion, I think." *Top of the onion. How did that get in there? I put it to the side when I sliced it.*

I turn, and rip a chunk of bread off, handing it to Alvea beside me. "I only used one onion," I turn toward Pevi, "so hopefully my stew won't kill anyone else." I offer a chunk to him. He glances at me, his mouth full of stew, and nods, his eyes bright, like a thanks that his mouth filled with stew can't express. *It hasn't killed him.* I half smile and turn. The last bit of bread is in my hand. I lift my bowl from my chair, and drop down, holding it to my chest.

Yore glances across the room at Pevi, the bowl of stew held loosely in his hands. "So, you said you came from a village, near the edge of Lakna?" Pevi nods. Yore lifts an eyebrow, half curious, and raises a bite of stew to his mouth. "Which edge?"

Pevi swallows his bite, as Yore takes one, and sets his bowl against his lap. "The southern edge, beside Hore and Glorman," Pevi says.

Yore shifts his hand. "How did you end up here? That is a fair bit of traveling. I did not think the middle cregfs had much interest in the Settling Lands. Not yet."

Pevi shakes his head, tapping his spoon against his bowl. "Lorneth is always eager to gain more of anything, in my experience. I think it is his way of covering up the fact that none of his wives have had any children to be the heir to his throne. He was very willing to send me up here, when someone suggested it. More than willing."

Yore shifts, leaning back, and his eyes are sharp now. "I thought his third wife had remedied that. Did she not have a child a few years back?"

Pevi shakes his head. "Nie. She lost the child and has not carried any since. So Lorneth has taken to other means. I don't think he'll marry again, now." He takes a bite, and Yore's eyes are still on him, heavy, as if trying to make him out, to figure him out.

Yore shifts his hands. "And why were you sent? Or did you come of your own decision?"

Pevi looks up, his throat bobbing. He nods, and sets his spoon down, his eyes flickering around the room. "My pakem, as I told you in the shed," he nods to my brother, and glances at Alvea and me, "was a law man. A lawyer. He was never well liked in our village, though he was a kind man, but since he was Lorneth's brother, everyone always assumed that he used that power for his own gain. I do not know whether that was true or not. I spent more time with my amani—my pakem's mamé—and my sister, before she married. My pakem was always off doing something, off seeing to the many things, or helping with disputes, so I do not know much of his character or his own work, only the little that I saw of him at home or about town."

He shifts his legs, settling, and his face darkens. "He died, from sickness. He was not in Lorneth's graces when he passed, and some of the men he had made enemies of took the chance to shame his name. Our name. My Amani was safe, as the mamé of Lorneth, but I was not in anyone's graces after that, especially since I had begun training in his trade in the south, before he became sick. I came back from training, and found my village to have changed, and they were not friendly toward me. I fooled myself and stayed a year, only to see it grow worse." He lifts his eyes, glancing at Alvea. "When my uncle offered to fund a new trade for me if I would stake out this territory for two years, I agreed, readily. There is no other path, now, and I did not have the means of making one on my own after that wasted year spent there in my pakem's shadow, learning his trade, one that I can never take up there. So, I am staking it out here."

Alvea leans forward, her eyes sharp, watchful. "As your cregf's nephew, are you not next in his line for the throne? Why would they cast you out?"

Pevi half smiles, shaking his head. "Lorneth has five brothers. My pakem was the youngest of them. He has nephews and nieces to spare, if none of his wives ever bear him any children. He is not lacking in heirs, even if they are not his own. As of now, the throne is set now to pass to my cousin, Lakni. She is the eldest and has already proven her ambition to be greater than my other cousins. She has cavene blood in her. And, she was plainly named ambitiously for that end, to take his place."

Yore is nodding "You are welcome here, Pevi the lawyer's son. We will see about getting you home in the morning. I'll go talk to our friend in the west. He knows these trails better than we do."

Pevi inclines his head, clutching the bowl in his hands. "Thank you. I will repay you for this kindness."

Alvea is shaking her head, moving to her feet. "There is no need for that. We are just glad to know you, Pevi Likloré, and thankful for your friendship. We do not often see lots here in this forest. And it is not the past that makes a man, but where he goes from that past. You will be welcome." She nods at him, moving to set her bowl on the counter.

Pevi glances up, nodding, to all of us. "Thank you. Your graciousness does not go unappreciated." He pauses, half frowning. "You all mentioned another man. Who is he? And you may call me Pevi. There is no need for formality." He nods toward Alvea.

Alvea inclines her head, a ghost of a smile on her lips. "Goran was his name." She turns toward the bucket.

Pevi is lifting his spoon, paused half to his mouth. "Did you all know him before you came out here?"

Yore shakes his head. "No. We met him in the woods a month or so back."

Pevi grins. "Ah. So, I am not special in the woodland greetings, a second random meeting in these woods."

I shake my head. "Third." Yore looks at me, sharply, his eyes locking on mine.

My face warms, I look down, lifting my bowl from my lap and clench my jaw. *Curses. I did not think before saying that. I never told them about the centaur. Curses.* I clear my throat and lift my head. "I met a centaur, not long after I met Goran, weeks ago. He was heading south, with his family. I never saw them or saw him again after that." Yore's eyes narrow, and he stares at me, hard. *I hadn't meant to not tell them. But there was not much conversation between us then. I am going to hear about this later.*

Nie. I won't. Yore would never question one of us, if we might question him back. Not after what he has done. He avoids any line of question and has for months. He shakes his head, and looks away, eyes soft and vacant again like maybe his mind went to the same place mine did.

Alvea drops into her seat, shifting her leg sideways, just a little. *Like it is bothering her, but not badly.* She shifts her skirts, placing her hands carefully on them, empty, folded. "You never told us about that, Oanéka." It's soft, and an accusation at once, like half of it is unsaid.

I shake my head, and stand, and my stew is still steaming in my bowl, uneaten. "I forgot to mention it." I wave my hand. "It was a brief meeting, and it was not long after we got here." *Everyone was quiet then.* "He was gone so quickly, it barely stuck in my mind." Yore glances at me again, and stands, moving over to the pot. He lifts the ladle, pouring himself more of the stew that nearly killed him. I swallow and stand. "I'm going to go find those blankets for tonight." Pevi looks up, a question crossing his face. I nod at him. "For you to sleep on." He moves forward, as if to protest, but I drop my bowl on the table, move for the ladder. *He won't interrupt me while I am already moving for it.* The wooden planks are cool on my fingers, skin chapped, and my throat is tight.

I pull myself up, onto the floor, and the room is dark, the shutter closed and the lantern cold. *Maybe time will heal things on its own, and we can leave things be and let them heal. Maybe it will be fine. But not now.* Voices are quiet downstairs, murmuring, Alvea asking a question, and the latch on my wooden chest is cold under my fingers. The air around it is cold as it shifts with the moving of the lid. *I would have done better not to bring up the centaur. He is only a reminder of a time unhealed, now.*

Chapter XVI

I step through the door. The water buckets slosh, bumping against my legs and I press the door shut and turn. The warmth of the room is heavy on my skin, like a living thing after the morning cold, pressing against the skin of my face, against my hands, and I can barely feel my fingers. *It was good that Yore cut the ice so early, or breakfast would have been late, with as thick as the ice was in the cold.* "Oh." A voice, a few steps away, groggy and low. "Let me help you." I glance up sharply. Pevi is stepping toward me. He slips his hands over the bucket handles, blinking, his eyes bleary with sleep, and lacking the alertness that was in them last night. The sleeves of his tunic shirt are rolled up, his dark forearms damp. *He must have been washing up for the morning.* I shake my head, step forward. "You don't need to..." He is already moving across the room, half gone to the sink.

He glances back at me. "Your hands are half frozen." His voice is still heavy with sleep. He glances at me again, moving to set the buckets down. "Do these go by the stove?"

I nod, and stoop, a smile brushing at my lips. I jerk my boots off, and stand, setting them to the side. My hands are awkward, puffy and red, and they sting with cold and warmth at once, tingling, burning. I look up at him, fingers strange on the cords. "Thank you." He nods, stepping away from the stove, and I move toward it. I shove my shawl back into place, tucked in my skirts. *It's cold.* There is a cloud of steam rising from the pot on the stove. I snatch the porridge bag from the shelf, and my hand fumbles, bag jerking. I grimace and set it on the counter. Turning, I pluck a spoon from the shelf, and lift the bag, pouring the grain into the pot bit by bit. *Bit by bit or it will be lumpy, and then it will be mostly uneatable like last night's soup almost was.*

There are steps, and the sound of a door. I glance over my shoulder. Pevi is gone, the door to the loo closed. Yore's door creaks open, his steps heavy and muffled on the floor. I turn back toward the stove, stir in a little more of the porridge. Steam licks at my fingers, hot and sharp, biting at my skin and my prickling fingers. I grimace.

Yore is stepping past me. His heavy coat is over his shoulders, on, and he is reaching for his boots. I look up sharply. "What are you doing?"

He glances at me, and away again, dropping into a chair with his boots in his hand. He is wearing the thick socks, the chunky pair he never wears. "Going to talk to Goran." He shoves the boot onto his foot.

I frown, shake my head. "But you haven't had breakfast yet. Is it because of the cold?" I tip the spoon, set it against the side of the pot.

He is still tying his boots, twisting the cords into place and his head is shaking. "The cold is not so bad today. It will get warmer as the day goes on. But I do not know how many hours it is back to his hut, how long it will take us to get there." He nods toward the loo door. "We need to leave if we are going to be confident of making it before dark sets in tonight, and if he plans to leave today."

I swallow, stirring at the watery porridge, and press a lump out. "Do you plan to take Goran with you?" *My porridge is going to spoil.* I stir faster, lumps hitting the spoon. I purse my lips, crushing one of the lumps of porridge against the side of the pot. It crumbles, flaking into the bubbling of the thickened water.

Yore glances at me. "Nie. He knows these woods. If anyone can help us find the man's hut, it will be him. And he knew our hut. He may know others or know a way of finding it that we don't. I don't even know which direction to begin to look based on the little info Pevi has about it." He twists off the laces of the first boot, his hands taking up the laces of the second.

I shake my head. "Could you not wait until..."

"Porridge is ready?" He glances at me and shakes his head tying off the other laces. "Nie. I don't know what Goran is doing today. He may not plan to be at his hut. Light is already breaking. If we wait, he may be gone before I arrive, and then we will be all on our own out there." He stands, moving toward the door.

I swallow, swirling the spoon in the pot of food that isn't needed. *Yore is leaving before it's ready. It will no longer taste the same by the time he returns, if he does not hurry, does not move fast, and he will be the one out there all day, in the cold.* He reaches for the doorknob. I swallow. "Take your hat." He glances at me, and feels his head, as if unsure that it is not there, and turns, snatching it from the rack. He moves, and is jerking the door open, gone into the chilled air, a wisp of it brushing into the room behind him.

* * * * * * * * *

Alvea steps off the ladder, and Pevi is moving across the room, over past a chair beside the mound of blankets on the floor. He drops into them, glancing across the room at my sister. Alvea's walk is stiff, her limp sharper, and she is holding her chin up, her eyes carefully averted from his. I swallow, and glance at the porridge. It is thick now, the creamy brown color that it should be. *Ready. It will be unpleasant by the time Yore is back, as I thought it would be.* I frown.

Alvea steps past me, and grabs a cup, dunking it into the new bucket of water. She lifts it to her lips, and her eyes travel to the window, surprise flashing through her eyes. She swallows, her throat bobbing, and pulls the cup back. "Why are you all up so early?" Her eyes flicker to mine.

Pevi laughs, short and breathy. "I just assumed you all always rise this early."

Alvea glances at him, lifting another cup from the shelf. Her eyes move toward mine. They look irritated, bright. She narrows them. "We don't, usually. My sister must have had something pressing to tend to. Would you care for some water?" She turns, glaring at me, and holding the cup carefully in her hands, eyes snapping to him. He nods. She moves toward him, pressing the damp side of the water up against her skirts. "I am sorry if my family woke you. We do not often have guests and are not accustomed to it."

My lips purse tighter. *Woke him? Yore is out in the cold, making sure that he can make it back to his home, because the man doesn't want to stay more than one night here, because he is worried about being an imposition.* I shake my head, and lift the pot from the counter, throwing a woven potholder on the table. I set the pot on it, and turn back, grabbing the bowls. I turn back with the bowls, their sides bumping against my chest. Alvea is speaking to the man about something, their voices even and light. *Perhaps he is assuring her that we did not wake him, that he was not troubled. I doubt we didn't wake him. I was not as quiet as I wished to be, as I'd tried to be going out.*

I lick my lips and lift the spoons. "Breakfast is ready." I glance at them. "Please come, sit."

Alvea nods, and stands, moving toward the back of the room. "I'll get Yore." She turns.

I shake my head, setting the spoon jar down. "He isn't here." She glances at me sharply, and her face pales a little. "He went to talk to Goran, to see if he has any knowledge of trails or huts to help us get Pevi home." I drop the ladle into the porridge.

She frowns. "How long ago did he leave?"

Pevi straightens. "He went already?" he shakes his head. "I wish I had known he was going. I would have gone in his stead. There was no call for him to go out so early on my account. I should have gone."

I shake my head, and dump porridge into the first bowl. The wood warms beneath my fingers. "It would have been ill advised for you to go. Goran owns several large hounds that do not take kindly to strangers. It is better that Yore went." I set the bowl on the table. "We will have to eat without him, or the porridge will be spoiled. He has not been gone for long."

Alvea pauses and glances back at me. She nods at Pevi, and he turns slowly, moving toward a chair. He pauses by it, his hand on it. I frown. Alvea drops into her chair. *He was waiting for her to sit. Curtesy I haven't seen used in years.* He turns, dropping into the chair at the end of the table, the chair where Pakem used to sit, back home. *Before he left us for something unknown. For nothing.* I swallow, and hand a bowl to my sister, and another to Pevi.

I drop into my chair, too quickly, my bowl half thudding against the table. Pevi glances at me, his bright eyes are sharp, clearer now. *But they are still puffy from sleep, like Alvea's are.* He inclines his head. "Thank you, Oanéka." My name sounds strange from him, the tone odd, sounds not uttered in any of the ways I have heard it before.

I swallow, and nod. "It was my pleasure. I am sorry to have woken you this morning." I take a bite. The porridge is simple, thick and smooth, the taste bland but for the hint of spice. Spice thrown in late, the way that Mavíkah always taught us to make it. Her voice is still a scold in the back of my mind, that baker next door.

Pevi takes a bite, glancing at me, and then at Alvea. He swallows. "So, Oanéka, what is it that you care for?"

My eyes dart up sharply and I choke, porridge caught in my airway, hot and scalding. I cough, press a hand hard against my throat. "What?" I wheeze. My eyes water. He is staring at me, eyes wide, alarmed. Alvea shifts, her hand moving to pound against my back. I shake my head at her. "I'm alright. I just swallowed incorrectly."

Pevi's brow twitches, and he is laughing, a bark of it, clear and simple. *Not like the clouded laugh that Yore gives, or the deep, strange, off thing that is Goran's laugh, mixed with a thousand meanings. His is there, plain, simple and real.* I smile, coughing. Pevi shakes his head. "I am sorry. I did not mean to choke you." His teeth flash white with his smile, and I smile back. Alvea glances at me, eyes meeting mine, careful, checking.

She laughs, and nods. "Most people do not ask Oanéka what she cares about, unless they plan to get a speech about flowers and colors and all things bright," she says.

My face warms. He turns toward me, his face openly curious, eyes flickering to mine. "Do you care for flowers particularly?"

I nod, and lift my spoon again, slowly. "Va. I raised and tended many of them. It was what I spent much of my time on back home." I swallow. "What do you care for?"

He grins. "I care for food." He laughs, as though to and at himself, and leans his arms against the table. "I care for life. And I care for stories of the world. It is good to have seen more of it, and I am impressed to get to see more of this side of it, up here, that so few have seen over the next two years."

Alvea nods. "Have you always thought of it that way? As a good thing, to be up here, to see this world?"

He shrugs, and lifting the spoon, his head half-cocked to the side. "Nie. For the first few months, I was not glad to be here. There is so much wildlife, close and creeping, dangerous, and few landlots. I enjoy company and did not care for the idea of living alone. Still do not. But it has grown on me, bit by bit, with the seasons. When I am here." He looks down again, takes another bite.

Alvea nods. Her eyes are vacant, staring aimlessly across the room, away from us. His eyes are on her face, for a moment, half studying, and half surprised, as if he did not expect her. No one expects Alvea. She is strong and weak, beautiful and harsh and gentle and rigid, my sister with her mystery and smile. He turns away, as if shaking off his thoughts, and lifts his spoon. "It is good porridge,

Oanéka. Did you put something in it? It is not so tasteless as mine is."

I half grin, and nod. "Va. I threw spices in it. We lived beside a baker, back home, and she would never let us make plain porridge."

Alvea laughs, and it is clear and low at once, and her smile is bright. "Mavíkah." She laughs again. "She would always say 'Poor porridge makes a poor wife, and poor wives lose their husbands. Spice your porridge, for heaven's sake, if you can sprice nothing else.'"

Pevi laughs. He shakes his head, glancing down at the bowl before him, and half grins. "Did the rest of your village know about this supposed power of porridge?"

Alvea breathes out a laugh. "I do not think they did, and for the better, that. Mavíkah liked to know things that she didn't think others did. But she had many good sayings, that will now be ingrained in both mine and Oanéka's minds. Her favorite was always 'Spoons do not make themselves.'"

Pevi's face crinkles, in an amused and confounded smile. "What?" He laughs.

I nod and twist my spoon. "Va. She would say it in response to anything. If you said that you had to make bread tomorrow, she would say 'Va. Spoons do not make themselves.'"

Alvea laughs, and waves her spoon, gently. "Or if you said you needed a new dress, she would look at you, tilt her forehead forward until there was only a slit of her eyes under her thick, gray eyebrows and say, 'Spoons do not make themselves,' and then stare until you agreed with her." Alvea laughs again, and Pevi joins, pressing his hands against the table.

He grins. "Did you know many people like her, in your city?" He glances between the two of us.

Alvea shakes her head. "Nie. It was hardly a city. Barely a town. And no one is like Mavíkah. But we knew many strange people. We have never been wealthy, and I think that the poorer you are, the more interesting lots you meet on the streets. Our father often switched his occupation." She sets her spoon down, resting her hand gently on the table. "There was this man, at the docks, that was always full of the best sayings. I never understood half of them, but he would always say them either in the most severe way, or with a grin so wide that all of his black teeth would show, and it looked like his face would split, and then he would laugh, and I have never heard a laugh like his. It was filled with all the best things in life."

Pevi grimaces. "He seems like quite the character."

Alvea nods, lifting a bite of porridge. "He is. One of the best men. I never got to ask him about where he grew up. He rarely spoke of his own life, beyond the stories he told of fishing."

The door creaks, opening. There is a gust of cold air, two figures step into the room, a hound behind them. It growls, dropping backward on its haunches, and I am on my feet, chair scraping the floor. The door slams shut.

"Gyaith. Quiet." Goran's voice cuts out sharply, low, and Yore is stepping forward, his feet pounding on the floor, boots still on.

Yore glances over his shoulder at the man behind him. "Have you eaten?"

Goran looks up, shaking his head, his hand still on the hound's back. "Nie."

Yore glances at me. I step forward, grabbing the bowls from the shelf and shake my head at him. "Stay there. I'll bring a bowl to you. Both of you." He nods, planting his feet.

Pevi is on his feet now, looking at the new man steadily. He steps forward, bowing a little, and Gyaith growls, her red fur standing up straight on her neck. Pevi straightens sharply, but he doesn't flinch away. *He is keeping his ground, though the great red hound is baring her teeth at him, growling.* He nods at Goran, over her head. "Gooddawn. I am Pevi Liklоré-Morfonnen and I am sorry that you were roused so early on my count."

Goran half nods, the hair bound at the nape of his neck moving a little. "It doesn't do to wait when storms are rolling in. It would have been better to have come for me earlier so that we could make a clean break of it." His eyes are sharp, scanning Pevi over, watching. "Where is your hut?" A dull question. *But he is plainly not asking him which direction, but what is nearby.*

Pevi folds his arms, gaze meeting Goran's. "It is wedged between the river and the mountain, not far from either." He shakes his head. "I was looking for the river when I got turned around in the woods. I have not the skill of direction, and the snow was not an earnest guide to me. I have never been out here in it before."

Goran nods, eyes flickering down, as if scanning the air. He looks up. "How far is the mountain? Does the sun set on the left, or the right?"

Pevi nods. "Not far. I can make it to the slopes inside of two counts of walking, a morning's trek, when I've tried. And it sets on the right, directly over the mountain."

Goran nods, and his eyes flicker over to Yore, a look passing between them. I pick a bowl up from the table, and hand it toward my brother. He takes it, breathing out a short thanks. I grab the other, and dump porridge into it. Goran is speaking to my brother. "It's a day's walk, nearly. We will not be back tonight, not with the storm rolling in." My eyes snap up. I hand him the bowl, and he half nods at me, his focus never leaving Yore. Gyaith is staring at Pevi, her head high, hair still raised on the back of her neck. *At least she is not growling.* "We will go back by my hut, on the way out and get the other two hounds." He glances at Pevi.

Yore is nodding. He sets down his bowl and the spoon rattles slightly against the wood of it. *How did he finish it so fast?* "I'll make sure the calli are tended for the night, before we go," he says, glancing at Alvea. "That way Oanéka will not have to. Pack some food, if you would. Thank you." His flicks his gaze toward Pevi. "You would do well to get your mule ready and get those boots of yours on." He turns toward the door.

Pevi nods, and half grins, glancing down at the red hound. She growls again, teeth baring further. "Are all your hounds as pleasant as this one?"

Goran glances at him, and something crosses his face, dark. "Nie. Crith likes strangers even less." Pevi swallows, his throat bobbing.

He nods, and steps to the side and he stoops, grabbing his boots from the floor. "I will keep a fair distance from your hounds, then, to keep from troubling them." Goran nods, and turns, the bowl empty in his hands now.

I reach forward, toward it, and look up at him. "Would you take more? There is more than enough, and you will be walking all day." His eyes flicker to mine. He nods. I turn toward Yore, but Alvea has his bowl, serving it. He is standing in place with melted snow pooling around his boots. I frown. *I will be cleaning that today.* I grip the ladle from Alvea's offering fingers, and dump porridge into the bowl. I turn back toward Goran.

He is looking at Yore, and Yore glances back at him, the bowl from Alvea in his hands. "Do I need my bow?" My brother lifts a brow, with the question, and Goran is shaking his head.

"There is little that will bother us in this forest with three hounds." Yore's eyes flicker to us, and a shadow of worry passes through his eyes, and is gone. He nods, shoveling the rest of his food into his mouth. Alvea's steps are uneven on the floor, moving toward the barrels at the back of the room, where the dry food is kept.

Yore is watching her, his eyes soft and hard at once, unsettled. He shakes his head, and his lips tighten. He turns back to his food, taking the last bite and setting the bowl on the counter beside him and the stove. "I'll tend the calli, then." He glances at me, and his lips tighten further, and he is gone, through the door, a gust of wind brushing in behind him.

I swallow, turn. I snatch Yore's sack from the floor where he left it, after it was cleaned from his last hunt, and turn toward Alvea. *What do we pack, for this? Yore always packed his own food and items for hunting, and for any trip he took back home, when he went out with the troubling men he journeyed with. What should we pack? Water?* I glance around. His water skeins are on top of a barrel, at the back of the room. I step across and grip them, turning toward the bucket.

Yore steps back through the door, rubbing his hands together. *He forgot his gloves, too.* He glances at me. His eyes flick toward Alvea, and they are back on me, settling, brows furrowed. "You'll have to tend the calli tomorrow, Oanéka." I nod and turn toward the bucket. I press the empty water skein into it, the cold soaking into my fingers.

"Will they need anything different than last time?"

He shakes his head, taking the water skein from my hands. Alvea already has the pack done, handing it to him. He nods at both of us, eyes flickering between the two of us. They are bright. *Excited.* And there is something else in them, perhaps worry. "Be careful. Stay close to the house." He looks at me with the last words, eyes finding mine.

I nod, and Alvea does too. "Be careful out there." She says. "I packed extra meat, just in case, but we will be looking for you tomorrow night. Be safe." Her voice is tight, eyes moving between the men. Goran nods at her, moving toward the door, and they are gone, out into the first traces of dawn.

Chapter XVII

There is a shriek, high and terrible, wailing high.

My heart thuds in my chest, eyes fly to the window. *The wind.* The world is white, and it is growing darker, something flying past the window in a thousand shards. *Snow. No no no. They should not have gone, should never have gone out there!* My eyes snap to Alvea. Her hands are motionless, on the threads, eyes staring at the window, wide, vacant. They flicker toward me. "They'll have made it." Her voice is curt, certain. She looks back at her threads. Her hand trembles, just slightly, face pale. "They've been gone for hours. They'll have made it."

I swallow, and it's thick in my throat. *Will they? What will we do if Yore is lost out there, if he doesn't come back? What can we do if he and Goran don't come back?* My heart pounds louder, thunders in my ears. *What can we do if we lose him, like those who got caught in the blizzard back home, years ago? They were found, frozen, a week later.* My heart shudders. *We won't even be able to find them, won't know where to look.* My eyes fly to the window. *We can't lose him. What will become of the agreement? Of staying out here for five years? He agreed to, we agreed to, but what if he is no longer... We cannot pay the debts. Alvea and I cannot make up what is left. What if...*

My heart is loud in my ears, and the wind is shrieking, screaming, noise growing louder by the moment. It slams against the house, and everything shakes, screaming in the growing darkness. *Elnial, please, keep them safe. Bring them to their homes safely. Please.* My eyes flicker to the window. Silence and screaming, and the house is filled to the brim with both, and my hands shake on the cloth in them.

* * * * * * * * *

The air shrieks, house shuddering beneath it. I drag my body upward. There is barely any light in the room. *Alvea's bed is empty.* Just a roll of blankets at the bottom of the bed. I slip my feet over the side of my bed and press them against the floor. It's cold, clinging to my skin through my night clothes. I shudder, and wrap a blanket around my shoulders, nightdress white in the darkness. I purse my lips, flick my eyes toward the ladder. *'Do not let the fire go out.' Perhaps she is just listening to Goran's words, checking the fire, like I am going to. Perhaps his words haunt her mind the way they do mine.*

"Where are you going?" My heart drops into my stomach. Alvea's voice is hoarse, soft and low. *She is still here.* I glance over my shoulder. The roll of blankets at the end of the bed has shifted, moved up to the top of her bed now. Her face is poking out of them, pale in the darkness.

I swallow and tighten the blanket around my shoulders. "To check the fire." My voice is a whisper, matching hers. *Can she hear it above the wind?*

Her lips tighten, skin pale, hair spilling dark over her pillow in the blankets. "You already checked it three times tonight." Her voice is dry, still drowsy with sleep.

Has it been three? I shake my head and step toward the ladder. "I just want to check it one more time, just to be sure." I step down onto the rungs below, and the air is warm and cold at once, the storm screaming. Firelight glows on the floor, sputtering as wind rips down the chimney. *But the fire is still going, still lit.* I lift a log and set it upon the stack in the flames, that is already high, stocked for the night, high enough. *But I can't let it go out. It has to be high enough. There will be warmth, here. There will be warmth.* My throat is tight. I glance toward the window, and the darkness outside. *Did they make it to the hut?* My skin is chilled. I shiver and pull the blanket tighter.

* * * * * * * * *

The air is sharp though the fire is going, and everything is too still, pressing on my ears. *I don't know when the storm ended.* Alvea's eyes have circles under them this morning, her face a little paler. *Mine is, too.* I saw it in the reflection of the water, white under the puff of wild red. My hair is plaited now, on my shoulder. I grip my hat, and pull it down, over my ears, over the curls. The wool is warm, and my ears smart against it. I shove my feet into my boots, and jerk the laces tight, twisting them into place. I stand, glance across the room, toward the window and the silence.

"Are you getting water or doing the calli?" Alvea's voice is soft, groggy still, and her eyes are puffy from sleep, her hair a little wilder than normal. *But her dress is neat and orderly, her posture sharp, her hands working at her hair.*

I turn back toward the window and grip my shawl from the rack beside it. "I'm doing both. I don't want to open the door much today, until Yore gets back." *If he does.* Alvea's lips tighten, like she knows my thoughts, and she nods, turning toward the stove, her hands still working at the strands of her hair. I wave toward the stove. "There is porridge, there if you would like some. It's still warm."

She nods at me. "Thank you. Come back in quickly. And don't forget your gloves." I snatch them from the rack, where they hang tied together. I loose the tie, throwing it back over the rack, and step outside.

The air is sharper, and still, so still. The world is furiously white, and nothing is moving, not a branch on a tree, not a brush of the wind. The endless white is over everything, coating every tree, every bush, each post that holds up the porch, like a blanket, over the whole world, complete, white and endless. *Beautiful. And horrible. White. White. And only time will tell if it is the white that came with the loss of life.* My eyes smart, and there is liquid swimming in my vision. I swallow, and it catches in my throat. *If I cannot keep hope, then what am I good for? Yore will come back. They will be fine.* I shake my head, and step forward, and the snow is delicate, perfectly soft and beautiful beneath my feet. I step off the porch. The snowdrifts slide over my boots, slipping down into them, and I freeze. It's cold and sharp and strange. And everywhere.

A laugh cuts through my throat. Snow. It is so strangely deep, a coat everywhere, horrible and vast and perfect. I kneel, press my gloves into it. My fingers sink easily down. It's fluffy. I grin, and stand.

I turn toward the shed, and slow. *I forgot the water buckets.* I shake my head, and glance back at the door. *It does not make a difference now, whether I go back for them now or later.* I turn toward the calli shed, and the snow is soft, damp and deep, puffing up in folds around each of my boots. *It's stunning, this everlasting whiteness that came with a scream in the night, more delicate than any snowfall I've ever seen.*

The side door of the shed is shut, the door to the calli fence, that they go in and out through. *Yore must have closed it before he left.* I step up to the outer door and jerk. It doesn't budge. I frown, and pull again, planting my feet harder in the snow. The last trace of snow slides off the handle as it turns in my hand, but the door does not move, doesn't budge. My feet skid. I look down. The snow is packed against the door, heavy and thick, pressing against it. *Curses.* I groan and step back. *I don't know where Yore puts the shovel. Curses. I'll have to find it...* I glance around, and there is only the world of white, white clinging to every part of the hut we cowered in last night, while they were out, either safe or lost in the darkness. *I don't know where he keeps the shovel.* My eyes flicker to the cottage, and over to the woods.

What would it be like, to die in a storm? Surrounded by the shrieking, the screaming fury of white, the swirling death? A shudder races up my scalp. I shake my head. *I cannot think like that. I cannot think that way, not right now. The calli have to be tended, water gathered. Don't think about it for now.*

I turn. *There is nowhere out here to look for the shovel, nowhere to have put it. He will have put it in the shed. We'll have to keep it in the cottage after this.* I stoop, and press my hands into the snow, shoveling it away from the door with my gloves. Only a little bit moves, a little more than a joint handful. I shove down, and my fingers scrape against something hard. *Ice.* The door is frozen shut. I drop back on my ankles and look up toward the sky.

Gray clouds are rolling overhead, with the early light of morning, and my nose burns with the cold.

I shove my hands back into the snow, pushing it hard away from the door.

* * * * * * * * *

The buckets are heavy, and my shoulders are tight, feet heavy beneath my skirts. The sky is still gray. Plain, gray, and simple, clouds a blanket across the sky, snow a blanket across the earth, and my gloves are damp, though they have been hanging in front of the fire all day since I finished digging this morning. *Sunset cannot be far. Sunset, and then what?* My lips tighten, cold against my teeth. I shudder.

I step forward, buckets heavy, water sloshing not quite over the lip on them. The snow is still soft, like earlier today, not iced over like it should be, like it will be in a few hours, once darkness fully falls over the earth and the little softening of the day becomes ice. I purse my lips and set the buckets down beside the door of the shed, and my hand grips the handle, jerking it open. I grab the buckets, and step through, water sloshing against my skirts. I grimace and puff out a breath. *I was going to change these skirts anyways. They have flour on them, and now mud, from the creatures in the shed. It doesn't matter if they are soaked to, so long as I head inside soon.* My throat is tight, and I don't know why. I shake my head and kick the door shut, moving across the shed toward the water trough.

The calli are lumped together, lying in the corner upon a pile of straw. Their shapes are dim, almost dusty in the fading light of the shed. *They are all chewing, none of them at the same time, their jaws working slowly, their strange, slanted eyes watching me.* I dump the water into the trough, one bucket, and the other. It splatters, colliding against the trough and catches the end of my shawl. I grimace, and step back. I move toward the door and set the buckets down beside it. The calli are still chewing, all watching, unmoving and unimpressed. I shake my head and jerk the door open. Whiteness stabs at my eyes, too bright after the dimness of the shed. I grimace and move across the ground, forcing my eyes up. The clouds are lazy overhead, gray, only gray, and the world is beginning to dim quickly, too quickly. *It's getting too late. Night is too close. What if they don't make it back soon?*

My steps tap against the packed snow on the porch, wood beneath it only barely making a crunching sound, muffled and sharp like everything else. I glance back toward the woods. *There is nothing there, but snow. Snow against every tree. No figures. No one out there.* I duck my head; I grip the doorknob, and step into the room. There are voices, more than one, and there's a man's voice, rumbling through the wall.

"...Oanéka...?" It's a question, the end of one, and Yore is in the middle of the room, half taking off his coat, his back to me.

My breaths catch in my throat, and he turns. I bolt across the room and throw my arms over his shoulders, crushing him against me. *He is alive. He's alright. He made it back. He is alive.* His coat is cold against my face, his shoulders stiff, awkward. *But he is alive.*

His arms wrap around my back, pressing it for a moment, and he steps back, his hands on my sides, setting me down. "I was not gone all that long," he says, and his eyes are half teasing, half hard. I shake my head and force a laugh. It hurts, caught in my throat. *He's alright. It was foolish to fear. He is alright. He's back.*

Alvea is smiling, a small, simple thing, and her eyes are bright. She grins at him. "Well then. Dinner is ready for you, Yore." She smiles again, stepping to the side. "I am glad you are back. Oanéka checked the fire every hour last night in your absence." My face warms. I look down.

Yore glances at me, pulling his coat off. He sets it over the rack, and kneels, pulling on his boot laces. *Boots. Mine are still on, still caked with snow. I will have to wash the floor again. Curse it.* I stoop, and tug at the laces, pulling them off as Yore pulls off the last of his. He works his jaw, standing. "I did not think she would take that much trouble, or I should have told her not to. It only needs to be checked rarely."

I glance up at him, and frown. "I wasn't checking it on your count. I could not sleep for thinking of it, after what Goran said about it going out." He nods, glancing at me and away.

Alvea steps forward. "You found his cabin then? Didn't get caught in the storm?" She asks.

He is nodding. "Va." He straightens his shoulders, rolling them stiffly, and stretches one arm, a little above his head. He looks down, almost sheepishly. "We found it just after the storm struck. His mule knew the way, or even with the hounds we would have missed it in the storm." My heart tightens, and my fingers fumble. *Praise be to Elnial. They made it, oh barely they made it.* Yore is nodding at Alvea, like she said something. "Goran is back at his hut. I told him that Oanéka would bring him some pastries next time one of you makes them."

Alvea looks up. "Oh?"

He nods. "Va. He had more work of it than the rest of us. Pevi lost a glove in the storm, and I thought he would lose his hand from the blue that was beginning to show. I've seen it before. But," he shakes his head, looks down, "Goran knew what to do with it, and tended him carefully through the evening, working with his skin until it was red again, normal. It was like he had some knowledge of the healer's skill." He shakes his head. "Good man, Goran." He glances at Alvea again, and steps past her, moving back toward his room. *As he always does.* I swallow, and glance back toward the window and shadowy white beyond, and my eyes are smarting. *He's back safe.* Reflections from the fire and the kitchen dance on the window panes, flames and shapes, faintly moving.

Yore's steps are heavy on the floor, Alvea's uneven. She is by the stove, lifting the pot, and he is moving toward the table as she sets the pot down upon it. He glances at her. "Is that food?"

She grins, and laughs. "What else would it be?"

He shrugs. "It might have been dye or sommat." She shakes her head, laughing again.

Chapter XVIII

I step into the room, and there is something moving toward me, sharply. *Yore.* His eyes flash, and he is bolting past me, out through the door and beyond. I move backward sharply, step sideways with the full water buckets in my hands. They slosh, water slapping the floor, and he jerks the door shut, gone into the morning. I purse my lips, and glance back at Alvea. Her eyes are bright, jaw tight, hands working furiously at her wheel. It is spinning faster than I have ever seen it, sound whirring across the room.

I swallow, and frown. "What is wrong? What happened?"

She glances at me, her eyes sharpening. She looks away. "You can take those pastries to Goran, and those bones to his hounds." She points toward the counter, where there are two bundles, her wheel not slowing.

I swallow again. "But has something happened?"

Her eyes flash, and her hands work faster at the threads flying beneath her fingers. "Everything is perfectly fine, Oanéka. You can mind your own tasks. Take those to Goran now, if you would not mind."

My lips purse harder. I fold my arms. "I just got in, and I do not want to track water across your floor." I gesture to my boots.

She lifts her eyes, glancing at me. "It's not my floor, and I won't be the one tending it if you get water across it." I my lips tighten. She shakes her head, and stands sharply and the wheel suddenly stills, her fingers pressing against it. She spins, marching toward the counter, her limp sharp, movements sharp, and she has the bundles. She turns, thrusting them toward my arms. I grab them, and snatch my hat from the rack, pressing it down on my head. She is already sitting again, the wheel spinning furiously beneath her fingers. I purse my lips, and jerk the door open, stepping out into the cold. It bites at my face, burns against the skin on my cheeks. I jerk my scarf up, over my mouth and nose, breath pressing against my skin.

I step down, off the porch and toward the creek, the snow packed beneath my boots, slick and frozen over. My steps wobble, sliding. I grimace, and step onto a rock, in the frozen stream. There is a hole, a few feet away, where Yore cut into it this morning so we could haul water up. I frown, step onto the other side. *He was fine then, happy when he told me he'd cut the hole for me.* The trees are everywhere, trunks still caked with snow, cut into their trunks from the storm, days ago. *Perhaps it will not leave until spring, perhaps it will stay there, clinging, like a blight. That would be a strange, pathetic thing. Curse it. Why did Alvea and Yore have to be snippy today? Couldn't they have held it together for a little longer?*

I step through the space with no evergreens. There is the trail, winding up to Goran's hut where it hides behind the trees, and there is the sound of metal ringing against wood. I move up the path, steps heavy and sharp at once, and I step around the trees. His hut is there, coated in white from the west like ours, a path cut in the white world, curling off toward his shed. The sound rings out again. I look up. There is a short bark.

I step forward, and glance to the side. Marin is moving around the edge of the hut, her eyes on me, head cocked to the side. Her eyes flicker to the bundle in my hand, and stay there, watching it. *She can smell the bones.* I lift one and toss it toward her. It thuds into the snow, and she is after it, blue fur streaking over the snow. She grabs it, and turns, prancing up the porch, head held high, feet lifted like a proud horse.

I shake my head. The ringing sound cuts out, twice, close together this time. I step around the hut. Marin is on the porch, her price between her paws.

Goran is standing by a pile of wood, the axe coming down is his hands, and a log splits in two with the force of it. He glances up, sideways, eyes flickering toward me. He lifts another log, setting it into place. My throat bobs. "I brought you pastries."

He glances at me. "I told Yore there was no need." His eyes flick toward the bundle, pause there.

I nod. "Va. But we would have brought them anyway, whether he asked me to or not."

His eyes flicker to me. "We?"

I nod, and half shrug. "One of us."

His brow lifts, and he moves, setting the axe against the logs. "You are the only one who comes here without needing anything."

My face warms. I look up toward the sky, pull my scarf away from my nose. "Well, I only come because..." *Why do I come? Because Alvea asks me to?* I shake my head. "Where would you like me to put these?" I lift the bundle. His eyes move to it.

He lifts a brow, just barely, and turns, lifting the axe again, and he brings it down with one hand, driving the blade into the top of an unsplit log. "I told you there was no need."

I shake my head. "I have already brought them."

He glances at me. "I can't eat two bundles of pastries."

I half grin. "This bundle is bones." I nod toward the one closer to me, and lift them a little more.

He half smiles, and nods, moving forward. He reaches a hand toward me and I offer them to him, his fingers barely brush mine and he has them. He steps around me, toward the hut. "Do you care for walking?"

I look up at him. He is moving around the hut, eyes forward. I step after him, and he is up the porch steps. I scramble up them after him. He hesitates for a moment by the door, waiting for me, and he is moving in, letting me slip in after him. His steps are light on the floor, sounding across the room. He sets the bundle on the counter. I swallow. "I enjoy walking most days, but I think you knew the answer to that question." My face warms a little.

He glances at me, adjusting the sleeves of his coat. "Then I would like to show you something, if you are not too busy. It isn't a far walk." He lifts a brow. "If you are up to walking more now. Today." He looks away, off toward the other side of the cottage.

I frown. *He wants to show me something? What would he show me?* I nod slowly. He is nods back, moving across the room. He grips the doorknob, pulling it open again. I step through, and he whistles, sharply, glancing across the room. My ears ring. The hounds shoot out the door, past me, their nails clattering on the wood, and they are off, in the snow, bolting into the woods, Marin after them, her bone forgotten. I smile.

He steps down the path, in a direction I haven't been, away from the road. I scramble after him, the hounds running in front of his feet, around his legs, their stride faster and sharper than mine, tongues lolling. He slows, and I am beside him. His eyes are still forward, watchful, careful. But his arms are loose, free at his side. *Does he ever not watch the woods? Is he ever free from watchfulness, or it is always with him?*

He moves around a tree and steps past a boulder. *He is moving out toward the mountain.* His movements are faster than mine, long, stretching out into the snow with each stride. My face is hot beneath the folds of my scarf. I jerk the scarf down further, suck in a hard breath.

He steps forward again, stride long, the hounds running just before his feet. "I saw this this morning, and thought you might enjoy it, though I did not think to see you today." I blink. He is still not looking at me, his eyes watching everything but me. *He thought of me when he saw something? Was it red? Or did it disturb his peace every few days?*

The sound of trickling water cuts through the air, very faint, almost musical and far off. I look up at him. He pauses, beside the branches of an evergreen. It is short, slender, the branches covered in ice and snow. He nods toward it. "This one." I frown. *He saw a short, sparse evergreen and thought of me?* I blink. He lifts a hand, pointing toward something tucked away to the side. *Oh.* I lean forward, and there is a tiny burst of color, orange, but nearly brown, and coated in ice. *An evergreen flower.* It is frozen, the ice catching in the light over the orange-brown of the faded bloom, half dead before it was frozen, but the petals are still long draped in the cold and ice. *And it is beautiful still.*

I swallow and jerk off my glove. I reach out my hand, half kneeling, fingers brushing the ice carefully. It is uneven and smooth under my hand, and the branch sways, swirling. I swallow. "It's beautiful." I brush my hand down it again, and it dances on the branch, swirling, the ice glinting just a little in the gray light. "What made you think of me?"

He is a few feet away now, two of the hounds beside him. Marin is beside me, her blue fur against my skirts. Goran inclines his head slightly. "You spoke before of your love for flowers. I thought you might enjoy seeing one, even if it is frozen like that. It is still colorful, after a sort."

I swallow again and look back at it. "It's beautiful." I drop back on my heels, snow crunches. "Maybe more beautiful." I stand, and glance back at him, and then the flower. *A flower, in the deep of winter.* "Thank you, Goran." He stiffens slightly, nodding. I turn toward him, my hand rubbing Marin's head beside me, glove still clutched in my other hand. "Thank you for showing me. It is lovely." I tilt my head, look up toward the trees, and there is silence for a moment. I swallow, and glance back at him, pull on my glove. "What do you do out here, alone every day?"

His eyes flicker to mine, and away, out into the trees, and I can't read them anymore, can rarely read them anyway. "There is always something to do."

I tilt my head, and I still can't tell what is in his eyes. "Do you enjoy it? The doing out here, alone?"

He nods too sharply, his gaze still out in the woods. "Va. I chose this life."

I tighten my lips. "But that doesn't mean that you enjoy it. We chose this life, but half the time, I think we would rather be anywhere but here."

"You could go back." He isn't looking at me, eyes still on the trees.

I shake my head, and my eyes flicker back to the frozen flower, stuck in place, the orange petals half wilted beneath the ice, frozen in another season and not this one. "Nie. We can't. Not for another five years."

"Five years?" I glance up, and he is looking at me, a question on his face as it was in his words. "What could bind you all to this world for five years?" His eyes are on mine.

My throat bobs. I look away, toward the sky. There is smoke rising, out where his cabin must be. I swallow again. *Has Yore not told him? Why would he not have? It has been months.* I swallow again and shake my head. "We are paying a debt. Pakem's, not Yore's... exactly. And our cregf offered to let us pay it by spending five years out here, to settle the place. He wants it to be claimed in his name and I don't think there was anyone else that he could get to go. Everyone else had roots in the village, family there. So we came to settle the debt."

His eyes narrow slightly, as if trying to understand. "With Alvea's leg, was there not another way? This is not the country for her." His voice is careful.

I swallow and look down again. There is a cedar branch, brushing my skirts. "He said the other option was sending Yore to the front lines in the war in the south."

He breathes out, harshly, running a hand down his arm. "I did not realize it was that strong a cause that brought you out here." He looks out, toward the woods again. "I knew it was related to Yore though. He carries himself like a man under a weight."

I look up sharply. "You think he blames himself?"

He looks down, glancing at me. "Have you given him reason not to? He brought you out here. And Alvea. This is not a world for her, with that leg. If she were to slip..." He shakes his head. "I would blame myself, in his shoes. I would blame myself for bringing you out here. I would curse myself every day that you had to stay here because of me."

I shake my head, sharply. "Alvea is fine. She rarely does anything outside, and she never complains of her leg or this place."

He glances at me again, and his eyes say something that his mouth doesn't. His eyes shift, face unreadable again beneath his beard. "Yore said you venture in the forest sometimes." He turns, starting back toward the cottage.

I nod, and look away, off into the trees. He is stepping, moving to the side, the hounds following him. My eyes flicker back to the flower, frozen, stuck on the branches. "Va." I shake my head. "But that is nothing new to you. I met you that way, more than once. I am perfectly fine at finding my way out here now." I move after him, snow half crunching beneath my boots.

His eyes flick back to mine, steps slowing for a second. "But have you asked Yore or anyone about walking in the woods, about doing it the right way, or are you just wandering?"

I glance at him sharply, my eyes tearing from the flower behind us. I frown. "I walk safely. I follow my tracks, like you said. And I don't 'wander' anywhere anymore."

His lips curl down. "That is only a small amount safer. What if dark comes? What do you look for? How do you stay alive if you are caught in the cold? What if the snow is frozen, or there is none? Do you know how to tell if a cabin is nearby? What do you do if you are truly lost?"

I blink, and my heart tightens. I look down. "Yore... Yore never mentioned any of that. He just told me not to go far from the cabin."

His head is shaking, eyes on the trees again. "I don't think he imagines that you walk as far as you do. You should ask him more about the woods." He steps past the trees, the hounds following him.

I move slowly after him, snow packed where we walked before, coming out this way. *There are other ways then following your tracks to return home?* "You know how to tell if a cabin is near?"

He pauses, and glances back at me, still half walking, the hounds moving around him. "Look up." I glance up, and there is the smoke, trailing above the trees. *His cabin. Of course. I knew that. But only halfway.* He strides forward. "And you may also look for cut trees. Most folks do not cut trees far from their own cabins. They'll cut the closer ones."

He steps back through the trees, and there is his cabin, beneath the smoke that is trailing toward the blue of the sky. I swallow, and glance at him. *He is about to go inside. I rarely get to talk with him, not like this.* He steps around the cabin, and I move after him. "Did you leave family, when you came out here?"

His gaze flickers to me, his eyes sharp, and he pauses, by the steps now. He stoops, brushing a hand over Crith's mangy brown coat. "Nie." My face falls. "They left."

I swallow hard. "How did they leave?"

He looks up, turning his eyes toward the trees. He flicks his gaze back toward me. "It is not what you are thinking," he says. He stands. "They got on a boat and sailed for the Fresh Isle, with hundreds of others who left things behind." He pauses, the steps now beneath his feet. "You should get back. They'll wonder what happened to you."

I laugh, and it's coarse and dry in my throat. My head nods, and I brush a hand along Marin's coat, and step away. *They won't miss me, not for hours yet. But I am dismissed just the same.* "Gooddawn, Goran. You should come to dinner again, when you like."

His eyes flicker toward me. "Or you all could come here."

My eyes widen. I pause. "You would have us here?"

He nods. "I could. If you all would not be uncomfortable coming here."

"We would not be." I frown and shake my head. "But Alvea couldn't make it, not after dark, not over the creek. Maybe once the days are longer, when it's a little less treacherous over the stream. She'll insist on coming then anyway." He half grins, and it brightens his eyes in a way that I've never seen. I smile back. "She'll want to see your part of the woods, once it is warmer."

He nods. "I only ask that you give me warning. I am not a man to be surprised." The smile turns wry beneath his beard.

I smile, and step backward, toward the trees. "We will plan on doing that then, when it is warmer. But you should come before then. I'll make a stew. Or roast vegetables."

He shrugs. "It is good, either way. I will bring the roast." I nod, and step backward, into the trees.

The snow packs beneath my shoes, still too high, and it clips the top of my boots when I do not step carefully. *I do not understand. What would drive a man to come out here alone?* My brow knits, and I step around the bough of an evergreen. *Why did he not go with them? Praise be that he didn't. But why didn't he? He could have gone across the sea. I have gone to the end of the world, for my family, but his left him and went over the sea without him. Why did he not go?*

I shake my head. *I would not go to the ends of the world. I did not even come here for mine. I came here because I did not have a choice.* My face warms, and my heart is tight in my chest., choking. *Does family stick close, any family? Mine is trying to tear itself apart, bit by bit, and has, ever since mamé walked out the door and never came back in, leaving no trace, no word but with a neighbor woman.*

A branch snaps, off in the quiet of the forest. My head whips up, and there is a shape in the trees.

The stag. He is huge, his head is up and his eyes are on me, sharp, foot frozen half in the air. His antlers rise to the branches of the trees above him, and his coat is thick, beautiful, strange, lit with the sun through the trees behind him, gold among snow. He is lifting his head. He snorts, one quick sound, and he is gone, bounding through the trunks of the trees and around boulders, steps sure, even in the ice of the last few days. *The stag. Yore would thrill to see him. Would he shoot him, that great of a beast? Or would he leave him be? I don't know. Would he shoot a beast like that for the prize of it, or leave it be for the mere chance of seeing it again someday, of knowing that you might come across it in the forest again, perhaps amid summer's light, when the world is again green, the way that Elnial made it?*

The stag is still out there, running through the first of the long months. I smile, and move down the path, back toward home, toward the cottage that will be quiet, Alvea spinning the wheel, and Yore gone in the cold and the shed.

Chapter XIX

My eyes are heavy, puffy. I yawn, my mouth stretching too wide, and rub my hands up my arms. *It's cold this morning.* My eyes flicker across the room. Alvea's bed is empty, the blankets thrown back. I frown. *She is up early.* I plant my feet on the floor, and pull my stockings on, fumbling with them. I yawn again, and grip my dress, pulling it over my nightdress.

My legs are stiff. I throw them over the edge of the floor and start down the ladder. Steam is curling through the air, from somewhere. I drop to the floor and turn, and there is a pot, on the stove, barely boiling, throwing steam upward. My eyes flicker around the room. *Alvea isn't in here.* I frown, and glance at the rack. Her shawl is still there, hanging from the hook.

I step forward and shove my feet into my boots and turn toward the stove. The buckets are gone. *I can't get water without the buckets.* My hands fumble with my shawl, and I jerk it over my shoulders and frown. *Alvea must have wanted water. Yore will have taken them.* I grip the doorknob, pulling it open. The air whips at my face, throwing my shawl back over my shoulders. It stings my skin, burning on my face. I grimace, shuffling. *It's too cold, bitterly cold this morning.*

My eyes flicker downward. Something dark is in the middle of the creek, bobbing in the wind. *A bucket.* I swallow, and step forward, my stomach tightening. There is another bucket, a little down from it. And something is moving, low, on the ice, scraping against it. My heart stops in my chest. *A figure. A person.*

I leap off the porch, and my feet skid on ice, throwing my steps sideways. The person on the ice moves again, and my heart sinks further, dropping into my stomach. *No. Alvea. Not Alvea.* I push forward, and am down the bank, slipping down the slope and my feet are skidding again. Water curls up my legs, sinking into my boots in the broken ice. I grip her shoulders. She is barely moving, and her skin pale, too pale, and she is muttering something under her breath, words only half audible. I slip my hands under her arms and jerk. She barely budges, water slapping around the hole gaping in the ice, gurgling in the creek. I jerk again, and she isn't moving, still in the ice.

My heart thuds in my chest, her hands fumbling with her dress, trying to grip, and her skin is icy, cold, too cold. I swallow hard. *No no no no no.* "YORE!" My voice cuts in my throat, and she is shaking, quivering, coughing, no longer grabbing at the ice. "YORE!" My throat burns. I jerk again, and she slides a little out of the stream, onto the bank, water everywhere, coating everything and ice grinds into my leg. My hands are stiffening, hard with the cold, and I can't feel them on her arms any more. I drop down, and wrap my arms around her waist, and pull. I grunt. Her body barely moves, water soaking through my sleeves, frigid. My joints are slow. I gasp, sliding against the ice. "Alvea?" She is just shaking, muttering. "Alvea! You have to use your legs. Listen to me. Try to stand. Alvea! Alvea, you have to use your legs." She mutters, her legs scraping against the ice, and it's not working. *I can't get her up, can't help her.*

A sob chokes in my throat. *I can't get her up alone. She's too heavy.* "YORE!"

There is movement, along the stream and Yore is beside me, his eyes wide, wild. He stoops, pulling her from my arms and he is lifting her. "What did you do?" His voice is sharp, eyes flashing.

I shake my head, stumbling; my eyes burn, arms shaking. "I found her there. She was in the creek, Yore. She was in the creek, just floating on the ice..." I point, useless. He is moving toward the hut, not paying attention to me, carrying her up the slope. He steps up the porch before I am beside it, shoving the door open with his shoulder, and he is inside. I step in behind him and slam the door shut.

"Get blankets." He nods toward the ladder, shifting her weight in his arms, and his eyes move upward. I bolt back toward his room, skirts slapping and wrapping around my numb legs, boots squishing with each step. I jerk a blanket off the shelf, and spin, back through the doorway. Yore is kneeling on the floor, Alvea in his arms, and water is pooling around both of them. I drop to the floor beside him, knees heavy on the floor and reach the blanket out toward them.

He snatches it from me, his eyes flickering toward mine. "You need to get her out of these clothes."

I freeze, my throat tightens. "How?" My teeth chatter.

He stands and is gone, moving toward the ladder. "Figure it out, Oanéka!" He grips the ladder, and is hauling himself up, gone.

I turn, my eyes flickering down. Alvea moans, softly, a shudder running through her, and her fingers move, gripping at nothing. She is pale, her face almost blue. I shake my head. *I don't know what to do. My hands are numb and her garments are heavy, wet.*

I grip the buttons on the side of her dress, and slip them through, one by one and my fingers fumble, awkward, stiff. I swallow hard, and my teeth rattle against each other. Steps tread the floor behind me, and fabric hits the floor. I glance down, fingers still working, still fumbling. *One of my night-dresses. He must have thought it was hers.* I swallow, and lift her arm, sliding it through her sleeve. It sticks, fabric clinging to her skin. I swallow hard. "Yore?" I pull her arm from the sleeve. It slaps the floor, like a fish, limp, fluid.

There is a shuffled step behind me. "What? Is she changed?" *Changed?*

My throat tightens. I shake my head. "Nie." I slip her other arm out, the skin clinging again, wet, frozen. It thuds to the floor, limp, slapping the wood. I grimace. *I should have been more careful.* "She's going to get sick." I purse my lips, sliding the dress down. "This won't be enough. Changing her won't be enough, Yore."

He growls, a step hitting behind me. "You think I don't know that?" There are steps behind me, pacing toward the kitchen, and they tread back again, loud, hard.

I swallow again, lift the dry gown over her head. Her hair clings to it, pulling, dragging against the fabric. I grimace. *Cold.* I slide her arm into her sleeve, and it drags against it, not sliding in like it should, limp, cold. *Wet.* I shake my head, pull her arm through, slowly, carefully, my older sister. "What are we going to do? Yore?" His steps are pacing, toward the kitchen his shoulders are stiff, hunched. "What are we going to do?"

He stops, and his shoulders tighten, hands fisting. "We are going to get her warmed up."

That will not be enough. None of this will be. We are going to lose her. He doesn't know how to tend sickness, and neither do I. I swallow hard, and stand, gathering her wet garments into my hands. "I am done." He spins sharply on his heels and is across the floor in a moment, kneeling beside her. He slides his hands under her legs and behind her back, lifting, and turns back toward the ladder his room. He pauses by the ladder, kicking his door open. I purse my lips. "What are you doing? Where are you going?"

He lowers her onto the bed and shifts, pulling the blankets up over her. "I can't carry her up the ladder, not like this." *But this is his room. His bed. Where will he sleep?* I look down at her. Her face is ashen, hair spread across his pillow, soaked, dark. *We will worry about him later.* He glances at me and looks away. "I'm going to make some broth." He moves past me, into the room beyond.

I spin, jogging after him. "Broth?"

He stops, sharply, and spins, eyes snapping to mine. "Va. Broth. When she wakes, she'll want it, and there is nothing else to do for now."

I shake my head. "When? Yore, if we don't get her warmed up, she may not wake up. We need to do something else."

His eyes snap to mine, narrowing. "Then what would you have me do, wise woman?! What do you want done? What else is there to do? I don't know what to do for this!"

I shake my head. My eyes burn. "I..." I shake my head again. "I don't know. You dealt with calli that fell in the lake in winter once, didn't you? What did you do for them?"

His lips curl. "You want me to treat our sister like a half-drowned calli?" He shakes his head, but his eyes are shifting, flickering back and forth. *He thought of something.* He steps to the side. "They were never unconscious. We'd hold them down in a tub of lightly warm water, just their head afloat for a few minutes to get their warmth back, then dry them off." His eyes flicker to the front door, and he ducks through the doorframe, gone out into the cold.

I glance back at the doorway to his room. *She'll be cold. We need to warm her up now, while he figures it out.* I move back into Yore's room, and drop onto the bed beside her, pulling her against me. She is shivering, her leg curled awkwardly beside her, and she is muttering, muttering low in her throat, words that I don't understand. *Curse it. Curse the water, and the ice, and her stubborn head. And curse the wagon that crushed her leg like that. She should never have received that leg, never have gone out for that water this morning, never have come here like this.*

Why did she not wake me? Why didn't she call to me before going out?

The front door creaks open, and shuts, steps tapping on the floor and it creaks. There is silence, but for the sound of her breathing, shallow, low. *Yore went for more water. He must have. He'll try the water, to get her warm. He's going to try it.* My throat is tight, and Alvea is shaking on the bed, her hair soaking my shoulder, my skirts cold, half-frozen against my ankles, against the soaking boots on the side of the bed.

Chapter XX

Yore lifts Alvea from the floor. I set a blanket over his arms, over her, tucking it in beneath her legs. He turns, her head bumping against his shoulder, a towel over her newly soaked hair and she's not shaking, not shivering violently anymore. I lift my damp nightgown from the floor. It's soaked, dripping onto the puddles already on the floor. It's thin and flimsy against my water-pruned skin. *Goran was right. We aren't made for this place. We aren't made for any of this. Alvea fell through. We aren't made for this, not for this broken place.*

I drop the nightgown over a chair and plant my foot on a towel on the floor. It's mostly soaked, water darkening over half of it. I press my foot, drag it through the puddles of water around the small tub. *She stopped shivering. She'll be alright. She'll be alright.* I still my foot on the towel. *What more is there to do? What more can we do for her? She's warmed up, dry. But she's still not conscious. Still too pale. She never woke at all, while she was in that water, while we tried warming her up. What more can we do, should we have done?*

"Oanéka." My head snaps up, and Yore is in the doorway, his brows creased. "What are you doing?" he says, a brow lifting at me.

I shake my head and bend over, scrub at the water on the floor. “Cleaning up.”

He grunts, stepping forward. “I’m going to do the calli. Go change your dress.”

My head shoots up. “Calli now?”

He pauses, hand gripping the doorknob. “What else would you like me to do?” He turns. “Stand there and stare at her?” His hand tightens. “I didn’t finish the calli this morning before you called me. I’m going to do them now. You can watch her, after you change out of that dress. Go change.”

My eyes flicker down. My sleeves are rolled up, water soaked into them making the fabric dark. Water soaked into the front of my skirts; water soaked through the hem against my ankles pressed against the floor. *This is my second dress of the day.*

He steps out the door, and pulling it shut behind him. I grimace. *Just watch her? There has to be more to do.* I drop to my knees, and look up, toward the ceiling. *Broth is already cooking for when she wakes. She’ll wake soon and she’ll be hungry. She’ll be alright.* I grip my skirts and stand. *The tub needs to be emptied, still. Wet clothes need to be hung until they can be washed, later. After she wakes. After she is awake again.*

* * * * * * * * *

Alvea shifts, her hair spilling across the pillow. I lean forward, my fingers fumble at my needlework. Her eyes are flickering open, face tight. She frowns. Her eyes flicker toward me, and they squint, unfocused. "...Oanéka..?" Her voice is hoarse, low, raspy.

I laugh and sit forward, pressing my hip against the bed from my chair. "Vea."

She coughs, her body shaking, and her face is flushed now, cheeks too pink. "How did I get inside? Did you... did you carry me...?" She looks around, as if trying to make sense of something.

I shake my head, set my needlework on the chair beside my hip. "Nie. Yore did. How do you feel? Are you cold? Do you need anything?"

She coughs again, her body curling. *It is thick, damp. Horrible.* She grimaces, glancing at me. "I'm fine. I'll be well in a minute. Just... let me catch my breath." She presses a hand against her chest, her breaths rising and falling too fast.

I shake my head, my heart drops into my stomach. "Nie. You are resting."

Her eyes snap to mine. They are too bright, fever bright, her cheeks flushed. "Nie. I'm not. This isn't even my bed. I'm going to make dinner, and you cannot..." her voice trails off, a cough cutting through her chest. She shakes her head. "I'm going to get up."

I grip my skirts, twist my fingers into them. "Alvea," my heart thuds in my chest, I lower my voice, soften it, "you need to rest today. You can get up tomorrow, if you feel well. I'll get you dinner in a minute."

Her eyes widen, the flush on her cheeks brightening. "Dinner? I've been out all day?" Her eyes swim. "This is ridiculous. I'm not going to be—" a cough rips through her body. She chokes, turning her head away, her body shaking. She stills, and her throat bobs. "I'm not staying in bed,

Oanéka. I'm not going to be an invalid. I'll be up in a minute and do the laundry. It's laundry day, isn't it? I'll do that."

Laundry day? That was yesterday. We did the laundry, together. I shake my head. "We already did it. Don't worry."

Her eyes snap to mine. "Don't tell me what I should worry with, Oanéka. And don't do my chores for me. I can do them myself."

I shake my head. "But Alvea..."

Her eyes flash, snapping to mine. "Don't! I don't want your help. I can manage perfectly well on my own."

My eyes burn. I shake my head. "Alvea. You did the clothes, yesterday."

Her face pales, eyes widening. Her hand is trembling on the quilt. "Yesterday?" Her throat bobs again. "That's not possible. Don't tease me. Yesterday, Goran was over, or Pevi was here... or..." She presses her eyes shut, her hands trembling harder. Her skin is pale around her flushed cheeks, too white. She shakes her head. "Go out. I need to think. Go out please, for a minute."

I shake my head. "You need to eat. It's been—"

"Don't instruct me!" Her eyes fly open, snapping to me. "I've taken care of things my whole life, managed things and I don't need someone telling me how to do it now. Please leave!"

My eyes burn. I grip my skirts, hands fumbling, fumbling. "Nie. I'm not leaving you. You need to eat while you are awake, please..."

She chokes on a cry, and tears burst down her cheeks. "Leave me alone. I need to figure this out! Leave me be!" She tucks her face against her hands, her shoulders shaking.

There are steps, and Yore is in the doorway. His eyes flash, narrowing on me. "Stop troubling her. Get out!" He is stepping forward into the room, moving toward her bed. I stumble to my feet, and my throat is tight, my face damp. I dart through the doorway.

Yore's voice hums in the other room, and then Alvea's snaps back, sharp, troubled. He growls something, and there is silence, and Yore's heavy footsteps. He steps past me, grabbing his hat, and he is gone into the outdoors.

I shake my head, throat burning. *She doesn't need to be alone. She just woke up. She should eat, needs to eat something. It's been more than a day and she's eaten nothing.* The broth is still steaming on the stove, untouched, and the loaf of bread is beside it, torn, on the countertop. My stomach is tight, my hands clenched on my skirts. I turn, toward the kitchen, and there is nothing in the room, just silence and the soft sound of sobs from Alvea's room.

I cannot remember the last time I heard her cry, not like this.

Chapter XXI

Yore steps through the door, cold air brushing into the room. He jerks it shut. I shiver, and lift the needle, pressing it through the fabric again. My hands are awkward, stiff. Yore glances at me. "What are you doing?" I lift the tiny needlework frame, eyes still on it. His brows crease. "You might rest."

I scowl, shake my head. "It's only a few hours past dinner time. I'm not going to sleep, not for hours." I pluck the needle through again, pale orange thread making the line of a sun-rimmed edge of the water. I grimace. *I might have chosen something other than water.*

He shakes his head, stepping into the loo, and the door slams shut behind him, closed.

My hand fumbles the needle, and there is blood, a tiny pearl of it on my fingertip, swelling, slipping down my skin. I swallow and brush it against the back of my hand. It won't stain anything there. There is a sound—a voice, soft and hurt—from the other room. Steps thud on the floor, and Yore curses. I stand. *I thought Alvea was sleeping again.*

There is a heavy step, and another curse from Yore. "Oanéka!" His voice is a shout, and my blood chills. I bolt through the doorway. Yore is beside Alvea's bed, his hand against her cheek, and her face is flushed, eyes shut. Her cheeks are flushed, bright red, skin still paler than before. *Fever. No. Please no. I thought it had left when it did not set in earlier, when she woke.* Yore's eyes flicker to me. "We need to..." His voice trails off, and his eyes are lost, searching for something that isn't there, isn't here.

He doesn't know what to do for fever. We've never had it, not any, not since Pakem left. I don't know what to do. My heart drops into the pit of my stomach, and it churns, twisting. I lick my lips. *What did they do for fevers? What was done? What would the healing man do?* I swallow hard. "Cold rags?"

The light dims in his eyes, and he nods, his hands tightening at his sides. "You get those. I'll get..." His voice trails off again. He swears, loudly, his hands balling tighter into fists. "This is foolish. What the stars are we supposed to do for this? For any of this?" His eyes are on the floor, shoulders slumped forward. My stomach churns. *I don't know what to do. We never had fevers. There has to be something we should do, something we can do about this, to mend it, to help her, to get her well again.*

I lick my lips again and press a hand against the wall. "Is there not anyone in the area who would know something?" He swears again, turning away from me. *There is only one person within a day's walk. Goran. He said Goran knew how to deal with blued skin, with Pevi's hands. He said he knew exactly what he was doing then. Perhaps...* I lift my eyes. "You said Goran knew a little about Pevi's hands?"

Yore doesn't look at me, his eyes frozen on the far wall. "That was only hands."

I shake my head. "But he may know more. You said it seemed like he knew something of the healer's craft and he is the only hope we have." I am spinning, move through the doorway. "I'm going for him." I snatch my shawl from the rack. "You get damp rags on her head, Yore. Keep them there." I shove my feet into my boots, and yank my coat from the wrack.

I jerk the door open, and am out, the cold sharp on my skin, and night is falling. The shadows are already long on the ground, and the ice crunches beneath my feet, each step sliding. I jump over the stream, and my foot skids, twisting. I grit my teeth and scramble up the bank, snow scraping against my fingers. I move around a tree and the air is colder within the shadows. Wind brushes through my shawl, throwing it sideways. I bolt around the trees, and I'm past them, and there is the clearing with no evergreen, only the black skeletons of the trees against the fading sky. My breaths burn in my throat, air too sharp, too cold, and it burns in my lungs. I turn, feet skidding on the snow. There is the glow of his cabin, barely a thin line in the darkness, warm.

I bolt up the path, pound up the steps. Hounds bark inside, muffled through the walls and I lift my hand, slam it against the door. The knock thuds, dull, small, barely there. *Let him be there. Let him hear me.*

"Who is it?" Goran's voice is sharp, low, and the hounds are barking louder. *Of course he is there. It is night.*

I twist my fingers in my shawl. "It's Oanéka." My breaths are heavy, wracking my chest. My voice sounds torn, hoarse. "Goran, please open the door."

The door swings open, and there is blood on a shirt, right before my eyes. *His shirt.* His brows are lowered, face dangerously unimpressed. "You shouldn't be out in the forest this late." He shifts, stepping to the side.

I move past him, into the room and shake my head, my hands twist tighter against each other. My chest heaves. "Goran. Alvea fell through the ice." All emotion is gone from his face. He is stepping backward, moving across the room. He pauses by a table, his hand lifting something. I swallow hard.

There is meat across the table, a half-skinned deer, by the shape. *He said something about leaving meat to freeze in the trees and cutting it down later.* The hounds are beside the fireplace, eyes all watching Goran, heads alert. He stoops, jerking his boots on, and stands sharply, spinning toward me. He snatches his coat from the wall, his gaze flickering back to me. "You ran?" I nod and tighten my arms. My skin is slick beneath my dress, sweat hot and cold and the room feels too warm. His eyes find mine. "How long ago did she fall, just now?"

I shake my head. "Nie. She fell in yesterday morning."

His jaw clicks shut, eyes snapping to mine. "Yesterday?" His voice is sharper, his eyes matching them. "What was done?" I open my mouth, and he shakes his head. He is steps past me, pulling the door open. "Go. You can tell me on the way." I move by him, and he is past me, down the stairs before the door has even slammed shut.

I move after him, pumping my arms, clutching at the shawl over my shoulders, and it is falling, slipping from them. I suck in a breath, chest heaving again. *His strides are too long, more than twice mine.* "She—" I suck in another breath, dodging a tree branch, "she went to get water, and fell through the ice." I puff out another breath, and stumble over a stone. The air burns at my lungs, bites at my nose and throat. Goran checks his movement for a second, glancing at me.

He is off again, strides long. I force my lips to form words. “We got her into dry clothes, and we tried to get her warmed up. She was shaking so much. And then, she was fine yesterday when she woke. She was alert, barely would rest and stay down.” He glances at me, and I can’t tell what is on his face in the shadows. *How does he know where to go in the darkness? The is no moonlight, only the faint glow of the snow through the shadows of the trees.* I stumble again. Water gleams in the midnight ahead, down where the hole is cut in the ice, swirling in the darkness.

Goran steps across the ice-coated stream in two strides, and he is already moving up the slope to the hut. I hop onto a rock, and then another. My knees strike the far bank, and I grimace, scrambling up. Steps pound on the porch. I bolt, up to the stairs, and the door swings open, light for a moment, and Yore’s voice is speaking.

“Goran.” His voice is tight. “Praise be.” I step through the door, and press it shut behind me as my brother speaks. My breaths heave. “Do you know anything of fever? I...”

Goran pulls his coat off, his eyes snapping back to me. “What have you already done?”

I tighten my arms over my chest and open my mouth. Yore’s voice cuts out. “We put her in lightly warm water and got her dried off and changed yesterday. Today, I tried to get her to eat some, and there are cold cloths on her forehead now, to keep the fever at bay.” Yore’s hands twist together. “She would only eat a little broth.”

Goran nods. “Do you keep chamomile in the house?”

I blink, and step forward, breaths heavy. “Va. We have some.”

He nods at me, pulling a pouch from his coat pocket. “Fetch some and heat a pot of water. Do you have any coriander?" I nod my head, stepping around the stove. I lift the pot and set the water on again. Goran's steps are light on the floor. "Get some. I want to give her an infusion." He steps through the doorway, back into Yore's room. *An infusion of coriander and chamomile?*

Yore glances at me, and nods, his eyes scanning me over. He nods again, and is stepping across the room, following Goran into the room beyond.

I turn to the pot. *It will be a spell before it is hot enough for herbs. There is nothing to do again but wait, just wait.* I twist my hands together. *What can I do?* Voices murmur together, back in the other room, and I can't make out what they are saying, and then Goran's voice cuts out sharp. Yore steps through the doorway again, his sleeves lopsided on his arms, one rolled up, one down and his hair a mess. His eyes flicker to me, and away again. "He is going to just keep changing out the cloths to keep her cool." His voice is flat. *Defeated. He doesn't think she's going to make it. Oh stars no.*

My heart is in my stomach again, and everything is too slow. *Not Alvea. Not her. She's strong and capable, always capable. She's always made it through things, her head up, everything orderly and together. Not Alvea.* Yore steps, toward nothing, and there is a ripple in the water of the pot, slow and small with each step across the room.

Chapter XXII

The threads are blurred, lines mixing together and there is blood on my fingertip, again, a dark spot swelling. Yore's voice mixes with Goran's at the back of the room, tones hushed and low, like the rumbles of a coming storm. I shake my head, press the heels of my hands against my eyes. Stars burst across them for a moment, and my head pulses, pounds. There is the creak of a board, somewhere off in the other room, and the word 'sleep' echoes.

I am falling, forward. I jerk my head up, and darkness jumps back, from the edges of my vision. I swallow hard and shake my head. *I'm not going to be weak, not going to fall asleep. I can stay up as long as they do. I can keep watch too.* I push the needle through again, and the color is in the wrong place, brown where yellow should be. *Curse it.* I pull it back through, pressing gently on the tip. My finger stings.

Yore and Goran are standing across the room, at the edge of my vision. I look up sharply. *I didn't see them come in.* Night is heavy on the room, and everything is too quick, everything but the snapping of the fire and the tones of their voices, low, rolling. Goran is half facing me, his back against the counter, and his mouth moving with words I can't focus on. His hair has come half out of the tight band that it is usually up in, and his face looks pale, in spite of the tan of his skin. There are dark rings beneath his eyes, but his back is straight, his eyes alert. *I think. Mine are blurry.* I shake my head. His eyes flicker to me for barely a moment, and back to Yore.

"Are you sure?" he says, to Yore and not to me.

Yore nods, his back to me. "I want it. I'm awake enough. I'm not going to rest yet even if I tried." Yore turns toward me, and his arms are folded over his chest. "Go to bed, Oanéka. There is no point in you sitting here."

My eyes smart; I jerk my head back. "I'm going to keep watch. She's my sister too."

Yore's jaw tightens sharply, his brows lowering. "Go to bed, Oanéka." My lips purse. His eyes narrow further, his arms tightening over his chest. He nods his head toward the ladder. "Just go. You've done everything you could possibly do to help here tonight."

I press my lips tighter against each other and drop the embroidery cloth against my lap. "I could just as well stay up with her while you rest, Yore."

His eyes darken, jaw clenching. "Get to bed."

My lips tremble. I stand, slowly, my hands tight on the embroidery cloth. "That's not a reason, Yore. You just keep saying the same thing over and over like it answers anything, but it's not an answer."

His jaw juts out, for just a second, eyes flashing. "Well maybe I don't have a reason!" His shoulders are tense, his eyes flashing, and he isn't just talking about sleep anymore.

I swallow hard, and my throat is thick, eyes smarting. I shake my head, and step past him. I grip the ladder rungs, dragging my body upward. My arms fumble with the top of it, clumsy, and the world blurs. My cheeks are damp, and everything is too big and too small at once, like a peg that will never fit, an oil lamp that sputters and goes out even though the oil is there, a wick that won't be trimmed, or a world without light.

* * * * * * * * *

"Oanéka." The voice is coming from far away, somewhere beyond darkness. *Something isn't right... something was wrong.* Darkness slips off; sleep slips off. *Alvea is sick*. I press my arms under me, force my eyes open. *Someone was calling*. I clear my throat, and the air feels chilled where the blankets have slipped from my shoulders.

"Va?" I call. My voice is hoarse, thick, and groggy.

"I need you to come down, when you are dressed." Goran. *He is still here.* There is light, barely, coming from the opening where above the ladder. *I slept too long.* I slip my feet from the bed, and shiver, bare skin slapping the floor.

I press my hands against my eyes. "I'm coming." My voice sounds wrong, thick and slow. My limbs are heavy, head heavy, there are strands of hair in my face, of curled red loose from my braid. I step into the corner and press my back against it. My fingers grip the hem of my night gown. I drag it over my head, tossing it to my chest on the floor. I grab my dress and pull it over my head, dragging it down. My teeth clatter together, shivers racing up my spine.

I stoop—my hands fumble with my stockings. *Curse it. I should be downstairs already.*

I kneel on the floor, and throw my legs over, stepping onto the ladder. I slide down it, step off, flick my gaze toward the door in front of me, Yore's door. *It's closed.* My eyes are blurry, hair still in my face. Goran is by the stove, stirring something. He lifts a mug, chugging the contents. The air smells strange, smells off. I wrinkle my nose, head pounding. He sets the cup down, his eyes flickering to me, and the dark rings are darker than before beneath them. His eyes flicker up to my hair, for just a moment, and back to my face.

My face warms. *My hair is still a wreck. I'd forgotten again.* He clears his throat. "I need you to make breakfast." He is speaking softly, his voice low.

I flick my gaze around the room. There is a blanket, over a chair, and the pot from last night is on the countertop, a ladle jutting from it, clean, but out. I glance back at him. "Where is Yore?" I should ask about Alvea. My heart shudders. *I don't want to know. I can make breakfast, tend things without asking. I don't want to know, not yet.*

Goran's eyes are studying me, watching. The edge of his brow lifts, like it does when he is questioning something he has decided, prodding it. He moves away from the counter. "Yore is doing the calli. And Alvea is resting."

My eyes widen. "She is?" He nods. "Has her fever changed at all?" My voice is low, hoarse.

He grabs his boots. "Her fever turned just after dawn."

I press my hands sharply against each other. "Oh stars. Praise be to Elnial!" *Her fever turned. She's alright, for now. She's alright.* My throat is tight. I lift my eyes to his, and I don't know what I'm looking for, scanning for. "Do you think she...? Will she... is she out of danger?"

His jaw works for a second, his eyes scanning over me. His features tighten. "Nie. But she's doing better. I think she'll be alright now, if she continues to rest, and not overdo anything." He is turning away toward the door, his steps heavier than before. My eyes dart to his feet. His boots are already on.

I step up to the stove, lift the empty water bucket. He is pulling the door open, stepping out into the cold. I lift my head. "Be safe." He doesn't look back at me, gone through the door. I grab the other bucket and move across the floor, stockings slapping against the wood. The house is silent, Alvea's loom is too still in the corner. *But she is alright now, safe for the time being, praise be.* I shove my feet into my boots, grab my shawl, my steps are soft against the floor. I jerk the door open, stepping out, and the clouds are low in the sky beyond the roof of the porch. Goran is moving through the last of the trees in sight, his form like a fluid shadow, moving through the trees. He's gone.

I step off the porch; the ground crunches beneath my feet, slick and sharp. Frozen, where water spilt, drug out of the stream with her body. I move down the slope, slowly, the buckets tapping against my shins. The ground crackles with each step, crunching loudly. I step down the bank. My heart drops. *The ice is uncut. I'll need to find the axe to open it this morning.*

I drop the buckets, and turn back toward the shed, steps crunching beneath my feet. The clouds are still low, rolling across the sky like foam.

* * * * * * * * *

Yore's back is tight, his hands white on the knot he is tying and untying on the rope. I drop the spoon into the pot of stew, steam puffing around my hands.

Something whistles outside, high and clear, almost a scream. *A storm.* I swallow hard, and my eyes flicker toward him. He glances at the window, pulling the knot free, his shoulders still stiff, tense. I step forward. "I'm going to check on Alvea again." *He doesn't need to know what I am doing. But I've told him already.* I step around the counter, move toward the doorway beside the ladder.

I step through the doorway, press the door open. The form on the bed is sitting up, her legs thrown over the side of the bed, her head in her hands.

My steps slow. "Alvea?"

She glances up at me, sharply, and her face is pale, just pale beneath the tangled mass of dark hair. I swallow, step forward toward her side. She shakes her head. "It's alright, Néka. I'm just stretching for a minute." She grimaces, shifting her weight to the side. *Like her leg is troubling her.*

I blink, hard. "You are alright? You don't feel poorly still?"

She shakes her head, shifting her hands on her legs. "I am only tired and a little sore." A shadow passes over the door. I turn, and Yore's shoulder is just leaving the doorway, gone again from sight. I frown. *Does he not want to see her?* Alvea's face is paler, her eyes staring at the empty doorway. She folds her hands neatly on her lap, her eyes still on the doorway. "He wasn't up all night, was he?"

I shake my head. "I don't know. I went upstairs. Do you want to eat?" I turn toward the kitchen.

Her eyes flicker to me again, and they are shadowed, but not fever bright anymore. She shakes her head. "Nie. I think I will just rest for a little while. I'll be alright then, after that. Like I was after I strained my leg a few years ago. I'll be alright in just a little bit."

I press my lips together, and step through the doorway. "Do you want some broth? Or tea?" I glance at her. She is half nodding, her back straighter than it was before. I turn back. *She wants a little food. That is a good sign.* I step through the door, flick my eyes across the room. Yore is by the door, pulling his coat over his arm. I frown. "What are you doing?"

He grips the doorknob, coat on and open. "Hauling more water to the calli. There is a storm nearly here." He doesn't look at me.

I lick my lips lift a mug from the shelf. "She wants a little food."

He glances back at me, nodding. "Good. Help her to the loo while I am gone. It may be good for her to move a little." He pulls the door open, stepping out into the cold.

I lift the ladle, dumping the broth into the mug. It swirls, swishing against the sides. I turn back toward Yore's room. Alvea is leaning against the pillows, her good leg folded beneath her. I step forward, reach the mug out toward her. She grabs it and takes a small sip. A smile slips across her face. "Thank you, Oanéka. It tastes wonderful." She takes another sip, her face a little brighter.

I shake my head. "Yore and Goran mostly made it. Yore thinks it wise for you to come with me to the loo while he's outside. Are you up for it?"

She is nods, taking another sip. "I heard him. We'll go in a minute." She sips again, long and slow. Her face is not flushed, her eyes not bright like it was last night. *And she is eating again. She is going to be alright. She is going to be okay.*

Chapter XXIII

Alvea's steps shuffle on the floor, one step, one drag, one step, one drag. She coughs, hard, her body bending forward with the force of it. *I hadn't noticed her doing that before. But she was asleep earlier.* Her hair is pulled back, a simple twist at the base of her neck, loose and low, and nothing like what she normally does. She leans against the counter, not looking at me. Her hand trembles. *She shouldn't be up yet. She needs to sit down.*

Her lips pale, and tremble, eyes flickering for a moment. "I..." She takes a step away from the counter. Her shoulders tremble, violently, and she is falling forward, toward the floor.

I gasp, and catch her shoulders, too late, and they slip through my fingers, striking my knee. Her body hits the ground, thuds against it hard. My breath chokes in my throat, and I can't breathe, can't drag in air. I pull her into my arms, shake her. "Alvea?! Alvea, listen to me..." Her body is still, in my lap. Her breaths are heaving in her chest, her face death white, and there is perspiration, slick across her forehead, cheeks flushed. I choke, eyes scanning. *I can't carry her to the bed. Oh stars. She should never have gotten up. This is my fault. Every bit of it is my fault. I should never have told her to get up. She should never have gotten up. I should have made her stay in bed, should have made it to her quicker.*

The door creaks open. There is a swear. It slams shut, steps pounding the floor and Yore's knees crash to the ground beside me. "What happened?" It's a growl, and he is lifting her off of me, picking her up.

I can't breathe. "She went to the loo," my throat is tight, and my voice is too thick, "and then she fell. She just dropped. I should have told her to sit down, Yore. She hit her shoulder... I should have helped her... But she looked so fine until..."

His fingers fumble with her neck, and he swears again. Her chest is rising and falling. *She is breathing. Why is he checking that.* His eyes flicker to mine, shifting her weight in his arms. "Go for Goran." His voice is hoarse, thick.

I jump to my feet, and bolt for the rack. I shove my feet into my boots, and spin. I jerk the door open, cold air blasting my skin, and I'm down the porch, across the snow. There is a new coat over the ground, and the air is sharp, flakes swirling in it, churning in the wind. They cut at my face, air ripping at my lungs. I jump over the ice-covered stream, rock and another rock, up the slope and the trees close in, snowflakes falling everywhere, coating everything, and the wind is soft for only a moment. Flakes whirl, my eyes burn, snow against them. There is a white cloud of falling snow between the branches of the trees. Wind rips across them, and they sway. I duck, and bolt up the path, and my legs are heavy, the snow deepening around my feet where the wind is throwing it.

The air cuts sharper, it howls through the trees. I bolt around an evergreen, and there is the glade where there are no more, only the white cloud of swirling flakes through the barren trunks. The air is heavy with snow, I stumble, moving through trunks. The path winds up, through the trees and I can't see the house through the swirling snow, white in the air. I can't see anything but the trees beside me, the snow ahead. I bolt up the path. Light cuts through the swirl, and there is the cabin, a dark shape in the dusk and snow, swirling in the mist.

I pound up the porch, and my fists collide with the door. The wind cuts, and my skirts swirl about my legs, twist around them.

The door jerks open. Goran is there, his eyes widen and his face pales for a moment. "Get inside." His hand wraps around my arm, jerking me in. I stumble, and the door slams shut, whiteness gone from everywhere. Everywhere but the edge of my vision. *It is caked to my eyelashes.*

I shake my head, wrap my arms around myself. "Goran..." My voice is strong, but my hands are stiff beneath my arms. "Alvea woke up, and she went to the loo. And then she passed out, Goran. She just collapsed. I didn't know what to do. Please. Can you come help her?" He turns away and he is grabbing his coat, jerking it on like he did before, when I came for him only two days ago.

I shiver. My hands are stiff, ears burning, face burning. My teeth knock against each other, once. *We need to go, need to get back.* He turns back to me, pulling gloves down over his hands. "Go sit down, Oanéka. Keep an eye on the hounds until I get back."

I shake my head. "What? N-no. I need to—"

He shakes his head, sharply. "I'll do what I can, but you cannot go back out in the storm. You are half frozen."

My throat tightens, eyes burn, I'm shaking, arms shaking. "Nie. I'm-m not staying here. My s-sister is dying, Goran. Please."

He runs a hand down his shoulder, his eyes flick to mine, meet them. He shakes his head. "Oanéka. You didn't bring your gloves, hat, coat or even a shawl, and there is a storm rolling in. If you go out there again like that, you won't even make it back to the cabin. I'll be carrying you halfway, and we'll be fighting for your life next." He turns, lifting the lantern from the peg where it sits. He turns the wick up, and the light glows brighter, flashing through the room.

I swallow hard. "Goran." I shake my head. "I cannot s-stay here. She is my sister. I w-watched her leg heal, when she was a child and broke it and I was barely old enough to understand. She's w-watched me through every sickness I've ever-r had in my entire life. Not mamé. Not pakem. She did. I can't s-stay here and just think-k. She's my big sister. Please. She's my sister." My voice cracks.

He doesn't look at me, his eyes on the fireplace across the room.

He moves, and his gaze flicks over to me, his eyes meeting mine. "I'm sorry, Oanéka. You are damp and shivering. You'll have the same thing she does as soon as you have reached the trail, and then you'll be frozen before we reach your cabin."

I swallow hard, and my eyes flick to the door. *He's right. And I'm slowing him up. He should have left already.* My body is trembling, my hand burning with cold, and my legs are numb beneath my skirts. *There is nothing for it. I can't go.* My hair is damp, the strands falling into my face as the white slips from them into droplets of water on my shoulders and neck. *I should have grabbed my things. I should have taken the time to get a coat, to grab my gloves before I came.*

My hands burn, aching, aching and I can't fight back the swimming of my eyes. I look down, and nod. My throat is too tight, and my hands shake beneath my arms. "G-go. she needs help. Go."

His feet are stepping toward the door, hand gripping the lantern. "Watch the fire and keep the hounds busy. One of us will be back as soon as we can, and we'll bring you back home. Keep an eye on the fire." The door opens, and shuts, and I am alone, in his hut. *Alvea is dying and I'm just here, watching hounds that do not need to be watched, warming my careless hands because I could not be bothered to grab a wrap before I came.* I bite my cheek.

My eyes burn. I shake my hands. Pain is crackling through them, fingers curled and I can't get the pain out of them. I lift my eyes to the ceiling, pain not fading in my hands, growing and they are awkward strange. "Elnial." My voice is clogged, thick, eyes on the ceiling. "Please." *I don't know what I'm asking, what to say. I should have done better at home. I should never have let her get up that soon. I should have grabbed my wrap, grabbed my gloves.*

And now there is nothing to do. I don't know what to pray. Elnial, save us.

The hounds stir, Gyaith watching me with only half her attention. I rub my hands together, and pain spikes from them, burning up my arm, colliding in my head. I grimace, tears swirling in my eyes, and press them together, out from me. The hounds are on the floor, watching nothing, and I cannot use my hands, can't bend my fingers, or even remove the pain.

Chapter XXIV

I press my hand against Marin's head.

The fur across my lap is thick, some creature I don't recognize, brown and just the hide now of an animal that Goran brought down. *A bear? A deer? It is too thick to be a deer, too thick to be a stag, like the one in the forest.*

I shake my head, press my hand against Marin's head again. Her mouth is shut, tongue not lolling out like it normally does when she is being petted. I purse my lips, turn toward the kitchen. *There is nothing to be done. The hounds have water. I don't know what or when they are fed. The fire is burning, stoked high. It has been all night.* I press my hands together.

Marin whines, and Crith barks, a single, high note. I whip my head toward the front of the house. The door swings open, cold air jutting into the room.

I jump up, fur sliding from my lap. Goran is standing in the doorway, white is coating the side of his body, sharp in the light of the morning. He presses the door shut, and my eyes widen, flickering to the window. "Is it storming out?" *My voice is too high. How did he come back in a storm? How did I not hear it? Would he risk it?*

He is shaking his head, not looking up. "Nie. An evergreen dumped its snow on my head." He drags a hand across his scalp, knocking piles of snow from it.

I suck in a breath. *Of course there isn't a storm.* My eyes flicker to the window again. My face warms. I look down. I lick my lips and press my hands together. "How is Alvea?" My voice sticks in my throat.

He pulls his coat from his shoulders, dumping it over a chair beside the door, and snow puffs off it. "Her fever turned again. She's resting." He moves away from the door. *There is something is his hands, wadded there, fabric.* He turns toward me, setting the thing on the table. "Your gloves are wrapped in it. You can go home as soon as you have a mind to. Breakfast is waiting there."

I blink. *Food. I hadn't thought of eating.* My stomach growls, faintly, gurgling beneath my skin. Gyaith whines. She presses her head against my stomach, fur soft against my hands. My face warms. I look down. Hair slides into my face, red, puffy, half out of my braid now. I nod. "Thank you, Goran." I lift my head. My eyes meet his. He looks tired, dark rings beneath his eyes again. I swallow. "I know where she would be without your help. Thank you."

His face darkens, a little, eyes flickering toward the window. *Does he blush?* "It was nothing. Go back. Make sure she stays warm, and get food. Yore hasn't eaten either." He turns, moving toward Crith. The hound lifts his head, his snout pressing against Goran's large palm. The hound's tail wags. I turn away, snatch the fabric from the table. *It's my cloak.*

I swallow. "Thank you, Goran. Will you come check on her, another day?"

He nods. "Just send Yore if you need anything." *Don't come yourself.* I swallow, and turn, moving toward the door. *He didn't mean that. Only I forgot my cloak, a problem and a solution, in sending Yore instead.* I shake my head, jerk my gloves on my hands.

I sling the cloak about my shoulders and step out the door glancing back. Goran is kneeling across the room, the hounds gentle around him, nudging him. I jerk the door shut and turn. *Alvea's fever broke.* I step down the porch. *Oh, praise be! She is alright, for another day.* I bolt beneath a tree, the boughs strangely bare of snow in the wood.

* * * * * * * * *

Yore looks up at me as I step into the room, my shawl is still clutched in my hands. There are dark circles under his eyes, matching Goran's, and his shoulders are hunched forward, almost sagging. He stands, slowly. "I'll go check the calli." I set my shawl down over the chair. He is stepping past me, moving through the doorframe. *Will he not stay in the same room with me? He didn't even greet me. Maybe he blames me for what happened, for this.* There is the sound of the door, opening and closing. I purse my lips.

Alvea is still, on the bed, only her head and shoulders visible beneath the blankets. Her dark hair is braided again, a simple plait, too loose, and strands of it have come free, sticking out around her face. Her skin is pale, far too pale. There is a bruise, dark on the side of her cheek. *Her head must have hit the floor. I didn't catch her fast enough, not even for that. I knew her shoulder hit, her legs hit, but I didn't realize her head did too.*

I shake my head. *She is still alive. I did not think she would even be that, through all of last night. She made it through the night again. That is hopeful, for now, for tomorrow.* My eyes flicker toward the door. *If Yore will ever look at me again, ever speak to me.*

I drop against the chair, folding my hands over my knees. *I should make food or clean the floor. It is muddy again, needs to be cleaned.* My eyes are heavy, and my arms are stiff, tired.

* * * * * * * * *

Steam is curling up from the pot, twisting into the air. I lift my hand, tossing dried carrots into the boiling, churning water. I turn away, and lift another handful, tossing the shriveled pieces in after the others.

"Oanéka." Alvea's voice. It's hoarse, coming from the back room. My head lightens. I bolt around the counter, rubbing my sweaty, steam dampened hands against my apron skirt, and move through the doorway. Alvea is lying flat on her bed, the same as she was when I was in here before, but her arms are above the blanket, her eyes just barely open. She licks her lips, the movement tiny. "Could you bring me some water?"

I nod, turn through the doorway. I lift a cup from the shelf, plunging it into the water below. She woke. She woke again. I scrape the droplets of water off the bottom of the cup onto the bucket lip. My hand shakes. I turn back, across the room, step through the doorway. Alvea adjusts a little, pressing herself up, and her face looks paler. I step beside her and hold out the cup. She reaches out, taking it from me. A tremor runs up her arm. She brings it slowly to her lips, taking a long sip, and I wait for her to hand the cup back. *She is weak, so weak.* My heart tightens.

Her hand offers me the cup, and she sinks back into the pillow. "I am sorry for causing you so much trouble," she says. Her eyes are soft, her voice a breath.

My heart sinks in my chest. "Alvea." I fumble with the half-empty cup, wrap my hands around it. "It's not trouble, it's never trouble. You are my sister. I only wish I could do it better, like you do—"

Her eyes snap to mine. "I know that it's... it's an inconvenience. Don't pretend, just for me, Oanéka. I appreciate it, but I already know." She coughs, the sound ripping from her throat. "I know it's an inconvenience, at best. Let me acknowledge it."

I shake my head, swallow hard. "I'm not pretending. You are not an inconvenience, not now, not ever. I am happy to take care of you for as long as you need it, because you are my sister." My throat is tight. "We take care of each other. That's what we all do. That is what family is supposed to do. I'm not lying to you—I know that lying to you never works if I had tried. You are not trouble. You are my sister, and I want you to be well. And I want to take care of you. You would be caring for me, if I was in your place. It's not an inconvenience. I want to see you well, and until then, I want to do all that I can for you, like you would do for us."

A tear slips down her cheek, rolling into her dark hair and it's gone. She swallows, her throat bobbing. "What happens, if I don't get well? What happens if I don't ever get well from this one? Will you stick around forever to take care of your weak, crippled sister?"

My throat tightens. I swallow hard, my eyes burning. "You'll get well, Alvea. Yore and Goran are both seeing to that. You aren't crippled and you will get well. You won't always be sick." I shake my head, press my hand against her arm, and it's pathetic, the only comfort I know. "Now you'll rest for a week, and then you'll be okay. You will be."

Her lips purse, her eyes turning away from mine. "My leg hasn't been right since I fell through." My heart sinks, hand tightening on her arm. She turns her eyes back toward mine, and there are tears swimming in her eyes. "I only ever went out there once, into the forest. What if I don't ever get to go out there again? Will you care for me, while I sit there, and waste away the years, a burden on you, a burden on Yore?"

I swallow hard, shake my head. "We'll figure it out. We can beat this, Alvea. You'll beat this, and you are not a burden and never have been." I shake my head, wrap my arms around myself. "I don't know where we would be without you. You have held everything together for years." My eyes burn. A tear slips down her cheek, and she turns her head away, down, hiding behind her hair like I do. I swallow hard. *What can I do? What can I say?* I turn toward the door. "I'll bring you dinner. Rest. We will figure this out, together, a day at a time." I step through the door and my heart shudders, eyes burning. *Her leg. Not her leg. Not her leg.* My eyes swirl. *I'm going to cry. She worked so hard, so hard to heal, so hard for it to work. I should never have let her get up. I should have been the one who went out to get water that morning. She should never have gone for that water.*

What will happen if her leg doesn't heal? What will Yore do when he finds out, that it is messed up again? He wouldn't look me in the eye earlier. He won't speak to me after this, after he knows what happened. My hands grip the counter, and they are white against it. *Why didn't I wake up when she did that morning? She wasn't supposed to haul water. It was too icy. Too cold. Why didn't I tell her to just stay sitting down? She should never have gotten up so soon. She knew better than to go out there. She never wanted to haul it before, not since the weather turned so cold. Why did she go?*

Maybe she is wrong. Maybe it's alright, just stiff from all the cold, from falling. I swallow, and it catches in my throat, a lump that won't go away. *What if she never recovers? Will she forgive herself?*

There is a hoarse cough from the other room. Silence creeps in, marked only by the crackling of the fire in the stove. My eyes burn, and I can't press it back. *Curse the poor eyesight of the driver, all those years ago, who did not see the child run in front of his horse until it was too late. She should never have had to wrestle through life with that leg. This should never have been her battle to fight.*

Chapter XXV

Yore steps out of the loo, his hands damp, his hair a tussled wreck. There are shadows, thick under his eyes still, no better than yesterday or the day before. He pauses by the room that should be his and looks in for a moment. Turning, he moves passed it, over toward the stove. He pauses by the counter, glancing at me. "Has she been awake at all?"

I nod, stirring the spoon in the stew. "Va." My hand shakes a little. "She was awake earlier, twice. She ate a little."

He nods, running a hand through his hair. "Did she mention her leg at all?"

My heart freezes, hand pauses on the spoon. "Why are you asking?"

His eyes flicker toward mine for a moment, but I turn my back toward him. He is shifting on the floorboards, the sound of them creaking beneath his feet, looking at me. "It seemed to be paining her, when she was unconscious before. She was favoring it strangely in her sleep. Did she mention it?"

I look away, press my hands against the counter beside the stove; they turn white, gripping it. *He'll never speak to me again after this. If he blames me for it, then he'll never speak to me again.* I pull a breath through my teeth. My heart drops in my chest. "She said...that it hasn't been working well since she fell through."

Yore is silent. No swearing. No shouting. Only silence, that stretches out. *And may stretch out forever.* My throat tightens. *He's not going to speak to me again after this. It has started already. He'll never speak to me again. He'll walk out that door, and it will be worse than when he never came home, worse than when he spent all his days with others bars.* I turn back to him. His head is down, shoulders sagging, a weight on them. "I should never have brought you two out here." His voice is hoarse, barely a breath.

I grip my skirts. "What? You didn't know this would happen., Yore."

His shoulders tense, hands turning white against the counter. "Didn't I?" His eyes snap up, meeting mine. "I knew this place would never be good for her, Oanéka. I knew it would crush your heart, and I took you away from everything you've ever loved anyway, even from flowers, because I couldn't keep my head on straight for two nights in a row, couldn't make myself do everything I knew I should be doing. It was folly. I should never have brought you out here, should never have crossed that border. I should have fought back before the cregf. There must have another way to pay off that debt, other than this or the front. Neither of you are made for this place."

I shake my head, hard. "Yore, you didn't know this would happen." *Goran was right. He blames himself. I thought he would blame me, but he still blames himself.* "This isn't your fault."

His eyes flash, his head snapping up. "Then whose fault is it?!"

"Pakem's!" My voice is too loud, echoing in the room.

He shakes his head, his lips tightening beneath his beard. "I was to take care of his debts. It was my job. My duty. And I failed. All that I did was add to them at my own leisure. That makes it my fault. That's why the cregf sent us out here. Because I failed, Oanéka. That is the truth of it. I failed and wasted my time and efforts and now you are here. Here with all this nothing, all this emptiness. That is on me. This is my fault. I didn't fight back. Didn't even try to do what I know I should, and instead, I just left you two alone for months and months, and then came back only to drag you both into this frozen wasteland. That's on me."

I shake my head; tears blur my vision. "Yore—"

"Yore, Oanéka." A voice cuts from the room beyond, low, hoarse. *We woke Alvea.* Yore's shoulders tighten, his head bowing, shaking. I swallow, and nod toward the back room. He turns, moving slowly toward it, and I step in behind him. Alvea is sitting up, only a little, her hair chaos, the braid all loose now. But her eyes calm, watching.

She glances at me and then him. "This wasn't your fault, Yore." Her voice is hoarse. His jaw tightens. Alvea shakes her head. "Yore..." Her voice is soft, low from sickness, from coughing, and it sounds weak, not like it normal sounds. "The cregf sent you here because he is a self-seeking man." She folds her hands carefully in her lap. "He did not need the labor debt paid. He took it from you because he could, even though it wasn't yours to pay. He saw a chance for more power at no cost to him, and he took it. He would have stood his ground if you had tried to fight him. It is a greedy man who takes that which he does not need from those who cannot afford to pay it. This was never yours to pay."

Yore's mouth twists. "If I didn't pay that debt, then who would? I'm Pakem's son, Alvea. It is my job. I should have paid it off, instead of roaming the wild places every night, and wasting my days."

Her lips tighten. "Pakem should have paid it off. It was his debt, and his alone from his love of games and seeds. The fault is on him, and the cregf and shop owners who never cut him off. Not on you." She shakes her head again, a tiny, slow movement, and folds her hands again. "You are responsible for your time, but not for the way he spent his."

His head snaps up, throwing his hands into the air. "What makes it not my fault? I was tasked with paying it off, years ago after he left, and I didn't, Alvea. I barely paid off a cent, too busy squandering, and too cowardly to fight, to try after the sentence was given." His fists clench, head shaking. "They told me this would happen. They told me, but I didn't listen, I saved my own skin, at the risk of yours."

I shake my head. "If you had asked us, we would have told you to, to choose this."

His eyes snap to mine. "No, you would not have. It's not worth it, not for this. I saw it in your eyes, when I told you. It's not worth it, for any of this."

Alvea straightens, pushing herself up on the bed, her eyes seeking his. "Yes. It is. It is worth every second of this, Yore." He glances at her, and away, his jaw tightening. She holds her gaze. "Your life should never have been taken for Pakem's debt. He didn't die. He left. He should be the one paying that debt through working, through years out here or wherever he is. He should be the one working to try and make up for every coin he spent that he never had to spend. Not you. This is his debt still, and we are paying for it together. That is not how it should be, but that is how it is, and that is on the cregf. Not on you. Never on you." She coughs, short and dry, her eyes watering.

His jaw twists, eyes on the floor. He shakes his head. I shake mine step forward. "And my garden isn't your fault either, for the same reason. I can grow more flowers here, someday."

Alvea shakes her head, her eyes flickering to mine. They flicker away again. "It wouldn't have been his either way. Your garden was leaving before this."

My eyes narrow, on her. "What?"

Yore looks at me, and his eyes avoid mine, skirting away. He shoves his hand deep into his trouser pocket. "The cregf wanted that bit of land to build a shed, for his hogs in the winter. He had already bought it, before we left."

My eyes widen. *What?* I shake my head, purse my lips. "He wanted it for his hogs?" He nods, slowly. My jaw tightens. "You two knew about this?"

He nods, his head still stooped. "I didn't want to tell you what was becoming of it. He told me he was taking possession of it the same day he gave me the choice. I knew it would hurt, so I didn't say anything."

A scoff rips from my throat. "Hurt? You didn't take it from me, he did! That mucus blossom!" My nails grate into my skin.

Yore's head shoots up, his eyes startled. "You aren't mad at me?"

I narrow my eyes. "You? Did you order us to leave home for a debt that wasn't yours? Did you lie to our faces about wishing that you could wipe out the debt but were totally unable to? Did you compliment me every day about my garden and then plan behind my back to put a shed over it?

For hogs? I could have been planning a new garden for the last two counts instead of pining for the old one!"

Alvea laughs, a soft, shaking noise. I blink at her, my breaths heaving. A cough rips from her throat, and she presses a hand to her chest, still laughing, breaths wracking. "You are mad at the cregf for complimenting your garden?" She is still coughing, grinning through it.

I stare at her, throwing my hands into the air. "He wanted to build a shed over it!"

Yore drops against the wall, his shoulders limp, head down, the fight gone. "Neither of you blame me for bringing you out here?"

Alvea shakes her head, pressing a hand against her chest. She coughs, her eyes seeking his. "Would you blame a horse for not being able to pull a cart that you filled? Would you blame a horse for the weight that was placed on the cart? I would have wished that you would have asked ut before, but this was the choice that should have been made." Her eyes seek his. He doesn't lift them, eyes on the floor. She shifts on the bed, her face paling. "Yore—" he doesn't look up, "—this was never your burden. You took it up, when it wasn't yours to carry. We should have left Longspur long before the cregf gave you a choice that was none. And each of us would have made the same choice you did, a thousand times. We would have chosen your life over any years out here. Five is a meager amount of time to spent to save a life."

Yore's eyes lift to hers, and the pain in them hits me full in the chest. *He's been carrying this for years, carrying all of this for years.* I can't breathe. My eyes burn. He shakes his head. "I would have hated either of you, if you'd made me leave that village for you. I would have hated every day that you'd spent on this world. I would not have forgiven you for it, not as long as we were here. I would have held that against you, Alvea, against either of you."

A tear slides down her cheek, and another, and another. She leans forward, reaching her hand out toward him. He steps forward, slowly, eyes down. Her hands grip his wrist. "Yore." Her voice is torn, thick. "You weren't the one that made us leave."

His shoulders shake, and his hand covering his eyes. "But I chose this place. You should never have had this work, and your leg..." His voice chokes.

Alvea purses her lips and her face grays. Her throat bobs, and her voice is softer, hand gripping his. "I knew better than to go out for water. But I did it anyway. That is my fault, and no one else's. I fell in that creek, because I was stubborn." Yore's eyes do not meet hers. Her lips tighten. "Yore." Her voice is solid, firm, though it is still so quiet. His eyes lift to hers, barely. She shakes her head. "You cannot carry this. I made my choice. Just like the leg was my fault, back home when we were young. This time it is mine again. You cannot blame yourself for this. You cannot carry this burden."

He shakes his head. "I should have said something to you. I saw that you were up, and Oanéka was not, and I should have said something to you, before then."

Her head shakes, sharply, hand tightening on his wrist. "No, Yore. That is foolish. You can't go around blaming yourself like that. You had no reason to think I would go out there on a morning like that and try something that foolhardy."

I look down, my throat burns. A cough rips through Alvea's chest. She doubles over, her face turning sheet white, lips a strange pink against her skin. She shakes her head, lifting her body from being doubled over with the force of it. My eyes widen, and hers lift to mine, calm, steady. "Did you thank Goran for me?"

Yore nods, reluctantly. "Va. But you can thank him again yourself. He will come by again, tomorrow or the next day."

Alvea nods, lifting her eyes to his. "Thank you, Yore, for saving my life. Thank you for dragging me from the creek."

He shakes his head. "I didn't do anything but lift you. Goran knew how to tend you, and Oanéka found you both times. She was already pulling you from the stream and she ran for Goran." *Found her, but before that, I left her. I didn't rise.*

Alvea's eyes flicker to mine and soften. She shakes her head. "Oanéka..." Her voice is more hoarse now.

I shake my head, press my arms around myself. "Don't, Alvea. Don't. That was my job. I didn't stop you, didn't catch you, and I know its foolish but I should have done something, and I didn't. I didn't even warn you how dangerous the ice around the stream was. I knew, and I didn't say anything." I turn toward the door. "The stew is going to burn."

"Oanéka." Her voice calls. I move across the kitchen, shove the spoon into the pot. Voices murmur behind me, and I can't make out what they are saying.

Steps thud against the floor behind me, and a hand brushes my shoulder. "Oanéka." Yore's voice. "Look at me." His fingers tug, just barely on my shoulder.

I shake my head, and lift the spoon, tap it against the pot. "Leave it, Yore. This one is my fault, and I will carry it."

The hand on my shoulder pulls roughly, spinning me. "Oanéka." His voice is sharp, his brows furrowed, low. I lift my eyes to his. "How is this your fault? How?"

I knock his hand off my shoulder. "How could this not be, Yore? How could it not be?" He looks at me, just looks, and he doesn't understand what I am saying. I puff out a breath, and spin back toward the pot, toward the spoon. "That was my job, Yore. That was my job, and I was lying in bed, while she was doing my task. I heard her get up, and I did nothing. I didn't make her sit when she tried to do too much, didn't tell you no when you said she should rise. Didn't even help when she was fighting for her life against fever. All I did was sit and wait, sit and wait for her to die with idle hands. She fell in because I was lazy, Yore." My eyes are burning. "She fell because I am lazy. Nothing has changed. And it was the same back home. I hid outside, hid in the garden because life hurt and let her do everything."

A hand grips my shoulder again. "Look at me." His voice is tight, thick. I turn, slowly, and my eyes are swimming. His find mine, earnest, careful, and the grief in them is heavier than I can take. I look down, press my hands hard against my skirts. "Oanéka—" his voice is careful, low, "—we all have made mistakes since we have been out here. We've all struggled and failed. But you are not at fault for not waking up when she made up her mind to do something. She is your older sister. You are not responsible for her. You were asleep, Oanéka. This is not your fault. It will not do to run around taking blame for things." I shake my head, and I don't know what I'm shaking it at. "Oanéka." His finger bumps my chin, lifting it. I look up, meet his eyes again. He shakes his head, eyes flickering across mine. "If you hadn't gone for Goran, both those times, she would have died. You saved her life. Twice. This burden is not yours. You are not lazy. You did more than all you could for her. Learn from the long past, but don't take up things that are not yours."

A tear slips down my cheek. "They are not yours either." I choke on a laugh, shake my head. "We all been doing that, haven't we, Yorevali?"

He lifts a brow, hand still resting on my shoulder, half there. "Doing what?"

I brush my hand across my cheek, swipe at the tears. "Hobbling along, carrying things and thinking that we are the only one to carry them, and the only one who lifts the weight of what has happened, of what will happen later. We all think we are carrying a burden that we alone are allowed to carry, but there are a hundred other people all carrying the weight of the same thing, carrying the same burden as us. It's foolish. And yet we don't know because all we can see is the weight we are lifting and our own griefs, our own selfishness. We don't speak to know that we are not the only one carrying it." I shake my head, swipe at my face again, and my hand comes away damp, tears smeared across my cheek. "We all think that we are so brave, so selfless lifting these things that we are too selfish to see don't even need to be carried alone."

A smile quirks at his mouth, his eyes finding mine again. He half laughs. "We do, don't we?" He laughs, dry and sad. His hand squeezes my shoulder. "Let's not do this again. We can talk better next time. We could have talked better this time."

I laugh and poke his ribs with my finger. He grunts, and scowls at me, his eyes half laughing beneath the fake scowl. I grin, and he is laughing, and it's enough. *It's enough, for today.*

I turn back to the pot, and lift the spoon, steam clinging to my skin as Yore's steps tap toward the door, lighter than before, a little lighter.

Chapter XXVI

Alvea slips her feet over the side of the bed. I grip her blanket under my hands, waiting. *She needs to try on her own.* My heart is tight, breaths tight. *What if what happened last time happens again? What if she falls?*

She looks up at me, pressing a hand against the wall beside Yore's bed, and straightens. "Kitchen?" She breathes.

I shake my head. "Just around the room. We'll go to the kitchen later."

She purses her lips, lifts her chin and nods. Her face is pale, too pale. *But her eyes are alert.* She steps forward, hand still against the wall, and hobbles a step, more than I've ever seen her hobble. I wrap my fingers into my skirts. She steps forward again, and hops, half pulling her other leg along. *She moving though, she's up and moving. Elnial, please give her strength, please help her make it back to bed.*

She pauses by the door and looks at me, face pale, perspiration on her forehead. "I don't remember it ever feeling this far to the door before." She coughs, a half smile on her lips, but it's faint.

I purse my lips. "Do you want to just go back? We can try again tomorrow." She nods her head, moving toward the bed again, slowly, her other hand pressed against the wall now, and her back half stooped. She reaches the bed and grips it, a cough wracking through her body. She presses her hands hard against the mattress, head bending forward. Another cough wracks through her. "I didn't imagine Goran meant this when he said to beware of frozen water." She glances at me, a wry smile on her lips, more like Yore than her.

She drops back onto the bed, and looks up at me, her lips pressed and her face white.

* * * * * * * * *

Alvea's hand lifts, brushing the blanket that is wrapped around her back onto her shoulder. Her steps are staggering, uneven. *But they are better than they have been this week, the few times she has been up.* She lowers herself onto the chair. I release her arm, step back. She is rubbing her leg, her hands working slowly, pulling the blanket over her shoulders. I purse my lips. "Does it hurt more now?"

She pauses, glancing up at me. "It's not bad today." Her breaths are heaving, just from that walk, her face flushed, cheeks bright. She puffs out a breath, settling her hands on her lap, and her eyes flicker toward the one un-shuttered window. They are clouded. I turn away, back toward the rising bread. My steps tap the floor. I lift the towel, glance underneath it at the dough. *It is nearly risen enough. Only a few more minutes and it will be ready to stick in pans.* Alvea's hands shift on her lap. "Do you think Pevi will come back?"

I look up at her. *Pevi?* I shrug and set the towel down. *I'd nearly forgotten him.* I turn for the pans, reach up toward the shelf. "He seemed a social man." I glance over my shoulder. "He'll come back, once it is warmer, I would guess. If he doesn't go traveling again. We are the only lots around. There isn't anywhere else to go if he doesn't want to be alone."

Alvea shifts, shaking her head. "He said he wasn't traveling this year. He cannot get his new vocation if he isn't at the cabin for the next 24 turnings. That was the requirement."

I pause, set the pans down. "Oh." I lift the top one from the stack, set it to the side. It taps against the counter. "Then I imagine he'll come around a fair amount this year." Alvea nods, her eyes on the wall, vacant. I turn back toward the pans, lifting the next one.

A cough wracks her body and she stoops forward, pressing a hand hard against her chest. She sucks in a long breath, dropping back against the chair. Her face is flushed; her eyes move to mine. " 'A man who breathes well does not crave air,'" she says. She grins, a half-hearted thing, her hand still pressed beneath the blanket against her chest.

A laugh bursts from my throat, and I shake my head. "Does that make you an unwell man?"

She grins, dropping her hand. "I would make a good unwell man, wouldn't I? I could sit here, cough grimly at people and give them sage advice about how they should be doing things and shake my stick at them. Mavíkah would also have made a good unwell man, but don't ever tell her I said that."

I laugh. "You would make a great unwell man. But you haven't got a stick." I lift the towel and flicker my eyes across the room to her. She laughs. I grin, and shake my head. "If you can keep your hands off your weaving. I do not know any unwell men who weave half as much as you do." She laughs, breathy and short, her eyes bright. She smiles, dropping back against the chair. I set the towel over the bread again, and glance back at her. *She looks pensive. Maybe she is thinking about home, about Mavíkah and all the others.* "Do you miss home?"

She glances at me sharply. Her lips purse, for just a moment, and she lifts her head, nodding. "Va. Why are you asking?"

I shake my head. "It did not seem prudent to ask before. I was not sure how you would take it."

She looks down, hands fumbling with her embroidery. She nods. "Va. I miss the people, and the smells and sights..." She pauses, her eyes vacant, closed. "But I do not miss the whispers. I do not miss the remarks made behind hands, behind closed doors, the scowls, the words, the glances when they thought I couldn't see. I do not miss what was said after Korta pulled my strings and left me with the whispers of the village as though I was nothing, not worth anything. I do not miss the days that followed, do not miss the glances, the looks and the bitterness."

I lift a pan, set it aside. "He was a pig."

She shakes her head. "Nie. He wasn't. He was a selfish man. But not a complete pig. He knew how to use words, how to weave them, how to use the skills his mother taught him, how to speak, how to gift, how to make people feel like something, how to speak to anyone, to make them believe what you want them to believe." Her lips purse, eyes traveling to the window and beyond. "I was blind not to see it, you know. Not to see how much he hated the way I walked, not to see what he was beneath the smiles, beneath the grimaces when he thought I wasn't looking. I saw them. But

I ignored them. It was easier to believe him, when he said that he loved me."

I lift the cup of flour and scatter it across the counter space. "We all were blind."

She shakes her head, looking out toward the window. "Paun wasn't." I grimace. *Paun. Paun the grimy, old fisherman with a beard to his knees and pockets full of years.* Alvea looks over at me, her eyes wide, earnest. "He saw, Oanéka. He said he didn't trust that merchant. I didn't listen to him. It's funny," she lifts her eyes toward the ceiling, and there is something lost in her gaze, like mine, "I have always said, 'Those who live unwelcome everywhere see what everywhere truly is,' but when it came to it, for me, I did not listen to my own words. He was an unwelcome man. He saw people at their worst. And I didn't listen to him, though he had only ever been kind to me. I told him he was wrong, because I liked the attention. Because I liked how it felt when Korta said my name."

Paun? Kind? Paun with the missing teeth, the invasive words, unwelcome? Paun the critical, with his words of remorse from the edges of the docks, called to those who pass by. How could he have seen anything that we could not see? How could he have any better sight from the edges of the village where no one was? Outside of everything, by the water's edge? I frown and clear my throat. "I never understood why you and Yore spent so much time with him. He did not seem... wise to me. He did not seem all there anymore. His mind seemed to be somewhere else half the time." A shudder runs up my spine. I drop back against the counter's edge.

Her eyes flicker to mine. "His words held something honest and raw. Real and blunt. No one else in the village was like that, not after Pakem left. They all said things they didn't mean or pretended we weren't there and you could see it in their faces. You must have seen that." She picks up her weaving, hands slow under it. "There was no lace around his words, no frills. Just earnest words from a little old man with an ashen beard and eye alight with a million memories." She smiles, faintly.

I grimace. "An ashen beard that usually had something in it, and his eyes wandered when you talked to him... never focused on anything..." I shudder.

Her eyes flicker to me, watching. She shakes her head, turning away, back to the loom. "You thought too much of beauty back then, Oanéka. You still do. He was a good man. But you still don't see that, do you?"

I purse my lips. "I don't mean not to. He always..." I look down. "He always seemed to think that he could see right through me. It made my skin crawl. I didn't like it. Or his teeth." I shudder again. "I didn't care for the way he talked."

She laughs, shifting her fingers on her embroidery, and coughs, lightly. "He made you look at your faults, didn't he?" I flinch, and nod. She is laughing, short and breathy. "He did the same to me. But you know, when Korta left me, and the whole village was talking, and Korta was talking, and Yore was gone and you were out, tending the garden, Paun would sit with me, and he never said a word in judgement, though he told me, he told me not to trust Korta. He just sat with me, and when I cried, he poured me a cup of tea, took the wool from my hands, and spun it himself."

I look up, sharply. "Paun spun for you?" She nods, and my throat tightens. *Paun, that Paun? I never listened to his words, never listened for a moment when I was around him. They seemed like shadows in a bright world, like words ill-placed, dry morsels. I didn't want them, never wanted to hear them when he called to me, or when he asked me to sit on the dock with him.* I grimace. *He cared for my sister better than I did, during those days.*

Alvea's eyes are on the window, blank, staring. "I wonder if we will ever see him again. If he'll make it through the winter months. Window Blackshaw wasn't there this year to give him shelter in her back cabin." Her lips purse, and they tremble a little, eyes on the window where the white things swirl in the cold beyond.

I did not think of Paun in the winter, of what he did when the cold settled in in the years gone by. Widow Blackshaw has passed. There is no telling what became of the ugly, strange fisherman, when the cold set in, what he did. My throat is tight, eyes burning. *I never thought of him.*

Chapter XXVII

Goran drops into the seat beside Alvea, his movements fluid like always. His hands fold between his knees, eyes moving to glance at her, one look over her and then done. He moves his gaze to meet hers, stoic like he always seems to be. "You seem a little better."

She nods, fingers fumbling a little with the threads beneath them. "Va. I feel better." She coughs, belying her own words. His eyes stay on her, studious, cautious. She shakes her head, half raising her embroidery. "Except for this cough." Her voice is hoarse. She coughs again, straightening, pressing the needle through her work again. "I am well besides that. Thank you, Goran. I owe you a debt of thanks."

Goran shakes his head, standing slowly. "You owe me nothing. But get well. There is much of this place that you have yet to see."

She laughs, soft and breathy, and a smile twists at her lips, almost wry. "I appreciate your humor."

He lifts a brow, a smile quirking for only a moment at the edge of his lips and it's gone. "I was not being humorous."

Alvea's eyes flicker down, her head turning away. Her shoulders droop. I drop the garment from my hands into the basket of clean and soaked clothes. My fingers fumble with the next one, and she is speaking. "I do owe you. And you are kind." She pauses, her head tilting. Her eyes flicker to his again, meeting them. "Have you heard anything of Pevi Liklоré?"

Goran's head is shaking before she finishes. He moves away from the chair, standing. "I have not heard anything of him, but I did not expect to. He is too far away." He glances down at her. "Have you?"

She shaking her head, her eyes still on her work, focused. "Nie. But I hoped that someone would. It...." She shrugs again, and it is odd on her. "It doesn't seem good for him to be out there all alone all the time, with only that mule." Goran's eyes flicker to her, and they stay for a moment, calculating. His brow lifts.

He turns away, moving toward the door. "I can go check on him, if you are worried."

Alvea's head shoots up. "Nie!" She shakes her head furiously, her hands trembling. "Nie. There is no call for that. I am sure he is fine. He'll be fine up there." Goran grins, his face turned toward the door where she can't see. He glances down at me, and his eyes meet mine, his grin growing. I tuck back a smile, turn my head down toward the buckets of wash water and the clothes, all soaked.

Goran tilts his head, his smile stretched across his face, eyes still seeking out mine. "If you are certain." I bite back a snort, grip the soaked shirt tighter in the bucket.

"I'm certain." Alvea's voice is high.

Steps hit the floor, one after another, and the doorknob jiggles, across the room, Goran by it now, his hand upon it. "I am going to see if Yore needs help before supper." He jerks the door open, a faint smile still on his lips, then he is gone in the outdoors. A burst of wind swirls into the room. I shiver, lifting my head.

Alvea's eyes are on the wall across the room, unseeing, her hands paused on their work still. I lick my lips. "Alvea." Her eyes flicker to mine, fingers moving on the needlework. I wring the garment in my hands, twisting it. "Do you worry about Pevi Likloré?"

Her face flushes a little, and she shakes her head, sharply. "Nie." She looks up at the ceiling, lips pursing. "Well, only a little. He was on my mind, while I was sick. I just kept wondering about him, wondering if he was alright, if he would ever come back through. I kept seeing his bold, bright smile in his dark skin, his eyes with that soft smile, and wondering if he was alright." Her face is red now, bright red. She shakes her head, pressing the needle through, hard. "It's nothing."

I blink and twist the water out of the garment in my hands, and the liquid splatters against the water in the bucket below. *Alvea is blushing?* I set the garment down, sharply. *Alvea has not blushed since Korta came around. I look up at her.*

She is working, her fingers plucking hard at a stitch. She shakes her head, pulling at the string. "I will put him out of my mind. I do not want Yore or Goran going after him. They are right. It is too long a journey in the winter. Perhaps spring will bring him," she looks up, "or perhaps not. We will just have to see in time." She nods, sharply, her hands lifting her work again. She tilts her head back down, as though the thing were settled entirely forever, put away and done with. "We'll just wait to see if he comes back," she says. Her face is still pink, her cheeks flushed.

I look down, tuck my face behind my hair and a smile pulls at my lips. *She blushed again, about a man. Alvea and Pevi. She blushed, when speaking of him. Goran knew what he was doing when he teased her. He read her faster than I did on this.*

I glance at her, lift the dish rag from the water and wring it out, the water trickling into the bucket below. *I wonder how much they got to talk, when he was here, her and the man from the woods who came from nowhere and everywhere with a flashing smile and a quiet mind.*

* * * * * * * *

Goran's steps thud against his porch, off beyond the trees in the distance. I press my hand against the tree next to me. *What am I going to say to him, here again? Pastries are too small a thank you, for saving a life. We might have invited him over again, rather than just bringing him pastries.*

His eyes flicker up, and he half starts. He straightens. "Oanéka." He presses a hand against the post beside him. "What are you doing here?" Marin stiffens beside him, her head lifting.

I swallow, and step forward. *Just walk up to the porch.* I step forward, and nod toward the bundle. "I thought I'd bring you these. They just got out of the oven a few minutes ago so they are warm."

His eyebrow quirks. He doesn't reach out, doesn't take the bundle, though we've done this before. "I don't need you to thank me, Oanéka. You all have nothing to pay me back for."

I swallow again, and my throat is tight. "And we do have something to thank you for. You didn't have to do what you did, all that you did. And I brought you pastries before you saved Alvea's life."

His face slackens, and he doesn't look impressed. "After she claimed I saved yours." My heart sinks into my stomach. *I'd forgotten that.* He folds his arms over his chest, lifting a brow at me. "If we are to be friends, we can be friends. But none of this paying back and working to earn what is given. I will not accept that kind of friendship."

My arm drops back to my side, and I frown. *We have to thank him somehow.* "Don't you want the pastries?"

His eyes meet mine. "No."

I reach the bundle out again. "They are not a bribe. A thanks. Take them. It does not do to waste food out here, and I will not be taking them back with me." He doesn't move. My arm sags again. "Goran, I would have brought them to you anyway, if we had made them. I offer you my friendship and these pastries. Take them. If it offends you, I won't bring you anymore after this, but take them. I can't make any promises for Yore and Alvea but I'll stop thanking you like this if it makes you glad."

He laughs, the smile lighting up his face, and he moves, nodding back toward the door. "I'll take them, this time. Will you come in for a few minutes?"

I purse my lips, twist my fingers into my skirts. "I can't stay." I shake my head, press a curl back from my face. "I need to finish supper, back home."

He quirks a brow again, smile still half there at the edge of his beard. "Then I take it you were just offering me pastries without the friendship. Take them back when you go."

I scowl, lifting the bundle. "Goran. I worked all afternoon on those. And Yore and Alvea will be waiting on supper soon. I have to get back to finish it, or she will and overtax herself."

He looks at me and lifts his chin, stepping up onto the porch. "You could at least come in for a moment and greet Marin after walking all that way." That smile is quirked in his mustache.

I purse my lips, step onto the bottom step. The sky is beginning to fade, shadows long between the trees, where the ice of the last snow clings. *I don't want Alvea overdoing it. She's been doing so well.* I shake my head. "I can't, I left soup on and I don't want it to burn. But you should come back to the cottage. There is more than plenty and I would be glad if you came back. We all would." My face warms a little.

He glances at me, hand still on the door, and his head waivers. "Well enough."

A smile brushes my lips. I half turn toward the trees. "Then I will see you in a few minutes, unless you are coming over now? You could bring the hounds?"

His head shakes just barely, and my heart lifts a little. I have time to get things ready before he arrives. He nods toward the door. "I have a few things to tend before I come. I will see you soon. Thank you for the pastries." He nods toward the bundle in his hand, and I turn, and move up the path.

Chapter XXVIII

Alvea is leaning against her chair, her face pale, but flushed with a gentle glow. She runs her hand over the square of material in her lap, moving it toward the basket. "I've nearly finished enough for that blanket." I glance at her. *She must be speaking to me.* Goran and Yore are talking in the corner, their voices a murmur.

I glance at her loom. The blanket squares are stacked together, enough to prove her words, a mound of them, all the undyed wool of the calli. "What will you do with it?" I shift my hands on my skirts.

She shakes her head, shifting a little in her chair. "Throw it over Yore's bed, I suppose. No one will want to buy blankets in the spring, when he can go back to the village."

I nod and lean forward. "When do you think he'll be able to go back in the spring?"

She tilts her head, eyes trailing toward the fireplace. She half shakes her head. "Maybe the fifth month? I doubt it will be sooner than that, but it would be in time for Yore to bring back news of the beginning of the warm months down home."

A smile pulls at my lips. I look down. "I could have him bring me more seeds. I may have found a place the other day to place my garden, if the soil looks good beneath all the snow in the spring."

She grins, setting her needle work on her knees. "Did you? Then you will have to show me a little later on. Is it near the hut?"

I half grin and laugh. "Where else would it be? There are only trees and rocks everywhere else. I would like to know how they cleared the field around us, because there aren't any boulders in it like there are everywhere else."

She glances at Goran and Yore. "There is a chance Goran would know. You could ask him and see. He may have been here."

I shake my head. "He said the family that was here when he arrived was not the one that built it. I asked about it a week or two ago, and he said that the dwarves had been gone for years when he got here."

She frowns, her hands moving to lift her needlework. "Are you certain? They must have used an ox or the like. I believe that was the way they cleared land back home, wasn't it? I wonder how many families lived here before we arrived." She glances up at the rafters, eyes half wistful. A cough wracks through her body. She grimaces and straightens.

I purse my lips. "I'll put some tea on. It's getting later." I stand, and glance up. My eyes meet Yore's across the room. He lifts a brow in question, and I shake my head, turn toward the counter. "Would anyone care for some—" Something screams and the house shakes, trembling. The men are springing to their feet and Alvea's face is sheet-white, her eyes too wide, hands clenching the needlework. *Storm.* Her hand trembles, the house shaking, and the storm shrieks again, high and in pitches I don't know.

"Storm." Yore's voice is blanched, and he is by the window. *I never saw him move.* "A blizzard." He turns, and his eyes meet Goran's.

Goran is still, his posture stiff, his eyes wide, and they flicker to the window. His hands clench by his sides. "I didn't see any sign of it earlier." *I didn't think they would be this close together. Will they always be, this soon? It's too soon for another. How can there be one already?*

Yore nods, and his gaze turns back toward the one unshuttered window. "You'll stay with us, until it is passed." He glances at me. "I need to check the calli."

Goran's head is shaking, sharply. "Nie. Leave them. You did them for the night. They will keep until morning."

Alvea shifts in her chair, her eyes still too wide, but her chin is lifted now, hand steady. "He is right, Yore." Her face is too pale, and it cannot all be from the storm. She glances toward the window, her eyes still wide. "I did not imagine they would come up so fast. There was warning, before the last one came, was there not?"

Goran nods his head, his hands gripping his knees. He drops back into his chair, runs a hand down his beard. "Sometimes there is little warning. It is good that we were all inside for this one. Normally you can see the cloud coming in, but I saw nothing of this one when I came over." The room falls silent, and my hands shake. *Good? Fortunate. What happens if next time someone is outside, if they get caught? What if we end up like those back home who did not see the storms coming? I thought you could see them out here. They almost didn't last time, almost got caught. There will only be more storms, won't there? With the months creeping on and the heart of winter?*

They are all just staring, Alvea's hands limp on her weaving. *We can't all just sit here like this. I can't just sit here and listen to it.* I swallow and stand. "It's late. I'll go grab blankets, then." *Will Yore put Goran on his floor or in here by the fire? I don't know what the etiquette is for this, not when it is a friend and not a stranger.*

Yore shakes his head, stepping away from the window. "Nie. We won't turn in yet. It is barely past dinner time. We can recall poetry or sing for a while." He moves back to his chair, and something behind his eyes is already weaving, the same way Alvea's fabrics come together. I do not move for my chair. *They are all sitting. I am alone, standing. I don't know what to do. Are we all going to just sit here, and stare at the fire and listen to that terrible howling? I know nothing of poetry, and the storm is loud.* It shrieks again, and the house trembles with it. *Will it crush the walls, or knock the ceiling in? I've heard of storms doing that before.* I twist my hands into my skirts.

Yore tilts his head and sits up, sharply in his chair. "Sit down, Oanéka. There is no need to stand there like that." I grip the back of the chair, and my face flushes a little. I sit.

His voice curls upward, song strong, beautiful as it always is. *He is going to begin, at least. But how can he sing at a time like this? How can they just sit there?*

"I walked along the grove at night,

Stars among the trees, clouds among the northern mountains.

Silent days drifted by, dancing, and the clouds vanished, nothing more above the sky.

A call sounds in the darkness, a whisper in the shade,

And I drift among the trees where I do not belong.

The world has spat me back, but I will climb the mountains and stand within the sun,
Light on the golden hills, with days forever more."

* * * * * * * *

The wail of the storm shrieks with the final note of the last song Yore took up, and Goran's voice takes up a note, a song that I've heard a hundred times before. My eyes flicker over to him. His voice is rich, not the smooth, deep tone of Yore's, but something that sounds raw in a different way, and the lines are rolling, thick and deep.

"In the darkness, the sounds rage, the storm comes, the grounds shake.
In the darkness, the waters flow, the tides rise, the grounds rumble.
By the firelight, the tides turn back, by the light of the sun, by the light of the star.
Though the darkness comes, it will not stay;
Though the darkness comes, so comes day.
I lift up my eyes: where does the light come from?
From the hills: from the hills.
To the hills we will look.
Upon the Guide I will wait.
In the darkness, thunder calls, rivers rage, boulders fall.
In the darkness, shadows streak, nights seem long, waters deep.

By the light of the lantern I see, for the light of dawn, and the new day, I'll wait.
Until the new day rises, and light streams ever deep.
Until the new day rises, and we begin to see.
What was covered in darkness and lost in the night.
I lift up my eyes: where does our hope come from?
From the light: from the light.
To the only light that is in darkness, we will look.
Upon the Hope in darkness, we will wait."

Goran's eyes are on the fire, watching something far away, and the wind is shrieking outside. I press my hands against my legs, my lip trembles. *What if this darkness doesn't abate? What if light doesn't come back? Does the light shine in this darkness, in the midst of the storm?* I glance at Goran again. *How many times has he thought of that song, along in the winter months, when the nights stretch ever longer, until there is only night? Does he long for the light too? The light to come in the darkness, the way Elnial promised?*

My eyes flicker to Yore. His eyes are on the one unshuttered window, watching the white streak past in the night.

I glance at Alvea. She is barely sitting up, her shoulders slumped, eyes on the fireplace beside her, drooping, face drawn. I press my feet under me. "It's late. I will get the blankets now, and then I am turning in, if you do not need anything else?" I glance at Yore, then Goran. Alvea looks up. Something crosses her features like a shadow in her mind, and I can't read it. She stands, swaying, and her face is pale, too pale, the blanket she's been wearing like a shawl drawn over her shoulders. The wind howls. She nods and moving toward Yore's room, her steps slow, measured. I move around her. Her eyes are on the ladder, half-hooded. *Wistful.* I shake my head and press my hand against her arm. "Goodeven, Alvea."

She nods at me, turning toward Yore's room that has been hers for the last fortnight. "Goodeven. Rest well."

I grip the ladder, and drag my body upward, step onto the rungs up. Voices are soft downstairs, the rumble of men speaking, and I can hear nothing of Alvea over the screaming of the storm. "...It should have stopped by then..." Goran's voice, "...rarely seen one that..." and his voice is gone again, gone behind the howling of the wind. *What about the hounds? What will they do if he does not come back until morning? What will happen to them? I did not think another storm would come so soon, or so quickly.*

I grip the stack of blankets, from the corner and turn. I step down the ladder, blankets tucked under my arm. The wind screams, the note raising, and it whirls off, the constant howl, swirling like a thousand screams. I drop my feet to the floor, and I cannot hear the boards creak, like they always do. I purse my lips.

Yore glances at me. "You look tired."

What can I say to that? I reach the blankets out, toward the guest in our house. "These should be warm enough. There is a pillow there, for your head. I'll try not to disturb you in the morning, when I get up, and if you want for anything, please ask."

He shakes his head, lifting the blankets from my hands. "Don't worry about that. I plan to leave early." He nods toward me. "Do as you will."

He is not worried about the storm then. We should not be either. All will be well. It will be fine, won't it? He moves away, toward the fire and the open floor. My brother is stooping, placing logs on the small blaze in its place. *Keeping the flame alive, like Goran said. Fire going out is death out here. Will he get up to keep an eye on it, in the night, or will Goran tend it? What will happen to Goran's fire, in his hut? Will they tend the fire in the night, or should I? Will it go out faster in the storm?* My eyes flicker to him. He is looking at the blankets in his hand, and I cannot read his expression. It is hard. Dry. Blank. *He'll tend it, surely. He'll be next to it, won't he?* I turn away and move for the ladder. "Goodeven." *They will work it out. Yore always tends it, so he will see to it. I don't need to worry about it.*

My brother glances up, nods at me. "Goodeven, Oanéka."

The wind howls, and I do not hear the words Goran says, though his lips form them as my hands grip the ladder.

Chapter XXIX

Something is heavy, heavy on my chest. *Darkness. Panic. I can't breathe.* I can't breathe. Something is wrong. I shove my body upright and there is something around me, something tangled around me, and I cannot get free, cannot get it off. Breaths wrack my chest, and a sob chokes in my throat. Everything is black, black and I can't see, can't see anything, can't push off the thing around me, and it's tightening. *Darkness. I can't breathe. I can't breathe. It won't come off.*

Something is moving in the room, moving through the darkness, large, lumbering, stumbling. *I can't breathe.* "Oanéka?" A hoarse voice, low, slipping through the darkness toward me. *I know the voice. I know it.* A sob rips from my lips. Yore. His hand brushes my shoulder, gentle, careful. "Oanéka? What's wrong? Is something wrong?" His voice is still hoarse, low. I shove at the thing trapping me, my chest tight. He nods, movement faint in the dark. "Hold on."

His hands grip the thing around me, pulling it free, and it's cold, everything is cold, my skin creeping and I'm shaking. *Quilts. I was wrapped in my quilts, trapped in them.* I shake my head, and he can't see me, but the bed beside me sinks with his weight. My cheeks are damp, cold air harsh against them, and I can't catch my breath, can't breathe.

He shifts, his hand on my shoulder, gentle. "What's wrong? Speak to me. What is wrong?" His voice is low.

I shake my head again, in the darkness that is complete with the midnight watches, still, and the wind is still screaming, still blasting, still shaking through the world with that echoing howl. *The storm. There was noise, noise from the storm. The screaming, the darkness.* I swallow—it catches in my throat, stuck, and another sob wracks my chest. I wrap my arms around my waist. "What if he's wrong? What if it lasts?" My voice shakes.

The bed shifts, and the storm screams again, howling, howling, higher. I shiver, and a sob wracks through my chest. *I can breathe. I can breathe. It's fine. I can breathe.* Yore's hand presses on my back. "Who? What if who is wrong, Oanéka?" Yore's voice is hoarse, irritated with sleep. "Take a breath."

I swallow hard and wrap my arms tighter. *I'm shivering.* "What if Goran is wrong? What if the storm lasts, Yore?" I'm shaking, hands shaking beneath my arms. "What if the storm lasts? What will we do? It's... it's still storming, Yore. It's still storming. What will we do? We can't stay here like this. It's too dark. There shouldn't be another storm so soon. I thought they would be further apart, not like this. It's too soon. What if they last for days? Weeks?"

An arm wraps around my shoulders, warm and solid, and he pulls me close, pulls me against him. He is warm, his arm firm around me, gentle, solid. "Oanéka." His voice is steady, low. "We'll be alright. Storms only last for a time. They all come to an end. It's alright. We have all that we need within the cabin. We have everything here, and when challenges come we'll face them. It's not too soon. We are alright." He rocks, gently, back and forth, back and forth, and my heart is slowing in my chest. The storm screams again, howling, and everything screams with it. "We brought everything we need, and I've been storing wood. We'll be alright."

I drop my head against his chest. His heart is steady, pounding barely beneath the sound of the wind. "What about Alvea?" *What am I asking? What about Alvea?* "She can't stay in the cabin forever, Yore, and the storms, this one came up too fast. She couldn't fight one, not if she got caught out there." *I couldn't fight one either, like as not.*

Yore shifts, his hand gripping my arm, gentle and firmer and warm. "Alvea will be fine. She is healing, and she won't be going out there for a while. We'll be fine, Néka, we'll be fine. We'll make it, we'll make it out here. I'm not going anywhere. The storm will end, and we'll learn how to deal with them. They'll not feel so bad later, you'll get used to the patterns of winter, and then it'll be spring." His heart is beating steadily, slowly, and the wind howls outside. *Still howling, like an angry thing. Paun said we were trying to settle an angry world; said we were foolish. What if we are? What if this is all foolishness, paying off the debt with our lives rather than running? Running would have been foolish, dishonest. But this debt should never have been ours. Running would have been cowardly, wrong.*

"This is foolish, all of it." My voice is low, and it cracks.

There is a voice, humming, near, clear and low, cutting through the storm, calm and gentle and here. *Yore's voice. Yore's tune.* His heartbeat is gentle and solid in his chest, beside my ear. A tear slides down my cheek, and splatters against my neck. The tune lifts, soft, beneath the voices of the storm, swirling with them, and it's gone.

* * * * * * * *

The wind is howling. I peel my eyes open. My joints are stiff, aching. *There is a new noise, somewhere. Where?* A step, across the room, and another, soft, stockinged. I pull myself up, cold air brushes my skin through my nightdress. Yore is moving across the darkened room, light barely flickering in from downstairs, soft against his white nightshirt. *Light from downstairs, the same as every morning, but the wind is howling today, and it can't be Yore's lantern, because Yore is here.*

I drop my feet over the side of the bed and reach down. I tug my stockings back into place on my feet, over my ankles, and shiver. Yore glances at me, and away, his mouth pursing beneath his beard. He grabs something from beside him, stooping. Turning back to me, he tosses something at me. I reach up and snatch the fabric out of the air, pulling it down against my chest. *My day dress.* "Thank you." My voice is hoarse, throat dry. *He won't have heard me over the storm.* I jerk the dress down, over my nightdress. *Yore had already pulled on his day shirt.*

He nods, stepping down onto the ladder. I pull the laces together beneath my arm, and my fingers fumble, stiff. *Too cold.* I twist the knot into place and shake my head. *It's not right. But I can't do it any better, not until my hands are warmer.* I step off my bed, and shuffle across the room. The light below is a little brighter, still the orange gold of the lantern light. I step down onto the ladder, down to the floor. Voices murmur together, faint over the storm and low, a rumbling sound. "She needn't get up. It's too cold to do any..." The voice stops. *Goran's.* His eyes flicker to me, and a brow raises. "You needn't have gotten up. There is nothing to be done in the cold with the storm still rolling. You might as well go back to your bed where it is warm."

I press my arms around myself, and my eyes flicker to the fire. It is burning, the flames leaping high, but the air is chilled, the storm howling. I tighten my arms. "Do you not care to eat, in this kind of weather?" My voice is hoarse with night, and I flinch. *I sound awful.* I press my hair back from my face, tucking it into place, and turn away.

Goran plants his feet, nodding toward the pot on the stove. "I've already started breakfast. Go sit before you freeze."

I move away from him, toward the coat racks. I grab my shawl, pull it over my shoulders and turn back, my arms tightening around it. Yore is staring at the window behind me; his eyes are vacant, his lips working. He sets his jaw. "It'll let up soon. It can't go on much longer."

My eyes flicker back to the window, and the storm screams. The house shudders. *It does not sound like it will let up soon. It is still so loud, still screaming just as much as in the night.* I shiver. There is a startled cry in the back room. *Alvea.* Yore moves to his feet and is gone into the room that was his. I press my lips together, turn my eyes toward Goran. He has not moved, his eyes on the fire now. He steps toward it. I lick my lips, shift my arms. "Would you care for some tea?" My voice is still hoarse, still wrong. My face warms. *Maybe he can't hear it over the howling wind.*

He glances at me and turns back, his hand moving toward the fire poker. "As you like."

I turn away, lift the bucket from the floor. Heaving it higher, I pour it into the kettle. I set it back on the ground. It thuds dully, the wind howling, howling outside. There is steam rising from the pot on the stove, beside the kettle. Heat brushes my leg from the stove. I step closer, the warmth seeping in through my skirts. My skirts feel cold against the back of my legs, through my stockings, away from the warmth of the stove.

Yore steps through the doorway from his room, his jaw clenched. He glances at me, his eyes meeting mine. He shakes his head. "She's not awake yet. She must just have been startled in her sleep."

Goran's voice cuts past his, sharp. "Does she usually sleep late?"

Yore's eyes flicker back to mine, searching. *He doesn't know. He's usually outside.* I swallow, my shoulders, arms still tight around myself. "Sometimes she does, when she's had a rough day before, when her leg's been troubling her. She may be fine." Goran looks away, stabbing at the logs with the stick in his hand. He is kneeling before the fire, his face profiled. I shiver, wrap my arms around myself.

Yore shifts, his gaze moving to me. "Go to the fireplace, take up a blanket. I can tend that."

I shake my head. "Nie. I am making breakfast. I am not that cold." *Half of me is warm, the other half cold where the warmth of the fire does not touch.* I shiver.

Yore's eyes narrow on me. "Oanéka..."

I shake my head. "I am alright, Yore. I'm making breakfast, and I am not going to take ill, I'm by the stove. And I am not going to sit around in blankets all day. This world is what we have, and I am not going to idle for a day when snow comes swirling in. This is my task." The wind screams, and I cannot control the shiver that races up my spine.

Yore's eyes have not left my face. He shakes his head, his shoulders tight, tense. "If you take ill, for your stubbornness,

I will not be to blame. Go sit down." He nods sharply toward the fire again.

I narrow my eyes, tightening my arms until it's almost warm, almost feels warm. "It was never your fault before." *I am still not warm, beneath the layers, beside the stove.* Steam curls up and the water is bubbling in the pot. I turn, grabbing the bag of porridge from the counter. *Goran must have got it out earlier, before we rose.*

Yore is still standing there, his hands in the pockets of his trousers. *He is not giving up.* He shakes his head. "Put more clothes on then. Wear your hat, or something. You are shivering." He nods toward me.

I purse my lips, pour porridge into the swirling, bubbling water. Goran isn't saying anything, isn't adding anything. My eyes flicker toward him. He is standing still, his eyes on the floor, somewhere else, on something else. I shake my head at Yore, turning my eyes back toward the water. "I am alright, Yore. I'll do it later. It's time to put this in." I pour the last bit of the meal in, and it swirls in the water, churning, mixing, thin and pale for now.

His eyes thin to slits. He spins, marching across the room, toward the window. *What is he going to do by the window? Stare? Brood?* I grab a spoon from the counter, shove it into the water. The tan of the water swirls, grains churning, bubbles rising to the surface and under again. Steps pound on the floor, and something shoves down over my head, clamping over my ears.

I squeal.

Something moves away from me, and I jump backward, fling my arm out toward the thing beside me. Yore is standing there, his eyes on me, just a few feet away. His lips are smug, eyes tight. My hand flies up to my head, and there is something fuzzy there, wool. *My hat. He shoved my hat on my head.* A laugh bubbles up in my chest. "Yore!"

He stares at me, arms still crossed, mouth twitching. "You wouldn't do anything about it."

Another laugh burst from me, and I can't stop, my knees softening. I press a hand against the counter. Yore is staring at me, his brow half-cocked, his mouth dry, unimpressed. I laugh harder, my hand fumbles with the counter. I grip it, my knees jelly under me, and my sides ache. Someone laughs, across the room, low, soft. *Goran.* He is standing, his eyes on me, a smile across his whole face and his eyes are laughing along with his voice.

Yore chuckles, his gaze on me, and then on the floor. I grin, slinging my arm across my stomach, and it hurts. He laughs, the grin splitting his face, and his pitch matches mine, breathy, his eyes crinkling at the corners and he's laughing with me, laughing with us.

I sniffle, tears running down my cheeks. *It wasn't that funny, but I cannot stop laughing.* Yore cannot either, his eyes on the floor, a smile pressing his lips so hard it must hurt, and Goran is grinning, and I can barely hear his laugh over the wailing of the wind. I smile, press my hand against my side. *This was good. This was good.*

I shake the spoon at Yore, turning back toward the pot, and he laughs again. His hand brushes my shoulder, gently. "Put more clothes on." The wind howls, as if echoing his words. I flinch. *The storm again. What will happen if the storm doesn't end? The storm will end. All storms end. There will be time before another one comes. They can't all be this soon. It will be alright.*

But when, then? When will they come? I turn toward the pot, and there are lumps of porridge, floating through the boiling water. I frown. My sides ache, cheeks hurt, and they pull back up, a smile pulling at my lips. I shove the spoon into the pot and press it against the side, bursting a lump of clustered meal.

Chapter XXX

Alvea's steps shuffle across the room, one step, and then a drag, her limp pronounced and slow. She lifts her head, holding it high. Her braid is tumbling down her side, long, dark and thick, her eyes rimmed dark with the last bit of illness, and with exhaustion. *It doesn't seem right, to see her head lifted, when she is still in her nightdress.* She is blinking at me. "What is it?" Her hands grip each other, head still high.

I shake my head, set the bowl down. "Would you like some porridge?" My voice carries evenly over the howling of the wind, and there is a step, upstairs, the men moving.

Alvea's head jerks up, her eyes widening. She turns. "Who is up there?"

I lift the ladle, dump the half-chilled porridge into it. *I wish it were easier to keep porridge warm. It is not pleasant when people get up at different times.* The porridge glops, unappetizingly. "Goran and Yore. They are looking at some of the woodwork from back home. Our clothes' chests and things."

"Goran?" Her face pales. She spins back, clutching at the skirt of her nightgown. "Curse it. I forgot he was here." There are feet, stepping onto the ladder, and someone is coming down. Goran drops to the floor, and she is standing just a few feet away, eyes wide, staring straight ahead. *Staring at me. Her face is slightly pale.* Goran moves forward a step, and pauses, glancing at my sister. Her hands tighten, shoulders straightening.

He looks away, moving to the side, toward the window. There are steps tapping on the ladder again, and a thud—Yore, jumping to the floor. He glances at her. "It is good to see you up." He looks at me, and a brow raises. He glances back at Alvea. Her face is red and white at once now. He steps away, toward the fire.

She nods at him, lifting her head, and wraps her arms over her stomach. "You as well. I am sorry. I meant to change before you two got down but did not get a chance to." Goran only nods, and stoops, lifting his mug from the floor. Alvea steps backward, her movements slow, shuffling. She steps through Yore's door and pulls it shut behind her. Yore looks at me, and shrugs. He moves over to the door and lifts his coat, slinging it onto his shoulder. My eyes widen. The storm shrieks.

"What are you doing?"

He turns, pulling his arms through the sleeves. "Checking on the calli."

My heart freezes, stuttering in my chest. "Yore..." I'm moving forward, a step. "No. You can't go out there."

His head is shaking before I've finished. "Goran and I are going out. There is the rope line, remember? There is nothing to worry about."

"Yore..." I press my hand against the counter, gripping it. *What will we do without Yore?* "You can't go out there. You can't. They are fine, Yore. They'll be fine."

He shakes his head again, pulling his hat down over his ears and his hair, snuffing out the gold strands. "I tended them for a night, not for longer. They are usually out of water in the morning as it is. I'll be right back. We put up the line for this reason."

I shake my head. My heart hammers in my chest, screaming. "What about frostbite? It's too cold out there. You can't... Storms are deadly, Yore. You remember the men back home?"

He shakes his head, pulling his gloves over his hands. "My skin will all be covered. No frostbite, and we will keep our hands on the line. We'll be alright." He turns. Goran is ready behind him, his coat, hat, and boots on when I wasn't looking.

Yore doesn't look at me, doesn't do anything but grip the door handle to walk out into the wailing, howling, screaming of the storm. "Yore!"

Goran's eyes flicker back toward me, and there is something soft in them, and I don't want it. He shifts his hand on the handle of the closed door. "We'll be right back, Oanéka. I've done this innumerable times. There is no other way to live with the storms. You cannot leave the livestock be. He'll be fine." *Live? Live? What if they don't live? What if they aren't fine?*

Goran pulls the door. The air screams, fury rolling into the house, and there is white, filling the room, white and then silence, the air going still and going cold.

The house shudders. There is nothing but the hint of snow drifting on nothing where they were before and a thudding against the house outside. Someone is walking behind me, steps slow. "Néka?" Alvea's voice is too high. "Where did they just go?"

My throat is dry. "They went to check the calli." *I don't want to see her face.* I turn. Her eyes are wide, watching the door that isn't moving, her skin too pale.

Her eyes move to mine. "They went out there?" Her throat bobs, her head lifting. "Goran must know what he is doing, if he went out." She clenches her jaw for a moment. "He had better." She turns, moving back across the room toward something, and I can't move. My eyes flicker to the door, and I can't move them away. *Elnial, please. Bring them back in, bring them back safely from the storm. Please bring them back in safely.*

The wind howls, but everything else is quiet in here, only the flicker of firelight, and the shuffle of Alvea's steps. *How can she be so calm about this?* She lifts the bowl of porridge, plucking a spoon from the jar on the counter. *I don't remember putting the bowl down.* I turn back to the door.

"Why did they do that?" My voice is dull in the room, like wood against curtains, like a brushing of air. I twist my hands, shove them under my arms. "Why would they go out there?" *She is too calm, eating porridge, her shoulders straight when they are foolishly out in a storm. Wasn't that the thing we heard about storms, about the weather in the north? The storms are deadly. Deadly storms. They take those who are caught in them, and they went out in one, for calli?* I press my lips together, spin toward her. "Why would he do that? That was foolishness! Doesn't he know what it would do to us, if he doesn't come back?"

Alvea's eyes flicker to mine, her eyes calm. She lifts the spoon, holding it just below her lips, her head high. *Too calm.* "He is just checking on the calli. That is what he does, Oanéka. We cannot just let them go thirsty in the storm. You know they will be out of water."

My chest tightens, heart hot. "Water? Alvea. It's a blizzard! Men die in blizzards. They aren't worth his life, are they? Calli aren't worth them risking their lives!" She takes the bite, her face still calm. My hands tighten. "Are they? Are they worth that?"

She lifts her head, plunging the spoon back into the porridge bowl. "There is no need to panic about it. You already know my answer. Of course they aren't."

I shove my hands further under my arms. "Panic?" My lips curl. "Panic? He's my brother, and he's yours too! What do you mean, 'no reason to panic'? He went out into the blizzard, Alvea! For calli! He is risking his life for big, stinky livestock! Storms take men like that! The ones that got caught back home were just checking their cattle, and he just went out there like that?" *We didn't go through all of this out here for him just to head out into a storm and die for some calli.*

Her eyes flash. "I know where he went!" She lowers the bowl, her eyes sharp, hands whitening on the dish, "But he went with the best that we have for now, and there is nothing we can do about it but hold our tongues and wait. Don't throw that at me. I know where he is. He'll be back in just a few moments. Nothing good comes of those who stress and rail about what cannot be changed." My teeth click together. She is right. He'll be inside in a few moments, or he won't. Hours of wondering, and then what? I tighten my arms. My eyes flicker back toward the door. "Oanéka."

I turn. She is watching me, that bowl still in her hands, her eyes still, calm. "You can't control him. He'll be alright. Let him be."

I swallow, and my throat is tight, the wind howling, howling. "Do I have a choice?" Her hand reaches out, pressing mine.

She looks away. "I do not care for many of the things Pakem often said." She grimaces a little, and my face mirrors hers. "But there is one thing that he said, that was good, that stuck with me, within all the rest of it." Her hand presses mine again. "'We cannot control the world that goes on around us. But we can control our response to it, and choose to grow, or to stay. To move, or to become a stone, immovable and lackluster. But you have to choose something.'"

I shake my head, my throat tight. "It seems strange that he would say that, since he ran from the world. From us. He chose not to choose."

She nods, her lips tightening, eyes past me. "Sometimes," she shakes her head, "I think the people who teach us the most are the ones that leave the most scars. That was how it was for Pakem. He could only teach what he wished he could be. He never lived up to what he taught. His life was more a warning than it was an example. Mamé's was the same." Her lips twist, a wry smile, more like Yore than her and she looks down.

The door swings open, cold air blasting and the storm screams. I spin. There are figures, moving into the room, the door slamming shut and quiet screams in, storm still swirling outside. Figures are standing by the door, white plastered to every part of them, their eyes a line in the whiteness. One of them moves, bolting across the room. *There are three. Three figures.* One of them is shaking.

My heart lurches. *That cannot be right.* "Yore?"

One of the figures shakes his head, grabbing the arm of the shaking figure. He moves, hauling it across the room. "Alvea, get blankets." Yore's voice, muffled, from the other man moving toward the coat rack. "Oanéka, help him out of those snow clothes." He nods toward the figure being hauled across the room.

Alvea is moving, away, toward the back where the blankets are. I step forward, grip the coat of the figure that Goran has pushed into a chair. Cold seeps through my fingers. I fumble with the buttons, snow coating each one. "Him? Who is this, Yore?"

The figure pushes down his scarf, shoving white away from his face clumsily, and grins, his midnight skin flashing. His lips are purpled, chapped and flaking. "Did you-u not-t recog-nize me?" Pevi's teeth chatter against each other, his skin stark against the white of all that he is wearing.

My stomach drops lower. "Pevi?" I stand, jerking the coat from his arms, and snow piles off it in small clumps, thudding to the floor. "How did you get here? What happened?"

Yore's hand nudges my arm. "Get him out of those." I glance up, and his eyes meet mine, earnest, urgent. He nods toward Pevi's feet, moving away quickly. "There will be time to talk later."

I nod, kneel beside Pevi. My fingers fumble with his boots, the thick fur strange, caked with snow and all white. *I can't see where to pull, and where to move them beneath it, the cords all running together beneath the fur. I can't get these off. He said they were trouble.* I slip my fingers into a cord, follow it, and it crosses with another and another, the cold slipping further into my fingers. I shake my head and pull my hand away, breathing on my fingers. *He needs to get out of the rest of these snow clothes.* "Hand me your coat."

I jump to my feet and turn, bolt across the room, snatch up the blanket from Alvea's chair. I turn, throw it over his shoulders and snatch the hat from his head, pulling the scarf with it. It is stiff, frozen to the shape of his head, strange and hard. Snow crumbles off it, falling with a dull puff to the floor. *Half the floor is covered in small piles of snow.* I look back at him, grip one of his gloves, and pull it.

I grimace. "I need you to tell me how to get your boots off. I can't get them."

He nods, his teeth still chattering, and another smile flashes across his face. "I am s-sorry to gi-give you such a fr-fright." He points, a stiff, half bent finger toward a cord, his movement slow, sluggish. "At-at the top. K-knot." I drop to my knees.

The cord is tucked beneath lumps of half melted snow, clinging to the fur and the leather, clinging to his boot and his trousers. I trace the line of the cord, pull and nothing moves, nothing changes. *It's frozen to the fur.* I pull again, jerk on it. The cord shifts. *There is the knot.* I pull it, pull at the twists of it, and it comes free, dragging along the snow. The cord runs into another, with another knot, and another, holding on each layer of fur, binding each layer together into a mass of boot and fur. I pull them free, down to his ankle, and the boot comes off, stiff and snow coated in the pool of growing water. My fingers are stiff, awkward, damp from the melting snow. I twist them, breathe on them again. I glance at the other boot. *Is it tucked in the same way?* I reach out, trace the cord and follow it toward the top.

Alvea is beside Yore, handing him a blanket. Her eyes are wide. *He is already out of his snow gear, just his pants are coated white now.* "What do you need?" she asks. Her voice is steady.

Yore's head is nodding, toward the kitchen. "Start a kettle. Just get it warm, not hot." She nods, her eyes still on him.

"And then what do you need? Your hands..." She steps toward the kitchen, glancing at him over her shoulder.

He shakes his head, moving away from her, toward the back of the room. He shoves his hands under his arms, a flash of pale skin, too pale for him. "My hands are fine. I am going to find clothes." He shuffles away, moving back into the room. I fumble with the cord, the knot buried beneath the snow.

Alvea's eyes do not even flicker to the man in the chair beside me, her head held high, eyes focused on the stove. *Is she not going to ask how he got here, what he is doing here, anything? She was asking about him only days ago, if he would come. She almost sent Goran after him, didn't she? And now he is here. Is she not going to ask how he is, if he is alright, how he came to be here in a blizzard?* The wind howls, and I shiver, hands stiff., damp. Pevi half smiles, and his body is wracking with shivers, foot shaking beneath his boot, leg knocking up and down.

I pull Pevi's second boot free. *His socks look dry, the woolen fabric mostly all one color.* Stink wafts up, under my nose and I gag, stand, stumble. "You need to get out of those pants." I point at him, half turn away. "Yore will find some for you, and then Alvea and I will leave so that you all can change." He nods, pulling at the glove on his hands, his fingers fumbling, movements slow and strange. He grips it, and his fingers slip from it, fumbling. I grab the end of it and jerk it off. He glances up at me, his head nodding, teeth knocking together. I nod back, and step away. He is still shaking, his pants the only thing left that is covered in snow, his shirt covered by the blanket I gave him. *What else can I do?* I glance at Goran. He is pulling his own boots off, his fingers slowed like Yore's were.

"I-I am sorry t-to have caused t-trouble." *Pevi.* I glance down at him. He nods at me, pulling the blanket about his shoulders.

I shake my head. "It's not trouble, so long as you are alright. Are you frozen? What do you need?"

Goran glances at him, his eyes sharp, snow clinging to the edges of his hair. He stands. "I do not know what you were thinking, Pevi Likloré. That was a dead man's journey."

Pevi grins, his teeth chattering harder, their sound clicking together. "Y-you will think-k me mad-d."

Mad? I swallow, twist my fingers together. They fumble. "How did you get here?" I say.

He grins again, eyes flickering to me. "Tatcha." I blink, and he half laughs. "The m-mule. S-she is usually real-ly good at predicting-g the w-weather. She gets anxious, when it w-will be b-ad." He shudders, pulling the blanket around his shoulders. "I am-m sorry for the t-trouble. I th-thought it w-would be safe. She seemed f-fine yesterday mo-morning." His hands are sliding up and down his arms over the blanket, rubbing over and over, and they are trembling.

I shake my head. "Yesterday morning? You should move closer to the fire. Here." I nod toward Alvea's chair, setting it close beside the fireplace.

Pevi stands, half hunched, moving slowly across the room. His grace is gone now, body shaking, shivering, movements stiff and slowed, his back bent. There is water, trailing behind him, dripping off his snow-soaked trousers—snow sliding off in chunks behind him.

Yore's feet hit the floor, at the back of the room, a bundle of cloth under his arm. I nod to him, step back from Pevi. My eyes flicker to Alvea. She is shifting the kettle on the stovetop, setting mugs on the counter with the other hand. She glances at me, and inclines her head, moving away toward Yore's room. I follow her, my stocking slapping a puddle of cold water. I shiver, half hop through the door after her. Her eyes flicker to mine. She moves, dropping onto the bed that is now hers. "Was he terribly cold? Did he seem alright?"

I shake my head. "I cannot tell. The healer back home said that shivering was good, if I remember right. But I cannot recall accurately. He may not have. He seemed talkative, that must be good, mustn't it?" I grimace, fold my arms together, shake my head. "We should have learned more from the medicine man. I wish he didn't mutter so much when he came around."

She folds her hands and refolds them. "He came around rarely enough. I don't know that it would have mattered if he hadn't." Her eyes trail to the door. She moves her hands again, shifting her fingers. "Do you think he is alright?"

A grin pulls at my lips. I press it back, shake my head. "You'll have to ask him. I can't say." There is shuffling in the other room.

"You can come back." *Yore's voice.* Alvea stands, pausing.

She looks at me, her eyes fixing on mine. "Go on." I blink at her. I turn, move slowly through the doorway. Goran is stooping, lifting the pile of soaked clothes into his arms.

I shake my head, dart across the room to him. "Leave that." I push his hands, move to take the pile. "Leave those be. I'll handle them."

He shakes his head, lifting the pile, and his hands move away from mine. "I'm already damp. Where do you want them to go?" He straightens, eyes waiting for me.

Where to put them? I swallow. *I hadn't planned to do anything with them yet.* I turn, point back to the washtub at the end of the room, empty and leaned against the wall, waiting for wash day. He steps forward, bare feet slapping against the floor. I move in front of him, grab the bucket and set it on the floor. Alvea's voice drifts over, speaking to Pevi, standing beside him. "...Take this. It is warm and may help." She hands him a mug, only the faintest traces of steam curling off the top of it. His fingers curl around it, and he is nodding, half smiling, his jaw still shaking, eyes less focused now. I shudder. *Surely he'll be alright.*

I glance across the room. Yore has one of the mugs in his hands, and a blanket slung over his shoulders, only his woolen long under-things over his legs. I swallow. "Yore?" He glances at me, a brow raising. I nod toward his legs. "Where are your pants?"

He shakes his head, shifting a little. "I own three pairs. Not four." A half grin stretches across his face. He shifts the blanket, clutching the mug closer. "Until today, I thought three was excessive. Now I am wondering." He grins.

I smile, flick my eyes across the room. The pants Pevi is wearing are long on him, bunching slightly where his stockinged feet meet the floor. Alvea is speaking to him, her voice soft and even. "...She's in the barn then? Were you trying to come here? Why did you come?"

I fold my hands together, move forward. I lift my head. "And how did you make it here in the storm?"

Alvea's eyes flash to mine, sharp, like what I just said was stupid. *I don't understand.* Pevi laughs, and his teeth chatter again. He clutches the cup closer to his chest. "I got to the shed before the storm hit." *Oh.* My face flushes. I look down, and his feet shift at the edge of my vision. "I've been wanting to come back, for a while, as you all are the only lots I know of out here and Tatcha seemed calm yesterday morning, so I thought to risk it, and bring you all some things that I'd collected in my travels that I thought you would enjo-y." He laughs, his jaw tight, controlling the shivers running up his spine. He pulls the blanket tighter with the tips of his fingers. "I failed at that. When the storm started rolling in, Tatcha bolted, and I think she lost the pack. It was not on her when we arrived in the shed." He looks up at Alvea and shifts his gaze to Yore. "I thought to try and make it to the house, if there was a rope, but with the thudding of the storm, I was not sure that you would hear my knock."

Goran nods, folding a blanket over his shoulders. "It was probably wise to wait it out as you did."

Pevi glances at him. "How did you come to be here, Goran Woodcutter?"

Goran straightens, just slightly. "I was here when the storm struck. I am glad you do not smell worse, after spending the night with a mule and six calli."

Pevi laughs, throwing his head back in a single bark of it. Alvea smiles, stepping backward. He shivers and pulls the mug back to his chest. "I do not know that there is much worse to be had. I imagine I do not smell pleasant." His eyes flicker to Yore, and then to Alvea, and me. "Thank you, all for bringing me in. I am sorry for the trouble."

Alvea's head is shaking before he is done. "Do not trouble yourself. We are glad that you are here. It is better to weather this storm in company than alone. I am just sorry that you had to spend the night as you did. Praise be to Elnial that you did not get caught out there in the storm." She shudders and turns away, her eyes flickering toward the window for a moment.

Yore stands, his movements stiff, like the other men. He pulls the blanket about his shoulders, tightening his grip on it. "It will like as not end before the day is up. What do you need for the food, Oanéka? Can I help you?"

My eyes snap to his. *Dinner? He is thinking of the midday meal already?* I shake my head, move toward the kitchen. "I have it. You all tend to yourselves, get warmer." I move away, pull a pot from the cabinet. Goran says something to Yore, and I cannot catch it. Yore half smiles, and folds himself into a chair, quiet again for a moment.

Chapter XXXI

Goran steps up beside me, his dish empty in his hand. The wind screams, white still swirling in the darkness beyond the window. I swallow, turn my head toward him. I could ask now. He is close enough. I lick my lips. "What will happen to the hounds?"

He looks at me, only a half glance. "How do you mean?"

I shift my hands in the soaped water of the wash bucket, turning the bowl over again. "You said that if we let the fire go out, then..." My words trail off, and I don't want to finish them. I shake my head. "What will happen to them, after being two days in the cabin without you? Without the fire? How long do you think it would take for it to go out?" His eyes flicker to mine, sharply.

He looks away, out toward the window and toward the night. He places his hands on the counter, spread against its surface. "They will either have found the supply of meat and grain I keep tucked into a corner in case." His eyes flicker down, to the counter surface. He straightens. "Or they will not have. They know to sleep close together. Heat will not have been the issue. But food will, if they have not found it."

I lick my lips, turning the bowl over in my soaked hands. "And water?"

He shakes his head. "Nie. I keep a barrel in the back of the house just for storms. I don't lid it. They are tall enough to reach if they get thirsty enough."

"Goran..." he glances at me, but I don't look at him. *If I do, I won't be able to finish.* My heart twists in my chest. I flip the bowl over, water splattering my soaked hands. "I am sorry that you got stuck here, through this storm, and pray that your hounds are well, but we..." I shake my head, "I am thankful for all that you have done. For you. I mean we are thankful for you. All of us." My face warms. I turn my head down, toward the bucket.

He is watching me, eyes flickering across my face. He nods, looking away. "It was a pleasure. And it is good to know you. Your brother is a good man. Your sister is a wise woman." My heart sinks. *What did I think he would say?* He glances at me again, and his eyes find mine. He nods. "I am glad you did not give up."

Give up? My face warms more. "Give up when?"

He looks away from me, off across the room and back. "In these last few months."

My cheeks feel like flames. I turn my face all the way to the bucket, and my hair barely slides into it. I grimace and knock it out with the side of my arm. "Did you think I would?"

He half smiles and shifts his weight forward onto his arms. "I was not sure at first. You seemed a little... stiff for this world. Not many women do well out here. Many of them have not made it through the first months, before they up and return home. There are several who seemed more suited to this world who are now buried in it."

I look down, at the dishes and my hands that have wrinkled in the water, like dried prunes. "Perhaps it is because I am softer that I have made it this far." I tuck my hands into my skirts, avoid his gaze. "Did you ever think to give up?" I look up, and his eyes are on my face still, watching. I look down again and pick up a dish, set it in the water. I purse my lips. "After you first arrived. Did you ever think about just going back home?"

He stiffens, lifting his arms from the counter. "Nie."

I shake my head, and the bowl skids in my hand. "Nie? How? There is nothing here, Goran. Nothing but endless barren trees and rocks and snow."

He stiffens further, his eyes looking past me at nothing. He shakes his head. "Some lots look for this kind of wilderness, Oanéka. Not everyone goes in a village or town. Some look for places elsewhere. Some want to be elsewhere. There was nothing for me back home."

I look down, lift a spoon from the bucket, and it is coated with soap suds, clinging to it. "I don't understand. Why would you want to be elsewhere? Why would you choose to be here? Any place like this. There isn't anything here to choose."

He looks at me, sharply, eyes flickering away again at once. "There are some things that are better to get away from. Some places that are better alone. And you don't believe that, do you?"

I move away from the sink. "Goran." He looks at me, and I hold my soaked hands carefully out from my skirts, my face warm. The water drips, pooling in the hand I have cupped beneath the wetter one. "Running away from problems doesn't fix them. And I don't think it's good for us to be alone." My face heats. "Lots. For lots to be alone. Any of them. Anyone."

He shakes his head, folding his arms over his chest. "You only know one part of the story, Oanéka. There are lots who are better off alone. Have you thought of that?"

Water splatters against the puddle on the floor beneath my hands. I tuck them against my chest, look down. "How? How can it be better for them to be alone? What could be gained in loneliness?" I look up at him. "I don't understand, Goran. All that I can see in that is just darkness. Emptiness. Gray and brown and barrenness. Why would you look for that? Why would you choose that?"

He looks away, out toward the window where white swirls in the darkness of night. The storm shrieks, and there is a laugh, loud and clear across the room. My head whips up, and there is Alvea, her head thrown back. Pevi is beside her, a grin ripping across his face. They are both glowing with the light of the fire. *She laughed.* My eyes flicker up to Goran. He is staring at her, eyes... proud. *He looks proud of her, proud of the laughter in her eyes.*

He looks back at me, slowly, eyes settling on my face, the pride gone now. "I wasn't looking for emptiness. I was looking for a place that was suitable to me, to the life that I wanted to live. Towns were not suitable for that. I sought out this."

I turn, tuck my hands back into the water, lift a bowl. My eyes flicker up to him. "What was suitable about this place? Why did you choose it?"

He looks at me again, eyes meeting mine and they move away again. "There was nothing to break. It was empty."

I furrow my brows, set the dish against the cloth on the counter, and turn, lift another. "There are a thousand things to break here. Trees, branches, vines and ice..."

His eyes look up, away from me, and his jaw tightens. "But those things don't matter to anyone but the forest. I can choose what I break and what I don't. I know what matters. There is no guessing." He folds his arms over his chest, his eyes going to the floor.

My brows knit together, fingers spinning the bowl in the water. "Whose property did you have to worry about at home?" I frown. "What did your pakem do for his living?"

He looks down at me, his eyes wide and lost like I've never seen them. They flicker down, his arms tensing about him. "He was a healer. A small man and a healer."

I blink. "Your pakem was a healer? Surely then he was in the business of working to fix what was broken."

His glance is sharp, eyes snapping to mine. "Aye. He was. But I was not. He fixed things and he told me that I broke them."

I flinch. "Surely you didn't break landlots."

His mouth grimaces, eyes turning back toward the window. "I've broken plenty. I was not a gentle child. I liked to fight, and there were plenty of boys in the village who liked to fight back. They were mostly smaller than me, so they would get hurt, and I rarely did. I was good with my fists and feet."

I shake my head. "That was when you were a child though. Surely as you grew..."

"So did his expectations?" His glance toward me is dry, bitterness in the slant of his eyes. "Aye. He expected more. He expected me to be small and gentle, like him. He expected me to have his small, skilled hands that could work any wound, tend any child. That I would have no bulk, like my brothers. I was not fit for his world, not as a healer, not as a worker. Not even on his ships. I was large like my mamé's brothers; like her family, not his. He expected me to be like him, a small, nimble man."

I frown and swallow hard. My heart is aching. "His ships? How did a healer..."

"Own ships?" His eyes move from mine again, up and across the room, to the window and the world beyond. "He left his profession. Became a merchant. My mother hated the blood and the lots always stopping him in the streets to ask him for help, people calling at odd hours. My brothers joined him in his venture at sea. Many of them were already half in the profession, like your brother was. My sister married his partner in trade, so she joined them as well. They were all on those ships of his." There is bitterness in his expression, grief in his eyes.

I swallow. "And you left that? Were you not more suited to working on ships?"

His jaw clenches, and he shakes his head. "Nie. I tried to work his ship, work with him, for two years. I had thought I could prove my skill with lifting, moving, charting. I am good with a pencil and stars. But I was always in his way. I was big, cumbersome, a problem when I helped, and a problem when I was out of the way on that ship."

My throat aches, eyes burn. "And then they chose to move to the East Isle? Without you? They left you?"

He nods, head low, jaw working. "My sister died just a month after her third child was born, and my pakem tired of the trade work on water. He said it was too much trouble, and planned to settle as an innkeeper, make the most of the goods he still had and sell the ships in the newer country. My brothers went with him. My mamé followed him, of course." The winds howl, the house shaking.

I swallow hard. "I'm sorry. About your sister. I did not know."

He looks up, arms still folded across his chest, and nods. His eyes flick toward mine. "How did your sister break her leg?"

He doesn't say Alvea. As though she would notice if her name was spoken. My eyes flicker to her. Her attention is all on the man sitting beside her. *What are they speaking of?* I swallow and set the bowl on the towel on the counter. "It was a wagon. She was not more than two summers old. Stepped in front of a man and his team of horses, huge and blundering. Her leg was snapped, I'm told, easily, before the man saw her."

His head tips, just barely and his lips grimace beneath his beard. "Why does Yore blame himself?"

I look up at him. "How do you mean?" My hand fumbles with the remaining bowl.

He glances at my brother, arms still folded over his chest. He nods his head, toward Yore, across the room with rope in his hands, tying and untying it, the sailor knots again. "He blames himself for that injury."

I shake my head. "I don't know. Perhaps mamé had asked him to watch her that day?"

He glances at me. "He is not more than a summer older than her, I would have wagered."

I shake my head. "Nie, but that can be the only reason I'd know of that he would carry that blame. And it would be like pakem and mamé to leave Yore with Alvea, alone. It would be like them even that early."

He glances at me. "What happened to them?" His voice is careful, and I don't have to answer.

I look down. "Mamé left years ago, when Yore was only fifteen summers. She'd had enough, and walked out the door, leaving messages sometimes with merchants and traders along her way. We haven't seen her since them." I purse my lips, run my hand along the bottom of the bucket, beneath the filthy water. "Pakem left a little more than a year ago." I lift my hands from the water, press them against the towel spread on the counter behind him.

He looks at me, eyes scanning my face for just a second and he looks away. "Where did he go?"

I shrug, fold my arms over my chest, mirroring his. They are damp, the coolness of the water seeping through my sleeves. "We never found out. We woke up one day, and he was gone. Yore was..." I catch myself. *Yore would not care if I mentioned to Goran how he spent those years. He has mentioned it to him himself.* "He was not around much then, and I thought maybe he was with him. But when Yore came back in the evening, pakem didn't and he didn't mention him, or ask about him. Alvea insisted he was coming back. He'd left before and had always come back, every time. But he didn't. Not that time. We waited for days but he never returned, never walked through the door." I swallow hard, shift my shoulders. "We found out later that he had taken all the funds we had when he left. And he had left debts with nearly everyone in town from gambling. Every store. Every tavern, all with our cregf." He nods. *The rest he knows.*

Alvea smiles across the room, her eyes moving toward the window as the wind screams again. She nods at Pevi, and stands, slowly, her lips half grimacing, as if she barely noticed the pain in her hip. "I'll get it," she says.

His head quirks. "Are you sure? I do not mind getting it." He moves to stand.

She laughs, shaking her head. "It is well. I'll get it and be done." She turns, stepping across the floor, her limp there and barely noticeable.

"What are you getting?" I say. I push myself off the counter.

She glances at me, stepping easily around us. "Just tea. Would you like some?" Her eyes flicker from me to Goran, her eyes bright.

I shake my head and Goran nods his. I move away from the sink, my arms cold beneath my damp hands clasping them. "I am going to get my needlework." Goran nods and moves away, toward Pevi, by the fire.

Yore only half glances up from his knots, eyebrow quirking for only a moment before his gaze is back on his hands, back on his work. *Was he listening before, or was he lost in thought, lost in what he is doing? His eyes told nothing. He may have been listening all along, or not at all. What would he have said, if asked about pakem and mamé?* Firelight dances across the room, and the wind is barely howling outside, the sound easy, gentle and fierce with the flickering of the flames.

Chapter XXXII

The air is warm, the fire crackling in the faint dark. There is a bundle of blankets like a shadow in the corner beneath the window, rolled up. *Pevi.* I lick my lips and glance toward the door. *Something is off.* I glance down. Goran's pallet is on the floor beside my feet. It is empty, blankets thrown back. *He must be in the loo.* I turn and lift the pot to the stove. I glance down. The buckets of water are brimful, water rippling across the surface. *Someone must have worked to melt the snow and stowed it in the buckets. Yore or Goran? Could they not sleep? Or were they just wanting to do something in the long hours of the night?* I lift the bucket and grip the base; the stream of water crashes into the bottom of the pot that is on the stove.

There are steps behind me, barely thudding on the floor. *Booted.* I turn and stoop, set the bucket down. Goran is behind me, lifting a cup from the counter. He sips at it, his eyes moving to the window. I press my hands against my skirts. "Goodmorn," I breathe.

He nods, moving the cup from his lips. "Goodmorn." His voice is low, barely a breath. "Tell Yore I am sorry I could not wait for him. I'll come back by evening to discuss things with Pevi."

I blink. *With Pevi? Wait? Wait for what?* I shake my head, my hand tightening on my skirts. "What? Where are you going? What do you mean?"

He looks at me, and that brow quirks, lifting. "I'm going to check my hounds. The storm stopped."

The storm stopped? I tear my eyes away from him, toward the window and the deathly, peaceful silence. *Silence. I didn't notice the silence. It was just there. Just echoing across the room.* "We could go outside?" My voice is small.

A smile pulls at the edges of his lips. "You hadn't noticed." He nods his head, the smile taking over his face, and he gestures toward the door. "You should go out there. It will never be more still than it is now." He turns, moving toward the door. *I should offer him breakfast, but he doesn't need food. He needs to check the hounds. Not wait for me to make something. They've waited long enough for him to make it back and he'll want to get back.*

I force a smile. "Goran!" He pauses by the door and Pevi shifts in the corner at the back of the room. *I've woken him.* I grimace. "Elnial be with you. I..." I swallow, pressing my hands harder against my skirts. "I've been praying. Come back and tell us how they are...?"

He half smiles and there is something sharp, pained in it now. "I've told you I'd be back tonight. I will." He pulls the door open and there isn't a blast of wind in the room, no whirling of the snow, no scream growing louder. Only the door open, and footsteps gone into the morning light, then it is closed again.

Pevi shifts in the corner, beneath one of the shuttered windows. He stifles a groan, pulling himself upright and his hand brushes across his head. I turn my eyes away, back toward the stove. "The storm is gone?" His voice is hoarse, scratchy with sleep.

I nod my head. "Va. At last, it has passed." My hands fumble with my skirts.

He is standing in a moment, rubbing the sleep from his eyes. "The storm is gone."

I blink at him. A half smile pulls at my lips again. "Va."

He shoves the blanket off his legs, stumbling and half falls. "Does Alvea know? Yore?" I shake my head and he stills, his eyes widening, too wide and he is still half crouched. "Wait. They are not awake." His voice is lower. I shake my head again and his gaze snaps toward the window and the world outside. "Curse it. I was too loud. I'll still now and keep my own countenance. It is strange how silent it is." His voice is a hoarse whisper now and he straightens, fumbling with the blankets.

I laugh and set a lid on top of the heating pot. "They are fine, Pevi. If they were not up from my call to Goran, they won't be up from your voice now."

He runs a hand over his head, the hair brushing against his fingers. He grimaces, drawing his hand back and his eyes flicker to his fingertips for a moment. He lowers his hand to his side. A smile quirks at his lips, wry.

I frown and lift Goran's cup from the counter, set it beside the washbasin. "Are your hands alright today? You can go wash up, if you'd like. Porridge water is on and Goran said that he'll be back to discuss plans with you later in the day. By evening, at the latest. There is salve for chapped hands and lips there." I nod to the crock that Alvea pulled out yesterday.

He looks at me and nods. "Thank you. But I am not certain what you are talking about with Goran. Did he leave?"

I nod. His brows lift and he nods back, stepping away from me. "I'll be back in a moment then." He turns, moving across the room, toward the loo. I smile and drop back against the counter. *The storm ceased. The storm is over for now. But now Goran has gone home. To whatever destruction or stillness awaits him out there, in the cottage. They'll be alright, surely.*

There are steps on the floor. I lift my head. Alvea is moving across the room, her eyes flickering around it. She looks at me, eyes wide. "Did they both go so soon? They left? Where is Pevi?"

I shake my head. "Nie. Goran has gone home, but Pevi is in the loo. You noticed the storm stopped then?"

Her shoulders relax, posture straightening back to its normal precision and a smile creeps across her lips, soft and gentle. She looks away, moving toward her chair. "The storm? Of course. How could anyone not have?"

My cheeks flush. I look down, turn toward the pot on the stove. I twist my hands in front of me, staring at the stove. "Did you hear it cease?"

She is shaking her head and her eyes snap back toward the other end of the room. The door to the loo opens and Pevi steps out of it. He stops short, grinning at her. "Good-morn, Alvea." He says her name gently, as though it were something delicate, priceless.

She smiles a little, turning away toward her chair. "Good-morn. I trust you are well? How are your hands and feet today?" She looks up at him.

Pevi crosses, moving past me. "All well. I'm going out to check on Tatcha and the calli for a moment." He nods at her and then to me, plucking his cumbersome boots from the floor. Alvea looks down, folding her hands neatly in her lap. He is tying his boots on, working at the cords on the floor.

I fold my hands, cross my ankles. "You won't go home today?" Alvea looks up sharply, her eyes snapping to him with a question in them.

He shakes his head. Her shoulders relax, her eyes going to the fireplace where the flames crackle. Pevi ties off the first boot and shifts his hands to the other, his head still half lifted. "Nie. By the time Goran gets back, it'll likely be too late to set out, especially if he said that he was not coming back until evening. We'll be here today." He looks up. "You all do not mind me staying another night? I do not wish to impose."

"We would not let you go home today if you tried." *Yore's voice stern and almost teasing.* My head snaps up. Yore moves past me, his hand reaching for a cup on the shelf. He glances at Pevi. "You should take time to rest after that feat. I'll talk to Goran about getting you back home later. Tomorrow may have good weather. If not, we will wait until there is. I'm not sending a man out into a storm, or the likes."

Pevi nods to him, straightening. "I appreciate your generosity and kindness."

Yore takes a sip of his water and raises an eyebrow. "It's not generosity. It's friendship, and we offer you that. We would be no friends of yours to cast you out today, or any day with weather uncertain."

Pevi half smiles, and there is a note of sadness in his eyes. "You can be generous and kind in friendship. They are signs of the real ones." He stands, turning toward the door, dragging his coat over his shoulders. "See you in a moment." His hand grips the door, and he steps out of it, pulling it shut.

Yore drops against the counter, his back straight, cup lifted to just below his lips. "What are you two planning to tend today?" *No comment about the storm ceasing, nothing but a question about what is being done.* He takes a sip.

I shake my head. "I don't know. I want to know how Goran's hounds are."

His eyes snap to me, and he takes a sip of water, his shoulders raising. "You should wait for him to come back, like he said he would."

I purse my lips, turning my head down. Steam is curling up from the pot, out from beneath the lid. *Is he worried about what he will find, what will be waiting for Goran?* I swallow. "What will you be doing today?"

Yore shifts his feet, just barely relaxing. "I don't know. Talk with Goran, when he returns. Haul wood from the shed to the porch to replenish the stock and cut more. Check the traps again for anything, reset them." He takes another sip of water.

Alvea looks up, her eyes flickering to his from her needle work. "Can anything have been caught during the storm?"

Yore shakes his head. "It's more about digging them out and resetting than finding anything." He sets the cup down, turning toward the door. "Call for me if Goran comes before I'm back." He grabs his coat, shoving his feet into his boots and grips the door. He pulls it open stepping out and it taps shut behind him.

Alvea looks at me. She blinks, a smile twitching at her lips. "Well. Now that they are all gone, what are we going to do?" She half laughs and a smile twists at my lips.

I turn toward the stove, lift the lid. Steam puffs out. "I don't know about you, but I'm going to eat before I head out into the cold to see the damage."

She laughs. "You mean you aren't itching to see snow?"

I look back at her, a half grin pulling at my lips. "Are you?"

She laughs again, turning her head away to lift her loom's shaft. "It's good to have quiet again. After so much storm. The snow comes with that. There is so much lovely silence."

I smirk, set the lid down. "So, you are going to fill it?"

She looks at me, her eyes narrowed, a smile still on her lips. "Not unless you tempt me." She laughs, shaking her head and her fingers go back to the loom. I shake my head back at her, lifting the bag of porridge from the counter space. *What would happen if I mentioned Pevi's name? Would she flush, or look away, that smile creeping over her lips like she isn't quite sure whether she belongs here, whether she has earned this? Or would she go on working, like she always has, weaving away?*

Chapter XXXIII

A knock sounds on the door.

I jump up, yarn hitting the floor, rolling away across it. My eyes snap to the door. Alvea's eyes glance at me and she doesn't stand, doesn't budge, but she half smiles. "Come in," she calls, her voice soft, calm. I frown.

What if he didn't hear her call to come in? The door creaks open and boots scuff, knocking off snow on the step of the door. Goran ducks through the doorframe. I press my hands against each other, press them against my skirts. His eyes flicker up, landing on me, an eyebrow raising, just barely. He looks away and stoops, pulling at the laces of his boots. "Were you expecting someone else?" His voice is dry. I swallow hard. *He isn't looking up, isn't making any sign of anything. Did they not make it?*

I swallow hard, shake my head. "Nie...Only you." *I shouldn't just stand here.* I drop back into my chair, snatch up the yarn from the pile where it fell on the floor.

He doesn't look up, his hands still working at the laces of his boots. "Why would you do that?"

I press my hands together tighter. "Because you said you were coming." *Should I ask? What if they didn't? If they didn't make it, he won't want to talk about it. Do I want to know how they died if they did?*

Alvea glances at me and back to Goran. She gives me a dry look. “Oanéka wants to know how the hounds fared.”

My face pales. “Nie. I... va. I do.”

He lifts his head, eyes flickering from me to Alvea, and he looks back at the floor. He tugs his boots off and stands. “They are well.”

“They are?!” The words burst from my lips and I squeal, clapping my hands together. Goran looks up, his eyes startled, hands stilled. I turn toward Alvea, pressing my hands tighter together beneath my chin. “They made it! They are alright still!” She smiles. I spin back toward Goran. “Truly, they made it?! All of them are well?”

He smiles, amused and it lights his eyes differently, real and deep and full. “Va. They are fine.” He stands, pulling the coat from his shoulders. “They found the food at the back of the room.” I clasp my hands together. He shakes his head, moving toward a chair. “I did not realize you were this attached to them.”

My heart drops a little. I swallow, lift my fingers from my skirts. My face warms. “Oh. Well...” I look toward the stove. “I have grown fond of them.” I grip the ladle. “You came just in time. Dinner is nearly ready, if you can stay for it.” My voice is flat, off. I swallow. He nods. My heart lifts a little. *At least he can stay, if I cannot go see how they are tonight. It is too late now.*

The door creaks open and Yore and Pevi are stepping through it. Yore looks up, and nods. “You made it back. Good. You want to come do chores with Pevi and I? We are heading out to tend the livestock.” Yore moves toward the wash bucket. *There is blood on his hands.*

My eyes widen, Alvea’s face matching mine. “What is that from?” Her voice is almost sharp.

He pauses next to me, pushing his hands into the wash bucket. "There was a hare in a trap. Looks to have been caught the morning of the storm, before it hit. It was frozen in the snowbank." He glances at Goran. The other man shrugs and Yore nods.

My heart sinks. *He's going back out already.* The men turn, all three of them moving toward the door and they file out, leaving Alvea and me in the stillness of the room. *But the hounds made it. That was the news I was looking for, and I have it now. I can focus, finish what I am working on and get things set for dinner. That was what I was waiting for.* Alvea is smiling, her fingers moving swiftly on her loom like they haven't done in weeks, not since her illness. *Maybe she is healing. Maybe she'll be fully well again within a few more days, another week.*

There is a howl outside, long and high, wilder than the sounds of the storm. *A wolf.* A shiver runs down my spine. Alvea's head shoots up, her eyes flickering to mine. "Are we hearing more of them now than we were?"

I shake my head, look down at the pot. "We heard them often enough at night, before."

She shifts, her hands still on her loom. "But it is not night now."

I shiver again and shake my head. "I don't know. You could ask Yore. I can't remember hearing them in the day, but I wasn't listening for them." *If I had, I don't know that I would have walked about in the woods, alone. Goran never warned about wolves, among the things he warned me against.* The loom whines again, Alvea's hands back at work, but slowly now, like they have been these last few weeks, before Pevi came back.

Laughter sounds, faintly, low and deep through the walls. My eyes flicker toward the unshuttered window. There is nothing but the edges of the forest, coated in white through it. I shake my head, stir the spoon through the stew on the stove. *It is thick, ready now. The sun will set soon, and then we'll gather again, one more time before Pevi goes home and we'll go back to days of emptiness.* I purse my lips. *Empty, but full of beauty. Perhaps it will frost again, or I can go walk out there.*

My eyes snap to the window. *The wolves. Nie. I won't go walking. Not far, at least. Maybe just around the cabin.* Alvea's eyes are on the mantel above the fire. *I can't see what is in them, only the light that dances on them from the flames. Thoughtfulness or hope? Dreams or despair? Surely not despair, after these last few weeks. So maybe hope. Maybe a little of it, now, filled with all of the last few days.*

* * * * * * * *

Goran is out on the porch, the hounds around his ankles in the morning light through the window. I glance at Yore, lift my head. "You have everything you need?"

He nods at me, pulling his scarf around his neck. "We'll be alright." He glances at me, and then at Alvea and Pevi. They are speaking softly, a few steps away, Alvea handing him something. *The blanket she finished.* Her voice carries, for just a moment. "This will fit in your pack?" He nods and she smiles, setting it on his hands. "Something to remind you of us, until you can come back here. Be safe." She smiles again and steps backward, her hands twisting together.

He grins and bows, that strange bow that he did the first day he came to Yore. "Thank you. It will be a welcome reminder until I can come back."

Yore half snorts, moving toward the door. I glance up at him and step after him. "Be safe out there. You have everything with you?"

He nods, again and grabs his gloves, pulling them onto his hands. "Keep an eye on the sky." His eyes find mine. "Make sure that you keep an eye on it while you are outside doing the calli and don't go out more than you need to. There is more than enough firewood in here for the next few days." *The last part is more to himself than me, and he is scanning the woodpile, as if assuring himself that it is enough. It's just two days. We have enough for more than a week in here, piled high beside the wall behind the kitchen stove.*

I nod and grip his arm. "Be safe out there. You'll keep an eye on the sky as well?"

He nods. "Goran always has one on it." He looks at me, again, the second glove on now and his pack on his shoulders, the water sack not hanging from it like it usually does. *He put it on the inside. It's there.* He shakes his head. "You'll stay inside as much as possible?"

I nod. "There is no call for me to go out there more than twice a day. It's too cold. We'll be fine. Be safe."

He turns and Pevi is moving through the door, nodding at me. He flashes a grin, and they are gone through the door, pulling it shut behind them and cold air brushes against my skirts, pressing them against my legs.

Chapter XXXIV

Alvea's hands are dropped against her lap, fingers stilled for once. *I cannot tell where her eyes are fixed, somewhere across the room where she has been staring, staring, her gaze unbroken.* It's quiet, empty. *Does she wonder if they'll make it back safely, or if there will be another storm? If Goran and Yore will be alright out there, coming back?*

I fold my hands, press them against my apron. *We just got through a storm, only days ago. There won't be another one so soon.* I reach for the end of my braid. The curls are loose and frayed beneath my fingers. I twist it slightly around my fingers. *They should be back today, Yore and Goran. If they are not slowed by anything, if all went well after yesterday, and Pevi is now home. They should be back today, by this evening at the latest.*

My eyes flicker to Alvea. *She will be thinking about the same thing, like as not.* I clear my throat. "Alvea."

Her head snaps around, eyes widen. "Va?"

I grimace, turn toward the counters. "Do you think they'll be back by dinner?"

Alvea's shoulders half sag, but she pulls them back, her head held high. She shakes her head. "There is no way of knowing." Her fingers pluck at the threads of her loom, carefully working out a thread.

I press my hands against the counter. The dishes are stacked beside the sink, only two bowls and a pot, waiting to be put away. *I should start supper, enough for them, in case they are back. There is no telling though, if they make it back, if Goran will stay for dinner or go home. I'll make something with bread then. Fresh bread.* My eyes drift to the window. *I should check the calli, before night gets any closer. I don't want to check them in the dark, like Yore does.* I press my hands against the counter and shove a strand of hair out of my face. *They will be alright. They always are. Yore always is. He always comes back.*

* * * * * * * *

My steps chunk through the snow, each one crunching beneath the surface, hardened by the coldness of the night, and water sloshes in the bucket in my hand. My skin burns. I grimace, stepping forward. I shove my shoulder into the barn door. It creaks, shifting as I shove it and moves backward, slowly. A calli looks up, her eyes wide and soft. She mewls gently. I fumble pouring the water into their trough. The calli mewls again, standing, shaking out her wooly coat.

I shake my head, grip the buckets again. *Will that be enough for the rest of the day, and the night? I don't want to have to come out here again later.* I stare at the water trough, only a little more than half-filled, though I've brought two bucket loads already. *I should get more, to be safe.* I turn.

There is a howl and something slams against the shed. I spin toward the door—snow pelts at my face, rips at my skin. I stumble, press my hands against my face. *Close the door. Close the door.* I stumble, snow biting my face, burning my eyes and there is a scream again, louder than the world, wind ripping at my skin. The calli are bleating, their cries mixing with the howling of the storm. My hand brushes the door, heart pounds, thuds in my stomach. *Shut the door. Shut the door.* I pull; the wind screams, the door barely budging beneath the force of it. My arms burn, thoughts scream and I can't get it shut. *It won't close.* My heart thuds. *Get it shut. Get it shut.* "Elnial..." My throat aches, wind cutting across my skin, snapping in my scarf.

I pull. The door moves, just barely. *Close... just close.* I jerk and the calli are mewling, their cries mixing with the wail of the storm, with the screaming of it. *I can't breathe.* "Creator, please." I pull. The door slides, too fast and it crashes, slamming shut. I stumble. My knees scrape at the earth, the air stilled.

The shed shakes, walls trembling beneath the wind and there is the scream again, that scream, ripping through the world, the calli bleating, and everything is covered with a layer of powdery snow. I cough. My throat burns, eyes burn, face stinging and the calli are still bleating, running in circles, mixing their cries with the wind. *I didn't keep an eye on the sky.* My heart sinks in my stomach, hands shake. *Storm. I'm trapped. What can I do? I can't stay here. I couldn't walk in the wind. Couldn't move through it. Couldn't even get the door shut. What if the shed caves beneath the wind? What will Alvea do in there, with only her thoughts of what happened?*

My arms shake, shivering. *Yore and Goran. No. No no no no. What if they were on the trail? What if they were coming back? Stars. What if they are dying out there, in the snowdrifts among the screaming of the wind, the howling fury of the storm, out in the woods?* My arms tremble. I press them around me and my coat bunches against them, jaw shaking, everything shaking. The calli are just running, hay kicking up behind them, eyes wide, voices lost in the howling of the air and the snow melting beneath their running feet.

I can't stay here. Alvea is alone. I can't stay here. I grip the door, pull it open, and the wind strikes me, shoving me backward. The door slams against the wall, gone. My fingers scrape at it, grab for it, and I grimace. Wind burns at my skin and the calli are screaming, louder than before, panic in their voices before the howling of the wind, blending, churning and I can't see. Snow pelts at my eyes, cuts at them from a hundred directions. I press my eyes shut, lift my hand and step through. My fingers fumble with the wall. *I can't feel the wall through my gloves.* The wind rips at my skirts and the wall scrapes against my shoulder, grating. There is a lump on the wall, beneath my glove. *A peg, sturdy and sure. Not a rope.*

My heart shudders and the wind slams against me, throwing me sideways and ripping at my hat, at my coat. Stars bursting across my vision, pain stabbing through my shoulder, through my head. *Cold cold cold cold cold...* My eyes swim, burn, body shakes, black swirling in my vision. *The rope, Yore's rope. I need to find the rope... I can't get back without the rope.* My hands fumble, there is nothing there, nothing but the peg and wind; nothing but the screaming and my vision swirls, ice cutting at my arms, at my face. I stumble, press my hands hard against the wall. *There must be a rope. They used it the other day and it is always hanging here, between the house and the barn.* Wind screams, and my hand fumbles with nothing. *The edge of the shed.* My heart sinks. Snow rips at my face, stabs at my eyes and I turn my head away, gasp. *The rope has to be here, it has to be somewhere.*

I grip the wall again, fumble with it and the wind jerks, yanking me sideways. A cry rips from my throat. I press my hand against the wall, grip at it. *There is no rope. They used it, but I never made note of where it was.* The wind slams again, and my head pulses. *Get inside... I have to get inside... I can't get inside with out the rope, can't reach the house.* Something slams against me, hard and there are stars, bursting across my vision and blackness. My head stabs, pain and the snow won't stop colliding with my eyes, won't stop ripping, pulling, spinning, whirling and it's everywhere, screaming and pulling and whirling and spinning. *I can't get inside.* My hands are stiff, awkward, and I can't feel anything with them. I stumble and my head pulses, darkness crowding in. *No. No no no no no. The shed.*

I stumble backward and the world swirls in, dark.

* * * * * * * *

Mewling... screaming... Calli. I press my body up, the world shrieks. My fingers fumble with something and it moves, sliding into place, pulling at my arm. *Door. It is heavy, tapping into place, dragging against the wind.* I tuck something into place and it's not moving anymore, not shaking anymore. My legs are stiff, head pulses, world turning dark. *It's cold. I'm cold. Oh stars.*

* * * * * * * *

The calli are bleating, screaming. There is the howling, and my head aches, pounds. I press my arms under me.

The wind is screaming, not the calli. My head aches, pounds. *The calli will calm down soon. They will quiet.* The hay is rough under my arms, pressing against my back. I push my body up. Cold washes across my skin, biting through the fabric of my dress. I shiver, cower back against the hay. My arms are shaking, all of me shaking. My eyes flicker over to the calli. I run my hands up and down my arms, over my coat. My teeth chatter against each other, head aches. *Calli. Should I try curling up next to them, once they calm down? If they are ever still?* I grimace. *They stink. The whole room smells of them, strong, blending with the sweetness of the hay. Will I freeze if I don't?*

I shake my head, and it pulses, stabs. I grimace, curl my arms tighter around me. *Stinking is better than dying of cold.* The calli bleat; two of them have boxed themselves into a corner behind the others, and their eyes are wide, voices curling into the howl of the wind, high and strange and barely there. My head stabs.

I flick my gaze toward the door. It's closed. *I closed it.* My teeth chatter. *I can't get anywhere, can't go anywhere.*

My head pulses, aches, hands cold around my sides. *It is better than being caught out there, then staying caught out there.* I shudder. *I almost got caught out there.* My hand fumbles with an empty feed bag. I shake my head, pull it over me. *It smells of hay and wood chips, dust and soil.* I pull my knees up to my chest, and shiver.

* * * * * * * *

Something brushes the side of my face. *Cold. Damp.* I groan, stiff, sleep is heavy. My eyes are heavy. *I can't. I'm too tired.* Something is moving next to me and it thuds, lays down, the hay rustling beneath the sound of the wind. *A calli.* I lift my head, push back the fogginess. It's dark, almost pitch dark. *Night. Night has fallen. I've been out here for hours.* Something shifts in the hay on my feet. *A calli.* Its shape is faint in the screaming darkness, body shifting, breaths slow and easy, though its stomach must be pressed against my feet. There is another one, its shape and coat faint beside me, body pressed against my arm. I shiver and curl closer to it. *Warmth. I won't freeze out here, like Pevi nearly did. I won't freeze while the storm rolls over.*

Elnial, please, let the storm roll over. My head aches, nose cold in the darkness, lips chapped, and the air is still screaming. *Let it stop. Let the men be safe. Let them not have left Pevi's home. Let them be safe. Keep Alvea safe. Keep them safe.*

The calli shift and the wind screams, the shed shaking in the night.

* * * * * * * *

"Oanéka." *The voice is soft, like the voice of the wind.*

Nie, the wind screams. "Oanéka." I shake my head, press my face against the straw. *It's warm. Ignore the voice, ignore the wind. Ignore the damp. It's cold.* Something grips my arm.

"Oanéka!" *It shakes.* "I cannot get you back inside without your help. Please. Get up." My head snaps up, bones ache in protest and a groan slips from my lips. I shiver. *It's colder, something gone from me.*

Alvea. She is standing beside me, her coat huge on her, a hat and scarf around her head. Her eyes are wide, watching me, back stooped forward. I press my arms under me and it's far colder, hay falling off my chest, off my arms and everything feels chilled. I blink and I can't get the film off my eyes. "Alvea?" I press my hand against my face and straw jabs. I grimace, pulling my hand back. My eyes are watering, face half-numb. "How did you get out here? The storm?"

Her lips purse beneath the scarf, I can see it through the tightening of her jaw, the tensing of her brows. "I prayed, and the storm stopped. Get up. You need to get back inside. It's too cold out here. Get up. You need to get up." Her hands grip my arms, pulling but it's barely a pull, barely a tug and she is favoring her leg. I drag my legs under me. Cold seeps into my bones. I shiver, teeth chattering against each other.

I grip her arm. "You shouldn't have come out here."

Her face is pale, dark circles beneath her eyes, but they are sharp, bright, her cheeks flushed, sweat clinging to her forehead. *What did she do? How did she get out here, with the snow?* "Of course, I should have," she says. "You need to get inside. Come along." I nod, my eyes flicker to the bucket by the door. The trough beside it is empty, bone dry. *I didn't make it out to get more water. They need more.* Alvea's hand is pulling on my arm and she is walking, not letting go. I shake my head, eyes blurry. *I'm shaking. It's cold.* I purse my lips, stumble. My legs are aching. *They will have to wait until*

I am warm. I cannot carry buckets like this. My eyes burn, throat is tight.

Alvea shoves the door open and her breaths are ragged, heaving, hand still gripping my arm. Light flashes into the room, white light and I grimace, squint. Everything is silent, only Alvea's breaths cutting the air. Everything is sheet white, snow white. Alvea is pulling me forward, her hand jerking, hard. I stumble, pry her fingers off my elbow. She looks at me sharply and I grip the door, pulling it shut behind us. She rolls her eyes and grabs my arm again, jerking. "You are shaking," she snaps. "Stop worrying about other things. I'll handle it later. You have to get inside." *She was going to leave the door open.*

I shake my head, teeth chattering against each other. "Th-they would h-have gotten ou-t."

There is a trail in the snow, from the door, crooked and strange down from the porch. *Alvea broke a trail to get here.* My eyes snap to her. Her shoulders are straight, back straight, face still flushed, cheeks still red and yet her forehead is pale, paler than the snow. She steps onto the porch and her mouth twitches, like a grimace hidden back, her leg moving strangely. She shuffles across the porch, dragging me with her and she is pulling the door open. I step in and it's warm, everything warm. I can't breathe. I jerk the scarf from my neck, pull my coat back. *It's warm, too warm.*

She spins toward me, grabbing my shoulders, pushing me toward something, toward the fireplace. I shake my head, pull away. "No. No I don't want to sit closer. It's too warm." I purse my lips, my hands shaking, teeth chattering. She gives me a look and I push it out of my mind, look down. "You...your leg." *She broke a path to get to me. What did that cost her? She only just healed, only just was able to get around and do normal things.*

She lifts her chin. "It's fine. Go sit down. You need to get warmer."

I drop into the chair beside me, away from the fire, jerk my arm from my sleeve. My fingers are awkward, stiff and fumbling with everything. *Gloves. I'm still wearing gloves.* I shake my head, breaths wracking in my chest. *I'm cold.* "I... I have to g-go do the c-calli."

Her head whips around, eyes narrowing. "Just sit still." She snaps. "They don't need your help. Stop trying to do everything."

I flinch, my heart shrinking. My lips trembles, hands tremble. "I'm not t-trying to do everything. I'm trying to keep the calli aliv-ve." I swallow, wrap my arms around myself. "Y-Yore put too m-much work into them for us-s to let-t them just die without w-ater." My hands are shaking. *I need to get the gloves off.* I grab at them and my fingers are shaking, fingertips missing fingertips. *I can't get the gloves off, can't grip them.*

She puffs out a breath, shaking her head, her eyes on the ceiling, breaths still heavy. "Please." Her voice is hoarse. "Please. Sit for a while first." Her head sags, back no longer pin straight. "Please just sit for a little while first. They will be alright for a little while more."

My breath catches in my throat, arms shaking. *What am I supposed to do? I'm cold.* It's cold, and the firelight cannot break the chill of the room. It no longer feels warm in here, my bones cold, everything cold. I stand, move toward the chair by the fire. *What happens to the calli if I don't tend them? How many hours has it been since they had water, since I filled it?* My eyes flicker to the window. It's bright outside, only bright through the window. I swallow. *Yore isn't back. They won't be back until this evening, if they left this morning, after the storm ended.*

If they did not get caught in it. I look down. A blanket drops over my shoulders and Alvea's steps thud on the floor, walking away.

Did they stay? What if they don't make it back? What if they were caught in out there? My head throbs. I press my hand against it, wince. Something wavers in front of me, a hand. *A bowl.* I look up and Alvea is standing in front of me, handing the bowl to me. *Soup.* I grip it and nod at her. "Th-thank y-you." The bowl is too hot in my hands, my skin burning beneath it. I drop it in my lap, jerk my hand away and my body is shaking.

Too hot, too cold. I shake my head and my lip trembles. *What happens if they don't make it home?* My throat is tight. *I can't breathe. Everything is cold.* Alvea looks at me, her eyes steady like they always are, but they more alert than I've seen them in weeks. Her eyes flicker toward my hands. "Are you alright? Are your hands cold?"

I shake my head, my jaw shaking against itself. "N-no. No, I'm alright." My hands are cold, stiff and burning in a thousand places. I press them against my skirts and it doesn't help, the cold in my bones and in my hands.

Chapter XXXV

Alvea's face is sharp, her jaw clenched, cheeks white. "Don't take any longer than you have to." She glances toward the window, the late afternoon light half-golden through the trees. My hands are shaking, but I am not cold. *I can't make them stop shaking, can't make my heart stop pounding. I just need to water the calli and come back in. It won't be that cold.*

I grip the doorknob, the glove thick beneath my fingers and Alvea isn't protesting, hasn't said a word against me going back out. *But her face is, her eyes that won't look at me. Is she thinking of Yore, wondering where he is?* I clear my throat, force back the shaking of my lungs. "I'll be back in a moment. It doesn't take long, you know." She nods, barely, her head drooped, shoulders tense, like Yore's when he's mad. *Yore. Where is he now?*

I jerk the door open, step outside into the snow-lit world. The air is sharp, still, white. The shadows are long on snowdrifts that are nearly past the porch steps, their lengths stretching out like fingers toward me on the wooden planks. *Like lace, or the branches of an evergreen, heavy with snow.* I shake my head, my heart tight in my chest. I jerk the door shut, glance down. The bucket is not on the porch where it should be. My heart slows, stutters. *Where could it have gone?*

I left it in the shed. I purse my lips, shake my head. *Foolish. I knew that.* I step off the porch. Something rustles, off in the trees. I freeze. My heart pounds in my throat. I press my gloves against my chest. *Surely it is a stag, or them? What else is there, out there?*

There are wolves. The shadows are long, trees stretching toward the fading sky. *I need to go.* I step forward and snow crunches beneath my foot. I shiver. There is a rustle again, a sound like my own step. My lips purse. Something is moving between the boughs of the trees, large. *Huge.* My hands shake against my coat. I freeze. *I should go back inside. But surely... surely it won't bother me on the way to the shed.* I press my hands against my skirts, hard. *I have no weapon, nothing. I can't fight off a wolf. But that's not a wolf.*

It moves out of the woods, by the shed, huge. My head snaps up. There is a tree growing out of its head. My heart slows. *Antlers.*

The thing moves out of the shadows and its antlers are massive, greater, thicker than the stag's, though it is like him. It is huge, its movements easy, slow, as though I do not matter, as though nothing in the world does but moving over the snow by the stream. It tosses its head, nuzzling the snow along the creekbed, its head low to the earth, antlers nearly brushing the tree boughs. My heart thuds in my chest. *That is no deer. It is thick, thicker than any deer, its height huge, form bulking. It is beside the door of the shed, down the slope where the creek is buried beside it.*

Something else steps from the trees and it is as big, but there are no antlers on its head. Only ears, barely flickering with each tiny sound of the forest. My legs feel like soup.

Who let creatures get that big in the forest? How have we not seen them before, these massive creatures? Why has no one mentioned them? The first one lifts its head, its eyes barely scanning the line of the woods. It snorts, breath puffing into a cloud, walking along the length of the creek. It lifts its head and steps through the trees, gone. I glance up. *The other one is nowhere to be seen.*

My lungs release, air puffing into a cloud before my face. *Just water the calli.* My legs feel frozen in place, clinging to the earth. *It could be safer from them in the shed,* if they come back. My heart shakes. *Let Yore and Goran not run into them. There is no telling if Yore took his bow or not. If Goran took a hound with him, if they took anything. Perhaps if they are like deer, they can be spooked like them. Perhaps they will run and not stay.*

I drag my feet from the ground, move toward the shed, steps crunching and my hand fumbles with the handle of the door. I pull—it barely shifts, ice cracking below. I grimace, slow. *It wasn't supposed to be that hard to open.* I grip the door, jerking again. Ice cracks, the door creaking and it moves, slowly, then jerks open. I gasp, falling forward and my knees strike the frozen ground. The door jerks sharply, bouncing back the other way and it takes my arm with it, jerking it above my head. I gasp, press my head against the wall. My body aches, head throbs, shoulders burn. I grimace. "Cursed door."

I lift my knees from the ice, drag my body up. My arms burn, shoulders ache. The door slides, and stops, running on its tracks. There is a shuffling of feet, mewling. I turn, press my hands into my skirts. The bucket is on the floor, empty beside the trough. The calli are huddled into the back corner, their eyes blinking, staring wide at me. I grip the bucket handle, turn back toward the open door.

I plant my foot back in the path I made through the snow. *What happened to Alvea's path, from the morning?* There is no sign of the trail she made out to get me. Just a sheet of snow, my steps the only mark on it. I step off the trail, down toward the creekbed. The wind is blowing along it, branches stirring, creaking with the cold. The snow is thin along the creekbed, bumped with rocks jutting from the ice. My heart sinks, a lump twists in my throat. *I didn't bring the axe. Didn't bring anything to cut the ice with.*

I look up. There is a figure, only feet from me, kneeling beside a tree across the creek. My heart slows. His eyes flicker up, face beneath his hood. *Yore.* I bolt, the bucket clattering against the snow behind me. "YORE." My steps skid on the ice, wind catching my hair. My toe collides with something and I stumble, slide. I grimace, arms flailing for balance and move forward again, jumping the rocks in the frozen stream. Snow crunches, jolting my legs. "Yore!" *How are they back so early?*

He steps toward me, eyes wide, hands reaching out as if to slow my flailing. "What is wrong? Are you alright?"

I move backward, shake my head. "Everything is fine. You made it back." My throat is thick. "You didn't get caught in the storm?" A shadow moves behind him, shifting. *Goran.* My eyes flicker back to my brother, face warm. I turn my eyes down, to anywhere but them. "You all should come in; you will be tired. I have to tend the calli..."

Yore shakes his head. "I'll tend them."

My eyes lift, back to him. "You will be tired though."

He is nodding. "I am but I will do them. Get back inside. It's too cold to be out today." His eyes are worried, scanning my face.

I turn away, toward the cabin, my throat tight and glance over my shoulder. "Will you come in first?" There are steps behind me, but they are quiet now, not the crunching of snow, only the squeak of it packing further together. I glance over my shoulder at them again. "You are alright?" I step, my leg plunging into the depth where my feet tread before, snow around my skirt, around my boot.

There are only steps for an answer. Yore grunts, after silence, with the porch beneath my boots. "We'll talk inside." His steps sound loud behind mine. I grip the handle of the door, my arms aching. My head feels foggy. It throbs.

I press the door open, step inside, movements clumsy. My face warms. I press my hands against my skirts, moving toward the rack too quickly. "Alvea!" She turns, and her eyes widen. Relief washes over her face. I smile, my throat thick. "They made it back." I wrap my arms around myself, fitting my gloved hands over my elbows. The men step in, pushing the door shut. There is a draft of cold air, cutting through the room like fever, hot and cold and I can't stop the shiver that runs over my scalp. Neither man moves to take off his shoes.

Alvea steps forward and stops short, eyes watching. I flick mine back to the men. She clears her throat. "Are you not staying, Yore?"

He shakes his head, half smiles. His face is pale with his scarf no longer over his mouth. "Nie. I am. I have to tend the calli first."

"Calli again? Curse them. Can they not wait?" Alvea's voice is sharp, a burst. I stare at her.

Yore straightens sharply. "If they are to be left overnight, they have to be tended before dark and it's nearly here." His voice matches hers for volume. His brows narrow. "You were not so opposed to them before. Why are you so angry with them now?"

Alvea trembles, her face flushed red, hands tight. "They nearly cost me my sister last night. Your sister." Alvea's voice chokes and she turns toward the counter. "She went out to tend them and the storm hit. I did not think she would ever come back." Her shoulders shake, lips purse, hands pressing against the counter.

Yore steps forward and stops short. His jaw tightens. "I won't be long, Alvea. I'll be right back." He turns toward the door, Goran visible behind him now.

Goran's eyes are on me. "What happened?" His voice is quiet, low.

Alvea brushes a hand across her face, turning toward the kitchen. Her back toward us is sharp, posture perfect again. "Oanéka went out to do the calli last night and then the storm hit. I found her in the barn this morning. And then she would go out and tend the calli, like you, Yore. We didn't know if you would be back or not. You could have been caught in the storm too. You could have died." Her voice catches. "I could have lost both of you to one foolish storm. One night. One storm and I could have lost you both because you went out there again." She shakes, her hands trembling beside her, back too straight.

Yore drops his hand from the doorknob, turning toward her. His eyes scan her and then me. I meet his eyes, my back straight, but everything aches and my head is foggy. He swears under his breath and his shoulders droop. "I am sorry, Alvea. I am sorry."

Alvea's head shakes, but she doesn't turn and Yore is gone through the door, cold air swirling behind him. Goran doesn't move, his eyes on the ceiling. I shiver, my head hot, fold my arms around me. "I'll make supper then." I turn toward the kitchen.

Alvea's head shakes sharply. "Don't." She hisses, turning toward me. "I've already done it. Sit down." I step forward. *Just sit?* My step sounds hollow. My eyes flicker to my feet. *I didn't take off my boots.* I stoop, and everything aches, everything cold. My fingers fumble with my laces, awkward and stiff. *Gloves. I'm still wearing gloves. I can't undo cords like this.* I grimace, gripping the gloves and I jerk them. My fingers fumble, pulling glove through glove. I swallow hard, my throat thick. My hand fumbles with the gloves again. My face flushes. I shove them into my pocket. I sway, legs betraying me, nearly throwing me to the ground, knees caving. I grimace, press my hand hard against the wall.

Someone releases a breath. "Oanéka, sit down." *Goran.* I grip the laces, shake my head. My throat is thick, a lump swelling in it. *I can do this.* I shuffle to sit on the floor, hands still fumbling with the laces. Steps tread toward me. "Not like that." His voice is low, hoarse. He stoops and hands are pulling at the laces of my boots and the cords come free easily, drop to the floor.

My throat tightens. I shake my head. "I can do that myself. Stop it, Goran. I can manage."

His eyes flicker up to mine, hand stilling. One of his fingers trembles, but the rest of him is perfectly still, crouching in front of me. "You are exhausted, Oanéka."

My lip trembles. "I'm not. And I can untie my own boots. I'm not a child, Goran. I can manage."

His jaw tightens and he drops back on his heels. "I know. I am not treating you like a child. You are tired. Did you not help Pevi with his laces when he was caught out there? Would you not help Alvea or Yore?" His voice is tight, earnest, raw and I don't know why.

I swallow, slowly nod. "I'm sorry. But I can manage." He nods, his hands moving to pluck the last bit of cord from my other boot. He stands, moves away and my laces undone for me.

My lips tremble. Goran moves across the room, his steps sharp and loud like I've never heard them. He turns, pacing back. I press my arms under me and half stand. My head is foggy, arms ache. I grimace and there is a hand before my face, reaching out. "Here." Goran. I grip the hand and his fingers wrap around mine, pulling me up from the floor gently.

I nod at him, tuck my arms around me. He moves across the room again, pacing, back toward me, back toward Alvea. He pauses, glancing at my sister. "Do you need water?" She nods, her back still turned to us. He grips the bucket and is gone from the room, the door knocking shut behind him.

I press my toes against my heel, toe my boots off my feet and sway. Alvea's shoulders shake. She swipes again at her face, the movement fast and gone. Her back is still straight. I swallow. "Alvea." She doesn't look at me. I step around my boots; stockings slap the floor. "Alvea." I pause.

She shakes her head, arms shifting. "Nie, Oanéka. Go sit down. Go sit down. I am alright."

I shake my head, step forward. "Alvea." *She's crying.*

"'Don't meddle in the tears of others, lest they should grow frustrated with you.'" Her voice is loud, sharp. My throat swells. I press my hands against my skirts, eyes burning. *Frustrated with me?* I shuffle over to the chair, plant myself in it facing the wall where no one is. *Is she going to quit talking again? Are we going to go back to silence and frustration and emptiness?*

My throat chokes. The door creaks open and closes again. There are soft steps on the floor, and the tap of heavy wood against it. The buckets. *Goran.* A second set of steps tread across the floor, heavier than the first. *Yore's.* "Tell me what happened." His voice is low and it's too thick.

There is a shuffle, in the kitchen, a soft swish of skirts. Alvea speaks. "There is nothing more to tell. Oanéka went out and was caught in the storm. And we looked for you last night. We looked for you and then there was a storm." She chokes, turns her head away. "I thought we'd lost you."

"Did she come in this morning then, or use the rope?" Yore says.

Alvea's voice is sharp, thick. "I found her this morning, beneath the hay asleep. And now she won't rest. Just like the rest of you. None of you will sit down for even a moment. I had to fight her to get her to warm up and you two are just the same." My shoulders tense.

"Was she cold?" Goran's voice.

Alvea's steps tread across the kitchen unevenly and something clanks. "How in the stars could she not be, Goran? Of course she was cold. It was cold out there, or didn't you know that? It was a storm. Winter. Ice."

"I know it." Goran says. "Has she been sick since you found her?"

Alvea's steps trail across the floor again. "Why are you asking all these questions? She was out there in the storm all night. Of course, she should rest, whether she is sick or not. She was out there all night."

I lick my lips, shake my head. *I am fine.* "How are you two back so early?"

Yore shifts, his steps moving away from the door. "We were out in the storm."

I toward him, in the chair. "What?!?" My voice is shrill. "What happened? You survived it?!"

Yore looks at me, his eyes steady, the gold of them caught in the light trailing from the lantern Alvea has hung over the stove. He runs a hand along his jaw, his eyes flickering to Goran, then to Alvea. "We started home yesterday, just like the last time we went. That mule was antsy and we'd gotten a late start after speaking too long with Pevi in the morn. He'd told us not to go." Yore shakes his head and a wry smile twists the lips of both men. "It seems he was right about that buggin' mule, even if she was wrong last time."

Alvea sets the spoon down in the pot. "Right about what?" She raises an eyebrow, her face hard.

Yore shakes his head. "That it knows the weather. The buggin' thing was antsy all morning and Pevi kept saying not to go, that it was usually right. After he got into that predicament by going when the mule was calm, I didn't think twice about coming home. But Pevi kept saying it until we left. We were only made it a few miles in. Then the storm hit."

I hug my arms around me, my lips feel dry. "What happened?" *He should have listened to the mule. They should not have tried.*

Yore glances at me, nodding toward Goran. He slings his coat over the rack. "He knew what to do, how to wait it out."

Alvea steps forward, her hand gripping the counter, her face pale. "What did you do?" Her eyes are on Goran.

Goran releases the fold of his arms. "We dug in a snowdrift against a tree and stayed there until the storm ended. We were dressed for the weather. It is the only solution I know, in a pinch."

Alvea blinks, her face paling. "You stayed in a snowdrift overnight?" I purse my lips, eyes scanning the men. *They do not seem ill, do not even seem to have weathered cold, do not seem chilled. They weathered the storm. It was alright. They don't even look as cold as I feel.*

Yore is nodding. "We did. It was not too bad, either."

Alvea's hand turns white on the counter. "But it must have been cold. You two will be ill tomorrow..."

Goran shakes his head. "Nie. We were not horribly cold." His eyes flicker to me. "Why didn't you think to use the rope to get back in?"

My heart sinks. "I did," I say and Alvea's face blanches of all color. I lick my lips, speak faster. "I could not find it, so I went back inside. I was only out there for a few moments. The wind was too strong for me. I couldn't move well in it, with the force of the gusts so I went back in." I look down. *It feels foolish to speak of my struggle, when they were out in it overnight, in the woods, in the storm, hiding in a snowdrift.*

Alvea folds her arms over her chest. Her eyes are on the floor. She looks up and shakes her head. "That is enough. We should eat. Talking of the past will do no more good."

Yore's gaze flicks to her, dry. He moves for the door, his knit hat gripped in his hand. "Talking of the events of yesterday cannot be called unproductive, Vea. That is not the past that was meant."

Alvea shakes her head. "We have spoken of it. Now it is time for food. You must be famished."

I glance at Goran. "Do you need to get back to the hounds?"

Alvea shakes her head, her hands lifting the ladle. "Don't try to get rid of him." She looks at Goran. "You are welcome to stay and eat. There is plenty and I am sure the hounds can wait." My face warms. I look down.

Goran nods. "I will stay. We've already been by the cabin." He moves toward a chair, beside me.

I stand, step past him toward Alvea. She gives me a look, and I don't know what it means. She turns, back to the pot, and sets another bowl full of stew down beside it. Yore is kneeling, pulling the boots from his feet. There is a trail of footprints across the floor, many, many sets from the day that is now behind us, mud and water, and all that was snow. *That will be cleaned tomorrow. Alvea cannot protest to me doing that work, for she cannot do it with her leg, and tomorrow, all will be well. Alvea is reaching a bowl out, out to me.* "Go sit down," she says. I take it, and look up toward her, but she is gone, back to the stove.

"Thank you," I say.

She shifts her shoulders, looking over them at me. "Just go sit. Goran, Yore, come get your bowls." She lifts one, turning back toward the table that I am beside. I drop into my seat. The stew smells warm, thick and good. *Spiced with whatever that strange herb is that she always insisted on sticking in her bread, once. Back home.* I half smile.

Yore drops into the seat across from me. He looks up, his eyes catching mine. "What?"

I shrug, looking back down at my stew. "I am glad you made it back alright. That you are alright."

He leans back, folding his arms over his chest, the stew still clutched in one hand. "It really wasn't bad. You should try it sometime. Made me feel like a fox in a hole for the winter. Or a bear in his den."

I shiver. "I do not care to feel like a fox. I'd rather feel like a hound."

Yore laughs, throwing his head back. "You are no hound, Néka. But perhaps a small squirrel?"

I scowl. "I'm not a squirrel. I don't even like squirrels. They are vicious."

He grins shifting his legs, leaning further back in his chair. "Va. So then you are one."

I shake my head, pursing my lips. "That does not make sense. And I am not that small either. You are just tall. I could be a hound."

Yore grins. "Alvea, who is the shortest person in the nearest twenty miles?"

Alvea slips into her chair, her movements cautious, smooth and awkward at once, favoring her bad leg. She half grins, something sparking in her eyes. She looks down, twisting her spoon carefully. "Why, I believe it's Oanéka. I cannot think of one person within at least that far that is nearly so short."

I glare at them, shake my head. "Someday, we are going to find out that there is a whole family of people all shorter than me nearby, or a whole dwarf clan."

Alvea tucks a grin away, moving her spoon to the other side of her bowl. "But you cannot contradict us for now, can you?" she says, tilting her head to the side.

I shake my head, a grin tugging at my lips. I cannot remember the last time they both teased me. "The stew smells amazing," I say. Alvea smiles, looking up sharply.

"Thank you," she says. She lifts her spoon but doesn't move it to her lips until Yore has taken the first bite.

Tradition. She has not forgotten mamé's training, so long ago, all these years later. And I have not forgotten her training, in mamé's absence.

Chapter XXXVI

I step around a tree. Pine bristles are scattered across the snow, hard now from the nights of freezing. The snow is strange, hardened into a shell over the world that does not break beneath our weight, but holds hard beneath my feet. The grain is rough beneath my shoe, strange, stranger here beneath the trees where the snow does not lay evenly, where the bristles and branches fall and jut out of the snow below. *I wonder if there is a way to measure the cold, one cold being more than another and causing a thing like this?*

I move around another tree, stepping away from it, around the drifts of snow that well up beneath it. The shadows between the trees are long, stretching out until they meet each other, endless lines across the white of the forest floor. I suck in a breath, and the air sticks in my throat, sharp like a blade. *Cold.* I pull my scarf up over my lips and the air is a little warmer with it there, brushing my own breaths back at me.

There is no song in the woods. I do not remember when I last heard a bird. The silence is gentle, vast, like a breath of fresh air on the wind of a breeze, and my heart is lighter. *Winter. Vast and beautiful. Winter. Harsh. It is no less harsh, for the beauty of the silence. Perhaps it is more beautiful, for the harshness of it. Water would not glitter so beautifully if it were not first frozen by the long nights. Frost cannot decorate without it.* My eyes flicker upward, out through the trees that stretch out, bare and empty forever. The light is pale, golden through them, cutting around each trunk of each tree, like a flame in the sky. *This silence would not have come without it, without this, without the brutality of winter that brings this gentle silence, like a sigh after a storm.*

I move around the trees, forcing my feet to go. A wind brushes the trees, branches knocking together a clatter above. The wind breathes, a hiss between the branches. There is smoke, curling up between those branches, up in the sky above that is streaked with a late brush of sunlight. My nose is stinging. *It's too cold out here to stand and stare.* The wind brushes the trees again and they sigh, branches knocking against each other above the frozen floor of snow.

I turn away from the smoke. *I am not going to see Goran today. He must be tired of seeing us after all that we have seen of him of late. I should not have ventured so close to his cabin, hadn't intended to. Perhaps he misses the solitude of these woods alone, the solitude of trees upon trees upon trees, whispering with the voices of winter that no one else knows. Does he miss this world without us in it to disrupt what was here before, without the voices, the help and the questions and pleading? Does he miss the everlasting silence of before?*

I press my hands into the boughs of an evergreen. The snow has frozen to its branches, clinging to each thread of the needles along the twigs that make up its thick, green coat. I duck, and look up, a stick crunching beneath my feet. Each needle is coated with the ice, glinting in the sunlight like the gemstones of old stories.

"Oanéka?" My head snaps around. *Goran*. My eyes widen. *Curse it. I just ruined his silence.* He shifts, slinging something over his shoulder on a long cord. "What are you doing here? It is cold."

I shake my head. "I was only taking a walk. I spent all day inside cleaning and so I wanted to come out, before the sun drops." I say. My voice is muffled through the folds of my scarf. *He is wearing a scarf over his mouth, but he didn't sound that muffled.* I shift the scarf, pull it away from my mouth. "I am sorry I interrupted your quiet." My breath is a cloud in front of my face.

He shakes his head, moving forward. He is wearing more layers than I've ever seen on him, a hat pulled low over his head, furs and wraps around him. He glances at me and back to the trail. "You didn't. But you should come back to the cabin before going home. Warm your face and ears or you will get frostbite." I nod, and swallow. He is stepping past me, back through the branches of the massive evergreen, with the frozen droplets clinging to the branches.

I step after him. "Do you..." I pause. "Do you ever miss the time before we were here, the quiet?" I look up at him. He is straightening, out from under the tree, holding back a bough for me to duck under. I step under it and look up at him.

He lifts a brow, turning away, moving up the path. "Why would you ask that?" There is a small bundle of sticks hanging off the cord on his back.

My nose is cold. I pull my scarf up over it, press it into place. "Because I know we have asked a lot of you since we have been here and you said before that you came partly to get away from everything. You did that, and then we came and brought a lot of everything with us; the trouble, the problems, voices, and opinions. The sound, and commotion. All of it."

He steps to the side of a low skeletal branch on a barren tree. "I do not miss it. It is good, not bad to have others nearby." He looks back at me. "Or would you rather that I leave you alone from now on?"

I scowl. "What? Nie. Of course not. Why would you ask that?" I pick up my pace, try to catch up with him.

He glances down at me, stepping around the large evergreen that I first pressed my back against those months ago. "Because you sounded as though you are tired of me being around."

I scowl. "Nie. I am not. I only thought you would be tired of us." *It's nearly dark. I did not realize how dark until now. There is no more sun between the trees. Only the light from the sky, faint, and the cabin only a few feet in front of us now.* I swallow.

He looks down at me, planting a foot on the step. "Before you all came, I spent the winter scraping fat from hides and listening to the vast emptiness of a life of nothing. Waiting for the howling of the wind. For the silence to be interrupted by weeks indoors and storms that rip through the forests." He turns back toward the door. "I do not miss that, Oanéka. I will never miss that life. It was a season and now I am glad, thankful to be rid of it, for a while. For the company. For the commotion and the noise. For this. Winter is better in company."

I swallow. "For a while?" He holds the door open, letting me in before him. The air of the room is thick, too warm. I jerk the scarf off my face, breathe. "Does that mean that you will someday wish to go back to it then?" My voice is clear now, the scarf gone.

He looks over at me, the scarf still over his mouth, over his nose and chin. "Nie, Oanéka. I just said I will not miss that time. What did you say?" He moves, turning away from me. "'It is not good for man to be alone?'" He turns back around and raises an eyebrow.

I shake my head. "But when we get to be too loud, as I think we will, you will tell us? Or maybe just walk away?"

He raises an eyebrow. "I am not walking away from anything. I have done that enough. If you start to be too loud, I'll tell you. Nothing more." He glances out the window. "We should get you back, if you are a little warmer now." He turns slowly back around, moving toward the back of the room. "I'll get the lantern." The hounds stand and Gyaith stretches her large teeth flashing. She shakes her tail, moving across the room toward her master. The other two follow, Marin's tail working fast, Crith's steps slow, sluggish.

Goran turns, the lantern in his hand casting a glow across the room. He nods at the hounds, moving past me, toward the door. "Come on." They follow him, eyes bright now, catching the light. *His hounds*. I tuck my scarf back over my mouth as the door opens. Cold air washes in, I can feel it through the layers of my skirts, through my shawl, through the scarf over my face. I step out the door and Goran holds it open for me, stepping to the side. I start down the stairs. Goran steps past me, his steps crunch on the face of the snow, like he always does, like they always do. He starts down the path, the hounds at his heels. Crith's tail smacks me, his fur strange by the light of the lantern, shadows bouncing around Goran. "Watch your step." He holds the lantern out to the side. I step over the rock, beside him.

I swallow and glance up, at the growing shadows of the trees, with the snow between them. "How long did it take you to notice the beauty of this place, out here?"

He glances at me and his face is all shadows. *I can't read it. So, I won't try.* "A while. It is not something I look for; not like you do."

He steps into the trees. I laugh. "I am not good at looking for it. That has been hard won." I pick up my pace, a hound brushing between us. My eyes flicker to the trees. "It is different here, like Elnial wove this place in a different way." I run my hand along the branch beside me. "Soul-filling. I do not know how long it would have taken me to see it, if I was out here alone. Years." I lick my lips, slow my steps. The snow is sparkling, just barely in the dark between the trees, the wind soft and sharp. "I used to think that the light needed to come here, Goran. That it needed to arrive before it could be seen." I look up toward the trees and he slows his pace a little, matching mine, his eyes still ahead. I shake my head. The trees are pale, lit by the orange fire of the lantern glowing in his hand. I flick my gaze up to him. "It was already here though, wasn't it?"

He glances at me, face half-lit by the lantern as we walk. "I am not sure I know what you are saying. I think you are speaking beyond me."

I purse my lips, shake my head and there is a smile pulling at my lips. "That light, Goran. That light that is poured out through all of creation." I pick up my pace. "I thought it could only be seen back home, with the flowers and plants and things. With living things. With delicate things. So, I would bring them inside in the winter to make things brighter, because I didn't think beauty could last through winter otherwise; it was so harsh. Because I thought I had to keep that light. I had to tend it, or no one would." I look down, step around a tree, broken across the path. I clutch my skirts, step forward again. "I couldn't see it, distracted by people, wishes, hopes and plans. It all seemed so dark. I was always too busy, with all the things I was holding close, my garden, friends who were here and then gone, chatter of women. Until we were here, and I couldn't be. And then... then it was like my heart was being ripped out. There was nothing here that seemed anything like everything I'd treasured."

He looks at me, eyes bright in the lantern, waiting. I step up next to him again. "But there was." A smile pulls at my lips, tugs at them and I look down. "The light didn't need to come here; beauty didn't need to come here, Goran. It already was here. I was too blind to see it, like you did. That was what I was looking for, in the dark months, and Goran, I couldn't see it, when it stuck to my feet, caught my hair, calmed my lungs. It's always been here, too, the light. And no darkness can overcome it, not in our time, and not in ten thousand years to come." I shake my head, laugh. "Can you imagine that? Light, that goes on forever, always, because Elnial is forever?" *We are to the creek.* Goran stops, his eyes flickering up to the sky. He stills.

"Oanéka." There is something in his voice, sharp and I look up. My breath pushes from my lungs. *There are colors, colors across the sky, dancing in it.* "The northern lights." His voice is careful, low, a breath like mine. I step forward and they shift, waving like a ribbon, more vibrant, more real than anything I have ever seen, under the sea of dark over the northern sky. Blue edges the green for a moment and fades back out, back to the green and the swirling, waving beneath the first of the stars. *Like nothing I have ever seen.*

I suck in a breath and wrap my arms about my waist. “They are beautiful, Goran.”

He laughs, and my eyes flicker over to him. His scarf isn’t over his mouth. “I didn’t make them.” He grins.

I laugh, breath thick beneath the woolen fabric of my scarf. My eyes trail back to the sky. “No. You didn’t. But you saw them first.” I smile. “They are beautiful.”

Goran steps over the creek. I suck in a breath, step over the snowed stream after him. He walks up the slope, to the porch. The lights are still dancing overhead. He pulls the door open, and my heart warms in my chest, my eyes trailing back to the sky for one last glance. *Light. It’s true. I can see it here now, even after weeks that did not go as planned.* I step through the door, rubbing the side of my head lightly. *It still hurts, from where I hit it. Va. Even after long weeks.*

I look up, toward the sky, as Goran presses the door shut. *Maybe growth can come in the darkest of places. Maybe there is hope in this present darkness.* Lights outside are dancing, over the world that is frozen over and my heart is warm in my chest. *This isn’t the ending, out here. This isn’t over, and there are a thousand new things to discover out there lit by that same light. Lit even in the cold, through the death of winter. When the darkness crawls in, it will not overcome. Not even in this place, nor in any throughout all the world and throughout all of time.*

Alvea’s good foot is steady on the pedal of her spinning wheel, wool whirling into something better, and Yore is by the fire with a book in his hands.

This book was written first and foremost, as is said in the first pages, to the glory of God. In that aspect, we have confidence through Him, that by His grace He will use all things to His glory, this work included. I hope, reader, that you have seen that goal however, in this work, because it echoed in my mind through many of its pages.

There are some people that I owe a huge thank you to, in acknowledging the work that they have done in critiquing and encouraging both in the writing of this book, and in all the years of writing that came before. God showed His abundant faithfulness through them, and so many more, so I want to acknowledge them here.

Susan Ojanen, with whom I had a conversation years ago that sparked my acknowledgement of my love for winter in her gentle words of goodness.

David Alford, who not only spent many hours on this story with me, refining and correcting it into what it is today, but also pushed me back into writing when I had stopped and started off the writing of this book.

Joshua, my brother, who had always been more than an encouragement in creative storytelling. (I hope you finish a book one day, because I am eagerly waiting to read it.)

Madeleine, who was always excited about writing before I was excited about sharing. Thank you for your help on this.

Katie Parsons, who's running commentary in notes was one of my favorite parts of this summer. Those notes still make my heart happy.

Cathryn McIntyre, my creative writing teacher and bonus aunt.

Annie Parsons, who was a fan before she was the artist whose work you see on the cover. Thank you for showing me this story was worth telling, and for being my alpha reader #2. You are the best.

Abbie, who put up with my ranting about stories before I ever finished a thing.

My family, who are all the best.

Hannah Rebecca Wilson, my editor, who poured so much joy into Frost Light. It made my heart rejoice to find you, and I am thankful to have had you onboard for this project. You are a blessing.

And each person who shared excitement in the early months and all along the way with the best enthusiasm. Thank you, Hannah Stam, Esther McIntyre, Rachel Mehl, Hannah Bailey, Hannah Brown, Hannah Easton, Joelle Canary, Joseph, Jeshua, Jesse, Timothy & Josiah Stam, Natalie Meredith, Olivia Lauger, Natalie Vernot, Becky, Sarah, Lydia and Sam Ratliff, the Salsbury family, Hugh & Julie Belcher, Ariane Hegarty, Laken Vaughn, Casey Barker, Suzanne Lort, Molly McCraw, Hayley & Kathryn Joyner, Lindsay Warhurst, Sue Gorman, Mary McCroskey, Bliss Brockmyre, Isabel & Sarah Elizabeth Smythe, Lauren Lovett, Jordan Gondy, Regina Green, Shiree & Dale Bullen, Chelle & Bobby DePriest, Joanna Morrison, Jenny Snyder, Abbie Kersey, Autumn Tremayne, Stephanie & Isaac Alford and so, so many more. It overwhelms my heart to think of all of the joy you guys shared over this, before you even knew what it was. Thank you.

And Anthony Lort. It turns out that the best spaghetti recipe is the one that you used to make the spaghetti you ate when you were hungry. All other spaghetti recipes are far inferior. Unfortunately, no one has yet created a true hungry man spaghetti, so I will leave a blank page in honor of the spaghetti recipe that should be here, but, after months of studying, has not yet been created. We leave it to the next generation of brave men and women, living up to the Italian dream.

@maggiesmithp hotography

About the Author

Danielle is from the heart of the Appalachian mountains and learned to soak up God's creation through the grasslands and woods of Southwest VA.

She writes to add her voice to the song that creation is already singing, in praise to God and to remind His people that He is good and that His goodness is evident in the world around them, through all time until its ending.

You can find her on her website @https://danielle-bullen-auth.com or scan the QR code on the back cover to get there faster and she would be more than honored to hear from you.

Printed in the USA
CPSIA information can be obtained
at www.ICGtesting.com
LVHW040809171223
766680LV00039B/626

9 798218 097387